BLOOMINGTON PUBLIC LIBRARY
W9-AWA-023
A11905 843346

4/02

BLOOMINGTON PUBLIC LIBRARY
205 E. OLIVE STREET
POST OFFICE BOX 3308
BLOOMINGTON, ILLINOIS 61701

DEMCO

Stolen Honey

Also by Nancy Means Wright

Poison Apples
Harvest of Bones
Mad Season

BLOOMINGTON, ILLINOIS
PUBLIC LIBRARY

Stolen Honey

NANCY MEANS WRIGHT

Thomas Dunne Books
St. Martin's Minotaur
New York

MYST
WRI

THOMAS DUNNE BOOKS.
An imprint of St. Martin's Press.

STOLEN HONEY. Copyright © 2002 by Nancy Means Wright. All rights reserved. Printed in the United States of America. No part of this book may be used or reproduced in any manner whatsoever without written permission except in the case of brief quotations embodied in critical articles or reviews. For information, address St. Martin's Press, 175 Fifth Avenue, New York, N.Y. 10010.

www.minotaurbooks.com

Library of Congress Cataloging-in-Publication Data

Wright, Nancy Means.
Stolen honey: a mystery featuring Ruth Willmarth / Nancy Means Wright.—1st ed.
p. cm.
ISBN 0-312-26245-0
1. Willmarth, Ruth (Fictitious character)—Fiction. 2. Women detectives—Vermont—Fiction. 3. Women farmers—Fiction. 4. Beekeepers—Fiction. 5. Vermont—Fiction. I. Title.
PS3573.R5373 S76 2002
813'.54—dc21

2001054787

First Edition: April 2002

10 9 8 7 6 5 4 3 2 1

To the Abenaki Nation,
the original Vermonters

Acknowledgments

Many people have helped bring this novel to fruition. I want to thank my son-in-law, Marc Lapin, ethnobotanist, for his special help with deadly nightshade and a hundred other details of nature; my daughter, Catharine Wright, for a critical reading of the work in manuscript; Greg Sharrow, folklorist at Vermont Folk Life Center, who led me into the world of the Abenaki; Mali Keating, Abenaki activist, who kindly granted me an interview; Cheryl Heath, who allowed me to watch her family video at the Folk Life Center; Jeanne Brink, basketmaker and Abenaki language expert; White Wolf Woman and Chaloner Schley; Cee at Computer Alternatives; and the helpful people at the Chimney Point Museum and at the Abenaki Tribal Headquarters in Swanton. I'd also like to thank Bill Mraz, who let me enter his world of bees, and Julie Becker, who lent me her taped interview with beemaster Charlie Mraz; my agent, Alison Picard; former editor, Jerry Gross; my copy editor, Dave Cole; and my assistant editor, Julie Sullivan, who all gave helpful suggestions; and of course, Ruth Cavin, my editor sine qua non and role model at St. Martin's Press. And finally, my wonderful extended family, especially my late husband and former agent, Dennie Hannan, who encouraged me, in the midst of his chemotherapy treatments, to write.

The following books were especially helpful: *A Book of Bees*, by Sue Hubbell; *The New Complete Guide to Beekeeping*, by Roger A. Morse; *Health and the Honeybee*, by Charles Mraz; *Breeding Better Vermonters*, by Nancy L. Gallagher; *Vermonters at Their Craft*, by Catharine Wright and Nancy Means Wright; *Aunt Sarah, Woman of the Dawnland*, by Trudy Ann Parker; *Many Cultures, One People*, edited by Gregory Sharrow; *The Original Vermonters*, by William A. Haviland and Marjory W. Power; *North Country Captives*, compiled by Colin G. Calloway; and the essay "After Two Centuries the Vermont Abenaki Are Visible Again," by editor Tom Slayton in *Vermont Life 36* (Spring 1982).

GODINEAUX FAMILY TREE

(family members mentioned by name in Camille Wimmet's notes)

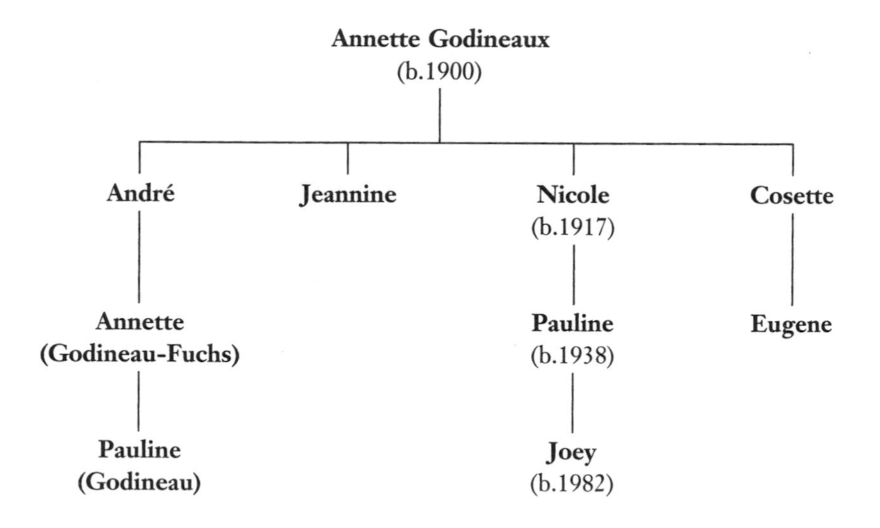

Stolen Honey

One

When Gwen Woodleaf's father died back in February, leaving the Woodleaf Apiaries to his daughter, Gwen was in the hospital recovering from viral pneumonia and couldn't "tell the bees" about his death. It was an old ritual, one that had been in the family for three generations of beekeepers. The way you did it was to tap on each hive three times and say, "Your former keeper has died—but please don't fly away, I'll be here to care for you." If the ritual was ignored, Gwen's father had warned, someone else in the beekeeper's extended family might die—or, at the very least, be severely traumatized—within a year.

But then Gwen was told by her doctor to rest at home on the bee farm for several weeks, so how was she to travel practically to the Canadian border to visit two hundred hives and tap on each one? After all, a beekeeper kept only a few hives on his property; the rest were spread out for miles. How silly it all was, she told herself at the time, and she'd curled up with a Victorian novel and watched the snowflakes fly past the window. The *bees* weren't flying then, of course—winters, they clustered snugly in their hives, dining on honey made from last autumn's asters.

But now it was mid-April and the worker bees were happily sucking up dandelion pollen and packing it into the baskets on their rear legs. Hearing their *hm-mm-mm* as she unpacked a case of new bees, Gwen felt optimistic about the future. At least there hadn't been anything so unthinkable as a death in the family—after her father's, of course. Nothing, she felt, could faze her today, not even the gloomy face on her helper Leroy Boulanger, just back from town, the truck keys dangling in his hand. Leroy's mouth looked like someone had sewn it into a down-curve; his rust-colored hair was standing on end from the wind.

"I run into Harvey Ball in town," he announced in his high-pitched, pebbly voice. "And he's mad as hops, all right. Seems the bees we left there got in the feed bins and spooked his cows. He wants you should come and do something about it."

He stood in the barn doorway; he slapped a feed cap onto the back of his head. He was wearing a blue and white Branbury College T-shirt—to impress her daughter, Donna, no doubt—Leroy had quit school after tenth grade. He had an unrequited crush on the girl. He couldn't see that Donna, at this point, was involved only in her studies at the local college—or so Gwen hoped.

"Is he sure they're bees and not flies?" she asked. "There's a breed of flies that look exactly like bees." She'd read, in fact, that Native Americans called the first honeybees brought over by the settlers "white man's flies."

"He says they're bees. He wants that you should go up right now." Leroy's lips squeezed stubbornly together.

Gwen sighed. "I'll go up this afternoon. Help me feed these new bees and get them into the hives, would you? Then I'll get some lunch going."

They were just finishing up when she saw Donna come laboring up the hilly road on her green bicycle. She jumped lightly off, a slim girl of medium height with her mother's dark blue eyes and the long shining black hair of her Abenaki father. She was home for the afternoon, she said—her chemistry class had been canceled. She ignored Leroy, who had managed to intrude himself on the walkway.

Gwen followed her daughter into the kitchen. Her father-in-law was already in there, fixing a huge tuna fish, onion, and chive sandwich. Mert LeBlanc was a basketmaker, a pleasant-looking man, dressed in loose leather moccasins and faded brown corduroys. His skin was weathered, his eyes a warm walnut brown; blue tattoos gleamed on his strong arms. He held up a braid of newly picked sweetgrass, his left hand shaking a little.

"It's not right, not quite," he said. "My damn fingers are too big. But yours, Donna, you could make 'em beautiful."

Donna had heard this before. "Someday, Grandpop. Not today."

Mert sighed, grimaced at Gwen. "Okay for now, but you'll see the light. Use the braid for a bookmark, maybe—those heavy college books of yours."

"Thanks, Grandpop." Donna dropped it into her book pack. "I'm going to a frat dance tonight," she announced, with a sidelong glance at Leroy, who was standing in the doorway with his lunch bag. He ate with the family but insisted on bringing his own fast food from McDonald's. The words "frat dance" had made the blood flare up in his broad cheeks.

"I thought you didn't like fraternities," Gwen said. "You and your friend Emily."

The pair openly boasted that they'd never attended a college football game or a frat party.

"Emily's been invited by a guy in her French class, and I'm going along. She's picking me up. The college is closing down any frats that won't take in girls—and ZKE won't, so this is the last chance. I mean, we want the *experience* of it. Look, Mother, it's spring."

" 'Spring' meaning the hormones are beginning to dance? Full moon tonight?"

"Really, Mother."

"Well, if you're going with Emily, I suppose it'll be all right. She seems a sensible girl."

"I'm not asking your permission. I'm simply telling you. So you'll understand if I come in late."

"How late?" asked Gwen, who locked the door nights now, since they'd been vandalized the month before, and three frames of honey taken. The bee farm was on the East Branbury Mountain Road, and relatively isolated. The nearest neighbor lived a half mile south, and Harvey Ball to the north had blinders on when it came to neighborly assistance.

"I'm eighteen," was the answer. "You and Dad don't seem to realize it." When Leroy gave a snorting laugh, she grabbed a red pepper and slashed it in half as though it were someone's head.

"Okay, I'll leave a light on. You have a key. But be careful," Gwen warned her daughter. "I don't like all the binge drinking that goes on in those frat houses."

"Don't worry, Mother." Donna leaned into the cutting board. Black hair falling across her face, she chopped the pepper into a hundred tiny pieces.

Donna and Emily had barely pulled out of the driveway that evening when an ancient Honda pulled up and Gwen's activist husband, Russell, got out, ablaze with silver: neck band, armbands, wrist bands, brooches, earrings. He hadn't removed them since his latest Revolutionary War reenactment. "Hey, Gwennie, babe," he bellowed even before he came through the door. "Any food in the house? Drove me straight here from Montpelier via Swanton, just stopped for one little drink at Big Joe's. All he had was Fig Newtons to eat, you know I hate Fig Newtons. Where's the girl gone? I got the one night home, have to shuffle off to Buffalo six A.M. You got any gas in the barn?"

He was all the way in the house now, filling it; his long black ponytail caught in the shutting door. She pulled it out just in time, let herself be enfolded into his muscled arms. The bear hug he gave her matched the bear tattoo on his right arm. He swung her around twice and then deposited her on a kitchen stool.

"Which question should I answer first?" she said, laughing. His original plan had been to go straight from Swanton across the lake and then down the Northway and over to Buffalo. But she didn't mind, did she? She rather liked the unexpected, the unpredictable coming and goings. And she certainly had those with Russell!

"The gas, I guess," he said. "Damn thing fizzled out right in front of the house. Hey, Pop," he called, "I'm home. Full moon tonight! Though it might rain later—or snow. God knows we need something wet. Got a pack basket I can take? The latch busted on my old case."

"What's it this time? More war games?" Mert lumbered into the kitchen, a beer in his hand. A silver earring swung from his left earlobe. "I got pack baskets, all right, come on in and choose."

"The usual, you know," said Russell, answering the first question, "the battle stuff. I got to run a lot, answer questions from the dumb tourists. 'Say, now, what *is* that thing you wear at your waist? Ooh, what side *are* you on, French or British?' Ha! I tell 'em I'm on the side gives me a good meal, a good deal. I watch their heads go click click, sure, he's an Indian, no loyalties, he's a cat: Feed him, he licks you." Russell laughed again and followed his father into the basket room.

"We're done eating, but I can fix you leftovers," Gwen hollered after him. "We've got venison left from last fall's kill. Just have to thaw it in the micro, okay?"

"Whatever," Russell sang out from the next room. "I'm so hungry I could eat *you*."

"Try me," she called back; then, hearing a noise, she felt her cheeks heat up. She hadn't realized Leroy was still there, guzzling a Pepsi, his face a morgue.

"Just going," Leroy said. He didn't look at her as he walked out. He was still put out with Donna. He didn't like Donna going off to a fraternity like that, not giving him the time of day—not that she ever did anyway.

Gwen wouldn't tell Russell where Donna had gone. Russell didn't approve of fraternity dances, either; he had nothing good to say about Branbury College boys, period. Anyway, there was no point telling him, he was only home on a quick overnight. Why would he have to know?

It was all so normal. A young woman going off to a dance. She'd gone to a dozen dances herself, hadn't she—in the year and a half she'd spent at the university? And nothing out of the way had occurred. Donna would be fine, just fine. Gwen would like to go dancing herself tonight. She would! She snatched up an aluminum pot and waltzed—onetwothree, onetwothree—around the kitchen. Until she banged—ouch!—into the center island.

It was only midnight and already Emily Willmarth had announced that she was going back to her dorm. Emily was lucky enough to live in the dorm instead of at home. But then, Donna knew, Emily had been paired with a rich, stuck-up roommate from Greenwich, Connecticut, and as early as October the society girl *and* Emily wanted to switch roommates. But the school wouldn't let them, so they were sticking it out.

"You can't go," Donna cried. "Not yet. Shep's coming back. He's making a beer run. The keg ran out. I mean, this is the last big blast. That's why you wanted to come, right?" She pulled her short black rayon skirt down over her butt. She'd bought it in town just that afternoon—hadn't realized how tight it was until she began to dance in it, and then it wriggled up.

Emily's roommate, Alyce, undulated past with a glass in her hand, a silly grin on her made-up face. "We don't usually see *you* here," Alyce gushed in one of her ingratiating, be-nice-to-the-locals modes. Donna never knew quite how to respond to her. She usually just turned her head and murmured something dumb.

Now Emily was arguing with Alyce, who had turned to her accusingly. "No, I didn't borrow your art book," Emily said, "why would I do that when I have my own?" It seemed Alyce was always losing things and then accusing Emily of taking them.

"It was there on my desk when I left for class, and it's not there now." Alyce lifted a painted eyebrow, like she'd made a weighty statement.

"Let's get out of here." Emily grabbed Donna's arm. "Anyway," she confided to Donna when Alyce had waltzed on past, "I want to leave before Bozo comes back."

"Bozo?"

"You know, Billy Bozeman. He's a nerd. He's always craning

back his neck and grinning at me in French class. I didn't realize he was in this frat. He went to get me a vodka and I don't want it."

"What happened to the guy who invited you?"

"He's out of it. They took him up to bed. Honest to God, it's been nothing but losers since I came to this school. Either they want to discuss astrophysics with you or they just want to get you into bed. Or both."

"Well, Shep isn't like that. At least I don't think so. I can't leave now, since he's told me to wait. You go ahead."

"How will you get home if I take the pickup? Mom needs it in the morning."

"Shep will take me. He's already offered. He has a motorcycle. Whee-ee . . ." Donna threw up her arms and whirled about. The black skirt spun with her and settled halfway up her ass. She yanked it down.

"You watch him, then, okay? I gotta go. Bozo's on his way with that drink. And you gotta bet it'll be le-thal." Emily ducked behind Donna and out the front door.

Now Donna was sorry she hadn't gone with her friend. Together she and Emily could face the collegiate world. She felt suddenly gauche with her black hair hanging loose down her back, while Alyce and the other girls all seemed to have blond hair done up in a sophisticated twist or, at the very least, an expensive short cut.

"Hey." She wheeled about to see Shep grinning down at her. He patted her on the rump. "Nice dress," he said, and handed her a glass. "Drink that," he ordered.

"It's only a little whiskey," he said, when she stood there staring into the glass. "I went all the way across campus for it." He held the glass to her lips and she sipped—spilled it on her blouse. He stooped to lick it up and she had to laugh. He kissed her lightly on the lips. "Come on. Just this one and we'll dance. You dance, huh?"

"Yes," she said, and drank. It tasted rather good, actually: It was icy cold and made with ginger ale, so it wasn't hard to get down. Her head felt fuzzy and free, like it was floating, unattached, beside her neck. The room smelled of smoke and perfume and whiskey and pot. She saw Alyce go upstairs with a blond boy. They would weave up a few steps, then drop down to giggle and kiss. Shep had dark hair—for some reason, she was glad of that. He was a junior already, majoring in political science, though he was in her sociology class. He wanted to be a lawyer. "The rich get richer," she remembered her grandfather saying, as he squatted in a pile of brown ash splints.

She must have finished the drink because suddenly her hands were empty; she and Shep were dancing. Shep's shaggy head was close to hers; she saw the fine hairs inside his ears, a cut on his cheek. She could smell the whiskey on his breath. Her father drank whiskey—too much of it, her mother complained. It was an Indian weakness, people said. But if that were so, then it was a white weakness, too.

As if he'd heard her thoughts, Shep said, "I hear you're Indian—uh, excuse me, Native American. That's cool."

She felt her face go hot. "Only half. My mother's not. I look like my mother." Though it wasn't entirely true. She had her father's nose, kind of flat. His hair, too, where her mother's was the color of maple syrup.

"I've never known an . . . uh, native before," he said. "We'll have to talk, hmm?"

She wasn't exactly sure what he meant by "talk." Talk about Native Americans? She didn't want to be some kind of guinea pig so he could go and tell his roommate he had the inside story on "Indians"—he'd "talked" to one.

But he must have read her mind again because he was pulling her closer. "I mean just . . . talk. About stuff, you know? Like what do you think of our soc prof? Something funny about her, you think?"

"Funny? Like what?" she said. Personally, she liked Professor Wimmet. But Shep just laughed and said, "Never mind. Right now, let's . . . dance. Close, like this, huh?" He pulled her to him until she gasped. His hand was on her buttocks; she felt her dress inching up, his hand pressing in, fitting itself to her curves.

It didn't matter. Her brain was comfortably blurry, she felt as though anything could happen, anything at all, and she'd go along with it. Because that's all she could do now. She couldn't think. Her brain was shrinking away from her body. The slow music crept on and on, and then suddenly sped up again, a heavy rock beat. She couldn't dance that kind of dance, she didn't know how; but it was all right, she swung out away from Shep and moved her hips. Surprisingly her feet moved along with the rest of her. When the music stopped and finally she looked up, Shep wasn't there at all. A red-haired boy with a purplish scar over his left brow was grinning down at her, handing her a plastic cup. "Shep said to drink this," he told her.

"Where's Shep?" she asked, hearing her voice plaintive.

"He'll be right back," the boy said, not answering the question. "Want to dance?" Someone had put in a Fugees CD and turned the volume way up.

She shook her head. She wanted to go home now. She was feeling out of control and she didn't like the feeling. She didn't like the way this boy was looking at her. As if she were something he had on his dinner plate and he was starving. She pushed past him and felt his hand brush her bottom. The loud music assaulted her ears, the laughter and shouts sounded faraway, although she knew they were there in the room with her. She almost tripped over a body—some guy, wasted, crawling across the floor. She didn't know where she'd left her coat but then remembered that the boy Emily had come to meet had taken it upstairs.

Did she want to go up there? No, but she needed her coat. She would walk home, even though it was four miles. And she didn't want her mother to see her like this, smell her breath. If she was going to walk, she had to have her coat. It was chilly out. It was snowing a little, she saw through a window: fat white flakes drifting lazily down, obscuring the moon, telling the world it didn't care that it was April, that spring had arrived. She liked snow. She liked rain. No sun god for Donna!

She took a deep breath and started upstairs. She found herself lurching, and grasped the handrail. Someone was coming down, another girl. The girl banged into her, she was drunk. "So sorry," the girl said, and Donna heard a crash at the foot of the stairs.

She heaved herself to the top, but the doors were closed to all the rooms. It was quieter up here; now and then she heard a giggle behind a door, a groan. She didn't know where her coat was, she didn't want to open the doors. She'd have to walk home without it—and how was she to get it in the morning? She went back down again, clinging to the banister for balance.

And there was Shep Noble at the bottom, smiling at her, a glass in his hand.

"Take me home, please, Shep. You said you would. You said you have a motorcycle."

Shep made a mock bow. His hair fell into his eyes; he pushed it back with a damp hand. "Whatever milady wants. One for the road?" He held out his glass. He had a rather nice lopsided smile.

"No, thank you." She didn't want it. He accepted her refusal with a shrug. She liked that; he seemed to understand.

Outside, she took deep gulps of the cool April night. The snow was clean and pure and fresh in contrast to the indoor scene with its mixed odors of people, pot, and perfume. She was surprised to see that at least a quarter of an inch had fallen, although it was a light, fluffy snow and would be gone with tomorrow's sun. She scooped up a handful and washed her face.

"Shit," he said. "Snow. And we have practice tomorrow."

Shep was the baseball captain—Emily had told her that. He was a skier, too. This was an athletic fraternity. What was she doing here anyway? Though if Shep asked her, maybe she would come to a game.

"Hop on," he was saying; his motorcycle loomed up beside her. It looked like a great black bear. Bear was the symbol of her father's clan. Her hand almost froze to the bike's cold metal, to the nameplate where Shep's full name was inscribed.

She climbed on behind him. He stuck his helmet on her head and they roared off. She was touched by the gesture. It seemed a small sacrifice. Her fears subsided. It was exhilarating to ride through the night, to feel the wind and snow in her face. She gave him directions to her house.

"Mountain road?" he called back, sounding surprised. She realized he didn't know, probably thought she lived in town.

"Just partway up," she said. "Not so far as the national forest. Though our land extends almost to there. My mother keeps bees."

"Oh, yeah?" He didn't ask any more questions; he was concentrating on the driving. He didn't want to be picked up again, he said—he'd been hauled into the police station one too many times. Just last weekend some belligerant cop had given him "the third degree—like I was some kind of criminal." The cycle slipped and swerved in the fluffy snow.

She wasn't worried, though, not a bit. She was enjoying the excitement of it, the thrill of hanging on to his black leather coat. They raced through town and then, more laboriously, up the mountain road and onto the dirt road that took them to the Woodleaf Apiaries.

"Here," she shouted over the roar of the cycle. "Stop here." He went into a skid, barely missing a tree, and pulled the machine up to lean against the sign.

"Those bees fly at night?" he asked. "I've got allergies."

She laughed. "No. And we only keep a few hives on the grounds. You won't get stung, don't worry. Mother keeps them well fed. She's got hives all over the state, on farms and orchards. She and Leroy are always on the road taking care of them."

"Leroy?" He was leaning against the tree now, pulling out a flask. She didn't like that, but he'd brought her home. She couldn't complain.

"Oh, he just works here—lives in a trailer up behind the house. He can heave those hives around while Mother can't." She thought she heard a rustle in the bushes and listened a moment. But it was only wind. Though she wouldn't put it past Leroy to wait for her to come home.

Shep grunted something and then said, "You don't wanna go in yet. We'll take a walk. Snow's practically stopped."

It wasn't a *question* about taking a walk; already he was yanking on her arm, pulling her along. But she didn't mind, did she? She hadn't gone out with boys much in high school, she'd had to study hard to get into college. Not many Abenaki girls went to college. But Donna had a special Native American scholarship. She was to finish college, the first in her family to do so; it was her mother's obsession. Her father was proud of her going, too. He never said that, but she felt it was true.

Shep was still pulling from the flask. But he didn't seem drunk, except for a little slurring of his words. He had asthma, he told her—that's why he couldn't play football; he had an inhaler, but he'd left it in the frat. She rather liked the idea of his asthma; it made him seem vulnerable, less the jock. His walking was steady enough. She would go just a little way with him. Soon they'd come to the swampy part of their land; it was where a stream ran through and spilled over, especially now, in spring. The ground was still thawing from winter and their feet would get soaked. She told him this.

He laughed. Everything seemed funny to him now. He put away the flask, pulled out a slim cigarette, and puffed on it. It helped his asthma, he said, to smoke.

"Smoking *helps* asthma?"

He laughed again. "Not nicotine—cannabis. Cures a lot of things. Like inhibitions." He handed her the joint. "Indians smoke, right? In ceremonies? Powwows?" He seemed amused by the word "powwow." He repeated it. "Pow-wowww." He gave a high-pitched giggle.

"Not marijuana, they don't." She felt indignant now. "Tobacco is a spiritual thing. The Abenaki used to think it had special powers that could help them communicate with spirit beings." Donna was careful to refer to the Abenaki as "they" and "them." Careful to use the past tense. "Today it's a kind of hospitality thing. You can't go visit my Aunt Thérèse without a gift of tobacco. You wrap it in red cloth with red yarn and beads to show honor. It's important to her," she said when he was suddenly quiet. "Of course, she herself doesn't smoke."

In case she had somehow offended the boy, she took the joint he offered and inhaled. And coughed.

He was once again amused. He laughed and laughed and drew her toward the swamp.

"There are toxic plants in here," she warned. "Oleander, nightshade. Mother grows them for medicinal purposes. She has them marked with red sticks so we'll stay away. As kids, my brother and I were never allowed in here." She didn't mention the marijuana her mother grew for her grandfather's tremors.

It was hard walking now, thick vines and roots twisted about their feet. He said, "Jesus!"—he'd tripped on a root. He backed out a few feet and paused to lean against a tree. He finished the joint. Then he grabbed at her hand and pulled her roughly toward him. She went, she had to, he was strong. He was kissing her now. She didn't like it, he was too rough. She pulled away, but he only yanked her harder against him.

"You want it, you know you do, you little squaw, you," he said, and kissed her again, a smothering, painful kiss.

She wrenched away. Her hand flew up and slapped his face.

For a moment he held her at arm's length, stared into her eyes. "I don't like that," he said, spacing his words. Then, before she could catch her breath, he'd shoved her down on the ground. A stone cut into the small of her back and she cried out. He grabbed at her blouse. She cried out again, it was a brand new blouse, he had no right. She yelled, "Stop!" but he didn't stop, he was pulling at her underpants, unbuttoning his belt with his other hand, and she screamed.

After that, things happened so fast she was dazed. She hit at him with her fists and scratched with her nails. She didn't care, she just wanted him to stop. "Little bitch," he finally grunted, and, pushing her roughly from him, he rolled off and fell back on the damp ground, his eyes shut. She stared down at him, then got up and tried to pull herself together. Her blouse was torn, her new skirt filthy.

There was someone behind her then, with a flashlight, yanking her up. It was Leroy. "Come on. I'll take you to the house. Here," he said, jamming his coat around her shoulders, "so your mother won't see your dress."

She was embarrassed, mortified! "I don't need your coat," she protested, but he was moving her along. She glanced back and Leroy said, "He's passed out. He's drunk as a skunk." He added, "You're not much better," and scowled.

"You're not my keeper," she said. "And we can't leave him lying there." She tried to release herself from Leroy's grasp, but he held fast.

"I'll take care of him," he said. "I'll get him back on his big old motorcycle. How far'd he go with you, huh? Not all the way, I'll kill him!"

"Who are you, my father?" she said.

He gave a grunting laugh and kept tugging her along with him. She heard her mother's voice calling from an upstairs window. "Donna? Is that you? Donna?"

"Yes, Mother."

"Who's that with you?"

"Just me, ma'am," Leroy called. "I was checking the hives—I thought I heard a noise—animal or somethin'. But it was Donna driving in."

"Well, be quiet getting in bed, then, Donna. Your little brother's asleep. I'm glad you're finally home." And the window dropped down.

Donna was relieved, she had to admit it. Her mother would think she'd come home with Emily. She wouldn't have to tell about the motorcycle. She wouldn't have to tell about Shep—not if Leroy got him out of there as he'd promised.

"You will help him back," she reminded Leroy. Not that she wanted to see Shep again—she was disgusted with him now. He'd been trying to rape her, hadn't he? If she hadn't fought back, if he hadn't been too drunk . . . She shuddered. Still, she didn't want him hurt. She should have realized he would expect something from her. Boys did. That's what Emily said, Emily had had more experience with boys than Donna. Donna's mother had home-schooled her until her junior year in high school. She waited for Leroy's answer before she opened her door. She was still embarrassed—how much had he seen, anyway?

"I said I would, didn't I?" said Leroy. "I said I'd take care of him. And I will."

Two

Gwen was loading the pickup, ready to make the rounds of the Branbury farms where she kept hives, when the police car pulled up behind, blocking her exit. She knew who it was and she didn't want to see him right now. She loaded in her record book, the smoker, gloves and bee veil, the sugar syrup, a few extra boards to put under hives that might need them, and then climbed into the driver's seat. "Olen," she shouted at the lanky, gray-haired man in the white car, "I can't talk now, I've work to do. Mert will give you a cup of coffee. He likes company while he works."

She was usually glad to see Olen Ashley, but now she was busy. He was a local cop, a friend of her father's. As a child she'd called him Uncle Olen, but when she grew older he became more of a big brother. In her last year of high school she grew aware that he had more interest in her than a brother might have, and for a few years she was rather pleased with his attentions, the presents he'd bring her. But six months into the state university she'd met Russell while she was doing a history paper on the Abenaki, and Olen took second place in her affections.

Shortly after that she and Russell married, and so did Olen. But two years later he was childless and divorced; he needed Gwen's ear, her advice. At least he kept his feelings in check, and for her sake he more or less tolerated Russell's activism. Although he'd told Russell point-blank that if he caught him doing something illegal he'd have to bring him in. They both understood that. It was getting to be sort of a cat-and-mouse game.

"It's not coffee I'm looking for," Olen said, sounding gruff, more like the police lieutenant he was and less the family friend, "it's a missing person." He leaned his arms on the cab of her pickup. His face looked huge and flushed in the window.

For a moment Gwen was worried. She counted mentally: Donna was home and in bed after a late night. Brownie, too, was in bed; it was Sunday, his sleep-in day. Russell's dad was in his workroom, surrounded by tangles and twists of split wood. Leroy was beside her in the pickup, staring straight ahead as though he didn't realize a policeman was present. His left leg, though, was jiggling a little from nerves.

"A missing college boy," Olen went on. "He was last seen driving off with your Donna on a motorcycle."

Now Gwen's stomach was doing twists and turns. A motorcycle? But it was Emily Willmarth who'd driven Donna home, wasn't it?

"I'd like to speak to the girl, Gwen. Not that she's under any kind of suspicion." He waved his arms, smiled a little. "But she was the last person to see the boy. He hasn't been back to his bed in the fraternity."

"Well, he's not here. Donna came in at ten of one from a dance. I know, I called out to her, I looked at the clock. Leroy knows. He was still up, weren't you, Leroy?"

Leroy jerked his head about, his mouth slightly open, as though suddenly aware that there was a police officer nearby. "Yeah. She went in the house then."

"You see," Olen said, still leaning his elbows on the open truck window, "his parents were coming up today to take him out to brunch at the Branbury Inn. He'd planned to meet them at ten-thirty. And he wasn't there."

"A college boy," Gwen said. "You were in college once, Olen. Did you ever take off on a Saturday night?"

"Sure, but I wouldn't leave my motorcycle out on a mountain road. We found it half a mile below here. Look, I've got two men searching the general area now. When I heard about the kid's bringing Donna home, I thought I'd come on up and ask." He looked sympathetic, his eyes on Gwen's face. "I'd like to talk to Donna, please, Gwen. These are New York parents. They're all in a twit."

Brownie appeared in the kitchen doorway. "Mom! There's no Froot Loops in the pantry. What'm I supposed to eat for breakfast?"

She saw her son the way Olen would see him, a slight, poor-complexioned boy with bowed legs like he didn't get enough calcium in his bones. Though she did try. Brownie had always been a fussy eater.

"Have the Raisin Bran," she called. "I'll buy some more Froot Loops. And go wake Donna, will you? Tell her Uncle Olen wants to see her."

She'd had the children call Olen "uncle" when they were small, and they still called him that. The word "uncle" made the mission seem more innocent. And it was innocent, wasn't it? What college boy wanted to have brunch with his parents when something more exciting might come along?

Another concern sprang up. Had he really brought Donna home last night—and on a motorcycle? She and Russell had had a few drinks, made love, and slept like babies—at least *he* had—until Donna came home. With Donna safe in bed, she'd slept soundly. Russell was out of the house by five-forty-five. Had he seen a motorcycle? She hoped not. It would blow his mind! She was suddenly upset with that college boy, upset with Donna. With Olen, too. It was a gorgeous April day. The pussy willows were out, the bees were overjoyed. Why was Olen pulling a shadow over her world?

And here was a second police car, pulling up behind Olen's. Would she never get away this morning? A short, robust-looking woman shouted, "The cycle'd been here, I could see the tracks. Shall we search the woods?"

Olen glanced at Gwen. "With your permission? He might

have just gone in the woods to, um, sleep it off. They'd been at a party, right?" His tone was more conciliatory, his voice softer, throatier. "He could have got lost, trying to get back to his bike. He's had a couple warnings for that thing—shouldn'ta been driving it. I suppose Donna didn't know."

"But why was the bike a half mile down the road if he was in our woods? Does that make sense?"

"Gwen," said Olen, poking his big gray head close to her face, "nothing makes sense when you're twenty years old. Right, Leroy?" For the first time he addressed the hired boy. Leroy nodded and pulled the bill of his feed cap down over his bushy red eyebrows.

"So we'll have a look," Olen said to the officer, a sergeant, who was out of her car now. "Tell Donna not to go anywhere," he warned Gwen. "We'll want to talk to her. The boy might've said something about where he was headed, you know."

"It's damp in there," Gwen said, resigned to losing half a morning's work. "You'd better let me come with you. You don't want to get those nice black shoes muddy." She wasn't going to worry. What would a college boy be doing in her woods? This "missing person" label was definitely premature. "So let's get going," she told Olen, who was lifting an anxious eyebrow.

"Stay here and explain to Donna what we're doing," she told Leroy. "Don't alarm her, though." She strode on ahead of the two officers. For one thing, she wanted to steer them away from the barrel she illegally burned her trash in.

They were partway into the swamp, picking their way slowly through the frosty grasses, when the sergeant, who had gone on ahead, gave a yell. "Stay back," Olen warned, and lurched forward. For a moment the woods were silent except for twittering birds and snapping twigs where some small animal had squeezed through.

But she wasn't going to stay back. If they'd found something—someone—in her woods, she wanted to see. This was a controversial area they were in now. A variety of unusual plants grew here: oleander, nightshade, pokeweed. Marijuana. She didn't want them to recognize that!

"Be careful, I told you," she called out. "Watch for any plants you're not familiar with."

"Too late for this kid," the sergeant shouted back, and when Gwen caught up, she heard Olen say, "Oh, Jesus Christ."

A dark-haired boy lay there, face down, the skin horribly red and swollen on the back of his neck and hands as though he'd been rolling in the leaves. When the sergeant turned him over—though Olen swore at her for doing that—she saw the hot red dry puffy skin of his face, the purple black bruises on the neck, something that looked like an unhealed cut on his cheek. Flies were buzzing about his head; she heard the hum of wild bees in the white Adder's Mouth that grew nearby. She saw the discolored place in the grass where the boy had been vomiting. He appeared to be sleeping—if that's what he had been doing—in a patch of deadly nightshade.

Gwen had a headache when she woke up the next morning; it was drumming and drumming in her temples. She had just had a call from Olen. The news was bad. She had asked Olen to give her time, to let her talk to the young people alone. She had had to turn aside his insistent questions yesterday. "You can see Donna later, not now," she'd told him, feeling disoriented, swept away. "She's upset enough without you hurling questions at her." Now she, Donna, and Leroy were walking the woods together. She wanted Donna to retrace her steps, Leroy to tell his part of the story. She needed the facts herself before Olen tried to elicit them in his plowmanlike fashion.

"I want the whole story. The whole truth," she insisted, "out of both of you."

"It was here," Donna said when they'd gone twenty yards into the woods. "I mean around here I left him—I can't remember exactly. He tried to—well, he tried to do stuff, I didn't like it. I fell—"

"She was pushed," Leroy said, his hands hanging like rakes at his sides. "She was on the ground."

Donna glared at him. "I fell. That's when he—Anyway, then you came, Leroy. You had no business following us in like that!

You should leave me alone. Stick to what you're paid for. The bees. My personal life doesn't concern *you*."

"Donna," Gwen murmured, seeing Leroy's stricken expression. "Enough."

"If I hadn't come by just then—" Leroy went on, and was shushed by Gwen. She didn't want to hear this part. She just wanted facts. Where and when, not what.

"It wasn't here," Leroy said. "It was over by that sugar maple. I remember, it's the tree with the red slash. I made it myself when Brownie wanted a path he could ski."

Gwen looked at the tree, at the ground beneath it. The snow had already melted in the April sun that snaked down through the budding leaves; there was no sign of a struggle, of a body lying there.

"He was there when I left," Leroy said. "He was out of it. He was drunk. I tried to wake him up, get him to go home. It didn't work. So I left him there. I figured he'd wake up sooner or later, get on his big motorcycle, and go home to his safe little bed."

"You said you'd take care of him. You did!" Donna cried, grabbing his arm.

"Well, I tried, didn't I?" He shook his arm free. "I told you I tried. It'd stopped snowing. The moon was back out. It wasn't that cold, he wasn't gonna freeze. He had a big fancy coat on. I noticed he didn't give *you* that coat to wear. You were the one would of froze if I hadn't—"

"Stop it, both of you!" Gwen shouted. She took a breath to steady herself. "But if you left him here, Leroy, then how did he get into the swamp? Tell me that."

Leroy was silent. Donna looked at him and he shook his shaggy head. "Not me. I just left him here, like I said. He must've got in there himself. Went the wrong way."

"They found the motorcycle down the road," Gwen said. "Is that where he left it?" She looked at Donna. The girl was clutching her hands together, as though trying to squeeze something out of them.

"Shep left it by the fence. At the foot of the driveway!" She sounded totally distraught now. One hand flew up to her forehead as though she, too, had a headache. A hangover, Gwen supposed, feeling her own head pounding. The girl wasn't used to drinking. Gwen had to understand. How could you go to a fraternity dance without drinking? How could a young girl say no?

"I didn't move it. It wasn't me," said Leroy, gazing off at something Gwen couldn't see. "I don't know how it got down there. Somebody else must've moved it."

"Somebody else," Gwen repeated numbly. "Then somebody else could have pulled the boy into the swamp. The police found him with his face in the nightshade—at least fifty feet from here." She added, "Atropine and belladonna come from that plant, you know. If it gets into the bloodstream it can paralyze the nervous system, it can kill."

How ironic, that word "belladonna," she thought. It meant "beautiful woman." It was said that, during the Renaissance, women applied an extract of the plant to their eyes to dilate their pupils, enhance their appearance. But the boy had been far from beautiful when they found him. His dilated eyes looked ghastly, shocked, as though he'd seen a horrible sight. It wouldn't—couldn't—have been her lovely Donna.

"You said he wasn't dead. You said there was a pulse." Donna yanked at her mother's sleeve, her hand shaking. "Please, Mom, you said he was still alive."

"Then, yes," Gwen said. "But Olen called. He's gone, Donna, the boy is dead."

Donna cried out; she turned away, her shoulders quaking.

"I'm so sorry." Gwen put an arm around her daughter, who seemed to need holding up. "Sorry for you. For the parents. But we have to face this. The police will be back here with questions. You'll have to remember everything. The time, the place, any other sounds you heard—the most minute details. And I'm not just talking to *you*, Donna. You, too, Leroy. You're a witness as well. Probably a suspect." She put her free hand on his arm. "I don't mean to scare you. I just want you to be prepared."

She saw Leroy give her a sidelong glance. She wondered if he knew what she was thinking about. Russell was there, too, that night, although he didn't know where his daughter had gone—Gwen hadn't dared tell him. But why would Russell go out in the woods? Unless he'd heard the motorcycle, suspected it was Donna—he'd have gone off soon enough then. He'd have been angry—she didn't want to think how angry.

She remembered now the dirty boots she'd found the next morning in the kitchen—she'd cleaned off the dried mud, put them back in Russell's closet. But of course it was mud from the Revolutionary War reenactments, not swamp mud. There was no need for Olen to know about Russell's presence at home, was there? No, definitely not. She held tight to Donna as they made their way slowly back to the house.

Donna slipped in through the side door of Emily's dormitory. There was no one in sight, thank heavens. Everyone would know by now about Shep Noble's death, about where he'd been found. She still couldn't believe it; it was like a nightmare she was breathing heavily through. She couldn't grieve—she'd hardly known Shep, she hated what he'd tried to do to her. But she never wanted him dead!

She reached Emily's room without running into another student and knocked, praying it wouldn't be Alyce who answered. But Alyce stood there, a small smile on her face. "Emily's inside," she said, motioning with a pale, ringed hand. "I expect you're here to tell her your troubles. I was just leaving." She swept past Donna like she owned the whole doorway, like Donna wasn't there at all.

A moment later she wheeled about. "We're all mourning Shep. All of us. The whole college. Shep was my special friend," she added, her face all puckery. Then she turned and ran down the hall.

When Donna entered, Emily looked up from her sociology book—they were in the same class—and said, "Hi, don't mind her," as though nothing had happened, although they both knew the sky had fallen.

Donna slumped back on Emily's bed and stared at the ceiling. Someone had stuck silver stars on it—last year's residents, Emily said. Emily liked to lie there and gaze at them. They made the future appear hopeful, she said.

But Donna's future didn't look hopeful at all—just the opposite. "You heard what happened."

Emily shut her book. She nodded, looking sad, sympathetic. "But I don't know all the facts. I mean, I only heard the rumors, you know. That Shep is dead, that he was found in your woods."

"And you're wondering where I was."

"Well, I've heard about Shep. A nice guy, an athlete, very popular. But a big appetite, too. For women. For drugs—he got in some trouble with that. They're oversexed, those athletes. He tried to come on to me once, did I tell you? We were coming out of soc class, he put his hand on my butt—and I pinched him, hard. God, I never should have let you come with me, Donna. Nothing would have happened if I hadn't made you." Emily's lip was quivery. She was pulling at her short brown hair.

Donna waved her hands. "You didn't make me. I went of my own accord. I should have gone home with you. It was *my* fault I stayed. And Shep, well, I asked him to take me home. I left my coat at the frat house. I was hoping you could get it for me. I can't go back in there!"

Emily sat on the edge of the bed, put her hand on Donna's arm. "I'll get it for you. Now quit blaming yourself. You didn't know he was going to come on to you."

"How'd you know he did? Is that what they're saying?"

"Well, it's not hard to figure. Kids know Shep. So you got him off, went back in the house, expecting he'd leave, right?"

"Sort of." Donna told the story: about Leroy's intervention, about Shep's passing out. "But somehow he got moved. Or moved himself. We just know he was in my mother's nightshade. It looks bad for my mother. Uncle Olen is working on the case. He's a local cop—not my real uncle, just a family friend."

"My mother's boyfriend, Colm Hanna, is a cop, too. He works there part-time. You should talk to him. Talk to my mother. She gets into these things. She—well, she helped me when things got bad a while back. Say, what are you doing tomorrow afternoon?"

"I don't know. I can't think straight. I guess I'm through after my one o'clock."

"Then we'll drive over, talk to Mom. It could help just to talk, right?"

"Well . . ." Donna didn't know why Emily's mother would want to help *her*. Ms. Willmarth was a dairy farmer, she had cows to take care of. However, Donna's mother kept bees on the Willmarth farm. There was some connection there. "All right," she said. "But I don't know what anyone can do. There weren't any witnesses."

"What about that guy Leroy? You said he was the last to see Shep alive, right?"

Donna held her breath a moment. Was it really Leroy? He had gone back after she went to bed. He was jealous. It drove Donna crazy; frankly, she couldn't move a step around the place without his watching her. She'd have to get a straight story out of him.

One thing she knew: She would ask her mother to get rid of those poisonous plants. Her mother even talked to them, apologized when she picked one or crushed it for some salve she was making. She would give a gift of tobacco to the plant in exchange for "taking its life." It was "Indian" to do that, her mother said. And all her mother had in her was one long-ago drop of Indian blood through some ancestor who'd been taken prisoner, marched up to Canada, and then married an Abenaki brave.

Well, Donna didn't need the traditions. She didn't need another identity. She was having enough trouble just figuring out who *she* was.

"Want some Sprite?" Emily asked. She went over to the small refrigerator she kept in a corner of the room.

"No, thanks. We've got that paper to write for soc class. I have to go see Professor Wimmet about what to write. I have to get my head together. I have to get my mind off what happened." But what happened was a shadow that would follow her even to bed.

"Sure, I understand. We'll talk about it tomorrow. Be here at two, okay?"

Donna nodded. When she went to the door, she saw that a sheet of paper had been shoved under it. She picked it up to give to Emily.

But it was for her, not Emily. In red ink were the words: *BELLA DONNA.*

She crumpled it in her fist so Emily wouldn't see, let the door bang behind her, and stumbled, on rubbery legs, down the hall.

Three

She's in her room, she isn't feeling well," Gwen told Olen Ashley when he appeared in the doorway, looking contrite, the cheeks of his big plain face working in and out, one hand fiddling with a jacket button as though he were uncomfortable with what he had to say.

"I can come back tomorrow," he said, his hand on the doorknob.

"No, wait." She needed to hear more—if he had anything new to tell her, that is. She wanted the facts; it was the unknown that was tormenting her. "Try some of my dandelion wine? We've had a great crop of dandelions this spring. The bees love them, too." Dandelions were the bees' first taste of nectar after a long cold winter. "Come on. Just a small glass? It's pretty mild."

Olen smiled. She knew he liked dandelion wine, even if he was on duty. They'd made it together once when her father was still alive, when they were both younger—before he'd gotten so law-and-order-fixated.

"Hi, there, son," Olen said, as Brownie came running in, straight for the refrigerator.

"Say hello to Uncle Olen," she said.

Brownie mumbled something and proceeded to spread a piece of bread with peanut butter and honey. Gwen didn't want to talk in front of the boy, so she poured the wine, and she and Olen sat in silence until Brownie started upstairs with a can of Pepsi and the sandwich.

"Lights out by nine," she reminded him, but there was no response. Brownie wanted more than anything in the world, it seemed, to be an ordinary kid. And so far he was achieving his goal. He was neither popular nor unpopular in school—he just went along, without trouble. She wanted life to remain that way for him.

"I suppose this will have to be in the local papers," she said to Olen.

"Afraid so, Gwen." He looked apologetic. "We have to report it, you know. A death that, well, could be homicide?"

"Homicide? It was the nightshade! And I didn't even plant it, it had been growing there for years. It likes a damp stony spot, a wasteland. I merely cultivated it, that's all. I mean, I sell it for the atropine. They put it in eyedrops, to dilate the pupils. Hundreds of ophthalmologists—"

"I know, I know," he said. "That's not the problem."

"What is the problem?"

"Cause of death. That's what they're asking down at the station." He licked his lips. He was nervous; she knew the dry lip syndrome.

"The nightshade!" she half shouted. "The boy had a cut on his face, you saw that. His nose was down in the roots. He must have dragged himself over there, dead drunk."

"That's what happened, I suppose—it was all an accident. But the coroner says—"

"Says what? What?"

"Gwen, if you keep interrupting, I'll never get to the point." He swallowed the wine, let her wait. There was always a flare of the dramatic in Olen, wanting to surprise, shock with his words. He'd protect her, though, that's what he liked to do. After a few sighs, he went on. "There were bruises on the forehead. Like he'd been hit, the coroner says. With a rock or something, I don't know. And where did that cut come from?" Olen looked upset. She could see he didn't want to make things hard for her. He wanted to get this over with as much as she did.

"Who would have done that? Dragged him and then hit him? Not Donna! You can't think that Donna—"

"No, no. I've known Donna all my life. She's like a daughter to me." He looked nostalgic; he rubbed his chest. Donna was still fond of Uncle Olen. It was Brownie who could take or leave him. Brownie wanted—needed—his father.

She sighed, finished her glass of wine. "So what happens next?"

"We wait. Until the coroner is finished with the body. Until the autopsy is done."

"Those bruises," she said thoughtfully, "were probably caused by the nightshade. It can turn the skin purplish. Make it look like he was hit, when he wasn't."

"They'll call in an ethnobotanist. Somebody who knows the indigenous plants around here."

"Why not let me talk to them? I know as much about nightshade as anybody."

"Conflict of interest, Gwen. We need an objective observer."

"Are you an objective observer, Olen? You're a family friend."

He flushed. "Now, look here, don't worry. I'll be on the case as long as they'll let me. I won't let anything happen to you. Or Donna."

"Or Leroy? What about Leroy? He was the last to see that boy. By his own admission. He's smitten with Donna, we all know that. But I'm sure he'd never hurt anyone."

"It's a motive." He was looking hard at her now, his lips pressed together. The look said she didn't know Leroy all that well. Leroy would have known where the nightshade grew, he could have dragged the boy over there, moved the motorcycle. It was possible. It would be manslaughter at the very least—if he'd deliberately pulled the boy into the nightshade. She cupped the glass in her hands, squeezed it until Olen took it away.

"You're going to break it," he said, smiling.

"You'll help Leroy, too?"

He thumped his empty wine glass down on the table. "We have to look at every contingency, Gwen. The boy's parents, I met them this morning. They have money up the wazoo." He rubbed his fingers together. "Poughkeepsie, New York. Father's a lawyer, they'll know how to litigate." He was looking angry now, bitter at the wrongful distribution of wealth in the world. "I can't come over here too often, though. I've got to appear impartial. Even though"—and his voice softened—"I'm not."

She was glad when he left. She was feeling flushed, uncomfortable. She opened a window, but only warm spring air blew in. And the familiar murmur of honeybees.

Tuesday afternoon, Leroy came down with a fever, and Gwen called Tilden Ball from the farm up the road to come and mow. Tilden was a tall, quiet young man, rawboned and awkward-looking—he seemed to have grown a foot every time she saw him. Like Donna, he was a freshman on scholarship at Branbury—the first in his family to attend college. He was there because of a farmer who'd sold his four-hundred-acre farm to a developer and then given three scholarships to local farm boys. Tilden wasn't especially bright, but driven by his father, he was a hard worker; he'd earned B's in high school. According to Donna, though, he was already in academic trouble at Branbury. He'd wormed his way into two of her classes, she said, so she could help him write his papers—which she wasn't about to do.

Tilden would be far happier, Gwen thought, as an automobile mechanic, as Mert had been. The boy loved old cars; he was always driving souped-up models.

Today, though, he was reluctant to come. He was done with classes by afternoon, but he had to pass chemistry and sociology—"No thanks to Donna," he said pointedly—or his father would "kill" him. But when she said, "Okay, Tilden, we'll find someone else," he changed his mind.

He'd be over in twenty minutes, he said, and he was, looking as though he, too, had a fever, he was so red-nosed and mad-looking. He'd had an argument with his father over his grades, was trying to calm down. He adored his father—or feared him—she didn't know which. The sad thing was that Harvey, a little martinet, seemed to favor the older two sons over Tilden. He just wanted Tilden to "achieve" so he could brag that he had a son who'd "graduated college."

Feeling sorry for the boy, she spent extra time showing him what to do, where to mow; and finally, around three o'clock, she went alone to the Willmarth farm, donned her gloves and bee veil, and inspected the dozen hives she'd left there. They appeared to have wintered well, but the hives were crowded, and there was always the worry about swarming. Bees wanted plenty of space in the hives, and since the queen liked to move upward to lay her eggs, the best way to give her more space was to rotate the hive bodies throughout the springtime, putting the full upper hive body on the bottom and the empty bottom hive body on the top. By May the top body would be filled with brood, pollen, and golden nectar—food for any queen.

When she opened the first hive, though, she found the bees in a defensive posture, their abdomens raised in the air in the sting position. Hungry, she decided, and defending their honey, of course—a metaphor for her own life. "Right?" she said aloud. But the bees only purred. She puffed smoke along the frame tops to quiet them, then medicated the brood against disease and closed the hive.

Would she be able to nurture her own daughter's life so easily? She'd hardly had a wink of sleep the night before, worrying about the college boy's death, about the oddities of the situation. Russell, too, claimed on the phone that he hadn't seen or heard a motorcycle when he left that morning. "You better go out and pull up that damn nightshade," he'd said. "Could have been our own kids got in it. And get rid of some of those hives while you're at it."

Russell was always complaining about her bees—he'd been stung once too often. You didn't *keep* bees, he argued, bees were wild creatures; let them inhabit the tree hollows, gather pollen where they would. His ancestors, he said (although he had almost as much French blood as Abenaki), never *kept* bees.

She sighed. She wasn't trying to *own* the bees, she was just *caring* for them. Surely an Abenaki man would understand that.

"Oh, well," she said aloud.

The hives checked and rotated, and a few of them fed with sugar syrup, she went back to the cow barn to report. She was surprised to find not only Emily there, but Donna, both girls squatting on upturned pails, in deep conversation with Emily's mother, Ruth. When Gwen started to back out, Ruth called her in. "We're talking about that boy's death. Emily thought it might help your daughter to talk."

Ruth got up, looking flushed and fit in her jeans and denim work shirt. "Let's all go in the kitchen. I'm done here anyway. Tim—he's the hired man—will finish up." She waved away Gwen's I-don't-want-to-impose plea and led the way to the house.

When they reached the house, Donna put her hand on Gwen's arm to stop her. "Mother, I told her everything," she said, looking weary, her hair shoved back behind her ears, in need of a wash—it looked stringy, Gwen thought. "She's helped people before. Emily brought me here. I told about *this*. It was under Emily's door at the dorm last night."

She pulled a rumpled piece of paper out of her pocket. Gwen read it and paled.

"And there's more. I didn't think so much of this. I mean, I thought it was Emily's roommate who wrote it—she's a bitch. But then this morning, on my voice mail at school—there was another message."

Gwen gripped her daughter's arm. She felt a little faint, needing and yet not wanting to hear. The thick fragrance of hyacinths came from the house garden; she had to steady herself on the porch railing.

Donna couldn't say the words. She pulled away from her mother, ran up the steps and into the Willmarth kitchen. Gwen followed; the smell of strong coffee strengthened her. Ruth put a steaming mug in her hand.

"I know how you feel," Ruth said. "I've had my share of these hate calls. Sick people, you have to realize that. Most of the people around here are okay. Full of the old fears and prejudices, maybe, but usually they don't interfere."

Gwen drank the coffee gratefully, tried to compose herself,

to catch Donna's eye to show her support, but the girl wouldn't look at her. "I don't know what anyone can do," Gwen said, hearing her voice hoarse. "We don't have all the facts yet, the blood tests. Olen Ashley—he's a policeman, a friend—is sympathetic; he's working on the case."

"I've heard of him," Ruth said, breathing in the hot coffee as though it were life-giving. "He's a good cop, my friend Colm Hanna says. Colm will keep me posted. His father's a mortician. He must already have the body. Or is it—"

"The coroner, yes." Gwen explained about the nightshade. "They said there were bruises, like somebody'd hit him. But I'm sure they came from contact with the plant."

"My son-in-law, Jack Sweeney's, an ethnobotanist—if you need him." Ruth leaned her elbows on the table, looked into Gwen's face. "He's my Sharon's husband."

"Oh, I'll remember that. Those parents, I understand from Olen, are litigious."

"It is their son," Ruth murmured. Her eyes had a faraway look. Gwen recalled something about Ruth's son, Vic, kidnapped at the age of ten. She couldn't imagine it. What if it had been Brownie in that college boy's place? What would she have done? She knocked her mug with an elbow, spilling the coffee. Ruth sponged it up, smiling, and poured a refill.

Not sue, no, Gwen could never do that. Money couldn't make up for a death. She didn't want to meet the parents, but they had her sympathy. Her eyes filled, and Ruth reached over to put a hand on hers. She heard the girls murmuring at the far end of the table.

Changing the subject, Gwen told Ruth what she'd done with the bees. Ruth seemed delighted with the idea of bees making honey on her land. They would make it in her stead, she said jokingly, her honey days were over. She herself was diversifying, she said, she was growing hemp—"if illegally." She was growing Christmas trees, she made maple syrup—although it hadn't been a good season, too dry, too few cold nights. "Vic has chickens," she added, "he brings in a little pocket money from the eggs. We're getting by."

Gwen had heard about Ruth's troubles, about how she was having to buy out her ex-husband's share of the farm. Milk prices were low, she'd read in the papers. She was thankful she owned her bee farm fair and clear. The profit from the honey went for food and clothing, not for loan repayments.

"I love to hear the bees," Ruth said, pushing back a sheaf of gray-brown hair. She had a broad-cheeked face, clear brown eyes, dark curving brows. She looked, well, open, compassionate; Gwen was glad she'd come. "They're in love with the wildflowers. I think the cows like them, too. They bring in the spring. They bring in life."

Gwen nodded; she felt it was true. About life, that is. But death was always there, that shadow across the land. It revisited on cloudy days when the bees were less active. And when she thought about Shep Noble.

Donna was standing up now, she needed a ride back to class; she had a conference with her sociology professor. She seemed obsessed with her studies, as though hard work and routine would get her through this trauma. Gwen stood up, too; she and Donna said their good-byes and drove off down Cow Hill Road toward the college. It was a lovely April day: sun out finally, gleaming on the yellow rocket that bloomed happily in the ditch. The bees would be ecstatic. Sometimes Gwen imagined how it would feel to be a bee, to visit the flowers, suck up the sweet warm pollen. Make honey. Such a richness! Her own life seemed drab by comparison.

There was something wasteful, though, destructive, in the air—the opposite of making honey. It lay in Donna's mood, something unspoken. Gwen was determined to bring it out into the light.

"All right, tell me, Donna. What was the message on your voice mail?"

Donna still couldn't say the words. She fished in her jacket pocket, thrust a note at her mother:

Go back to your teepee. You don't belong.

Enraged, Gwen shoved her foot down on the gas pedal, shot the truck forward.

“Slow down, Mom,” Donna cried out. “There’s a dog in the road!”

Gwen swerved and the dog, a scrawny black Lab mix, dashed across in front of the truck.

“Don’t let anyone ever tell you that,” she shouted at her daughter. “That you don’t belong. It’s the Alyces who don’t belong, the hate people—not you!”

But Donna was shaking her head; her thick unwashed hair fell across her eyes, making a shadow on the dashboard. “Not in that college, Mom. I’m the one who doesn’t belong there. And it wasn’t Alyce. It wasn’t her voice. It was a male voice.”

“Be right with you, Donna.” Professor Camille Wimmet looked up briefly and then back at her computer. She was frowning into it.

“I’ll come back another time. You’re busy.”

Donna backed toward the door, but the teacher said, “No, no, sit down. We had an appointment, didn’t we? I was just working on something.” She quickly saved her work, then exited the screen.

“Just a project,” she said when she saw Donna looking at the blank screen. “Nothing to do with our class. A somewhat controversial project, something people might not like to read.” She smiled. She had a nice smile, a little crooked. A light-colored mole to the right of her lips added mystery to a rather plain but cheerful face. “Sit down, Donna, please. Tell me how I can help you.”

Donna drew up a chair. “Professor Wimmet—” she began.

“Call me Ms. I don’t have tenure—not yet. I may never have. Not unless . . .” She waved a hand at the computer again. “Well, it’s all right.” She laughed softly and fluttered her hands. Her fingers were long and slender—Grandpop would say she should make baskets, Donna thought. “Who really wants to be in that rat race?” the teacher went on. “This is a male-dominated faculty.”

Donna felt uncomfortable. She didn’t want to hear about her teacher’s personal life. Nor would she tell the professor—Ms.

Wimmet—about her own troubles. She just needed a subject for her paper, that was all.

Ms. Wimmet was looking at her, waiting for her to speak up. She took off her gold-rimmed glasses. The violet-colored sweater she wore was the exact color of her eyes.

Donna took a deep breath. "It's about my paper. I was thinking of writing about the early settlers coming into this state. Why they came, who they were, what they did when they got here. What problems they might have faced. Still do, um, face."

Ms. Wimmet was looking intently at her. Donna felt herself blush. Her own skin had a cinnamon cast, her eyes almost a blue-black. She didn't look like the progeny of Anglo-Saxon Vermont settlers. She felt she had to explain herself.

"My ancestor on my mother's side was captured by the—the Abenaki people," she said. "In a Massachusetts raid. Her name was Elizabeth Jackson. Her daughter who was also captured, was separated from her. The daughter married an Abenaki man and even when she later had the chance refused to come home. My mother has a journal Elizabeth wrote later in life."

The teacher looked interested. Her lips parted in an O. "I'd love to read that," she said. "Is it published anywhere?"

"Oh, no, my mother just has it."

"So you want to trace that history? Know more about your ancestors? The Abenaki side, I mean? You'd have to study the Indians of the period, as well. That is, if you want to bring in the capture, and then the reasons why the daughter refused to come home. You could use the journal for part of your research."

Ms. Wimmet seemed excited now; she looked as though she would really like to know about the journal. "But your paper is for a sociology class. You'll have to focus on the structure of the world your ancestor lived in, the structure of the Abenaki society. Where was she taken to? St. Francis? I know many of the captives were."

"Odanak," Donna said, using the Indian word for the St. Francis Reservation that was just north of Vermont, in Canada. Her grandfather could help her with some of that history. He had come originally from Odanak. He still had relatives there on the reservation. You had to be at least one-quarter Abenaki to live there.

The teacher was leaning on the desk now, her elbows like lavender wings. Her violet eyes bore into Donna's. "I think this will be an absolutely fascinating paper. I'll learn from it, too. You see, I've been interested myself in, well, the Abenaki culture. Not just the Abenaki, but the Franco-American connection. There has been a lot of intermarriage, I know. I have French-Canadian blood myself."

"Really? But you don't look—"

"It's the Scandinavian in me, on my grandmother's side, some recessive gene. Strange the way genes work." She was smiling at Donna now, like she really cared about Donna, like she wanted Donna to write a really good paper. Then she looked back at her computer, as though she longed to get back to the paper she was writing, the one she was calling "controversial."

It seemed the interview was over. Donna stood up. "Well, then," she said, "I'll get going on it. And if you want to read the whole of my ancestor's journal—I'm sure my mother would be glad to have you read it."

The teacher sounded interested, like she might really come up and read it. "Where do you live?" she asked.

When Donna told her, she cried, "Oh! Where Leroy Boulanger works? I knew he had something to do with bees. I keep meaning to go up and see him. He's a cousin—on my mother's side." Her mother's sister had married a Boulanger, she explained, then divorced him. Leroy was the child of that brief marriage, and her only cousin. "A bit of a black sheep, my mother used to say." She laughed a little as she said this. The distance between a college teacher and Leroy Boulanger was vast. Donna had to smile, too. Leroy wasn't dumb, but he certainly wasn't a college type.

Anyway, Donna was feeling at peace for the first time since Saturday night. She felt as though things might work out after all. Ms. Wimmet was on her side. She stood up, too. They were both smiling. Shep Noble had said there was something "funny" about the teacher—Donna had no idea what he'd meant. And she didn't care. She liked Ms. Wimmet.

Outside in the corridor, Donna drew a deep breath and hurried to the main door. She would have to ride her bike home today, her mother needed the pickup. Leroy was always willing to come when she called, but she didn't want to see Leroy, even if he was Ms. Wimmet's cousin. She didn't like the way he'd been looking at her since that awful night. He acted like he was her guardian; he was far too possessive. She didn't want anyone possessing her.

She walked outside to unlock her bike. She hadn't used it since yesterday; she'd gotten a ride to school. There were students moving about the campus in different directions. She thought she saw heads turn, fingers point. It had to be her imagination, she told herself, not everyone could be watching. A girl had come up to her just that morning, to say, "How awful it must have been for you, Donna."

Her green bike was in its usual spot, but it wasn't wholly green anymore. Someone had painted words on it in red. *SQUAWS FUCK*, the red paint shrieked at her. And on the other side, *SQUAWS KILL*. She saw two ZKE boys in a doorway, grinning at her; they went back inside when they saw her looking at them.

She rode home in a daze. She wanted to get as far away from Branbury College as she could. She wanted to get her bike in the barn, paint out the cruel words. She couldn't find any green paint, so she slapped on black over the red. When Tilden Ball appeared in her driveway with a mower, she held her breath to keep from screaming at him.

"I need your help with my paper," he said, stalking up behind her on his long skinny legs. "I don't know what to write about. I could fail the course! Dad will kill me."

"Let him kill you, then," she shouted, exasperated. "What do I care?"

Four

The hate notes could have been someone from the fraternity. Shep was popular there," Emily told her mother when she came home to do a wash. "Most kids wouldn't blame Donna. But some asshole evidently has. Donna's a basket case."

"Can you blame her?" Ruth said. She'd had the experience herself, the implication that she didn't belong—not in the college world, but in the cocktail world of the new arrivals from downcountry. As area farms failed, Ruth had felt her psyche shrinking; hers was one of a handful of small dairy farms left in the town of Branbury. Her ex-husband, Pete, wanted $100,000 for his share of the farm; she'd paid off a quarter through loans from the bank, from friends like Colm Hanna. Now Colm was offering to buy up Pete's share himself, become her partner.

But Colm wanted more than just a share of the land. He wanted her, Ruth—as a bed as well as business partner. Did she really want that—was she ready for it? She had to decide. If she didn't, it wouldn't be fair to Colm: to take his money, but withhold herself. Did one ever know an answer to a question like that?

Emily was talking again. "I feel like that myself, Mom, rooming with Alyce Worthington. She makes me feel like a dumb little farm kid. Which I am, I suppose. I've never even been to

New York City, where she goes at least once a month. She talks about the Met and the MoMA, and the Park Avenue apartments where her friends live. Her father's a big-time architect. Her mother spends her afternoons pouring tea at the charity gigs. I can't stand it, Mother. I can't! I might . . . stab her one day. With a pitchfork. I've been thinking of taking one to school."

"Stop that talk. The year's almost over. You can cope. Then you can change roommates. Or live at home."

"And smell like a barn when I go to class every day?" Emily slammed down the can of soda she was guzzling.

"I might remind you we put in a new shower. For you and Vic."

"And you? For Colm Hanna? I've seen how you jump in the shower before he comes to visit." Emily gathered her books; she was headed for the college library, she told her mother before Ruth could respond to the latest innuendo. "And sometimes *he* needs a shower," she shot back as she waltzed out the door with her soda and book bag.

Ruth laughed. What else could she do? Then, feeling self-conscious, she headed for the shower. Colm *was* coming over, in fact. She hoped Emily would be gone before he arrived. For one thing, she wanted to talk to him about the belladonna crisis.

Colm knew all about it, of course. Here he was in the usual outrageous garb: bright green corduroy pants he'd worn since St. Patrick's Day, a cobalt-blue shirt, and mismatched socks: one higher than the other when he hiked up his pants to sit down at her kitchen table. He'd been showing land earlier in the day; he'd left his boots at the door. Was she supposed to thank him for that? Just now he'd come from his father's mortuary, he said. The dead bodies wouldn't care how he looked, but the real estate clients? She supposed they'd be amused by a down-to-earth Vermonter-Realtor-Cop.

He told her the latest on what the police were calling the "deadly nightshade case."

"The boy's parents are suing the college for a million bucks. They claim it was the college's responsibility to look after him.

Crazy, right? And Gwen Woodleaf may well be next. It may not be homicide—unless they can prove the kid was deliberately immersed in it—but the belladonna was on the Woodleaf property. Not just growing there, but cultivated, along with—wait'll you hear this—a couple of marijuana plants. Of course, Gwen pleads she does it for the grandfather's shakes. But jeez, it's illegal, Ruth." He reached for a doughnut while she sat back in her chair to weigh his words.

"Well, I think it's ignorant to show this whole world in black and white. I've seen the old man up at the bee farm. I went there once to buy honey—though she brings it for free now. He makes baskets, they're really nice. Gwen says he got started when he had a heart attack and couldn't do his autobody work. And he remembered how his own Abenaki grandparents used to make baskets—till galvanized pails came in in the thirties and they couldn't sell baskets anymore. His hands do shake a little, but the marijuana helps. Gwen doesn't grow it just to smoke it, for heaven sake!"

"Okay, okay," he said, backing off. "What about the kids? Donna? What do you know about her habits?"

"Oh, stop, Colm. You're starting to moralize. It doesn't become you." Any more than that outfit he was wearing, she thought, and had to laugh. She could smell her own boots, for one thing. How hypocritical was *she*?

He invited her outdoors for a walk then, through the pasture, where her cows were soaking up the sun. The mountains were crowned with white clouds; the sky was a sunny bath. She put her face up to it. Already she was getting lines in her skin; soon, the wrinkles would come. But who cared? She wasn't going to carry around a parasol.

She asked Colm what they could do to help Gwen and Donna. Herself, she was drawing a blank at this point. "I don't for one minute believe that girl dragged the boy into the nightshade patch."

Colm shrugged. His hungry-looking face tilted up to hers. "Noble had a reputation for womanizing. He probably came on stronger than she wanted. But the girl had been drinking, too.

Olen Ashley questioned the other guys at the fraternity, a couple of girls who went there. By all accounts, Donna was three sheets to the wind when she left with Noble."

"Olen Ashley told you that? He's a friend of Gwen's, you know. She told me."

"Then he might have to drop the case if Gwen—or the girl—gets charged. Or that hired guy, Leroy."

"You'd take over then, Colm. Promise me you would."

"I'm only a part-timer," he said stubbornly, and changed the subject. They were walking past a patch of tall, coarse-looking plants. A white stick merely read the letter *H*. "That's not hemp you've got growing there, Ruthie." He pointed. "Tell me it's not."

"It's not," she lied.

"Tell that girl to hold her head up," Russell was ranting on the phone from Buffalo, "never mind those fra-ter-ni-ty boys. He drew out the word to show his scorn. "I told you she should go to a state college like you did. She'd learn just as much there as in this hoi-ty-toi-ty school in Branbury."

Gwen could visualize Russell as he pushed his nose up with a finger and said "hoity-toity" in a mock British accent. Russell had never forgiven the British for defeating the French and Indians back in the eighteenth century. They wanted to own the aboriginal soul, Russell claimed.

"Russ," she said, not wanting to worry him away from home or tell him about the message Donna had found, "it will all work out. Donna's working harder than ever at the books. She has an ally in the Willmarth girl. The only problem now is, well, the police have found the plants I've been growing for your dad. It was that Sergeant Hammer. She and another officer came back today with a dog."

"Tell the police to bug off. So what'll they do to you? Throw you in the jug? If they do, I'll come down, tell 'em it's *my* pot. It's for my dad, after all. Stupid they don't legitimize it, damn government."

Gwen laughed. "Just a fine, I think. Olen will help. He'll be coming over to question Leroy."

She was sorry then that she'd said it. Russell was muttering something about Leroy being a fool after Donna; he didn't like it. "He's not right for the girl, he's not good enough. Donna's going to graduate college."

"Of course she is. She'll do us proud. So tell me how it's going out there in Buffalo. They have you running around in war paint?"

Gwen let her husband wax on about how little they paid him for a long day's work of dodging and running and shooting, about how fat the role-playing British general was, how little the other reenactors knew about Native Americans—other than the stereotypes: Indians drink, Indians steal. "Hey, they drop their mouths open when they hear me speak regular English. They think I should sound like Tonto. Ug, me go-um soon, um, Paddy's Bar." He laughed hugely at his imitation.

It was the way Russell laughed aloud at the world that had drawn her to him: his Rabelaisian belly laugh that shook the room, shook the worries out of her own head.

"I'm sure they're astonished at how good-looking you are." And he *was* good-looking: his coal black hair in a sleek ponytail, tied with bright feathers. She pictured him in his native regalia, in that British redcoat he told spectators he'd "stolen" from a dead officer. Russell was the one the tourists photographed over and over again.

"When're you coming home for a decent stay?" she asked.

"After Saratoga." His assignments read like a map of revolutionary battles.

"Donna would like to see you. So would Brownie. Especially Brownie."

"I'll be home for a bit next week. You tell them to keep the faith. Love ya, babe," and he signed off before she could answer back.

"Love you," she whispered to the dead phone. She didn't know why—she and Russell were as different as apples and oranges. But down inside she knew it was love.

Her reverie was interrupted by a knock on the door. She went to it, thinking it was Olen, and she wanted to hear about the marijuana verdict. But she was surprised to see Harvey Ball with his three sons. Harvey now owned the land on both sides of the bee farm. He'd made money on investments, and he seemed to be quietly gobbling up land. She hadn't even realized he'd bought the sixty-acre place to the south of her until she saw the truck arrive and the furniture being carted out of the house.

"Harvey," she said, "can I give you a cup of coffee? I have things to do this afternoon, but I've a few minutes now. Apple or grape juice?" she offered the boys, who stood behind him in the doorway. She wondered why Tilden was home at midmorning—no classes? The older one, Sidney, taller than his father but slighter than Tilden, was working the farm with his father. Ralphie, the Down's syndrome boy, plodded right over to the refrigerator and poured himself a mug of apple juice.

Harvey realized she was busy, he said, but he had something he wanted to run by her, a bit of business, a proposition. She didn't like the sound of that word, "proposition"; she busied herself with coffee, slapped a cup into its flowered saucer. Sidney preferred coffee, too, he said, looking unhappy to be here with his father when he was obviously, his attitude said, perfectly capable of being on his own in adult company. Tilden refused anything at all. He sat on a kitchen chair looking uncomfortable. She smiled at him, but he glanced away, as though they had no relationship at all. She supposed Harvey had heard about the dead boy. A new issue of the local paper had come out yesterday afternoon, though she hadn't read it yet. She didn't want to, to tell the truth.

He cleared his throat. He was a short stocky man, with a fringe of graying hair combed carefully forward over the balding head and a complexion ruddy and pocked from hours in the sun. Like some short men she knew, Harvey seemed to feel that he had to make himself highly visible; he had to take the initiative. He leaned toward her on sharp elbows. His gray-striped sleeves were rolled up tightly on his muscled upper arms. He got right to the point. "I read the papers," he said. "I'm sorry to hear of your troubles. I'm sure it was just an . . . accident?"

She wasn't going to answer that. He could think what he wanted. The question mark in his voice showed that he didn't think it an accident. After all, the nightshade had been cultivated—by her. She gripped her coffee cup, shrugged, to show that she was concerned, yes, but not worried. Not worried about her own family being implicated.

"Must be hard for that girl of yours."

This wasn't a question. She nodded. "Hard, yes. She hardly knew that boy. But she's coping. She has her studies at the college."

Harvey glanced at Tilden, who was staring into his hands. Harvey hadn't gone to college. He'd been known to be highly vocal at town meetings about rising school taxes, the college not paying its share, what he considered "town takeover" by the college, et cetera, et cetera. Now, it seemed, he would live through his younger son—for the moment, Gwen thought. Only an hour ago Tilden had roared down the road past the beeyard with a noise that would outshriek ten lawn mowers. It scattered the bees.

"Now Sidney wants to take over the farm and I'm glad of that. Too many kids wanting out of farming. It's a damn shame. The old man works his nuts off—pardon my French—the kids quit on him."

She kept her eyes on him, sipped her coffee. She heard Sidney clear his throat, Tilden's chair creak. Ralphie slurped his apple juice and wandered in to look at Mert's baskets. "Pretty, pretty," she heard him say.

She hoped she could get the Balls out of the house in ten minutes—Leroy was waiting in the barn. Leroy had nothing good to say about the family, with whom he'd had a few run-ins. When Tilden came down to do chores or plead with Donna for help—and she had helped him in high school but had no time for it now, in college—Leroy went out of his way to antagonize.

"I want the best for Sidney," Harvey said, twisting slightly in the chair to nod at the boy. "He took a course at the university summer school, you know, he learned how to deal with a big farm, a megafarm, he calls it. Maybe a thousand cows, right, Sid?" Sid shrugged. "None of this twenty, thirty cows, like some barely hanging on down in the valley."

"Uh-huh." She waited for him to make his point.

"Now, I'm keeping the herd down to sixty so long's I'm in charge. But when the kid takes over with his new methods—I mean, I'm phasing out, wanna spend some R and R time in Florida, you know, take Ralphie here with me—Sid'll want to change things a little. He'll want—well, I might's well say it. More land. We got a hundred fifty acres to your west here, another sixty to the south. You're right in the middle. To be frank, we need your land."

He leaned forward, stuck his fat-nosed face close to hers, and she drew back. "And when I read the papers," he went on, "I thought, well, this might be the time to act. Deadly nightshade growing on this property?" He chuckled. "It might be to your advantage to move down into town. I mean, you only keep a couple hives here, right? What difference to live up here or down there? Right, Sid?" He appealed to his older son, who was drinking his coffee with a dull expressionless face.

The blood was up in Harvey's cheeks; the long speech had cost him his equanimity. And hers. She set down her coffee cup. "I'm sorry, I've run out of time."

He got up, too. His face was mottled pink, his forehead shone with sweat. He was trying to remain civil. "I understand, I just threw this at you. I didn't really expect an answer right off. Just wanted to broach the subject, you know. You'll want to talk with your . . . husband." Harvey had seen Russell once in his full regalia, complete with tomahawk—he'd looked stunned.

But of course she wouldn't sell! For one thing, this was sacred land. There was a grave here: a female child from the late Woodland period, buried sideways in a flexed position, along with a copper awl, a notched point of jasper, a copper bead necklace, a few shell beads. The land could never be sold, Russell said, and she agreed. She imagined Sidney plowing up that grave, tossing the bones into the woods. It would be sacrilege, yes. She wouldn't tell Russell what Harvey had proposed; he would be too angry. Russell did have a temper—slow, but potentially explosive.

"By the way," Harvey said at the door, the three boys halting behind him, " 'spect you won't be going to the funeral this afternoon, right? I hear they stopped classes for it. The college, I mean, big man on campus he was, hey, Tilden?" Tilden shrugged. "You'd feel, well, a mite uncomfortable, right?" He tried to look sympathetic, but it came out a smirk.

"I never met the boy," she said. "But of course I'm going. And so is Donna."

Harvey just smiled.

Ralphie stuck out his hand in parting, a grin on his lopsided face. He was really quite sweet, in spite of being a Ball. "Shiny," he said, "Ralph see a shiny," and he pointed toward the woods.

"Is that right?" she said, looking for a dropped coin, but not seeing any. It was a buttercup he'd seen, perhaps. Simple pleasures.

Harvey pulled him along then, and the trio walked slowly back up the road. Just as they were at the curve, where her land touched the Balls', and where she kept a half dozen hives, she saw one of the boys—it might have been Sidney—turn around and spit.

She clapped a hand to her cheek. It felt sticky, unclean, as though the spit had been intended for her.

Five

Professor Camille Wimmet hurried back to her office after sociology class. She didn't have any students signed up for conference; this was her sacred hour. She had completed all the coursework for her doctorate; now there was only the real work, the paper she would turn into a published article and ultimately, she hoped, a book.

The subject was fascinating to her. It had all started when she learned from her mother that back in the early thirties a woman named Eleanor Perkey had lived for eight weeks in Camille's hometown of Corning and interviewed the inhabitants to learn their reactions to a recent influx of French-Canadian farmers. Perkey had talked to Camille's grandmother, who had moved down from Quebec with her husband and six children to take over an abandoned sheep farm. Camille was shocked to learn that the "old residents" had complained that their town was no longer "one big family" and predicted that soon all the farms owned by "old Yankee pioneer stock" (which, translated, meant white, Anglo-Saxon Protestant—WASP!) would be sold to French-Canadians.

Eleanor Perkey, she found, was the wife of William Perkey, a university professor, who was conducting a eugenics survey in the state, hoping to edge out the "feebleminded" and other "degenerates," with a narrowing eye on poor Franco-Americans, homosexuals, and so-called "gypsies," some of whom turned out to be Abenaki Indians. It was Eleanor Perkey's report on "degenerate women" who were sterilized in the Brookview Reformatory in Rutland that gave Camille the true focus of her paper.

Two families, in particular, were of interest. One from the present day, and the other from the past. The present-day family was the Woodleaf-LeBlanc family, whom she knew to be of mixed Abenaki and French-Canadian blood—her student Donna had interested her in that genealogy. The woman from the past, and her principal focus, was one Annette Godineaux. Annette had been put in the reformatory on a charge of "sexual promiscuity," a "crime" of which many poor, uneducated, and abused women in that period were accused. She'd been recommitted for numerous petty crimes: larceny, breach of parole, thefts in the five-and-dime, bounced checks. And, according to a Stanford-Binet test administered to her, she scored a borderline seventy-five.

But then Camille had discovered in Mrs. Perkey's report that Annette wrote poetry. There were only four poems extant, used largely by supervisors and local police as "evidence" of her promiscuity. How could a woman with an IQ of seventy-five write such lyrical verse? Unless in some way she had fudged the IQ test, deliberately written in false responses. It was Camille's assumption that this had been the case and that Annette, whose grandfather had married an Abenaki woman from St. Francis, was as intelligent as Camille herself.

So Camille was out to prove that this woman, who had been in and out of prison no less than fourteen times, and who had ultimately submitted to the indignity of sterilization, had been horribly exploited. Annette was most likely dead, since she'd been born in 1900, but dead, Camille was out to prove, because of exploitation by the state of Vermont, which had aided and abetted the Perkeys in their eugenics project.

It was abuse, it was hate. And she meant to expose it for what it was.

She opened the folder of *ANNETTE* papers she had so far

copied: the police and social worker reports, the poems, the IQ tests, and most intriguing of all, a copy of Annette's personal journal, written prior to her disappearance from the written records and left in her room at the reformatory. Annette had had four children before her first arrest for adultery, all sent to foster homes; there was reference in the diary to an older child's offspring. Camille would have to track them down as well. There was so much work to do before she could write! First, though, she would put the reports, poems, and journal onto disk, and copy that disk so that she would have a double record. Camille was paranoid that way; she even kept important papers in her home freezer to be sure they weren't burned by a chance fire.

She took a long draft from the bottle of spring water on her desk and leaned eagerly into her task. She had to work quickly because of the four o'clock memorial service for Shep Noble. There were so many deterrents to her work! Her teaching, of course, student conferences, the interminable faculty meetings. And only yesterday Leroy's mother, who was in an institution with cystic fibrosis, had called, with an aide's help, to ask her to look up the boy. He hadn't been to visit for six months, Aunt Denise said, and would Camille do her familial duty? She was, after all, Leroy's only active relative.

Although Camille wasn't looking forward to the visit, it did have an added dividend: an introduction to Merton LeBlanc, whose sister, she'd discovered through her research, had been one of Eleanor Perkey's victims. And then the real business would start: the search for Annette, and interviews with the Godineaux family—at least with whatever members of that extended family she could ferret out.

She heard male voices out in the hall and got up to shut the door all the way. But not before she heard Frazer Manning, her department head, say to a colleague, "Tell that fruitcake to buzz off," and then laugh. Frazer was a known homophobe, and she detested him. She'd like to run out and yell, *Who do you think you are—God? Calling someone a name like that?*

But she had to be careful. Camille was lesbian. She couldn't come out yet in public—not until she had tenure.

* * *

Gwen felt awkward and sweaty where she stood at the back of the college chapel that was already jammed with mourning students. The fraternity had come en masse: The boys sat near the front in a dozen pews, a sea of bright heads, some of them still wearing baseball caps. Gwen craned her neck but couldn't pick out Donna from the crowd of girls and a few boys who had swarmed up into the balcony or on the ground floor behind the fraternity. The first two pews were reserved for the Noble family. Should she speak to them? No, they would all meet in court eventually—though she mustn't let them get her down, Russell had warned when he called again just before she left for the service. *She* hadn't made the boy drink, he reminded her; *she* hadn't given him an expensive motorcycle on which to drive her daughter and then try to rape her. For it had been attempted rape, she'd gotten that out of Donna. And now Russell was threatening to quit his job, to come home and "keep an eye on Donna." The girl wouldn't like that. He'd once "destroyed" a high school relationship, according to Donna, with his "unreasonable behavior."

The service was a series of testimonials to the boy. One by one, the fraternity brothers scuffed up in their dirty but costly Reeboks and told stories: how Shep had helped one brother make the baseball team by practicing with him each morning before breakfast; how he'd never missed a ski meet, even when he had the flu; how he'd held the fraternity championship in chugalugging—she wondered what the parents thought of that feat! Two of the boy's coaches stood up to affirm his sportsmanship and athletic prowess, and then three girls wept out abstractions like love, beauty, and soul. One of them might have been the Alyce whom Donna disliked. She matched Donna's description: blond hair swept up on top of her head, designer jeans, and silk shirt—something steely about her, the way she stood poised and dry-eyed, eliciting tears with her sentimental words. The girl who sat beside Gwen in the back pew was sobbing into a flowered hankie. Gwen wondered what she'd think if she knew who Gwen was—the instrument, the girl might say, of Shep Noble's death.

Don't feel guilty. You're not guilty. Still the tears sprang up in Gwen's eyes. Shep Noble's was a young life, unfulfilled. Who knew, after a few knocks in the world, what he might have become?

At the final burst of organ music Gwen slipped out; she couldn't bear another moment of it. Just as she stood, gulping in the outside air, she saw a dark figure slip out a side door. It was Donna: The girl's head was lowered, she was crying openly. Gwen called out, but Donna didn't hear, or chose not to respond. The girl ran down the path to the road, jumped on her bicycle, and raced off toward town. She looked like a refugee fleeing a war, her hair in long black ropes from the wind, her legs pedaling faster than any human, it seemed, could go. Up a hill, around a corner she careened, and was gone.

Would she escape the war after all? The persecutors? Gwen prayed that she would. But knew in her heart it would be a long uphill battle.

Coming out the rear door of the chapel, Professor Camille Wimmet saw Donna Woodleaf-LeBlanc ride up the road on her bicycle. Had the girl attended the service? She supposed it wouldn't have been easy for her, under the circumstances. Camille herself had gone with mixed emotions. Shep Noble had been her student—an average student, usually prepared, if not brilliantly. Rather narrow-minded, though, she'd noted in class discussion—like his ancestor.

And this was the question in Camille's mind: Should she should tell the Woodleaf family about the Perkey connection? Was it relevant? For Shep, she had discovered, was a descendant of William and Eleanor Perkey, who had done such irreparable harm to the state's poor that their project had turned into a veritable holocaust. Shep Perkey Noble, alive, might have helped her; he might have had letters, documents, family stories to offer. She might even have persuaded him to write his paper about the eugenics project.

And yet, when she'd invited him to remain after class for the purpose of interrogating him, and he'd stood before her desk looking handsome, confident, arrogant, like his maternal grandparents, she'd felt such an anger fill her throat that she could only mumble something incoherent about his latest quiz and quickly dismiss him.

But who else would know about this connection? And who would kill for it—if indeed, that had been the case? The poor "degenerates" whom the grandparents had abused? The babies they had, in effect, denied life to? But the poor had no clout. They were mostly absorbed now into the general population; in hiding, like the Abenaki, who, in order to survive, for decades had been trying to assimilate themselves into the white majority.

Yet the Abenaki of late, she'd read, had been emerging, protesting, asserting their ancient rights. Was Shep Perkey Noble's death part of this protest? The notion seemed far-fetched. She would have to consider carefully before putting the Woodleaf-LeBlanc family at risk. After all, Donna was her student.

"Professor Wimmet—are you free? Can I talk to you about my paper?" It was Sue Coletti, a plump, sweet-faced girl—overly conscientious.

"Why not?" she said as the girl trotted alongside her. She'd been thinking abusive thoughts about the dead. She wanted to push them out of mind. "So what is it you were planning to write? This afternoon has blotted everything out of my head."

"Oh, yes, sad, wasn't it? I know he was in your other section." The girl, a declared lesbian, put a hand on the teacher's sleeve.

"The paper," Camille reminded her, and hearing voices behind her, she pulled away and walked on faster.

Donna rode her bike to the local Ben & Jerry's. She didn't want to see any of those college kids, not even Emily, who had offered to go with her to the service, but at the last minute had to help with a freshening cow.

She'd sat in the balcony, seen the parents when they came in, looking tall, well groomed, terribly grieved. It had broken her heart to see the mother suddenly slump into the pew, a handkerchief clutched to her face, the father patting her shoulder. That one gesture, the patting of the shoulder, was what destroyed Donna. She was suddenly drowning in tears—not for Shep so much, whom she didn't know, really, but for the parents. She hardly saw or heard the rest of the service. As she stumbled down the stairs after the final benediction, someone grabbed her wrist and twisted it. It was Alyce Worthington. "You'll have to live with this," the girl said, looking hard into Donna's eyes. And then, with a little push, she let her go. And Donna raced downtown to console herself with ice cream.

It was no consolation. Her tears kept dripping into the plastic dish. She was getting up to leave when a voice spoke up. She knew that voice, jammed both fists into her eyes.

" 'S'not worth it," Leroy was saying, "you shouldna gone. Look." He snatched up her hand when she tried to pick up her bowl. "He was an SOB. *You* know he was, he wasn't worth your little finger. You can't go mooning over 'im."

"I'm not mooning over him. That's not why I'm crying!" Leroy didn't understand. He couldn't understand it was the boy's father comforting the mother that brought on the tears. And then that mean-spirited Alyce, telling her she'd have to live with the guilt. Leroy couldn't understand all that.

"You should have minded your own business, Leroy. You had no right to come out that night and peer at us. Like we were . . ." She couldn't find the right words.

"Like you were gettin' laid," he said hoarsely, running a nervous hand through his rusty hair. "That's why I came out. You were yellin', you don't remember that? I'm supposed to sit by, let that son of a bee attack you? What else could I do but—but stop him?"

She felt her heart go slack. "Stop him—how?" she asked. "Did you drag him into the nightshade? Did you hit him with something?" She was awed at her own words. Horrified. Her breath came in ragged gasps.

He didn't answer. Not right away. Finally, leaning his elbows on the table, the whites of his eyes brilliant, he said, "Maybe. Maybe I did. For you, Donna. Anything I did, it was for you."

"Don't come near me. Ever again," she said, and kicked his leg, hard, as she left the table.

* * *

Leroy stomped into the kitchen late that afternoon. He needed to borrow the truck, he told Gwen; he didn't say why. "If I had my own car, I wouldn't *have* to borrow yours."

"Save up for one," she said brightly.

"Save what? What you pay me? I need to make more money. I need a car to get around. I got a friend looking for a better job for me. He finds one, I'll take it."

"What? Why, this is our busiest season, Leroy, you can't leave now! Maybe next year I can pay more, I'll try. It's been hard, with Donna in college."

"I need my own car," he repeated through stubborn lips, and turned on his heel. A minute later she heard the truck screeching off down the road. He's punishing us, she thought. Punishing Donna for ignoring him, punishing me for not being able to pay a better wage.

She dropped to her knees to scrub the kitchen floor.

Six

Mert LeBlanc was surprised to see a taxi pull up in front of the house and his grandson climb out, dragging his green book bag. Then when Mert reached in his pocket for a few bucks the taxi drove off and Brownie said the school nurse had paid and he could bring her the money the next day. He was throwing up "all over the place," he said, and she was afraid he had a bug. A couple of throw-up bugs, Brownie explained, were still going around, and he didn't want to spread them.

"So you're bringin' 'em all home to us, thanks a lot," said Mert, and laughed when his grandson frowned, taking him literally. "Better go right to bed, then, son."

Mert went back to the pack basket he was making for the local craft center exhibition. He'd made egg baskets, apron baskets, thimble baskets, laundry and pack baskets, even a large cradle with a canopy over its woven bottom. He was pleased with those baskets. It beat putting auto parts together the way he'd done the first thirty-five years of his adult life.

He was part of five or more generations of basketmakers on Abenaki and French sides of the family. The baskets had kept both sides alive through depressions and oppressions, like the time a woman with a fancy WASP name had come knocking on the door to take his Aunt Maxine to the hospital for "a little procedure," as she called it—*Sign here, please*—to keep her from having more babies. The woman had looked hard at *him*, too, but Mert managed to run out the door and only his father and aunt were visited by the simpering social worker. Aunt Maxine had blasphemed the woman to her dying day. It was something Mert would never forget.

He was tightening down the ash strips when his grandson walked back in with a peanut butter and honey sandwich. "You must be feeling better now," he told the boy. "You'd think you never ate breakfast." And Brownie said, looking defensive, "Well, I lost it. I threw up, I told you."

Mert began to suspect something then. He began to suspect that Brownie's being sick had something to do with the college boy who'd died in the patch of nightshade. "Somebody say somethin' to you about that dead boy, did they?" he asked, still concentrating on his pack basket. It had sixteen uprights all tapered out; now he'd have to weave in the strips. He didn't want to alarm Brownie, just let the boy speak it out.

The boy did. He told how the whole busload of schoolkids that morning began hissing his name, calling him Brown Bear, the baptismal name he didn't want people to know. How the driver, Mrs. Bump, stopped the bus and they finally quieted. "Then, when I was getting off, a kid yelled, 'Your sister's a murderer!' and they started up again."

Brownie was crying now. He cried right into Mert's uprights that had taken three days to dry. But it was all right. Mert laid down the work and put his arms around the boy. The body felt like a basket, all ribs and strips of flesh. Mert felt his shirt soak up the tears.

"There, there," he said. He told Brownie about when he was a boy growing up in the thirties. "If you had any Indian blood in you," he said, "the other kids wouldn't play with you. Most tried to hide it, like my wife, Estelle, who was your grandmother you never knew. She dropped dead one day, kneading dough, yes, she did. She was a hard worker. She wouldn't admit she was Indian—all her life pretending to be somebody she wasn't. Me,

I had my own friends, French and Abenaki. I was almost a half-blood and proud of it."

He told the boy about how he wanted a certain brown ash tree and the ranger said, "Mert, you can't cut a growing tree on government forest land. I said, 'Yes I can, I'm Abenaki, you look it up.' So the ranger looked into it and he come back and he says, 'Mert, if you want that tree, it's yours.' You see, the government can't take an Indian's livelihood away from him. And if there's two hundred maple trees in the forest up behind our place, I can hang fifty buckets and he can't stop me."

Brownie looked skeptical. "The police would stop you. Mr. Ball would call them. They'd send over Uncle Olen."

Mert laughed again. "I'm not afraid of no police. Neither's your dad." He put both arms around his grandson, pulled him close. "And don't worry about that dead boy. Olen's a good man, he's trying to help us find out what really happened."

"Shep Noble died from the nightshade!" Brownie cried hotly. "Mother says so."

"Sure. Now go lie down so I can tell your mother you wasn't just playing hooky, she won't like that. Don't think about them mean kids. Don't think about the nightshade."

Donna drove back to the farm with Emily after their sociology class. Her mother would pick her up after her bee rounds—Donna's bicycle had a flat tire. Anyway, Donna didn't want to go home. Home reminded her of Shep Noble. Home reminded her of Leroy, who might or might not have killed Shep. It reminded her of being a "squaw," like the note said.

"Penny for your thoughts," Emily said as she parked the pickup in the farm driveway. Donna glanced out at the two round silos, the red barn, the cows browsing beyond in the pasture that was full of wildflowers. It was peaceful here, unlike the war zone of her own home, the yellow crime scene tape still strung across the path into the woods.

"Oh, nothing much. I was just thinking how nice it is here. And worrying about the paper we have to write. Have you got a topic?"

"Well, I thought I might do something on farming," Emily said. "You know, all the attitude problems?"

"What problems are those?" Donna needed to get into other people's worlds, into *their* problems. She had to stop thinking about her own.

"Oh, the way people feel about farming. That it's the kind of job you don't need an education for, just to milk cows. When that's not true at all." Emily was warming to the subject. "You have to know about nutrition, and milking machines, and artificial insemination. My mother works all day at it. And we're still living on the edge!"

"I know," murmured Donna, feeling she should make a noise of some kind after that impassioned speech. And she *did* know what living on the edge was. Her family was a good example of it. Milk and honey, she thought. It sounded romantic, but you couldn't make a real living off it. Herself, she'd *do* something one day. She'd be a professional, like Ms. Wimmet.

She got out of the pickup and slammed the tinny door behind her. It popped open again.

"Damn the thing," Emily said. "I mean, this is what I'm talking about. We can't afford a new pickup because my mother is trying to buy my father out—and so she keeps patching together the old machinery. Frankly, I'd be just as happy if she'd let him buy *her* out. Move us to town. Then I wouldn't have to share this old truck. Alyce has her own Volvo, you know; she looks at me like I'm just a local hick—an outsider."

"Somebody painted *Squaw* on my bicycle," Donna said, suddenly blurting it out, then reddening with the confession. "It was one of those ZKE boys, I'm sure, I saw them afterward, laughing." Emily looked at her.

"It was worse than that. It was horrible. It said, *Squaws Fuck. Squaws Kill*. Like they really think I killed that boy!" The tears were crowding her eyes again.

"Hey," Emily said, "the ones that count know you didn't hurt that guy. The frat boys are just looking for a scapegoat. Not to mention a good lay. That dumb Bozo thinks I'm a lay 'cause

I'm a town girl. Well, you can't give in to them or they'll take advantage."

"I know," Donna said, wiping her eyes with her sleeve. "That's what Mother says. I mean, that's what she'd say if she knew what I've been going through. But I don't tell her everything. She's in trouble enough with the police for planting marijuana."

Emily laughed. "My mother plants hemp illegally. They're a pair, your mother and mine. Mom's getting to be a living example of civil disobedience. Now she's burning her trash out in the pasture, and that's against the town ordinance."

Emily got Donna blowing her nose, laughing about their unruly mothers. Donna told how her mother burned her trash, too, because she couldn't afford to pay thirty dollars a week to have it carted away. "Now Uncle Olen's found out about it, but he doesn't say anything because he's in love with her."

"Really?" Emily sat down on the porch steps and Donna sank down beside her, shrugged her book bag off her back. It felt good to do that; her shoulders straightened and she felt lighter.

"Sure, he is. Of course, he's ages older than she is. I mean, like fifteen years. He's ready to retire, practically. Mother's forty-six."

"She's younger than my mother. Mom just turned fifty and she doesn't like it."

"Who would? Anyway, Uncle Olen's a bug about obeying the law, but because of Mother he has to make compromises. He's having a struggle."

"Does your mom like him? I mean, you have a father, right?"

Donna glanced at her friend. She knew that Emily's father had left the family for another woman. But Emily's face was expressionless.

"As a family friend, that's all. Mother knows how he feels. She just ignores it. But he's helping now to clear our names. So I want him to keep coming around. I want to get this behind us. I want to go on with my life."

"Yeah, I know."

The girls sat in silence a few minutes. Donna heard a tractor grinding up from the pasture. It was pleasant here, with the pear trees in delicate white bloom, the mountains rising lavender-blue across the road. At home Donna lived *in* the mountains, she could hardly see them for the trees.

The tractor struggled up the drive and quit, and Ruth Willmarth climbed down. She didn't look fifty at all, Donna thought. She was, well, young-looking, with gray-brown hair pushed haphazardly on top of her head, a blue denim shirt open to her sweaty neck. But when she turned to face them, Donna saw that she was upset about something.

"Is your mother coming by?" she asked Donna. "Something's happened to the hives. The upper ones have been knocked off and some of the bees are dead. Another bunch have swarmed up in a maple tree. It could have been an animal, I suppose, a bear looking for honey. I only hope it wasn't one of my heifers—Zelda, maybe. That beast!"

"Mother's coming to pick me up," Donna said. "I don't know why the bees should be dead." She looked up at Ruth Willmarth's flushed face.

She did know, though. She knew. And it wasn't Ruth Willmarth who was under attack. It was herself—and her mother. Someone was blaming them. Someone wanted to destroy their lives, the way the nightshade had destroyed Shep Noble.

She dug her hands deep into her pockets, felt the lining rip.

It was nothing Ruth had done, Gwen assured her when she pulled in an hour later to pick up her daughter; it might well have been a bear. "Last spring an old black fellow knocked over one of my hives searching for honey." Gwen sent Leroy to tend to the damaged hives while she undid the swarm. Already part of it was on the ground from the weight of the few thousand bees that had dragged down the maple branch. She placed a new hive body on the grass with the entrance near the bees and spread a sheet in front. The bees would have to walk over the sheet to get into the hive and the white sheet would make the queen easier to spot.

"It's possible that somebody did this to get back at me," she told Ruth while they were waiting for the bees to catch on. She didn't want to worry Ruth, but she had to tell someone. "There was a letter to the editor in the paper, a woman deploring my conduct. Meaning more than the nightshade—meaning, oh, yes, my 'mixed' marriage. The backwoods bigot!" Gwen felt confused, wanting to disbelieve; wanting to accuse. She felt better, though, for having shared her thoughts.

"Seems to me you're a backwoods liberal," Ruth said, and Gwen had to smile then.

"The longer I live, the more oddball I get," Gwen said. "Honestly, I'm sick of conforming to someone else's norm."

"You got it," Ruth murmured. The queen bee was moving across the white sheet now, a golden yellow with three black stripes that marked her as Italian. Gwen preferred the Italian to the Caucasian bees. They were more sunny, colorful. Gwen hoped she wouldn't have to kill this queen, she was such a beauty. She'd have to see first what kind of egg-laying pattern the queen had made.

Now the rest of the bees followed into the hive, and the two women walked back toward the barn, where Donna was helping Emily to grain the cows. Or trying to help, Gwen thought, smiling. Donna was all thumbs when it came to manual labor, be it dishes or vacuuming. Not that she couldn't do it, it just wasn't a priority with her.

The girls were coming out of the barn with a new calf. It had a huge black head and long spindly black and white legs. It had been born the day before, Donna told her mother: "Isn't it sweet?" She had her arm around it. It was one of those moments. Gwen nodded but couldn't speak. Donna released the calf and went back toward the pickup, where Leroy was stacking the broken hives in the back. He looked hard at Donna, his face pinkening. When the girl frowned, he turned a deeper color and sucked on his lower lip with his teeth. One upper tooth was black, as though he'd been struck by someone or something. Gwen saw Ruth watching.

"He has a crush on her, Ruth. Though at this point I think it's more of a love-hate kind of thing. And I know what you're thinking. He was there that night, like I told you. Olen's planning to question Leroy about it. I'll back up anything Leroy says, I will! He's been a good worker; my father hired him—I guess I'm sentimental about that."

At least there had been no more talk lately about finding another job. Leroy had been quiet, maybe too quiet. "Brooding" was the word that came to mind.

"An obsessive love can take over the brain," Ruth said. "I've seen it happen. Not long ago Emily had an emotional affair. It turned out badly."

Gwen nodded her sympathy—that boy's death had been in the papers. "Well, we're off to Glenna Flint's," she said, motioning Donna into the pickup. The girl sat in the passenger seat, leaving the back for Leroy, who glared at her, and climbed in beside the smoker. "Glenna called to complain about a swarm in her mailbox. She says they won't let her get at her Social Security check."

"I should be so lucky," said Ruth, waving them off, "to have a check in my box."

Ruth looked after the departing pickup and felt uneasy. She didn't like the way Leroy had looked at Donna. She knew what an obsessive love like his could do. It could warp one's sense of right and wrong, it could blind. Until nothing mattered beyond the desired object, and then anyone who came between it and self had to be eliminated.

She would ask Colm to check on Leroy, to see if he had a police record. It was just a hunch. But one couldn't rule him out as the Noble boy's killer. Personally, Ruth couldn't accept the accident theory. Someone had moved that motorcycle. Someone had dragged the boy into the nightshade. The boy wasn't stupid—after all, according to Donna, he knew he was asthmatic. But no asthmatic would lie facedown in any unknown plant, would he? And Donna had warned him.

No, someone had killed the boy. If not Leroy, then who? They had asked for her help. She had to try and do something. But what?

* * *

Gwen was humming as she drove into the beeyard. She'd dealt with Glenna's swarm, then dropped Donna at the library, Leroy in town—he'd hitch a ride back, he said. It had been a pleasant visit at Ruth's, in spite of the damage to the hives. An animal was the culprit, she really thought so. Things would get better. She had to keep her optimism.

For one thing, she was sick of this yellow crime scene tape, she wanted it down. Taking a scissors out of her bee kit, she stepped resolutely to the edge of the woods and cut. Snap! and the woods opened up, like a door to a magic kingdom. Her kingdom.

She hadn't been in here for days. It smelled of spruce and moss and fresh leaves. She threw back her head and breathed in the fragrance. Something caught her eye then—something hanging in an oak tree. At first she thought the police had hung it there. But as she drew closer, she saw that—oh!—it was a dummy, a dummy of a woman in a bee veil, crudely drawn. On the dummy's belly, in red paint, were the words *HANG THE WITCH.*

She quickly cut the obscene thing down and stumbled through the underbrush to the trash barrel. She threw it in and lit a match. Breathless, she watched it burn. Was it her imagination, or did it have a sickly odor, like old blood?

She sank to the ground and sobbed into her smoky hands.

When Camille arrived at the Woodleaf Apiaries, she was surprised to see a souped-up sports car pull in behind her. It was her student Tilden Ball; she saw the narrow face behind the wheel. The car made a terrible racket; it reminded her a little of Tilden, to tell the truth, full of excuses for late work, full of bullshit in a paper on which he was an "authority" but which never came up to standard.

"I saw your car," he said, unfolding his tall, gangly body from behind the wheel. (How, she wondered, did he know her car?) "I followed you up the mountain. I went to your office to see you about my paper, but you weren't there." He sounded put-upon, accusatory. He stared at her as if to ask what she was doing up here anyway.

Had he been spying on her? Did he know something about her? She and her partner, Esther, had tried to be discreet. They'd lived in separate apartments, gone to movies, bars, and restaurants in Burlington or Rutland—never locally. It was easier now that Esther was gone. But God, what she wouldn't do to have Esther back. . . .

"I live up there." He narrowed his hazel eyes, pointed up the road. Did he think she was coming to see him? He was standing between her and the entrance to the house. "It's the paper," he repeated. "I don't know what to write about this time. Dad says farming. I can't write about that, I don't like the subject."

"What are you interested in?" she asked. They were standing near a hive of bees; it made her nervous, although she was fascinated by bees. "Bees?" she said, moving away, pushing past him, gaining the upper ground. "You want to understand sociology, take a close look at bees, their social structure." The bees didn't seem to be aware of her, though. They were buzzing about the dandelions. Dandelions were done blooming where she lived in town; she supposed things were a week late up here in the mountains.

The boy had a labored smile on his face. "I help some here with mowing and bees. Just for pocket money, you know. I can write a paper on bees?"

Ordinarily, no, she thought. But she might be able to stretch the limits of sociology to include bees. Besides, already she saw a young man standing at the corner of the barn. It would be Leroy. She hadn't seen her cousin for six years; he'd have been a short, scrawny fourteen-year-old then. A boy could change a lot in six years. For the better, she fervently hoped, remembering how unsavory he'd been, how crude.

Leroy was standing there watching her, his hands on his narrow hipbones, thumbs stuck into the side pockets. His belt was low-slung, a gold chain hung from it, with jackknife, keys, she didn't know what else. She waved briefly at him. She was anxious about their meeting, to tell the truth. She turned back to Tilden.

"How they hive together, form a community, how humans relate to them. Read Maeterlinck's *The Life of a Bee*." Camille wasn't a botanist, but as a girl she'd been fascinated with that essay, the universal mysteries it probed.

"I'd rather write about cars," Tilden said, "the relationship between people and their cars. That's part of sociology, right?" He took her smile for approbation, grinned back.

When Donna came out of her house, running toward her teacher, frowning at Tilden, he backed away and jumped in his car. It screeched off down the road.

"Picking your brain?" Donna said, glaring after the car.

"Oh, just the paper, you know. He said he saw my car. I was surprised he knew it was mine." She patted the hood of her ten-year-old Honda.

"People remember red cars," Donna said, and Camille grimaced. Red provoked. It had been Esther's car, Esther had liked bright colors. Camille couldn't bring herself to give it up. Well, she guessed she'd have to accept Tilden's paper on people and cars, but she certainly wasn't looking forward to it.

Donna said, "Come in and have a soda or tea or something. Mother's just gone to town—you must've passed her. But Grandpop's here. He makes baskets. You might like to see some of them."

"Yes. Though it's actually Leroy I came to see. I told you he's my cousin? He's my only living relative, in fact, other than his mother, who's in a home. But I'll drop in afterward—just for a minute. I've a faculty meeting." She wasn't looking forward to that. Not with Frazer Manning at the helm. The way he looked at her—as though he could see through to her bones.

"I'll put on a pot of tea, then. You like herb tea? My mother makes it herself from ginseng. Or you can have lemon and honey."

"Either would be lovely." She waved again at Leroy, who'd remained by the barn, one spread hand on the wall as though he were holding it up—or it, him.

Leroy didn't offer to take her back to his trailer. " 'S not fit for company," he said. "I don't exactly have a live-in maid."

Instead he offered a green Adirondack chair out beside the house. She was glad she'd worn a woolly sweater; there was a cool breeze on her face. She could see patches of dirty snow in the woods.

She asked about his welfare and he answered in short clipped sentences. He wasn't about to give away any secrets. He hadn't been to see his mother lately because, "What's the point? She can hardly talk. She just twists around in that wheelchair like somebody wound her up wrong. I can't hardly stand to watch her, makes me dizzy. Jesus—I ever get that disease, I'd off myself."

Camille thought how fragile human beings were, how traumatized by disease and society. Her work on the eugenics project had only strengthened that feeling. Had Aunt Denise lived back in the time of Eleanor Perkey, she might never have had Leroy. She'd have been sterilized first.

"Well, you're lucky to be alive," she told Leroy. His raised eyebrow said he wasn't sure about that. "Things aren't going well? The job here seems interesting. Ms. Woodleaf must be a nice person to work for. You might think of becoming a beekeeper yourself one day. You're young, this is a learning experience for you." She took a breath, coughed delicately. His face was clouding up. He didn't want a lecture. She was his cousin, not his mother.

"No, they're not going well," he said, straightening up in his chair. "I need a lawyer. The police are after me. But I can't afford one." He caught her eye.

"You mean for that nightshade death."

He leaned toward her and she could smell the sweat. It was an unpleasant smell, like dirty socks. "I thought you could lend me some money. For a lawyer. I need a car—I can't keep using the truck here. I only got a bicycle to get around. You're in that rich college, you get a good salary, you can lend me a couple thou anyway. I'll pay you back." The bill of his dirty cap was almost touching her breast, his eyes brooding on her, like the sky getting ready to rain.

She got up; the conversation was taking an uncomfortable

turn. "I don't make a good salary at all," she told him. "I don't have tenure. That's what I'm working on now. Trying to earn it."

He stood up, too; he was not much taller than she, but squarely built. The red was slowly creeping up his neck, his chin; his nose was a carrot. She'd come in good faith to have a pleasant talk, to tell Leroy she was available anytime—for talk, for sympathy—and all he wanted was money.

"So I'm the black sheep. Nobody wants to be related to me. No high-and-mighty college professor." He stood facing her, arms on his denim hips, the eyes blazing into hers. He followed her back around to the front of the house. "I'm not asking a fortune. Just a thousand. Even five hundred'll help. I said I'd pay you back. Who else I got to ask? Mother's on Medicaid. The old man gone off. Like that," and he snapped his fingers. What he didn't mention was that he was her heir—that is, if she didn't have a child of her own, and that was unlikely. Did he know about her and Esther? Aunt Denise did. Camille had confided in her one day, and then was sorry afterward when Denise looked shocked.

She hesitated. She didn't want him talking to Donna about her, word could spread. She turned back. She would have to placate him. "Maybe five hundred. When I get my next paycheck. I'll let you know." She didn't want to ask exactly why he'd need a lawyer, what precisely he'd done. She didn't want to know. When Donna called her into the house, she went, but reluctantly. She was suddenly worn out, devoid of small talk.

Yet she did want to meet the grandfather, break the ice, so he'd be ready to talk when she asked the tough questions. This was her mission now: the eugenics project. Everything else—family, faculty affairs, failing students, would-be lovers—had to take second place.

She accepted the cup of fragrant tea Donna proffered. She thought briefly of what she'd wanted to tell the girl's mother about the Perkey connection. But the mother wasn't here, and once again, as the old man padded into the room, she put the thought aside.

Seven

Gwen was making honey cakes in the kitchen when Olen Ashley drove up in an unmarked car. She was glad of that; he was here to interrogate Leroy. Leroy was fragile. She'd sensed it as they worked together in the beeyards. She'd heard the short quick breaths he took, the groans as he emptied out the dead bees. She wanted to think it was a bear or heifer that had knocked over those hives. Or an accident of some kind—she always lost bees on the apple orchards when the orchardists sprayed or, for that matter, the farmers. But there had been no aerial spraying at Willmarth's, an organic farm.

Stop worrying, concentrate on your work, she told herself. She was making a honey cake with soybeans. You had to heat the honey, stir in a gelatin mixture until it dissolved; then beat it like crazy and roll in soybeans after it was thoroughly chilled. She was just putting the cakes into the refrigerator when Olen banged through the kitchen door. He was breathing heavily. Obviously the interview with Leroy hadn't gone well. She wanted to lift his mood; she told him she might make a honey cake out of mountain laurel—toxic to humans. She'd send it to her neighbor Harvey Ball. "If you want to get rid of someone, here's the way to do it," she quipped. But Olen just looked at her and growled; he lowered his hulk onto a stool. He said, "I'm not planning to bake a honey cake with mountain laurel. And you better not say that out loud to anyone else."

"Oh, Olen, it was just a joke. Lighten up a little. Here. Have some walnut fudge."

He usually liked her walnut fudge. Today he shook his head. "It's Leroy, isn't it?" she asked. "What did he tell you?"

He spread his thick fingers on the cutting board. She had a moment's fantasy that she might chop them into small pieces, mix them into a salad. She looked, bemused, into his earnest face. He was disturbed. Well, damn it, so was she.

"Nothing, that's just it," he said finally, lifting his fingers from the board, flexing them. "He just repeated what he'd told us when we found the body. He was there when the pair arrived; he saw the boy, uh, abusing Donna. Leroy kicked him with a foot—nothing to really hurt him, he *said*—nothing to cause the kind of dark bruises we saw. And then he told Donna to go into the house. Left Noble facedown in the mud. Figured the boy would come to, go home on his motorcycle. But . . ."

"But?" She drew a breath. She waited.

Olen groaned. "He was lying, I'm sure of it. It was the way he wouldn't look me in the eye. The way he kept licking his lips. Little things—after a while you get to read the signs. Leroy dragged him into that nightshade, must've done. It was Leroy responsible for his death, damn little prevaricator."

His fingers were tapping on the cutting board, tracing the curve of a knife cut where Brownie had tried to whittle a bear out of a hunk of hardhack. "Speaking of nightshade," he went on, "that marijuana, Gwen—"

"I don't smoke it," she said, "can't you explain that to the police? Lessen my fine a little?"

"It's the law,' he said stubbornly. "You can't grow marijuana. It's illegal."

"I know that. But will they be coming around again? Can't I grow it in a jar?"

Olen groaned, dropped his face in his thick-veined hands. "You drive me crazy, Gwen, you know that? If it weren't for your father . . ."

"If it weren't for my father, what? You wouldn't come around anymore?"

He met her eyes. His were dark brown, like walnut fudge. "You know the answer for that, Gwen. You know. I don't have to say it, do I?"

"No. And please don't," she said softly, and went to clean up after the honey cakes.

The supervisor of the Brookview Women's Reformatory was a huge man—not fat, but big all over: a beefy neck, an oversized head with eyes like black buttons, and thick horn-rimmed glasses that gave him a startled, owlish look. The hands were baseball mitts: A baseball—or a neck—would be quickly swallowed up inside them. His hair was the color of garlic salt, his skin weathered but not wrinkled—he might be fifty-five, even sixty. His name was Richard Godwin.

He didn't look up when Camille entered. He was busy, his desk strewn with papers. Filing cabinets lined the walls. They were alphabetized, she saw. She would like to get him out of the room, search the files—but Godwin looked as though he'd developed roots in his desk chair.

When finally, uninvited, she dropped into a facing chair, he said, "Yes?"

She introduced herself; she had made an appointment. She would be brief, but firm. She wanted to know when Annette Godineaux had been released for the last time, where she'd gone. Was she alone, or were there relatives, her children, perhaps, along with her? Most of all, she wanted to know whether or not Annette had been sterilized. "And if so, had she given her assent or was the procedure forced on her?"

He looked up, his face stern, self-righteous. "Lady, this institution has never *forced* an inmate into anything like sterilization." It wasn't done anymore, he insisted, "the old law went off the books in '73." He smacked his giant hands together; she felt the reverberation in her neck. As for Annette, "The files are confidential." Then, his face reddening with his indignation, "Of course she would have given her consent! Vermont law demands it. My father—um, my predecessor—would never have forced an inmate into such a procedure. And I can tell you one thing, young lady. He would have advised against it, oh, yes." Godwin had obviously learned his lesson from the Holocaust. He would be politically correct.

"Your father was supervisor before you?"

"Happened so." He looked defiantly at her. "He passed on in '70. I took over."

"He would have known Annette Godineaux, then, he would have admitted her?"

"He came here in '32. If she was admitted then, he'd have known her. Now, look, Miss . . ."

"Wimmet," she said. "Ms. I called yesterday. I spoke to your secretary."

"Yes, now I recall. From the college." His voice softened, grew indulgent, as though she were some flighty young student. "Well, it's all in the past, isn't it? What do you want to dig it up for? Like I said, the law's off the books. Back then, well, this Godineaux woman was obviously a petty criminal. Had to be, if she was in here. Probably unable to take care of her, uh, offspring. Not that I hold with such a law, but there are some it might make sense for. For the children's sake, I mean." He drew a snuffly breath, shuffled papers on his desk. His fingernails shone pinkish; he'd obviously polished them. Her own were down to the quick—from typing and nerves.

"I might have evidence that she was sterilized in this institution. And that the patients didn't always give their consent." She hadn't finished reading and recording the diary yet, but somewhere there would be a definitive statement.

His face was a closing door. "I said our files are confidential. Are you a relative?"

"I don't believe so. Are you?" Flushed with her audacity, she plowed on. "Godwin? Godineaux? Was there a slight name alteration somewhere?"

He rose up; the shadow on the wall behind was enormous. She'd struck a nerve. The father, she conjectured, had had Annette sterilized, so that he could write off that potentially decadent branch of the family. He took a step toward her, his arms crossed on his massive chest. He was busy, she would have to leave. She wasn't going to get anywhere today. Well, she would finish recording the diary, find proof, confront him again. She wanted the whole truth for her paper.

Outside the office, she felt she'd climbed a beanstalk, escaped from the giant. But she'd have to catch him sleeping if she was to defeat him. She imagined she felt his hot breath on her neck even as she hurried down the long hallway. Almost to the main door, a hand grabbed her sleeve; it was a young woman, hardly more than a girl, holding out the other hand—for what? A coin? A touch of friendship? Camille pulled a five-dollar bill from her wallet, pressed it into the prisoner's palm.

The girl-woman held her eyes for a moment, then, blinking, pocketed the money and scurried off.

Camille's late afternoon visit was just as frustrating. She was trying to explain to Eugene Godineaux that she was only doing research, that she wouldn't use his name in her paper, should it be published, but he was deaf to her entreaties. He wanted her out of the house. The "house" was a trailer up in the mountains of Ripton, half a dozen smudgy-faced kids hanging about, an exhausted-looking mother in a drab green housedress sprawled on a dirty beige plush sofa, legs splayed as though, with so much to do, so many things and people to tend to, she didn't know where to begin and was therefore rendered immobile.

An old woman squatting over a basket of potatoes looked Indian, with her brown complexion, gray-black hair pulled back on her head and pinned up in a braided coil. She seemed to be the only one actually working in the place. It might be the Depression thirties still in this household, except for the giant TV squealing out a soap opera and a computer on a rickety corner table where a boy with acute acne was playing a video game.

A child's cry in a far corner of the house took the man out of the room for a moment and the woman on the sofa whispered, "Nicole was the one got away. Nicole got a husband. Pauline can tell you what you need to know. Go see Pauline."

"Where does she live—Pauline?" Camille asked, dropping her business card in the woman's lap. Pauline, Camille had discovered in her research, was Annette's granddaughter. Nicole was Pauline's mother. "And where can I find Nicole?"

The woman opened her mouth to reply but was silenced in midsentence by a .22 rifle, lifted up off the wall gun rack in an explosion of anger and pointed at Camille. "Git out," the man shouted. "We don't wanna be part of your goddam research." He backed Camille to the door with the gun; she went. He followed her to the car, the gun at her head. She wanted to scream, she wanted to shoot *him*. For a long moment she thought that maybe she was all wrong, that the eugenics survey had something to say for it, that men like this *were* degenerate, unfit to propagate.

He was running after the car, firing shots in the air. "Don't even try to write about us Godineaux, don't even try!" he bellowed, and she drove erratically down the mountain, taking the first curve too wide, twisting the wheel frantically to avoid plunging into the river that surged and fumed one hundred feet below.

She was mad, she was furious. When she saw the *TAKE BACK VERMONT* sign outside a house near the foot of the mountain, she veered into the driveway, jammed on the brakes, flung herself out of the car, and yanked up the sign. She knew what it meant: It was a protest against the civil union legislation the Vermont legislature had recently passed, giving basic human rights to gays and lesbians.

"Homophobes!" she shouted. "You killed her. You killed my Esther!" She scurried across the road with the sign and slung it down the embankment. She stood there, watching it slide toward the river, gasping for breath. Finally it hit a rock and broke up.

She ran, crazy-legged, back up to the car. A small boy was on the porch shouting for his mother. Camille revved up the engine, roared off down the hill; saw the woman in her rearview window, shaking her fist, yelling.

"Lesbian," her lips seemed to say. "Pervert."

* * *

When Colm Hanna happened to "drop in" that evening, Ruth told him about the damaged hives. The two were sitting in her kitchen as usual; the TV was blaring in the living room where Vic, done with his homework—so he said—was watching *Wheel of Fortune*. She heard him yell out, "Chicken every Sunday!" and wondered where on earth he had heard that phrase.

"My mother used to do that," Colm told her, "every Sunday. And beans or scrambled eggs the rest of the week. A habit left over from the Depression. Mother was always sure the bad times would come back."

"It did, in our house," Ruth said. "Though I don't dare cook a chicken or Vic will think it's one of his. He's into chickens in a big way now. More coffee?"

He shook his head. "But I could use one of those Otter Creek Ales. I'll get it," he said, motioning her back into her chair. "Maybe it was the chickens knocked over those hives," he suggested, grinning, as he returned from the kitchen. "Ten of them together could do it." He leaned back in his chair, guzzling his beer. He had that contented look that meant he was here for an evening of togetherness. She didn't mind, really; it was just that she had paperwork to do. She was behind in everything these spring days, what with plowing and discing, getting ready for May planting, and two cows freshening any given week.

Now here was Emily plodding downstairs, looking pointedly at Colm as though he might disappear if she stared him down. Emily liked Colm, but she'd never wholly given up on her father coming back. Tonight, though, Colm was simply a rival for her mother's time.

A cry went up from the living room TV and then a raucous cheer as someone raked in a pile of money. Colm took the hint. "I'll listen in with Vic. I could use ten thou."

"I guess," Ruth said. "After you lent me that amount to pay off my ex."

"That's me," Colm said from the doorway, "Mister Fla-hool." She smiled. "Flahool" was an Irish word; it meant generous, throwing around one's money. Colm was generous, she had to admit that; it was one of his good points.

"Right," she called back. "So what do you need to know about farming?" she asked her daughter. "If I can't answer your questions, I'll make something up."

"It's not really about that," Emily said. "Not yet anyway. I just wanted to talk about what's been going on. I don't like what happened with the hives. And there's more. I don't want *you* to get hurt from all this. I mean, I'm the one who made Donna go to that frat party."

"Whoa, hold on. You asked her as a friend, she went. It could have been you coming home on that motorcycle. It could have been that boy dead in our hemp garden. It just happened, that's all. Now tell me what the latest is. Other than the hives."

Donna told her about the graffiti on the bicycle and Ruth's stomach turned sour. She banged her knuckles together. "I hate that, hate that!" she cried. "It happens over and over. Why can't people let people *live*?"

The TV roared with excitement and Colm hollered, "I got it right! Lemme on that program. I'll buy this farm back for you, Ruthie. The fat lady in sneakers just won twenty thou."

Ruth sighed. The world on the brink of disaster and Colm would calm it with a glass of beer. An unkeepable promise. He should be a politician. "Why didn't you want Colm to hear about this?" she asked Emily. "Did Donna go to the police?"

"That's just it. She made me promise not to tell anyone. She thinks it's Shep's frat buddies getting revenge. Their house is off bounds, but they still meet. There's some old guy in town who was a frat brother, he lets them meet there. The college administration is using Shep Noble's death as a lever to break up all the fraternities. So the boys are fighting the college with the help of a couple of old ex-Zekes."

"Who are these 'old' guys,' do you know?"

"No, but Billy Bozeman will tell me. He's still after me. The more I ignore him, the more he gets in my way."

"I hope he's not a stalker." Ruth was suddenly alarmed.

"No, he's just a jerk. I can handle him."

"I'm not sure I like that, either. You can't encourage him. Remember that last one you brought home and he tried to commit suicide on our front steps?"

"Just a little blood, he was bluffing." She lowered her voice. "And don't go telling Colm Hanna about that graffiti. Donna doesn't want her Uncle Olen to know, either. Already he keeps showing up on campus, following Donna around like he's her big protector. She doesn't like that."

The living room was quiet now. Colm was standing in the doorway, his ears sticking out through his wild hair. "I'll talk to you tomorrow about that paper," Emily told her mother. "I have to have a proposal in by tomorrow. It's about the impact of farming on the town, what's happening to the family farm. I figure you have strong ideas about that."

"You bet your boots I have. You want me to write the paper for you?"

Emily stood hesitantly at the foot of the stairs. Was her mother serious? When Ruth grinned, she said, "Okay. I didn't expect you to do that. But I do need you for a source."

"You got me," said Ruth. Vic strolled in from the living room and she swatted his bottom. "Get that homework done, kid, and then take a shower."

"And get all smelly again cleaning the calf pens in the morning? What's the point?" He started up the stairs.

"Well, take the shower in the morning if there's time."

"There's never time."

"Then get up a half hour earlier. At least you get picked up later than some of the others. Brownie is picked up an hour before you, Gwen says."

Vic came down a step. "He's been skipping lately. And I think I know why. Something that happened on the bus."

"What was that? Tell me."

"The kids started hissing his name, 'Brown Bear.' Then when we were getting off the bus someone called his sister a murderer. Jeezum!"

"And what did the bus driver do to stop it? What did *you* do, Vic?"

"She—she tried. I guess I did, too."

"You guess?"

Vic hung his head. "I could of tried harder. I was afraid they'd get after me, too."

"And call *your* sister a murderer? Come on, Vic. You have to stand up and speak out. I've taught you that, haven't I?"

Ruth was really worked up now. Mad at Vic, mad at the bus driver, mad at the frat boys, mad at whoever had vandalized the Woodleaf hives. "Shit, shit," she said, and saw Vic scamper upstairs, knowing she was in one of her "injustice" moods. "I'd like to—"

"To what, Ruthie?" said Colm, coming up behind, kneading her tense shoulders. "Arrest them all? Bring them to justice? Reform the world in a day?"

"You're so sanguine, Colm. So damned patient. I don't want to wait. I want the world perfect in my lifetime. *My* lifetime, Colm." He was holding her close, rubbing her back. Unable to come down off her high horse so soon, she said, "Did you look up Leroy Boulanger, like I asked?"

"Oh, yeah. I forgot to tell you. He's got a record. Well, nothing big—just a stolen car, you know, that sort of thing."

She grabbed his shoulders, made him look her in the eye. "What does that mean—'that sort of thing'?"

"He jumped a guy once at Alibi. Knocked out his teeth. Got clobbered himself. Police had him in overnight. Aggravated assault, they called it. That's all I know."

"Aggravated assault," she repeated, and thought of the bruises on Shep Noble's face. She had to be diplomatic, though. Gwen seemed to favor the boy.

"Ask your colleague Ashley to tell Gwen about the police record, would you, Colm?" It was a cop-out and she knew it. But she didn't want to be one to damage a friendship.

Camille was fixing herself a cup of tea, ready to go back to the computer, when someone banged on her door. It was a tall, wiry woman in her sixties, plainly dressed in a denim skirt and blue cotton blouse, a necklace of pale pink shells around her neck;

she gripped her black leather purse with strong tensile fingers. Her name was Godineaux, she said. She'd heard from a relative that Camille was poking her nose into the family's privacy.

She spoke rapidly in a coarse voice. Camille imagined her throat full of frogs and salamanders—her threats, too. Camille was to halt this project at once, the woman cried. She had "no goddam business dragging old dirty linen back into the light—who you think you are, the Virgin Mary? What's my family to you? Some things we don't want hung up on the line for everybody to see, you understand?"

Camille was impressed by the laundry metaphor. She struggled to keep her cool. "Who are you?" she asked. "Are you related to Annette? Annette's a wonderful woman. I only want the world to know she was wronged. Of course I'll use a pseudonym!" She resisted an impulse to fling herself on her knees, clasp her hands together to show her good intent.

The woman was unconvinced. She stood inside the doorway of Camille's apartment, swaying a little on scuffy black heels, her mouth a straight line. How had she known where Camille lived? She would have done some research herself. Or maybe Eugene Godineaux's common-law wife had summoned her. Camille had asked about Nicole.

"Do you know Nicole? Is she your mother?" Camille was desperate now. She couldn't give up her project, no. "I said I'd give fictitious names," she shouted at the woman, and then softened her voice. "No one will know. Your lives will be the same as always. This will be an academic paper, it won't reach the general public."

Although she hoped it would, didn't she? She dreamed of a book?

The woman saw her hesitancy. She narrowed her black eyes; the wrinkles fanned out into her cheeks. "Sure," she said, "sure, and somebody gets ahold of it, and does his own dirty work, and digs up our lives. And people know. And the cops find us and say they been looking for us and we . . ."

She stopped; she'd gone too far. Her face was chalk-white. She looked clownish with those two small red spots in the center of each cheek where she'd dabbed on rouge. "I said you can't do this. I said it's gotta stop." She was nearing hysteria, clutching at her necklace as though it were Camille's throat. "You'll be sorry if it don't. You'll be sorry!"

"Pauline?" Camille threw out the name—Nicole's daughter would be about this woman's age now. She would have kept her own name. It was a ploy. But it worked. The woman jerked at her necklace; it broke, the shells scattering on the floor. Her face was tomato-red; her fingers tightened into fists. She rushed at the computer where it sat whirring on its stand, the exam Camille had typed into it still on the screen.

Camille gripped her shoulders. "Leave that alone. It's my work. Don't you dare! That doesn't concern you—it's for my class. Get away now!"

Pauline was strong. She shoved Camille down into a chair, spun back to examine the screen. She stood panting in front of it, then wheeled about, placed two hands on the edge of the chair where Camille was struggling to get up, shoved her back down. "I said leave us alone. You hear?"

She turned and ran out of the apartment. When Camille looked out the side window, she saw the woman fling herself into a beat-up black car. The license plate read *LIVE FREE OR DIE*, a New Hampshire plate. Camille jotted down the first three digits of the license—CP3—but then the car sped away in a storm of exhaust.

Camille sank back down in her armchair, spent, and angry. She couldn't let some Godineaux relative browbeat her. The woman, Pauline, didn't understand. Camille was trying to help the family, not hurt it. Why couldn't the woman understand that?

"I won't give up the project," she told her black Persian cat, who'd come whining into the room, wanting food. "I won't!"

Eight

Saturday was the day for visitors, it seemed. In a moment of hiatus, Gwen was rushing about, cleaning up the kitchen. No one understood that bees didn't take days off, that spring was a busy time for beekeepers. Gwen's goal each spring was to have all hives in place at least a week before the daffodils came in bloom, and then the clover that gave the first major nectar flow and sent the bees back to the hives so loaded with golden pollen they could hardly remain airborne. With April nearing an end, she had only a short time to accomplish this.

Oh, but the house was a mess! Dirty clothes piled up by the washing machine and schoolbooks and papers sprawled everywhere. Brownie was skipping school every two days, it seemed, claiming a stomach bug, or a bone spur in his heel that the doctor couldn't find; and today Donna was shut in her room with Emily Willmarth to work on the sociology paper—too busy to do dishes. Mert, as usual, was squatting in a heap of brown ash, working furiously to create baskets for the craft center exhibit. *He* had no time for dishes. He'd only damage them anyway, poor man, with his shaky hands. She suspected Parkinson's—she'd have to get him to a specialist.

The morning had started with two "patients" wanting bees for stinging. Gwen did a little "bee therapy," though not for pay. She believed in the use of bee venom to treat autoimmune diseases like arthritis and multiple sclerosis. Young Chuck Minor had just left with a jar full of bees to sting his arthritic grandmother with. Then the phone had rung off the hook with only an ominous silence on the other end. She let it ring five more times, then picked it up, only to hear an oath from an irate Russell. "Can't you answer the fuckin' phone?" he'd hollered. "Jeezum, Gwen, I been calling and calling."

Russell wanted to come home, he said, he wanted to see what was going on, how everyone was, what Donna was up to. "Keep an eye on her, Gwen! But, damn it all, I got three more gigs this month and it just won't pay to come back to Vermont first." She told him about the Ball family's visit, but not about the offer to buy land. When he signed off, he reminded her to keep Harvey Ball "off the property. Don't let him put a foot on it, Gwen. He'll turn the grass brown." And they both hung up, as usual, laughing.

Now, just as she was knocking on Brownie's door to remind Vic to take a jar of honey back to his mother, there was a knock on the kitchen door.

"Hello, hello," a female voice rang out, and when Gwen dashed down the steps she found a small, tidy woman standing tentatively in her doorway, glancing about. "I'm Camille Wimmet from the college—Donna's teacher," the woman said. She thrust out a hand.

"Why, hello." Gwen snatched up the hand, which might have belonged to a child, it was so unblemished. Her own hands were scarred from a thousand bee stings. The rest of the woman looked as pristine as her hands: She wore a longish black skirt with a lavender cotton sweater and a crisp white blouse. She wasn't exactly pretty; she had a plumpish nose and jet-black eyebrows that gave her an earnest look, round eyeglasses that dimmed her violet eyes. She looked more like a schoolgirl than a college professor.

"I'm so interested in Donna's paper," Camille went on, "I can't thank you enough for letting her—and by extension, myself—have the use of your ancestor's document."

Document? Gwen hadn't thought of the journal as a "document," but she supposed that was the way sociologists saw it. For a moment Gwen couldn't think who it was the woman wanted to see. She stared blankly at the young woman.

The teacher saw her confusion. "Donna told me about her grandfather. You see, I'm working on a paper myself, and the LeBlanc name came up in my research. I thought your father-in-law might not mind talking to me about his family. I mentioned it to him. I was here last week to see Leroy—he's my cousin—did Donna tell you?"

Here was a disparate match! Yes, Donna had told her about the relationship. She was glad, actually, to know that Leroy had a relative nearby. "Mert doesn't go out much," Gwen said. "He doesn't drive anymore. His hands aren't always steady on the wheel."

"I understand. I heard about . . . your helping him with the, um, marijuana."

Gwen flushed, but the teacher was smiling. Gwen smiled, too. She spread her hands in a gesture of peace. "Well, go on in. He works in there. Coffee?"

The teacher shook her head, and Gwen led the way to Mert's workplace. "You have a visitor, Mert." Her father-in-law grunted but didn't look up from where he was concentrating on the star bottom of a new basket. Gwen followed the teacher's eyes. One wall held a gun rack, another a photograph of Mert dissecting an old car. Shelves held twists and curls of split wood and, rising up out of them, framed photographs of the family. The largest photo was a ten-by-fourteen color shot of Russell, taken at one of the reenactments, looking virile even in his forties (actually, he was two years younger than Gwen) with his hard lean bronze body, a tomahawk stuck into the sash that held together his striped loincloth. Oh, but he was a handsome devil! She wanted to reach right into the photo and embrace him, feel his sinewy arms around her back. Smell that fragrant mix of sage and tobacco.

Mert was making a basket with a Demijohn bottom. "It's a better basket than the Abenaki Star," he told the women's feet.

"I mean, the Star is made the same, but you got eight straight uprights and you got eight tapered. It was my Aunt Sylvie on the LeBlanc side made the Demijohn bottom—the old way's lost now. So I only make the Demijohn on special order." He looked up. "You're the one wanted to see me?"

"I'd like to ask you a few questions," Camille said. "About your family. Your Aunt Sylvie, *her* sister Maxine."

Mert cocked his head, stared up at the visitor; he put down his work. "What you want to know about her for? That Maxine, she got in trouble. Not all her fault, though."

Camille sat down on an overturned box. "I'm here because I'm writing a paper about the French-Canadian impact on this state. I'm a Franco-American myself, you see. I came across Maxine's name in the university archives. Some of those women were unfairly committed. Your aunt may have been one of them."

Camille's voice softened toward the end of the speech. Mert nodded and went back to his Demijohn bottom. Gwen liked the professor. She felt that the young woman wouldn't come on too strong with Mert, that he could take care of himself. She tiptoed out of the room, shut the door on the pair.

The phone rang just as she got to the sink to wash up a few dishes. It was Harvey Ball. He had an offer, he said: "You won't get another like it. I can go a hundred thirty thousand on your place. That's twice as much as it's worth—we'd have to tear down the house. I'm just doing it for my son. For you. You can move into town like I said, out of town if you want. I'd think you'd want to, with all this trouble. What people are saying about you. Saying—"

She slammed down the phone. She didn't want to hear any more. Couldn't. Her legs were buckling, her face was on fire. The nerve of the man! She banged her fists against the wall, leaned her body into it, felt the tears well up in her eyes. Maybe she should sell. Maybe she should.

She felt rough sturdy arms grab her elbows, pull her about. "It's all right, all right," Olen soothed. "We'll get you out of this, Gwen. We're working on it. No one on the force thinks *you* did it. Or Donna. My feeling now—it's all a tragic accident. Like you said, the bruises came from the nightshade. Who'd ever think a boy could die like that from nightshade?" He coughed, looking troubled. "If you'd just pull up the nightshade, other stuff that's compromising . . ." He handed her a clean white handkerchief. She blew into it.

"I tol' you, Olen. I can't. My father-in-law." She heard him groan. She was naughty, she was an irate child. Was she being unreasonable? Was she really a witch for growing healing plants? Why, in her ancestor's day she might have been hanged! She had to think things through, straighten out her priorities.

She pulled away. She had to get to work, she told Olen. Work was therapy.

"You're taking him with you?" He pointed through the open screen to where Leroy was piling mended hives into the pickup. "Did you know he was arrested once for stealing a car? And there's more. Oh, yes, we've got a file on him. I wish you wouldn't keep him here. It worries me. For Donna's sake—think of Donna. Think of your boy."

Now she was feeling stubborn. "I need Leroy. He knows bees. I haven't time to train anyone else. You'll have to accept that, Olen. Now, if you want a cup of coffee, there's some left in the pot. I have to go. Donna's in her room if you have any questions. Mert has a visitor. Donna's professor," she explained when he raised an eyebrow. "She's writing some kind of paper on French-Canadians."

"Oh? Well, I just came to look at the site again, where Noble died. To see if there's anything else there—a thread, a fiber we missed. By the way, the tests showed Noble had more than marijuana and alcohol in his blood. He had Ritalin—that stuff they give kids these days to calm them down? Mix it with alcohol and anything can happen. Did happen—goddam irresponsible kid!"

"He's dead," she reminded him, blowing her nose again.

He sighed. "Anyway, thanks, I could use a cup of coffee. Then I'll be off. But remember what I said," he called after her as she flung on a red plaid wool shirt over her jeans and gathered up her bee apparel. "About those plants. It's not just me you have to worry about. It's the others. The chief wants it all pulled up."

She didn't answer. Leroy was already in the pickup, waiting; he was wearing a Red Sox cap; his face appeared frozen shut under the bill, which was pulled down practically over his dark eyes. She knew he didn't want Olen coming around.

But Olen's words worried her. How much did she know about Leroy? Had he really stolen a car? She wondered if her father had known that.

"Where to?" the boy muttered. Seeing her frown, he glanced away.

"Shoreham. I want to check the hives on the Pomainville farm."

She revved up the truck. She didn't look at Leroy. But she could feel him scowling at the police car that was still parked in front of the house. She started to put out a hand, to tell him not to worry, that she would protect him. But she pulled the hand back. There was something about his anger that frightened her.

Olen Ashley watched Gwen pull out of the driveway with Leroy in back. It worried him, yes, it did, having that fellow on the property. He hadn't wanted to tell Gwen about Leroy's past—Hanna had asked him not to. But she was so stubborn. So vulnerable. If anything happened to her, well, he couldn't take that. He couldn't live without Gwen. Not that he'd ever push himself on her—he'd never do that! Never! She had her husband, though they weren't suited at all. He'd never understood that marriage. He was still with Jennie when Gwen first brought Russell around. Russell was handsome, athletic—a runner. But he was Indian. Indians . . . well, they had a different way of looking at the world. They had no concept of the law. They were always protesting this or that, felt they had a right to the land just because it happened they'd gotten here first.

Olen pulled up a couple of deep breaths, poured himself a mug of coffee. He was comfortable here in this kitchen. Though less so since Donald Woodleaf's death. With Don alive, he'd been able to drop in more often. Don liked to talk, Don was an American Revolution buff like himself. He and Olen were brother Masons, shared the secrets, the hand grips. When Don was almost struck that time by a falling tree, Olen had saved him. "May my body be cut in two," Olen whispered, remembering, "my entrails burned, ashes scattered—should I fail a brother in need." Would a brother Mason ever have to do that for him?

Don, of course, had been a buffer between him and Gwen. The three of them could share a coffee or a beer, laugh a little. After he died, things got awkward. Gwen always jumping up in the middle of a conversation, feeling self-conscious, even guilty, he supposed, with her husband away. He wasn't always able to disguise his feelings. Sometimes the feelings just popped out in his face and he'd have to leave before he lost control.

Now there was this nightshade case. Someone—Leroy, he figured—had dragged that boy into the nightshade, though that hadn't killed him. It was the boy's asthma, the inebriation, the Ritalin in his blood that did it. Absolutely. The whole thing had been an accident, like he'd told Gwen. He would try to prove that. Get her off the hook when the court case come up. But not Leroy. Oh, no. Leroy still had questions to answer.

The voices grew louder in the next room. What did that woman want with Mert? What could the old man tell her that would help some paper she was writing? He heard snatches of the conversation—she had the louder, higher voice. Something about a Mrs. Perkey, the word "sterilize" . . .

Finally there was the sound of a scraping chair, words of farewell. He squinted at the woman through the door, then left the house. Backing out, he almost hit her red Honda. That would never do. Olen had a perfect driving record. He was proud of that.

There was an apple tree in blossom by the fence when Gwen and Leroy got to the Willmarth farm. Gwen took it for a sign. Things would work out. She opened the window wide to breathe in the fragrance. It was almost May, Branbury's orchards were bursting with apple blossoms. It was a time of promise. Nothing untoward had happened for several days now. Gwen was getting back her native optimism.

Here was Ruth, driving up to the barn in the John Deere. She jumped out lightly, glanced at Gwen's pickup. "You're on fire, I think," she said, and Gwen laughed and showed her the smoker.

"But I do need a good fire," Gwen said, and showed her an infected hive they'd brought back from old Glenna Flint's place. "It might not be foulbrood at all, but I can't take any chances. I know you're like me, you burn your own. Olen made me remove my barrel. But I'll put it back when all this is over. The prices they charge to haul the stuff! It's unconscionable."

They loaded the hive full of dead brood onto the tractor, drove it deep into the pasture, to a damp area by a narrow stream. There, behind a grove of birch trees, Ruth kept a rusted barrel. With Leroy's help, they rolled the hive into it. It wouldn't fit and they had to break it up. Pieces kept falling, dead bees scattering, and they got to laughing. Even Leroy, trying to look bored with the women's giggles, smirked now and then but finally made his way back to the truck. Ruth had three bags of trash ready for burning herself. It was a little windy, but it had rained overnight.

"One for the governor," she said, and tossed it in.

"One for the local constable. One for Olen Ashley, and one for the garbage collector," cried Gwen.

"One for my ex-husband Pete and his beloved town dump," shouted Ruth.

"One for Harvey Ball and his three little Balls," yelled Gwen, and the women howled with laughter. It was silly, it was outrageous, but Gwen felt, somehow, renewed.

Afterward, the ride back through the cow pasture was gorgeous. The landscape was green and white with pear and maple trees in bloom, the mountains purplish with new leaves. Yellow rocket and a few early white clover were popping up, full of glad and thirsty bees. It would be a good harvest this summer. Every cow they passed had her head deep down in the lush grass.

Gwen told Ruth that bees saw the white clover as blue. "Whenever I see a white blossom, I try to imagine it blue. All the apple orchards in deep blue bloom."

"I love it," said Ruth. "And what about red? Do they see red?"

"Oh, no, they don't see red at all. The red flowers are all bird-pollinated—mostly hummingbirds. So I plant white geraniums in my porch pots."

As they approached the house, they saw a reddish glow, a column of smoke. Ruth was alarmed; she put the tractor in high gear. It was Gwen's truck. The back of it really was on fire. Leroy was already there, slapping at it with an old car blanket, his face red and sweaty.

"I'll grab some pails," Ruth shouted. "There's an outside faucet."

In twenty minutes they had the flames out. But the back of the pickup was badly charred. "It wasn't the smoker," Leroy said. "Smoker was almost out when we left to burn. And I found this." He picked up the remains of a box of kitchen matches. Someone had lit one, he claimed, and tossed it in the back. Gwen wanted to think it was the smoker, though—she didn't want to think that someone had deliberately set fire to her truck.

But inside Ruth's warm kitchen, where a pitcher of apple blossoms sat on the table, smelling like the most fragrant of incense, she mentally added this latest bit of malice to the growing list that had begun with the note to Donna in Emily's dormitory room, and her mood darkened.

She saw Ruth look out the window where Leroy was sitting in the truck, guzzling a Pepsi. He hadn't wanted to come into the kitchen. Could he have set the fire himself?

No, no, she scolded herself. Why would he set a fire and then try so valiantly to extinguish it? It made no sense. Yet the car Leroy had allegedly stolen haunted her mind. She had meant to question him about it on the way to Willmarths', but his grim silence had stilled her tongue.

* * *

When Camille Wimmet read Annette Godineaux's diary entry for Friday, March 18, 1937, she understood why the young woman had faked her IQ test.

Fooled em today. When they asked me who was the president of the United States I said uh, Jimmy Stewart? and they didn't even smile, just scratched on their pads like cats in a litter box. Well, I won't play their game. I tell em, oh yeah, I broke into old lady Flake's house, stole her money sock, I tell em what they wanna hear. But why did you do that when you were on parole? You'll end right back in here. Cause I want a soft bed, good food, I tell em, which is not altogether a lie. Not after Billy, the bastard, locked me out, said he had a new woman, wouldn't pay alimony for my kids he claimed weren't his. Where was I to go? I won't live with Maman. Not with that asshole boyfriend wanting nothing more than to get in bed with me nights after he's done with her. I'm sick when I think of waking up with him on top of me. My André, maybe Jeannine, maybe Cosette, could be his kid, Jesus. But not Nicole. Her father would of married me if he hadn't been saddled with that bitch of a wife. And then got run over by that tractor—thought I'd die myself to hear it. Nicole must be 20 now. My God. One day when I'm outa here, when I get a job, make some money, I'll round up my kids outa those foster homes. We'll live on a farm somewhere. Some other state. Maine maybe. Or upstate New Hampshire.

The eugenicist, Eleanor Perkey, was wrong, Camille discovered: There weren't three children, but four: a boy, André, and three girls, Nicole, Jeannine, and Cosette. Was their surname Godineaux? And Billy—who was he? And that married farmer? Well, somewhere she'd find answers. She'd had more luck with Mert LeBlanc's great-aunt Maxine; Camille had found her in Perkey's report, first arraigned for vagrancy (selling her baskets, no doubt, up and down the state), and then released, then back in again and sterilized, according to Perkey (no records extant), before she was finally let go.

She wouldn't find the answers, though, with that arrogant man down at Brookview. He was a relative, she'd just bet he was. She'd look into that. She imagined his father sleeping with one of the female inmates—this 'Godwin' a bastard son. He wouldn't want that little morsel coming to light!

The horror for Camille was that they had sterilized Annette. Had she really consented? All they needed, according to the "voluntary sterilization" law passed in 1931, were two physicians to decide that the patient was feebleminded, insane, disabled, or whose welfare would otherwise "be improved" with sterilization: if male, a vasectomy; if female, a salpingectomy. Imagine the women tricked into that procedure! How else, if not tricked, would they have given their consent?

It was a mystery, as so many things were still a mystery. Like where were those offspring today? Where were the grandchildren, if she had more than one? What kind of lives were they leading now, and where?

Camille was determined to find out. This afternoon she would visit the Willmarth farm, where a foster boy named Joey Godineaux worked. After all, Annette's offspring might well have taken the distaff name, since she'd never married. She copied the notes she'd been making on her computer and stuck the disk in her purse. She was feeling paranoid. When she'd come after class yesterday afternoon she'd found her papers shuffled about on her desk, as though someone had been in here, looking for something, had heard a noise, and run off. It was probably a student, she rationalized, looking for a paper; she'd left the office door unlocked, she'd only been gone the one class hour. She hadn't been careful about locking up, the way she had to rush from class to class to conference to faculty meeting.

The students, too, ate up her time, like Tilden Ball, barging in here this morning, demanding a retake for a failed quiz. Well, she didn't give retakes. He had to accept that. Though he obviously didn't like it. She didn't care for him, not a bit. She didn't like the way he looked at her, either. He definitely knew something. Or suspected . . .

But this paper would bring her tenure, respect. She would declare herself then, proudly, the way Esther had wanted, the way she herself should have done, risking the tenure. If she had,

Esther might have stayed in Vermont, not driven west on a motorcycle, prey to that homophobic trucker. Now Esther was dead. And Camille had only Esther's cat for comfort.

Out in the hall a dark figure scurried around the corner. A colleague? A student? "Hello," she called, but the person didn't answer. She locked the door and ran out to her car.

She found the hired man and his teenaged ward, Joey, in the barn milking the cows. The Holsteins stood impatiently by, waiting their turn—it was obviously the highlight of their day. It was an average-sized farm as farms went these days: a red barn and two cement-block silos with *WILLMARTH SONS* in peeling paint. Where were the sons? Yet how good, Camille thought, that the farm had survived, when only the megafarms seemed to hold on these days. In this case, without a man, too—only the woman farmer, this cheerful-looking fellow, and the foster boy, Joey, who was thrusting a mud-caked hand at her.

"This is my Joey, I'm Tim," the man said. She took Joey's hand. She wanted to put the boy at ease. Tim brought out a chair from some inner sanctum; he and Joey went on with the work. The boy appeared to be cleaning teats or something, the process was a mystery to Camille. Everything was shiny and steely: the milking gadgets, the pipes, the pails, the pans of food and water. The barn was ripe with smells: cow dung, the sweetish odor of new milk, hay that got her sneezing and then blowing her nose.

She laughed at herself, said she was "fascinated by all this—look, I just spend my day in a dusty classroom. Anyway, Joey, I wanted to ask you about your parents, if you knew them. I'm trying to trace some relatives of a woman named Annette Godineaux. She had a daughter named Nicole, a granddaughter named Pauline. Ever hear those names mentioned?"

"Nicole, Pauline. Thoth are good names," said Joey, grinning through bad teeth. He had a slight lisp, she noticed. "But who they?"

"He lived with foster parents early on," Tim put in. "He doesn't know much about his real parents, do you, Joey?"

"Nope. Tim, here, he my parent now, right, Tim? My . . . surra—surra—"

"Surrogate father," said Tim, shooing out the four cows they'd been milking and ushering in a new batch. The cows were huge, Camille noted; she'd never seen them up close like this. They were terrifying, actually. One bellowed, practically in her ear, and she jumped. Tim laughed. "That's Bathsheba. She's a wild girl. She likes to spook you." He slapped the cow on its rear end and it mewled again, turned a wild dark eye on Camille.

She moved her chair back. She didn't think she'd get very far with this interview. She would have to talk to the foster parents. "Do you have their address, Tim?"

Tim stuck his tongue in his cheek, screwed some metal milkers onto Bathsheba's teats; they hung down like pendulums in a grandmother's clock. "Let's see, now. The Petits moved—to Winooski, I think. But I did hear that Joey's mother was once in Otter Training School. I don't know about the father. About thirteen years ago they closed the school, let the residents out on their own. The mother couldn't cope, she walked out on the kids—there were two of them, and Joey here was taken in by the Petits. They were kind enough as far as I can see, right, Joey? They treat you okay?"

"Okay," said Joey, rubbing on a cow's teat, "but not so good as you, Tim. You the best." Tim squirted a bit of milk at the boy, and Joey giggled.

Camille knew about the training school. It had done its share of sterilizing, too. Joey's mother—was it Pauline?—would have brought the two Tim mentioned with her. She'd bet the mother didn't have any other kids after that, though. She thanked the pair, gulped in breaths of fresh air outside the barn. It was raining now. She had on heels that sank into the muddy earth. She'd parked her car out by the main road. There was a light on in the kitchen—perhaps Emily was in there, her student, she'd have a newspaper Camille could hold over her head; she didn't want to get her leather jacket wet. She ran up on the porch and knocked.

It wasn't Emily, but the girl's mother who greeted her, she'd just come in from the fields. She offered coffee and popovers with fresh butter, sat Camille down. She was curious about Camille's work—"Something about the thirties?"

Warmed by the coffee and Ruth's enthusiasm, Camille told a little about Annette Godineaux. "I'm trying to trace her progeny, to find what happened to her and her offspring—Nicole, Pauline. Joey here is the first evidence I've seen myself of any so-called "degeneracy."

"Degeneracy!" Ruth cried. "Why, I'd trust him with my life! He's a wonderful boy, a big help around the place. We all adore him."

"Look, I didn't mean 'degeneracy' in that way. I was speaking, well, of brain power." Camille didn't quite know how to put it. "I should say 'developmentally disabled.' " She spread her fingers, helpless to find the right words. Ruth could be touchy, she saw.

"I'm quick to argue these days," Ruth allowed. "All these double whammies from the Department of Agriculture. They're telling me I should milk three times a day when I can barely do it twice. I won't do it, I tell you! I won't doctor my corn, either, to make it 'bigger and better.' I won't use BST on my cows." She let out a breath, grabbed her coffee mug in two hands—the knucklebones stood out, bluish white. Then she laughed. "Never mind me. I have to sound off now and then. Everyone's after me with advice."

Camille could only nod. She felt a sneeze coming on, there was an odor of barn in here, too—Ruth's rubber boots, maybe. The boots were standing by the door as though they had a life of their own. She sneezed twice; reached in her pocket for a Kleenex. A disk came out with it. She looked at it, surprised, then laid it on the table.

"You know, I feel—oh it's crazy, but as though someone's after me, too. Not with advice or warning—I don't know what they want, actually. You see, I found some papers had been gone through on my desk. Then I saw someone disappear around a corner when I came out. When I called, he—she—didn't answer." She held out the disk. "Look. You'll think I'm crazy, but would you keep this for me? Of course, there's more work to do, I'll keep updating. I've a copy at home."

She stopped, embarrassed at her words, her cheeks hot. She groped for the disk. But Ruth already had her hand on it.

"Of course I'll keep it," Ruth said. "And, hey, I keep the deed to my land in the basement freezer. That's *my* safekeeping."

"Thanks, but a desk drawer will do."

Camille refused the loan of an umbrella after all and ran out into the rain; it felt good on her face, fresh, clean. Her research on the eugenics project had been getting to her. The project was only one step below the Holocaust, wasn't it? Why, it was 1943 when Annette was sterilized, along with her daughter and grandchild! Camille wondered if Binet tests had been given to the Godineaux children. Probably not. Probably in his infinite wisdom the administrator had decided that the children were miniature Annettes with her "subnormal" IQ score.

She would find out. She was on a roll now; she didn't want to eat, sleep, or go out to a bar. She just wanted to do her research, write her paper, get tenure. Then she'd let the world know who she really was. What a relief it would be.

She opened her office door—and gasped. "Oh, no!" Papers and notebooks were scattered on the floor, books pulled off the shelves, scraps from the wastebasket swirling about in the breeze from a half-open window. Who? Why? Someone wanting to steal her notes, maybe, get ahead of her on this eugenics project? Another faculty member? She'd mentioned the project to a few colleagues, wished now she'd kept mum. Was it Frazer Manning, aware of rumors, wanting her out of the department? Breathing shallowly, she booted up her computer, put the mouse on *ANNETTE*. Clicked.

It was gone. "No!" The screen was blank. Her months of research, erased. "No-oo-ooo . . ."

Oh, God, why? Had someone copied the work? Someone wanting to discourage her from going on with the project? And, oh—where was her briefcase with the copies she'd made from the university archives?

"Hail Mary full of Grace," she moaned, the way she used to

as a child when something bad happened. She spun down into her desk chair; her head reeled. But she had to calm herself. She had to think.

Yes, the briefcase was in the car, yes. But had she locked the car? She couldn't recall. She must phone the police—campus security, town police. She dialed, gasped out her message. Then she ran to the car.

Ah. It was there, the briefcase. She drove back to Willmarths'—thank God she'd left her disk there. She would take it back, enter it into her home machine. She would stay up all night if she had to—at least to finish copying Annette's diary.

Ruth would think her crazy. Maybe she was. Oh, yes, she was.

Nine

Donna was at the family computer working on her sociology paper when her grandfather shuffled into the kitchen. She wasn't happy about the interruption: He liked to talk, she needed quiet. She wanted to get a good grade on the paper, finish the year with a B average at least, then transfer to the university. Or quit college altogether, she hadn't made up her mind. She only knew she didn't want to stay at Branbury College.

When Grandpop pushed a dish of chocolate ice cream under her nose, she gave up. She'd visit for a few minutes, then explain to him that she had to have quiet. Perversely, she told him about the Indian raid on Deerfield back in 1704, the enforced march.

"They killed our ancestor's husband because he tried to escape. They killed her father because he was too old to walk. They knocked women and young children on the head because they couldn't keep up. Those were *your* ancestors, Grandpop!"

"Sure," he said, spooning up his ice cream, "but to them it was humane, see? If they just left 'em there to die or be eat up by wolves, it'd be worse than a quick knock on the head. And your mama said the natives carried some of the youngsters on their backs. *Your* ancestors, too," he said, referring to Elizabeth's daughter.

"Well, maybe. But they shouldn't have captured them in the

first place. Why, those poor captives had to walk sixteen miles a day. Through a thick forest! It was awful. Listen to what Elizabeth wrote: 'I must lie between two Indians, with a cord thrown over me and passing under each of them.' Imagine! She was still a young woman, Grandpop."

"Uh-huh."

" 'Occasionally, though,' " she read aloud to her grandfather, " 'the savages kindled a fire to warm me into life.' "

Her grandfather chuckled. "You mean, the savages wasn't so savage after all? You see, it was war, my dear girl. Someday I'll tell you the story from how the Abenaki viewed it. The way my Abenaki grandfather told me and his dad told him."

"I know. I know all that." She was feeling impatient now. "Grandpop, this paper is due soon. Ms. Wimmett expects it. And this isn't my only course."

"I can take a hint." The old man padded back into his workroom. And padded out again. "You like this pretty sweetgrass basket? It's for you, Donna, keep your earrings in it."

He thrust it at her. "Thank you," she said wearily, and went back to her paper.

Donna was glad that Elizabeth's daughter Isobel had remained faithful to her Abenaki lover. Herself, she longed for a lover. Last fall she'd been briefly smitten by a boy who'd sat beside her in Art 101. But then she'd seen him one weekend embracing a girl who'd come up from some other college, and she realized he wasn't interested in her at all, not local Donna.

The kitchen door creaked open and Leroy stood there. He coughed to get her attention and, frustrated, she said, "I'm busy. Can't you see?" He was such a sad sack—nothing like Isobel's lover. His shoulders were slumped, his hair like shredded carrots. "Leroy, you can't barge in here like that. If you want to talk to me, you can do it in the daytime. I have work to do."

He sat down anyway, he was that obtuse. "I need to talk to you. Now," he said.

She leaned into her work to discourage him.

He didn't take the hint. "It's that Olen again," he said. "He gave me a parking ticket. I was in Alibi only a half hour, the lot was full. He's on my tail. He thinks I killed that guy. I want you tell him to get off my back. Tell him you saw me come back to the house that night."

She looked up, indignant. "You want me to take back my story? That I went to bed and you were still there?"

"I want you to say you were looking out your window when you got to your room, you saw me coming back to the trailer. I wouldn't of had time to drag the guy into the swamp."

She stared at him. "Leroy, that's ridiculous. I could say that, sure, but I wasn't looking out my window, was I? I could have seen you going back, then you could have sneaked out again to drag him off and hit him on the head. I mean, really, Leroy! If you didn't do it, then don't worry. No one else was around that night to accuse you."

Leroy seemed to sink lower in the chair. "Someone else *was* here. Your father. He was already here when you came home. He left before you got up."

"What!" This was the first she'd heard of her dad's being home. Why hadn't someone told her? She jumped up, furious. "You know my dad had nothing to do with that death, Leroy Boulanger! He wouldn't kill anybody. And don't you tell Uncle Olen Dad was here. I know Mother wouldn't, that's probably why she didn't tell me. Now go to bed. I don't want to hear one more word out of you." She sank back down in her chair. She was feeling a little sick, a little teary; she just wanted to go to bed and not talk to anyone.

Leroy got up, but hung in the doorway, looking at her. He was sniffing, he had a cold. Donna wrote gibberish on the computer, waiting for him to leave. Finally he said in a small cracked voice, "I already told Olen your father was here. Tonight I told him—when he gave me that ticket. I said it to get him off my back."

When she looked up and gasped, he said, "It's a murder case, maybe, right? You got to tell everything. You can't keep back evidence."

He backed through the door; it banged shut behind him.

* * *

It was eight o'clock Tuesday morning and Russell was home. He pulled up with a grind of brakes and a broken muffler, a cloud of exhaust, and a "Gwennie? Where're you, babe? I'm home. Donna? Brownie? Pop? Got a whole twenty-four hours this time. Answer me, huh?"

They all came running out: Gwen, Brownie, Mert. Russell liked a welcoming committee. Gwen was her own person, of course, but when she came home from a beekeepers' conference or from the hospital with flu, Russell was always there with balloons and beer to welcome *her*. He liked ceremony, that was all. He caught her up in his arms, danced her about while the others looked on, smiling.

"Brownie's here," she whispered in his ear, "give the boy a hug, he's missed you." He did, and Brownie smiled for the first time, it seemed, since that college boy had died. "Only twenty-four hours?" she pleaded. "Stay longer, Russ, never mind the money. We need you."

"Yeah, but I got to go to Swanton, I got a meeting there with the chief. A short one," he conceded. "What happened to the pickup? The Ball kid's out there painting it. The Mongoloid kid with him. Can we afford that, huh? Jeezum, though, I could use some shut-eye. I been driving all night. Then bacon and eggs—I'll fry 'em up. I brought a hunk of ham."

"Give it here," Mert said, "I'll cook it. You go and sleep. Okay, Gwen?"

"Okay." She told Russell about the burned back of the pickup—an accident, she assured him. "I might've been careless with the smoker. I know you can paint it," she said before he could expostulate. "But Tilden Ball's pretty good with cars, and besides, I only pay him minimum wage."

She could see the boy beyond the window, on his blue-jeaned knees, painting the rear a blue slightly lighter than the original. Oh, well, she'd have a two-toned truck. She smiled to see Ralphie, the Down's syndrome boy, grab the paintbrush and dab a blotch of blue on Tilden's rump. Then—uh-oh—Tilden gave him a shove.

"There's high school kids would do it," Russell said. "I wouldn't hire those Balls to dig shit."

"He's a nice enough kid, Russ. He can't help it if his father's a martinet. He gets the wrong end of the stick as it is. But look, sweetheart, I have to work today. Weather's right for bees—sun out, not much wind. I have to go clear to the Canadian border. I'll drop Brownie off at school on the way—he doesn't like that bus. If you'd told me you were coming . . ."

"I didn't know," Russell boomed. "Buffalo had a late snow, shut down our last day. Kee-rist, I drove ninety miles an hour to get here. And you complain," he teased.

He hugged her again and she had to smile. She was glad to see him anytime, any day, any hour. "I'll make it short," she told him. "I'll be back early afternoon. But I want you to call Swanton and tell the chief you have to miss this meeting. We'll take a long walk. Then when Donna comes home—we'll do something together. The four of us. Five," she said, including Mert, who was already fussing about the kitchen. He dropped a knife and retrieved it with a groan—which reminded her: She'd have to plant more marijuana. "I'll put the marijuana in an outdoor pot," she told Mert, and he grinned.

Russell was in the bathroom when Tilden gave a soft knock at the door. Had he heard her remark about the pot? She hoped not. "It's done," the boy said. "It looks rough, but it's the best I could do. It needs body work first." He pushed Ralphie away where the boy was trying to rub the blue paint off his pants.

"It'll have to do, I'm afraid. What do I owe you, now?"

Tilden consulted a notebook, peered at his watch, then made some figures with a stubby pencil. He came up with $15.86. "I had to sand it first—that took an hour. You gotta let it dry a half hour before you go anywhere."

A half hour? She couldn't wait that long. "Just load the smoker in, will you, Tilden? A couple of extra supers. Leroy can help." She added on a dollar for his extra time.

He pocketed the money, loaded in the smoker, and left the way he'd come, head down, eyes on the ground as though he'd suck up nourishment from it. Ralphie started to follow, then stuck his head back in the door. "Ralphie see a shiny in the woods."

"Yes, how nice," she said, and shooed him out the door.

The Balls had been gone a mere ten minutes when Olen Ashley arrived in the police cruiser, muttering about "that license plate." She supposed he'd seen Russell driving into town with the Abenaki Nation plate. Sometimes, she felt, Russell screwed it on just before he arrived in Branbury, to bait Olen. "Please, not today," she pleaded. "Russell's only home a few hours. Let him go now, Olen. Ignore that plate."

"Well, if it's not Uncle Olen," Russell said, emerging from the downstairs bathroom, grinning ear to ear, his black ponytail still stuck with feathers, a spot of vermilion on each cheek. From Olen's viewpoint, though, it would be a personal insult: an illegal plate; an Indian in war paint. She saw his cop face darken.

"Another time, for both of you," she said, playing mediator. "Let's not spoil the day. Go rest now, Russ, you've had a long, all-night drive." She pointed her husband upstairs, motioned Olen to the door.

Neither man moved.

"All right. Just remove it before you leave the grounds," Olen said, looking stiff, intractable, in his blue cop uniform. "But I have to ask you some questions. That's why I came. About the night of April nineteenth. The night that college boy died here."

Gwen sucked in her breath. Who told Olen that Russell was here? Did Russell think that she had? She stepped between the two men, ready to speak up, but Russell moved her carefully aside. "We'll discuss this outside," he told Olen, and strode out the door.

Olen glanced at Gwen, then followed. She had the feeling that he relished this confrontation. And so, she had to admit, did Russell.

"I'll be down in a minute," Brownie called. "Is Dad still there?"

"He's outside," she called back. "I'm packing your lunch box." Life went on in the midst of war. She squeezed in his tuna fish sandwich, the pears, chips, and cookies. Then she stood in the doorway. She couldn't leave until she saw this through.

For a few long moments the two men stood facing one another, like opposing armies—waiting for the leader to call the charge. Russell kept smiling. Olen was frowning. Each moved back a step and then forward again, in a kind of dance. Gwen caught snatches of words: "nightshade" . . . "blow" . . . "I wasn't" . . . Olen's face grew redder and redder until there were two scarlet patches, identical to Russell's. Now, she thought, they truly are at war.

Olen suddenly whirled about, ripped the license plate off Russell's red car; the screws went flying. No longer smiling, Russell dashed after him. "Stop that!" Gwen ran out between the men, snatched up the offending plate. "That's enough! You're two grown men. Give me that plate."

Olen handed it to her, breathing hard, his eyes still on Russell. "See that he doesn't use it again. And I won't press charges." His hand was on his gun—a reflex, she supposed, but she instinctively flinched. "You're lying," Olen told Russell. "You were here that night. He'd bothered your daughter. I can understand that. But then he woke up and you hit him on the head, did you?"

"No! He was asleep!" Gwen cried. "Go away, Olen. Just go away!"

"I can speak for myself," said Russell, his face a red flag. "Sure, I could of done all those things. But you see, I really was asleep. I didn't know the kid was here. I didn't know Donna was with him." He paused, took a step closer to Olen, his eyes yellow with sun. "Or I would have killed him—like you said. You gotta believe it. I would of."

He stalked away, back into the house. Olen's hand left his holster. Gwen held the license plate tight to her chest. "Just go away," she told Olen. "Leave us alone. You've gone too far now."

He took a step toward her, but she backed away. "I'm sorry, Gwen, I'm just doing my job. Russell was here that night. You didn't tell me. I have to question everyone."

"I didn't think it mattered. He was asleep, I told you."

"You were awake all night?"

"No, but—"

"Then you can't swear he didn't go outside, see a motorcycle? Go looking for its owner? Find that boy?"

"He wouldn't." A defenseless boy, lying drunk and drugged on the ground? But then she thought: What if the boy woke up? Defended himself against Russell? Jumped him?

She shook her head to get rid of the suspicion, sank onto the step. The license plate clattered down beside her.

Olen explained again that he was "only doing my job—if Russell would comply. Look, I'd like us all to be friends, Gwen, I would. But he *will* push me to the limit!"

After he drove off, giving one more pleading glance through the car window, she realized she hadn't asked who "told" on Russell. It's not the children, she thought, not Mert. It could only be Leroy. Leroy would have heard Russell arrive—that broken muffler, who could miss it?

"I won't need you today," she said when Leroy came down from the trailer, coughing into his hand. "You stay home and nurse that cold." She turned away to show that there would be no more discussion.

Despite the setbacks—the reformatory director still refusing to let her see his archives, an abusive phone message from Pauline ("Do you remember what I said? Have you quit nosing into our lives?")—Annette's family tree was growing on Camille's computer. She'd bought a more powerful PC; she wanted to work longer hours; the destruction of data in her office had made her doubly paranoid. College security had said they'd keep an eye on her office, but they were a small force and busy elsewhere; she was better off at home. She'd visited the town police as well, although Chief Fallon looked either annoyed or bored with her concerns. She'd felt like a small girl complaining that someone had stolen her teddy bear. Seeing the man leaning back in his swivel chair guzzling a Pepsi, she wanted to remind him about the sugar, about ruining his teeth. But she'd kept her mouth shut. It wouldn't do to antagonize the police.

Now, in her two-room apartment on Seminary Street, she brewed herself a cup of green tea and sat down to work, the cat purring at her feet. The Perkey files informed her that Annette had left the Brookview Reformatory for the last time on July 23, 1943, along with her daughter Nicole, born 1917, and with Nicole's small son, who'd been allowed to stay with her. At this point Annette was "dying" to get out, she wrote in her diary. They had offered freedom in exchange for sterilization.

They said they'd take out my cherry, squeeze it dry, get rid of my bad blood was how they put it, they want to breed a new swarm of Wasps. The idea of it I don't like. But I look out the barred window and there's a tree. A mountain. I could get a place of my own on that mountain, nobody to tell me, Annette eat your soup, Annette sit on the pot, Keep that light out, No reading or writing, you hear? So I let them do it. And then I find they do it to Nicole too. But Nicole's got two kids. She don't mind they dry up her cherry. But the boy?

And then a poem, written after she got out:

Up here at dawn I'm a bird
on a merry go round of clouds,
I make my own music.
Town's at my feet, I
swoop down
then bird and clouds
fly up into fire.

Now it was Nicole that Camille wanted to find or, if she was dead, her son. Surely Pauline, with all her threats, was a dead end. Camille might find the son more reasonable—or even a grandson. The implication was that the son, too, had been sterilized. Was he "feebleminded"? Were he and his mother still alive? If so, was it possible to pull oneself up out of poverty or institutionalization? Mert LeBlanc seemed to have done it. And what about Nicole's husband? Camille had only just found out his name. Was there inbreeding? Who was that judge who was arrogant enough to declare someone "unfit" for Vermont society?

There was a knock on the door; she opened it to find Emily Willmarth—she recalled now she'd asked the girl to bring her paper here to the apartment since it was a day late. Emily was full of apologies, mumbling something about "two calves yesterday and one of them breech, so Mom needed my help."

Camille smiled; she'd heard all the excuses. In this case it was undoubtedly a genuine one, although the problem was that students started the paper late to begin with, allowed no time for last-minute traumas. "Thanks," she told Emily, "I'll look forward to it. My grandmother had a farm, but I'm afraid it was gone by the time I came of age."

"I wish mine was, too," Emily said in a small voice, and then grinned to show she didn't really mean that, but yet she did.

"It's a nice farm."

"I suppose. It's just . . ." Emily looked up at the ceiling lamp. "It would be good to live in town, that's all—like people who get off work at three or four in the afternoon."

"Like teachers, you mean? But teachers bring work home with them."

"Sure, sure, I know that," the girl said quickly. "But teaching is different. It's more, well, nice to do." She looked pointedly at Camille's high-heeled boots, her slim teacherly pants; then down at her own mud boots, and grimaced. "Well, I'm off. Back to the library—I've two more papers. All due within three days of each other."

She looked a little put out, as though Camille were in deliberate collusion with the other professors. But then she laughed, and Camille smiled, too, and, shrugging, held up her palms for truce.

"Get some rest," Camille said. "You look tired. Exams coming up in two weeks."

Emily was on her way to the door when the screen on Camille's computer went suddenly dark. Camille cried out, then realized it was because she hadn't written anything on it for a quarter of an hour or so. But the blank screen had given her a start.

"Wait—Emily," she said, and reached in her drawer. "Here. Take this to your mother." She thrust a disk at the girl. "It's just something I'd wanted her to keep for me. She'll know. It's not classwork," she added. "It has nothing to do with exams." And then, when Emily frowned, "I wasn't suggesting . . ."

"It's okay." Emily pocketed the disk, and with a swivel of sleek brown hair and the clack of a loose leather belt against the metal knob, she was out the door.

Emily's visit, the imagined footsteps, the screen going dark had made Camille feel vulnerable again. For some reason the dead boy, Shep Noble, came back into her mind. She still hadn't told Gwen Woodleaf that he was a Perkey. There was probably no connection at all with his death, none. But the thought nagged at her. She took a breath, picked up the phone, dialed the Woodleaf Apiaries. The phone rang four times and finally the answering machine clicked on. So she left a short message, mentioning Shep Noble, and asked that Gwen call her back. It might be important, she said. She didn't want to say exactly why it might be important, on a machine.

She went back to work. After an hour on the computer, she felt a kind of paralysis creep up her back and knew that she had to move her body. When she got up, something snapped in her spine. She had a pinched nerve that required surgery—she'd kept putting it off. She lay on her back on the floor and pulled her legs, hard, up to her chest. But it didn't help. She'd have to walk out the kinks. It was these late nights on the computer, the anxiety to get this paper researched and written, that had done her in. She would walk once around the block—twice, maybe.

It was a cloudy but warm night. Camille's apartment was over a garage; the near-deaf couple who lived in the house were in bed by ten o'clock. Oddly, she felt safer out here on this quiet street than she did in her apartment: The houses were close together, a few had lights on upstairs. A car went down the street at least every ten minutes. She strode out, feeling her back unwind, her muscles stretch. She heard her heels click on the sidewalk, but when she paused, the street was quiet. She thought about her paper—walking stimulated the brain. So did the rain that was just starting to dampen her skin and hair.

For a moment she had the illusion that Annette was moving along with her, pouring out her story. *Help me*, the woman pleaded, *pull me up so I can breathe in the fresh air. Get them off my back!* Camille was sure that someone was behind her then, and she walked faster. But when she reached her apartment steps and looked back, there was no one. The footsteps were in her imagination. Annette, too, had disappeared. A car drove slowly by and then turned into a driveway up the street. Two cars were parked on the street—it was too dark to see the color or plates. It was a perfectly normal evening. It was her own paranoia she had to struggle with and overcome.

She fumbled for her key, discovered she didn't need it. Usually the lock clicked shut automatically, but she realized that she had left it open for Emily, and afterward had forgotten to push the bolt. She went in—and gasped. Someone in a black hooded raincoat was seated at her computer, reading what she had written, then deleting it; she could hear the quick raspy breaths. Now, as she stood in the doorway, gripped with anger, the gloved hand reached down to yank the plug, both hands pulling the machine toward the table edge as though they would steal or destroy it.

She snatched up a chair by the door, went at the intruder, struck the back of the head. They were suddenly face-to-face. Her vision blurred. Things took on a life of their own. The computer crashed to the floor. The chair rose, sailed through the air. In a fury she attacked, barehanded. She was caught; she broke loose, dashed for the phone, dialed 911. Felt herself pushed; she fell, rolling over, hands, wires coiled about her neck, tightening on her throat.

And the room blinking slowly black. . . .

Ten

Colm Hanna was the first on the scene, alerted electronically by a 911 dispatcher. He was the only one in the building when the call came in; the chief was home, nursing his aches and pains, watching a ball game. The others were off duty or on a beat somewhere: Sergeant Hammer at a fire in New Haven, Olen Ashley helping campus security—a fight in one of the dormitories. If they couldn't have fraternities, they'd raise hell in the dorms. He was stunned at what he found. A young woman with a phone cord twisted around her neck, her face and throat a dark red, deep purple bruises on the back of her neck. The phone lay bleating beside her head. An Epson computer lay on its side, a black cat crouched nearby, wary.

A pile of papers rustled in the breeze from an open window. Colm picked up a pack of Juicy Fruit gum and a shiny key painted with a purple X that had fallen on the rug; he wrapped them in a handkerchief for forensics. There was no sign of activity in the bedroom; if the attack was sexual, it had happened on the living room rug. There was no pulse, poor kid. She didn't look over twenty-five, though she might have been thirty. These things were hard to deal with. Colm could never do this police thing full-time.

The outside door was unlocked. Had she known the stranger?

It was a man, it would appear, judging by the marks on the throat. "Jeez," he said. "Jeez." And then, "Too late for her." And, "Don't move anything," when moments later Sergeant Hammer ran in, then Olen Ashley, who'd just checked back into home base. Ashley had heard of the woman; she was a college professor, he said—the department had listed her home phone after her office was vandalized, her files deleted. Ashley was still shaken—and shaking, he said—"at the degree of intoxication" he'd seen that evening in one of the men's dorms. Could one of the drunks have stumbled into the professor's apartment? He called the medical examiner while Colm alerted his father—Hanna's Funeral Home was two blocks away.

The response wasn't wholly unexpected: "Christ, Colm, it's after eleven. I was sound asleep—my arthritis bad, bad! Can't you take care of the body? I mean, if it's homicide, they'll wanna keep it, right? You know where the limo keys are."

As it turned out, his father was right. The medical examiner had the body photographed, then wrapped and transported to Burlington for a complete medical-legal autopsy. Ashley and Hammer took charge of searching the apartment for evidence. Colm went home. Then, looking up at the darkened windows of the mortuary, he backed out of the driveway and just drove. How could he sleep anyway, after what he'd seen? He imagined what it must have been like for the young woman, finding an attacker in her apartment—or did she let him in? What had he been after, anyway? A copy of the exam? A kid might have panicked, tried to stifle her screams. What would drive him to do that? A demanding father? "Pass that course or else"? It happened, Colm knew. Parents wanting to make over a kid in their image.

When he drove past the Willmarth farm—for some reason the Horizon headed itself that way, like an old horse to Paddy's Bar—he saw a light on in the barn. The car turned in, parked next to the green pickup. He and Ruth were vying, it seemed, for "oldest running vehicle." He found her rubber-gloved and cleaning up a newborn calf.

This one was already rising up on unsteady legs; the mother—

up, too, after her ordeal—licking at the calf, bawling her pleasure. It was a bull calf, Ruth said—it would go to the slaughterhouse. "Vic hates that. He gets overly fond of these calves." And then, "What are you doing here at this hour?" She glanced at her watch, reported, "Eleven-thirty-five. Last week it was two in the morning. I hoped Emily would stay home tonight, but she had to hand in her paper to that sociology prof."

He told her what had happened, and she cried out, "No! Can't be! Who would do that?" and she sank down on an overturned pail. When she caught her breath and started talking, as if to chatter away the shock of the death, she explained how Camille had come to her, left a computer disk. "She was feeling paranoid. I didn't take her seriously enough. I could have done something to save her, couldn't I?" She pulled off her gloves, dropped them in a pile of hay. They were wet with mucus and blood. Colm felt queasy all over again to see them.

She brought him into the house. It was a warm evening, rain stopped, stars just beginning to wink through the clouds. The universe was carrying on, a young woman's death nothing to that vast nonchalance. Inside he hit the Otter Creek Ale; she kept it for him, didn't drink much of it herself. It kept her up peeing, she said. Tonight, though, she'd be up anyway. She had two young grandchildren upstairs in bed, the little one with a cold—Sharon and Jack at an overnight ecology conference.

"Someone wanted to see what was on that computer," she said. "Or destroy what was there. That's why Camille was worried. Her research had something to do with a eugenics project back in the thirties. Past history."

Colm had read a piece about it in the *Boston Globe*. "Another religious war. At least your people were Protestant, Ruthie. We Irish Catholics were among the degenerates, you know. But in the pecking order, a hair above the French—mainly because there were more of them in Vermont. At the bottom, the Native Americans."

"But who would kill over something that happened in the past?" she argued.

"Maybe she named names. People who think the past would

hurt the present. Or it could have been a student. We'll have to check the class lists. It could be a random killer—that's the worst." He poured a second glass. He needed it. Ruth was nursing a cup of herb tea. It helped her to sleep, she said. He'd help her to sleep, too, if she'd let him, he reminded her, and she only smiled and put out a hand. It was still smelly from the birth. He didn't mind, did he? He'd take whatever she'd give him. Her divorce was final now. But she was still carrying some kind of cross. Or maybe the bitterness at Pete's defection hadn't yet subsided—she didn't seem to be done with the old marriage.

He could wait. It seemed he had to, if he wanted her.

She jumped up, startling him. "What did I do with that disk she gave me? We can read it, see if she names any names." Then halfway across the room she halted, slapped a hand to her head. "What a ninny I am! She took it back. She came rushing over after her office was vandalized, asked for the disk. She wanted to copy it onto her home computer, the office one was too accessible." Ruth sank back into her chair, dropped her chin in her hands. "I should have reminded her to bring it back afterward."

"How could you know someone was going to kill her?" He grabbed one of her hands. Patted it. Jeez, he felt like her father.

"I know, I know," she said. "But someone wanted her work, she thought—maybe a colleague. Or it could have been an outsider. She was looking up the Godineaux family. It could have been any one of them. She throws her business cards around. She even gave me one. It has her number, her home address, her office at the college. How public can you get? She struck me as being rather naive."

"They'll take the computer to the station. If there's still anything on it, I'll get it copied. We can track some of these people down. You got a little time on your hands?"

She looked at him; he knew she didn't. But he knew she'd make time. She said, "Emily. Emily was going over there tonight with her paper. She would have been one of the last to see Camille. I'll call her tomorrow. She'll have heard the worst by then."

They sat in silence for a few moments while Colm finished

his beer. He started for the refrigerator and she stopped him. "I'm going to bed, I'm bushed. I need to sleep this murder off, clear my head. If you want another one, you'll have to drink it in your car. I'm locking up."

Once he stood up, he decided he didn't want another one anyway. He had stronger stuff at home. Guckenheimer whiskey. It would do the trick—for tonight anyway. Tomorrow he'd take a look at that computer. Jeez, two dead in the same month—and both from the college. Weird.

Upstairs a child cried out. Ruth was racing up the steps like the kid was about to leap out a window. "I'll phone you tomorrow, okay?" he hollered.

There was no reply. He couldn't compete with a grandkid.

The *ANNETTE* file was blank, someone had managed to delete all but the last few sentences, Colm said on the phone the next day, while he was lingering on the line. Receiver cradled between bent head and shoulder, Ruth was sweeping out the barn: bits of hay, feces, caked blood, dried urine, straw. What a smelly world Ruth lived in! The granddaughter, Willa, was squatting on an overturned box, cooing to a stuffed rabbit, her honey-colored hair falling across her round face. That blank file, Ruth thought. If they didn't know what was on it, how could they find any leads to the killer?

"But they didn't get her date book," Colm said. "Olen found that in her bedroom. She'd written down three or four Godineaux addresses—that should give us a lead. At least there was no sign of a sexual assault."

"Thank God for small favors," she said dryly.

"There was a key, though, something I picked up from the floor. I'll have forensics check it for fingerprints. Might not be anything important. But it didn't fit her door."

They were silent a moment. She heard the new calves bleating in their stalls—they wanted their mothers, out in the field. Willa said, "Mama?"

"Soon," she told the child. "Mama will be home soon."

Colm said, "Now we've got two deaths and we haven't a clue

about either one. Although . . ." He stopped talking. A cluster fly buzzed in her ear.

"Although what, Colm? You're getting to be like your boss, Fallon. You don't finish sentences. It drives the listener crazy, you know that?"

"Now you've knocked it right out of my mind, Ruthie. I don't know what I was going to say. Wait—yes, I was going to say that Olen has a new suspect for the Noble boy's death. Russell LeBlanc. Evidently he was there that night; he had means, he had motive. He knew where the nightshade was. He could've dragged the guy there."

"What are you, Colm—undertaker, Realtor, or cop? Which is it, pal? If cop, remember that Russell is Gwen's husband, even with a different name. I don't like the idea of his being accused without proof. *She* won't like it." She surveyed the mess at her feet. She wished she could afford to buy a machine that would sweep it all away.

Colm sneezed. " 'Scuse me," he said.

"The fire in Gwen's car," she said, forcing her mind back to the two deaths. "Any fingerprints on that charred box of matches I gave you?"

"Not a trace. The guy must've been wearing gloves. So was the fellow who murdered the professor. No clues, I told you. Except for the key. And the date book."

"Well, keep looking. Colm, I have to finish cleaning up in here. Talk to you later, okay? Unless you want to come over and help?"

"Uh, no, thanks. I'll phone first."

"Sure," and she hung up. She rubbed her aching neck, swatted a fly. Help might be on the way, though. Two bicycles whirled into the driveway. "Just in time," she shouted at the girls. "Come give the place a mop-down, will you, Em?" Though she knew what the girls really wanted, what they needed. "I know, I heard," she said, hugging them both with her smelly arms.

"I was the last to see her," Emily said. "Two cops came over to question me. I still can't believe it. It's so awful." Her eyes filled, and she opened them wide to hold in the tears. "She never got to read our papers." She was breaking down now, blowing her nose, while Donna stared blankly at the sloppy barn floor.

Ruth carried little Willa out into the fresh spring morning. It smelled of earth and new grass and wildflowers. It was hard to go back inside, but the girls needed solace. She sat all three females down in the kitchen with hot chocolate. Willa slurped it contentedly out of her bottle. The older girls held the mugs in cupped hands, their faces spreading gloom.

"So what exactly did you tell the officers?" she asked gently. Of course it was a shock, losing a favorite teacher. There was an absence here that couldn't be filled. The young women were still in shock.

"Just that I went in for five minutes," Emily said, "around ten o'clock—I don't know the exact minute—with my paper. She seemed glad to get it, she said I should get some rest, I looked tired. She was concerned about *me*, when *she* was about to be—to be—to be—"

Ruth put an arm around her. "She didn't know that—not then. So that was all? When you left, you didn't see anyone, well, skulking about?"

"No. A couple cars parked on the street, that's all." Emily reached in her pocket for another Kleenex. "But she gave me something for you. A disk." She dug deeper in the pocket. "I had it, I know I never took it out. Damn! It must have fallen out."

"Her research," Ruth said, alarmed at its absence. "I'm sure it was. Keep looking, Em. You've got to find it."

Emily stood up, searched her pockets. A pencil fell out, two pens, some chalk, a pile of coins, crumpled Kleenex. But no disk.

"Think back," Ruth urged. "Where did you go after that? Who did you run into? Did you fall off your bike? You have to retrace your steps."

"Not now," the girl said, her eyes filling again. "Mom, the whole school's in a panic. Kids wanting rides everywhere. Nobody wants to go out at night in case the killer strikes again. You've got to find out who did it!" She started upstairs and motioned Donna to follow. Ruth sat there, feeling helpless.

Halfway up, Donna called back. "Ms. Wimmet left a message for Mother. It was weird. She asked her to call back. Something to do with Shep Noble's death."

"No idea what it was?"

Donna shook her head, and the tears spilled out again. She climbed heavily up the steps to Emily's room. Alone with her granddaughter in the kitchen, Ruth felt she could use a good cry herself. For Camille, for Shep Noble, for Gwen and Donna. For Emily. For the whole goddamn mixed-up world. . . .

Willa stared intently at her grandmother. Her face puckered in sympathy. Ruth opened the door—she had to vent her feelings. "Let people live out their lives the way they want!" she shouted at the sun.

But the sun went behind a cloud. It was the old cop-out.

Donna skipped her afternoon chemistry class; it was no use, she wouldn't be able to concentrate. Instead she got on her bicycle, rode toward home. Home was safe, away from the fresh crime scene that the entire college had become. It was like her world had spun crazily about and then crashed. It helped to ride, to try and make sense of what had happened. To remember Ms. Wimmet as she was, alive and in love with her subject—with Donna's paper, with Donna's ancestor Isobel who refused to leave her husband, the village they lived in together. Isobel had left no words behind; no one knew her feelings, her dreams. But she was an equal there, Ms. Wimmet had pointed out, it was a matriarchal society. Women were farmers, corn huskers, creators of pots and baskets.

Donna was impressed with that. The natives weren't "savage" at all. People today just didn't understand. They didn't *try* to understand.

But Camille Wimmet had understood. She'd talked to Donna like a person, an equal, she said Donna was lucky to have that background. She said she hoped to look for some intermarriage in her own family, after she finished the research on this French-Canadian woman—a woman who had Abenaki blood in her, too. But that research had led to Ms. Wimmet's death.

Donna held tight to the handlebars; the tears scalded her eyes. She blinked repeatedly to clear her vision. She was cycling through a wooded section of town, just before the road that led up to the mountain where she lived. It was growing dark; the trees leaned over the narrow pavement like they'd lurch forward any minute. Thoughts of death and murder made the foliage look darker, the mountain ahead look grimmer. She was sorry now she hadn't called her mother for a ride. She thought she heard a whirring noise behind, another bicycle, and she pedaled faster. When she glanced back, she saw it wasn't a bicycle, but a car. She edged closer to the side of the road. The car roared up behind her. She bent over the handlebars, her legs like logs on the pedals. Suddenly it was on her! She lunged hard to the right—and it struck her wheel. Bike and rider crashed into a ditch. She lay in it for long minutes, dazed.

When she stood up finally, her knees bruised, hands bloody where she'd tried to stop the fall, the road was empty. There was only dust from the car, which had raced on up the road. If she hadn't swerved at the last second, it might have killed her. She stood there, numbed with the thought, her hands hanging like weights at her sides. It was a long time before she could propel her body toward home.

This time the bees had swarmed next door at the Ball farm. Mert had answered the phone, assured Harvey Ball, in his unruffled way, that someone would take care of it. So now Gwen had to do it. And then, at four o'clock, she would drive over to the memorial service for Camille Wimmet, which was certain, like Shep Noble's, to be a damp one, full of fond students, including Emily and Donna, whose papers she would never get to read. But Donna had hardly said a word to anyone since she'd arrived home the night before, scraped and bleeding from falling off her bike; she hadn't wanted to see or talk to anyone. "No one!" she'd shouted, and Gwen complied.

The problem was, with so many other things going on, Gwen hadn't taken care of the hives on her own land, or on Ball's—they had become overcrowded, and now the bees were taking off on their own. At least she assumed that was what had happened.

She saw Harvey plowing the field with his older son and so she knocked on the door, thinking Tilden or Ralphie might be there, know where the swarm was. She would prefer to take it down quietly, then steal away home without any words from the father.

Tilden looked surprised, then wary when he opened the door—she seldom came over in a neighborly way; she didn't feel welcome. He had a book in his hand, but she didn't comment; she merely inquired about the swarm.

"Toolshed," Tilden said in his laconic way, and pointed to the east, beyond the red cow barn.

"Would you mind coming with me? I could use your help." She glanced at his bare feet, wondered how he found shoes to fit. His toes were long and bony, almost fingerlike.

Without looking at her, he put down the book and led the way, still shoeless, to the shed. The swarm was wrapped around a lamp to the right of the shed door. She let Tilden hold the smoker while she got it down. As they worked, she asked what he planned to do when he got out of college. Small talk, but she felt he needed a little attention. The mother had died of breast cancer three years before; she knew he'd been closer to the mother than the father.

"I won't farm," he said. "I don't like cows. I don't like stinking barns."

"You like the smell of diesel fuel and old engines," she teased. He started to smile, but then frowned, as though the smile might be used against him. "You could start your own business, then. Sell cars?"

"Not if I graduate college. I'll have to sell insurance or something."

"Your dad would want you to do that?"

"It'd be my decision!" Tilden rose to the defense of his father.

"Well, then. You know what you'll have to do."

He didn't respond, so she changed the subject to a more controversial one. "Your father wants me to sell my land so he can have a bigger farm. What do you think?"

"Dad wants it for Sidney. Dad loves the farm. It's important to him."

"The land is important to us, too. It belonged to my father—his father before him. I want to pass it on to Donna and Brownie." She thought of the grave site, but decided not to mention it. Though it was no secret; there'd been a piece about it in the local paper a few years back.

Tilden walked on ahead. His father was rumbling up on his tractor, and the boy looked nervous. "She asked me to help," he told Harvey, backing away as though he'd done something wrong. "I had to show her where the swarm was."

"You're not in class," his father said, the dark brows clouding his eyes.

"Dad, I don't have a ten o'clock. I'm going now." The boy turned on his heel with a withering glance at Gwen as though it were her fault he wasn't in class. He might have helped her back to the truck with the smoker, she thought, but then, the father's appearance had changed the atmosphere.

She picked up the smoker, started back to her pickup. She could hear Harvey behind her—she could smell him, he'd been spreading manure. She moved resolutely along, but then he planted his bulk between her and the driver's-side door. "I didn't like it," he said. "I needed a special tool of mine. Damn bees wouldn't let me in."

"Of course they would. Bees are benign when they're swarming." She waited for him to move so she could get into her truck.

"Quiet, is it? I got two stings. Here—and here." He indicated his forehead, where there was a slight inflammation.

"You must have angered them. Harvey, I have to go now. Please."

He moved aside and she climbed in. But he held on to the door handle. "I could go to the police. Tell them you planted that marijuana again. Even after they made you pull it up. Oh, yes, I saw. It was in a jar behind your house."

"You were spying! You had no right." The anger was up in

her throat now, she was choking with it. She started the truck. She'd drag him along if he didn't let go of her door handle.

"Sell!" he cried. "I'll give you a good price. Only a hundred twenty-five thousand. How's that? That's a fair price. You don't need all that land. You don't use it right. You can keep the bees and live somewhere else. Down in the village. Some other place. Sell and I won't tell the police who dragged that boy to the nightshade. Who left him to die there."

"What?" Her foot trembled on the clutch.

"Sure. It was my son saw him. Ralphie. Ralphie can't sleep on a full moon night. He was out walking, edge of our property. He saw a "shiny man," he said, dragging that boy along. It was your husband."

"No! How can you say that? Ralphie meant buttercups, that's what he meant by 'shiny.' I pointed at them, and he nodded."

"That getup your husband wears. All that silver. It shines in moonlight. You bet it does. Ralphie? Come over here, Ralphie."

The little Mongoloid trotted over, smiling. "Shiny," he said, "Ralphie see a shiny."

"Shiny *man*, you said," Harvey coaxed. "Shiny *man*. Right, Ralphie? Say it now."

But Ralphie ran off, giggling. "Shiny," he called back stubbornly, and his father's ears reddened.

Russell was covered with silver, it was true, when he was wearing his full regalia. But that night, he'd been sleeping in the nude—except, of course, for the earrings he seldom removed, maybe an armband or two, she couldn't remember. But why on earth would he have gone out stark naked?

"Russell was in Buffalo," she said, going out on a limb. "You couldn't have seen him."

But Harvey just smiled. "Farmers are up early. We run out of orange juice—Ralphie had a cold. I went to that convenience store down in the village. Passed your husband, oh, yes, coming back up the road. He was just leaving your place quarter of six. Shiny man, you bet."

She pressed down on the gas and the truck lurched forward. For a moment Harvey ran along with it, his hands still on the door handle. Finally he dropped off, shouting, "A good price, a fair price! And the police won't know."

She didn't answer—couldn't! She bumped down the stony driveway to the main road, tears crowding her eyes like angry bees.

"You'll be sorry," he hollered after. "By Christ, you'll live to regret it!"

Eleven

Colm and Ruth had divided up today's visits—Camille's murder had goaded Ruth into action. This time she'd known the victim, bonded with her—so had Emily. Colm was to interview the four remaining male students in Camille's sociology class, then follow up two leads from the professor's date book: the director of the Brookview Reformatory and a Eugene Godineaux family in Ripton. Ruth was off to see the Petits, the foster family who had taken in Tim's Joey, then chat with several girls from the sociology class. She dreaded those interviews. The young women were still in shock; according to Emily, they were lined up daily to see the college counselors.

The Petits, she found, had moved from Branbury to Winooski, Vermont, a mill town where Thaddeus Petit, a construction worker, had found a more lucrative job. "So we ended up here. And I don't take in foster kids no more," said Mabel Petit, who was "thrilled" to hear about "my darling Joey. He was the sweetest kid when we got him, never a bit of trouble—well, hardly ever, kids being kids. But," she added, tapping a finger on her temples, "missing a couple of bricks, you know."

She gave a tinkling laugh. She was a tinkling kind of woman, a dozen colored bracelets hanging from her arms, and dangly glass earrings that kept tangling up with her orange hair. She'd extricate them with her orange nails and say, "Ooh, ouch!"

After the amenities, the tour of the small two-bedroom house that was filled top to bottom with trinkets, Ruth settled in with a cup of tea and told Mabel about Camille Wimmet's visit to see Joey, and then her death by strangulation.

"Oh, my gawd," Mabel bawled, "I saw about it on TV. How aw-ful, the poor woman! Who you think would of done such a thing?"

"That's what we'd like to know. That's why I'm here." And when Mabel said, "Ooh, ooh," again, and shrank back into her overstuffed chair, Ruth said, "I mean, it's because of Joey being a Godineaux. The name might hold a clue. Can you tell me about Joey's parents?"

Mabel was cautious. She pulled back her shoulders, examined her fingernails. "I'm not supposed to say. I mean, they didn't tell me much. Really."

"But you know something," Ruth urged, holding the woman's eyes with her own.

Mabel swallowed up her lower lip with her yellowish teeth and considered. "We-ell," she said, "we-ll, Godineaux was the mother's name. The father run off, you see, before Joey was born—I mean, they never married, Joey's parents."

"Do you know the father's name?" Ruth leaned forward. Somehow the male line seemed important, she didn't know why. Though, to tell the truth, she was wholly in the dark. She didn't know what she was searching for.

Wincing, Mabel pulled out another hair from her earring. "I'd tell you, hon, if I did, but I don't, I just don't. You'll have to go talk to the foster child agency. You know, where I got the kids from? In Argennes? Gawd, I forget the name of the woman what runs it. I'm going through menopause now, you know." She lowered her voice, leaned forward confidentially. "I get these hot flashes. I sweat in the sheets at night, my belly's a balloon, you know what I mean?"

Ruth sucked in her stomach. She was wearing a skirt in deference to the visit—a striped cotton one that billowed out in front. Yes, she did know what it was to go through menopause:

the heavy periods, the hot and cold nights. But she wasn't about to discuss it with this woman. She nodded, in compromise. "Can I call you for that address—that name? I have to get back to my farm. Your Joey is there with my foreman—he's a big help. You brought him up right."

Mabel grinned. She'd just remembered the caseworker's name. "Evangeline Balinsky. You can look the number up. I got my foster kids from different places, you see. Some of 'em Catholic like Evangeline's, some not. I can't remember them all."

"Of course not." Ruth smiled through a cup of Lipton's tea, fifteen minutes more of conversation that yielded no rewards, then took her leave, smoothing down her puffy skirt—there was too much fabric. She made a mental note to give the skirt to Sharon, who was smaller-hipped than herself. From now on she'd stick to pants.

On her way back, she stopped in a used clothing store called Neat Repeats and bought a pair of black cotton jeans for $5.50. She looked pounds thinner in them. In the store mirror she wiped off the lipstick she'd rubbed on before the interview. Now she was Ruth again, ready to take on the college women.

She was halfway home when she realized she'd left the striped skirt in the store's dressing room. Oh, well, she thought, skimming down Route 7 past red barns and open land rimmed with mountains, Sharon wouldn't have liked that skirt, either.

Ruth was glad to get home after her hour's meeting with the female sociology students. It had been a dead end, the girls still teary-eyed, blank when it came to any motive for the murder. They were saddened for Camille; they were worried for themselves—a killer was on the loose. It worried Ruth as well, to tell the truth: for herself, for her family. The grandchildren were in the pasture when she arrived, picking buttercups that stained their noses a bright yellow. Robbie ran at her with a bunch; the stems were crushed in his small hands. Not to be outdone, little Willa raced after him, thrust a dozen blossoms in Ruth's arms. All heads, with no stems.

"Put them in water, Nana," Robbie urged. The boy knew how

to make things live. It was a comforting thought. She shepherded the children into the kitchen, gave them hugs and juice. Sharon was there in the usual outrageous getup: tall green rubber boots and blue long johns under the purple skirt, an embroidered vest, and an Indian cotton blouse. Her heavy brown hair was pinned up on one side of her head, hanging straight and bushy on the other. Ruth embraced her. She was the perfect antidote for Mabel Petit.

"Colm called. He's coming over at seven," Sharon informed her. Sharon was always trying to get her mother together with Colm; she didn't like Ruth living alone. Ruth didn't know which was worse: Sharon pushing her toward Colm or Emily trying to respark a burned candle with her ex-husband, Pete. Although Emily had cooled in that regard since Pete's efforts to make her buy back his portion of the farm.

"He say anything else?" Ruth dropped her jacket on a chair. Sharon eyed her mother's new black jeans. "Mother, they use a shoe horn to get you into those?"

Ruth was offended. "They're a perfect fit." She sucked in her stomach and pulled on a sweater. Admittedly the jeans were a little tight when she bent over. She'd change before Colm arrived. She didn't need *his* opinion, too.

Sharon smiled snidely and hollered at the children, who were pounding up and down the stairs. "Oh, and earlier there was a call from Gwen Woodleaf. She wants you to sound out Jack, see if he'll testify for her next Tuesday. About how those bruises could come from the nightshade. I told her he would, but she wants *you* to call him. Mom, I have to go. Jack's coming home. It's my night to cook."

"Tofu stroganoff with seaweed?" It was her turn to tease her vegetarian daughter.

"Nah. A tempeh stir fry."

"Yuck," said Ruth, who, though she'd given up on red meat—partly because it might be one of her slaughtered bull calves—still preferred fowl and fish to soy and seaweed.

When Sharon and the children left, it was like a storm gone out to sea. It was still early for milking, so she fixed herself a cup of peppermint tea, breathed in the steam—she might be on the verge of a cold. She relished these few moments of peace, alone in the house. Vic would be home from school late, he had softball practice. Of course, Emily might pop in at any time, depending on whether or not she needed something: an article of clothing, a book, Mom's shoulder to wax indignant or bereaved on. She'd given Ruth an earful about her latest encounter with Billy Bozeman. Emily was convinced it was disgruntled fraternity boys responsible for the graffiti, even the damage to Gwen's bees. She might have a point, Ruth thought. In college, Ruth had stayed clear of the fraternities, except for an occasional foray into Pete's frat that had wholly abashed her. Too much rah-rah. Too much booze. Too much grabbing ass.

Then why did she marry Pete, a good ole boy?

To make babies with, she guessed. Pete had good genes. He was low-key, where she was apt to be high-strung; calm in a crisis, while she sometimes lost it. Outgoing, while she tended to be introspective. You needed those opposites to make babies. She'd never regret hers! She supposed these inverse attractions went back thousands of years.

Her teacup empty, she called her son-in-law to see if he'd testify, and Jack was intrigued.

Though he'd have to study up on nightshade, he hadn't come across much about that plant before. "I'll call the lady back," he promised, "then do a little research. I oughta learn more about it anyway. First thing you know, Sharon'll be growing the stuff."

"No doubt," Ruth said, and hung up.

Colm Hanna arrived promptly at seven. He was an on-time kind of guy; Ruth liked that about him. She tended to be on the late side herself. Of course, one couldn't always count on cows making one available for appointments. But tonight the milking had gone smoothly. While they cleaned up the milking apparatus, she'd quizzed Joey about his father—with no results. "He left," Joey said, perhaps quoting Mabel Petit, "he just gone. Poof!" He flapped his arms like a bird. The mother had taken off with another man when Joey was four, Tim told her privately, and the grandmother was ill at that point; she couldn't care for the boy.

Where was that mother now? That grandmother—if *she* was still alive? Ruth made a mental note to find out. Still, she told Colm, "It would help to know what we're looking for. What answers to what questions."

He shook his head. His interviews had yielded little beyond "one hell of a headache. That guy up in Ripton—a good ole mountain man if I've ever seen one. You should see that gun rack. How does he get a license for all those guns?"

"How do thirteen-year-olds?" she asked, reminding him of the latest high school rampage out West. It made her so afraid for Vic. For children in schools everywhere, for teachers and students.

Colm went on with his "day of woe," as he called it. "I got nothing out of the man. When I mentioned Camille's death, he just said he 'wasn't surprised, the way she was poking her nose in other people's closets' was how he put it. I asked him what she was trying to find out, and he shrugged. Took one of the guns off the wall, said he was going hunting. I said it wasn't hunting season. He just grinned. He has a whole Green Mountain National Forest outside his door. Why should he wait?"

"He had no alibi for the night Camille was killed?"

"Said he was right there at home watching TV. His wife could verify. She looked at me like a scared rabbit and nodded. I know damn well he was lying."

"When he left the house to go 'hunting'—you didn't ask her again? She might have been mum in his presence."

"How could I? He wouldn't leave till *I* left. He ushered me out at the point of a .22."

She laughed at the picture Colm must have made: the rabbit running from the hunter. She poured him a glass of Otter Creek Ale and warmed up some leftover turkey and broccoli.

"The guy I liked even less," he said, "was that administrator down at the reformatory. He was definitely hiding something. He wouldn't say why she'd come to see him, just said she was writing some kind of paper. Well, I knew that anyway. He said he'd heard about that eugenics project, 'but it was all in the past, wasn't it?' "

"This woman Annette she was writing about, she was probably there in that prison, don't you think? That's all I know from Camille, it was something about Annette that interested her. And her offspring—I recall the names Nicole, Pauline. What happened to all of them? We have to find out."

"I asked about Annette like you said—you could see he knew something. I asked if there were records we could see. Flashed my badge to put the fear of Jesus in him."

"Yeah, yeah," she said. Colm was not your typical cop. He was too laid back. He couldn't spook a cow.

Colm was insulted. "Well, I did unnerve him, damn it. He jumped up out of his chair, said he had things to do. Said there were no records on her anymore. They'd had a fire, he said, all those papers got burnt."

"I'll bet. Send somebody else down there to get to the truth of it, would you? If they're burnt, he probably did it himself."

"I'll send Olen Ashley. He's a stickler about that kind of stuff. He's been a madman lately, holds the record down at the station for traffic tickets, sniffing out bad checks."

She asked about the college student Tilden Ball—"the one who's failing two courses? Did you talk to him?"

He consulted his notes. "Tilden Ball. Yeah. He was doing chores for his father that night, he says—though I haven't verified it. An odd kid. He needs a friend, I'd say, but he won't open up to people. He seemed relieved Camille wouldn't have to read his paper."

"Would he kill because of it?"

"Hard to say. But sometimes it's the quiet ones who hold things in."

"Mmm. What about Camille's will? You were going to check on that."

"I did, didn't I tell you?"

"Nope. What about it, then?"

"She died intestate, according to the lawyer. Hell, she was a young woman, never got around to a will. So it all goes to some aunt—I forget the name. But the aunt's in an institution. And oh, guess who's her legal guardian?"

"Don't make me guess, Colm, just tell me."

"Leroy Boulanger."

"Ah. The plot thickens."

"He'll get the money, I suppose—whatever there is."

"Not a lot, I'll bet. A young teacher, without tenure? Though she might have something put away from her parents. Interesting. You think he'd kill for a little inheritance? Talk to him, would you, Colm? Remind him we know about that stolen car."

"Why don't *you* talk to him, Ruthie? Seems to me you're pretty flahool, handing out all these jobs."

"I have the cows, Colm, remember that."

"I have Dad's dead bodies. My real estate."

"You can handle it. More broccoli?"

"Jeez, Ruth, you know I don't like the stuff. It's like eating shrubs."

"You should eat broccoli. Broccoli loves you. Grown in my own garden, too."

"Do you love me, too, Ruthie? I'll eat the whole damn dish if you'll tell me that."

She smiled, an enigmatic cat; she could feel her tail starting to swish—and helped *herself* to more broccoli. "Delicious," she said, smiling at him through leafy teeth.

When Gwen went out back behind the barn to check hives—and pay her respects to the grave site by leaving a gift of tobacco—she was confronted with a mound of dirt. For a moment she couldn't understand what it was. But when she looked beyond and saw, she lost her footing in a wave of panic and fell on her knees.

The grave had been dug up! She hauled herself to the far side and looked down in. The hole was empty. The low white fence Russell had erected around it was in pieces. A few shells and birdstones were still there, the dirt the color of red ocher paint. But the skeleton was gone. Gone, too, the ancient copper beads some caring mother had put into the grave to adorn her girl-child for the hereafter. Gwen sat back on her haunches, staring, until she felt dizzy, ready to fall in herself, head first.

Was this one more punishment for the nightshade death? But digging up a grave! It was the worst kind of sacrilege. As if that young Indian girl were some old heap of bones, no more important than a dog or horse—and less so than the mammoth bone some archaeologist had recently dug up in the area.

Outraged, she struggled up off her knees and ran back, panting, to the house to phone Russell. The number he'd given her rang and rang, and she gave up. She heard her father-in-law's hesitant footsteps, felt his hand on her shoulder. She looked up into his questioning face and blurted out the news of the theft.

He dropped into the chair beside her. "Why, they can't do that," he said.

"They did, Mert. Somebody did. Somebody who knew where that grave was, who wanted to show their disrespect."

"Call Russell. Russell will know what to do."

"I tried, and no one answered."

"Then call that fella Olen. He'll know what to do."

He'd be right over, Olen shouted, sounding outraged. And he was. His fury calmed her own anger as they stared into the empty grave. "How dare they!" he cried. "You didn't hear anything in the night?"

She shook her head. "Did you, Mert?"

"I took a sleeping pill," he said. "Some nights I get the wakes. Then I go walking. Then I can't get up in the morning. Then when I get up I get the shakes." He glanced at Olen, who'd wanted the marijuana plants pulled up, but Olen was still staring into the empty grave site.

"Leroy," Olen said, as though he'd just discovered him in the act.

Seeing Olen's tight lips Gwen said, "Leroy knows how sacred that grave is to us. He wouldn't harm it."

Olen scowled. "Maybe not. But he might have heard something. Seen something. It took a powerful lot of digging." He walked around the site, picked up handfuls of dirt to examine under his nose as though he might find fingerprints.

"Leroy's not here, it's his day off," she said. She thought of Harvey Ball, who coveted her land, but she was afraid Olen would march up there and Harvey would give him an earful about the shiny man. The shiny man, whom Harvey had insisted was Russell. So she kept quiet.

"I'm sorry about this, Gwen. But let me work on it. Don't tell your husband. He might, well, do something crazy."

She nodded. Olen was right. Russell called this dead girl his "princess." He would go crazy if he knew. Olen put a hand on her arm, squeezed. She heard Mert cough and she drew away. She must keep calm. She told Olen about Jack Sweeney, the ethnobotanist. "He's going to vouch for me in court next week. He agrees with me about those bruises. They *can* be the result of the nightshade. And I'm planning to pull it all up, Olen, honestly I am. Oh, and Olen—did I tell you about Camille's message? It was just before she was killed."

He shook his head, looked attentive. He waited.

"She wanted to tell me something about Shep Noble. How he was somehow connected to the project she was working on. I can't imagine what it was. But maybe you can find out. If so, it would suggest that his death was a murder, not just an accident, wouldn't it? And here I am trying to prove it an accident? Should I try to postpone the court proceedings?"

Olen stuck a tongue in his cheek; his hands squeezed slowly together. Finally he said, "No, don't cancel. It might have nothing to do with that death. The boy was in her class, Donna said? Some connection there, maybe. I'll look into it. You have to go through with the court case, Gwen. To prove your innocence. The state's attorney called it, right?" He waved his arms at the dug grave. "Now, don't walk here, Gwen, till I can get somebody else up to look at it. How old you say those bones were?"

"Maybe ten thousand years."

Mert grinned. "She was an oldie, all right. A good old girl."

"We'll get her back," Olen said, "don't you worry. They can't go digging up graves. It's not right. It's against the law. I won't allow it!" He sounded, she thought, as if he were the law personified. His hands were trembling again with his anger.

"Maybe *you* should try a little marijuana. To relax," she said slyly. "I can fix it up for you."

Now she'd gone too far. Olen thrust his hands in his pockets and strode off with a curt nod.

"They've gone too far this time, whoever it is," Ruth told Colm when he phoned to tell about the latest mischief on the mountain. The idea of digging up a grave horrified her; she knew how the Abenaki people revered their ancestors. For one thing, their buried dead proved their Vermont identity—that they had lived here and not just wandered through. "They deserve recognition by the state," she cried hotly, "and they're not getting it. Gwen told me that."

"Write a letter to the governor," he said.

"I will!" She took a sip of coffee. It was too hot, it burned the roof of her mouth, making her madder than ever at the state of affairs in Vermont. "And have you seen these signs that are springing up all over the county? *TAKE BACK VERMONT. VERMONT FOR VERMONTERS.* They say it's mostly because of the civil union legislation. I mean, I could agree with them if it meant 'Go Back to Small Farms,' 'Go Back to Independent Stores' everywhere. I can't find a damn thing I want in those huge warehouses, and nobody to wait on me. But don't go back at the expense of human rights! Even some of my farmer friends are posting the signs on their barn doors. What do I say to them? What do I tell them?"

"Write a letter," he said again.

"Oh, you're so goddamn sanguine, Colm. And I will, I will. Tonight. Today I'm on my way to Argennes to that foster care agency. To see if I can find out who Joey's father and grandparents are—if they're still alive. Where that will lead us, I've no idea. I feel like a mole creeping about underground."

"That's not a good analogy, Ruthie. You're at a loss, but creeping underground is what moles do. They're blind from birth. The underground's their home."

"Oh, stop being a smart-ass." She waved him away, spilling her coffee. She hung up the phone and sponged the liquid—it had dripped into her boots. She could smell the manure on them. She'd have to take a shower before she went to see any foster lady, who was sure to be impeccably dressed, coiffed, and perfumed.

Evangeline Balinsky, though, was a surprise. She was short, plump, and frumpy in a shapeless blue checked cotton jumper that couldn't hide the balloon of her belly. Under the jumper she wore heavy lisle stockings that might have been her grandmother's, and blue Adidas sneakers. On her head was a purple wreath with a jingle bell on top.

"It's to cheer up the children," Evangeline said. "I'm just back from visiting a new foster mom. She took in one of our quieter ones, a five-year-old who hasn't spoken a word since her dad went to jail and the mother left her with an aunt, who brought her to us."

"Poor child," Ruth murmured.

"Well, then," Evangeline said, with a lift of her head and a jangle of her wreath bell. "Down to business. What exactly brings you here?"

Ruth explained about Camille and her own blind mission. "And my daughter can't find the disk Camille gave her. There might be something on that disk that would give us a key to her death. Someone who might be hurt if his past were revealed. At least, that's my theory." She gave a short laugh. "I don't know why I say *his*. It could be a *her*."

She looked at her own hands, hard and blue-veined from working in the fields. *She* could strangle a person, couldn't she? She hoped she'd never be forced to do such a thing, but she *could*. If someone tried to hurt a child or a grandchild . . .

Evangeline saw her flexing her fingers. "We're all capable of violence, aren't we? I recall pummeling a child once—not my own, no, I never married; it was one of the foster boys. A fourteen-year-old who wasn't going to conform, no, ma'am, he was going his own way. And the foster mother was kind and loving. The boy would have had so much if he'd opened up. But one day he attacked her with a knife. She managed to run in the bedroom, bolt the door, call me. She was bleeding terribly when I got there. The boy went after me then, and I grabbed him around the neck. I never realized how vulnerable a neck can be. . . ." She touched her own neck. "All these thin cords and muscles. I had to stop myself before I killed him, I was that angry." Her bell rattled with the memory.

"Did he change? Did the foster mother ever forgive him?"

"He ran away. We never found him. Lord knows where he is—Canada, maybe. There are miles of unwatched border."

"His name wouldn't have been Godineaux?"

"No, it was Wasson. Nick Wasson. You looking for a Godineaux?"

Ruth told her about Joey, her search for a father and grandparents. "I thought you'd have records here in your office." Again she felt so vague, so confused. What would she ask these people if she found them?

Evangeline pulled out a huge green drawer, selected a file, her bell jingling all the while. Ruth wondered if she wore it to bed. A jingling bell would be company for a single woman. She might try it herself. But Evangeline was frowning as she stared at the folder, her folds of chin almost touching the page.

"The mother's name was Pauline," she said. "And so was the grandmother a Godineaux, name of Nicole. It was the grandmother brought the boy in, as I recall. The mother was in prison for something or other. Forging a check, shoplifting—I don't know. There was no money to bail her out. She got six months, but it wasn't the first time." She frowned. Here was a woman with a conscience. Ruth liked her.

"Annette," Ruth said, recalling the title on the disk she'd kept for those few hours. "Was there an Annette in that family?"

Evangeline puzzled awhile longer, flipped a page. "I don't see an Annette. But there could have been. It could have been the boy's great-grandmother. We don't keep a whole family tree on these people."

"Of course not. But this Pauline—or Nicole—do you have an address? And what about the father? Any information on him?"

Evangeline's chins swung; her bell sounded with the sweep of her head. "He was a no-good, that's all I know. Pauline was never married to him. He fathered young Joey and took off. By then Pauline was in her mid-forties."

"Any other children?"

"Oh, yes. One other besides Joey. Or was. Where, I don't know."

Pauline hadn't been sterilized, then. Ruth explained about the eugenics project, but Evangeline already knew; she grimaced. "Obviously not. But maybe Nicole was. There's no evidence of children after 1943. Nicole was let out of the reformatory in that year, along with her mother—whom we might assume was this Annette you speak of. Could be they were both sterilized. Where they went after that—who knows? The next we have on them was when Nicole came in with young Joey."

"What was she like—the grandmother?"

Evangeline smiled apologetically. It was so long ago, so many clients and children, her face said. She flipped another page. "Ah. Here we are. She brought Joey here in '86. I take notes, you see. I've a terrible memory." She squinted at the page. "Terrible handwriting, too. But here's what I wrote: 'Handsome woman, in her sixties, long gray braid, amber-brown complexion—might be part Native American. Seems smart enough, a survivor.' " She looked up. "That's all I wrote. She was alone, no mention of a husband or live-in man. She seemed to be doing migrant work: apple picking, farm work. But she wasn't well. I remember that now. She asked for two aspirin, her spine ached, and I gave them to her. I thought bone cancer. I don't know why I thought that. The pesticides, maybe, on those farms."

"You don't know where she is now?"

Evangeline shook her head. "All I know is where she was then. In Bridport, on the Papineau farm—cleaning barns and so on. She was supposed to keep in contact with us, but we didn't hear after . . ." she peered at the chart. "After 1992. You might check the local hospital. The obits."

"Poor woman. You've no mention of her husband—or Pauline's whereabouts?"

"Nothing at all about the men. They don't seem to enter the

picture. Screw 'em and leave 'em," she said. Then, "Sorry about my language. In this work you hear it all. End up using it yourself. But it's mostly the women, it seems, left with the babies they can't take care of."

"Pauline?" Ruth reminded her.

Evangeline spread her hands. "You might check with the Brookview Reformatory down in Rutland. They should have records. Last I knew, she was behind bars."

Ruth thought of Colm's abortive interview with the Brookview director. Olen Ashley had checked on that so-called "fire" that burned the records prior to '79 and said it was true. But wait. She had a thought. "What was the date Joey was brought in?"

Evangeline checked her records again. "July 1986. He was four years old."

"Then Pauline would still be in their records. Good." She shook Evangeline's hand good-bye. "You've been a help, thanks. And our Joey—you helped him. He's a joy." The smile lit up Evangeline's face. She looked like a Cheshire cat. Her bell jangled as she opened the door for Ruth and purred good-bye.

Maybe, Ruth thought, getting into her truck, a woman would soften up that irascible director. She would have to go down there, knowing it might lead to nothing.

Twelve

Gwen wasn't home when Ruth arrived at the bee farm—a last-minute detour to sympathize with Gwen over the grave robbery. Gwen had been gone most of the day, the father-in-law said. "Up to Richford, on the Canadian border. She got hives up there. Should be home half hour or so. You want to wait? Want a soda or something? Coffee?"

Actually, she could use a little caffeine. "Coffee would be great," she told the old man. "Then I wonder if I could walk the grounds a bit. Gwen has told me so much about her healing plants. She offered a cutting off some of them. Not that I'd take anything till she comes—I just thought I'd look. I run a dairy farm, down in the valley."

Sure, Mert knew who she was, knew she was Emily's mother, knew she helped folks find out who did this or that. He didn't like this latest trick, this dug-up grave. Not a bit. "I start by grinding the beans, see? I make you a good strong mugful. You look like you could use it."

Did she? Well, she supposed she did, all this running around, trying to find out who did what and why, and maybe when, too. She should be a journalist.

Mert was just pouring the boiling water, carefully, into a

brown plastic cup, over the ground beans, when there was a crashing noise out back.

"Uh-oh, it's Russ," Mert said, looking out the window. A moment later, Gwen's husband walked in, dressed in jeans and a T-shirt that said *ABENAKI NATION*. He was rather slight, but well put together and quite good-looking. The two pair of silver earrings he wore looked incongruous with the T-shirt and jeans. He glanced at Ruth, a glint of malice in the yellowy irises, and for a moment she thought, yes, he could have killed that college boy. But then the eyes smiled when Mert introduced her as "Gwen's friend. Gwen's got bees on her farm."

"Well, you must be a saint, then," Russell said. "Those bees get away now and then. Look, I got me a sting." He held out a tattooed arm and sure enough, there was a red welt below the elbow.

"That's 'cause you moved that hive," said Mert. "I saw you. Bees don't like that."

"I was trying to put it back, dammit," said Russell. "It got knocked over when they stole my girl's bones. You know about that?" he asked Ruth.

"Russ came in last night unexpected," Mert told Ruth.

"Oh," said Ruth, "I did hear about the theft, yes." She looked properly contrite. "Could I see it—the grave site?" Was it sacrilege to ask?

Russell gave a bitter laugh. "There's no grave site to see. Well, site, yeah, but they took the bones. They took some of the grave goods. The copper beads."

"Could that have been what they were after?"

Russell scoffed. "What they were after was our land. It was that pack of rats up to the next farm, you can bet. They want us out of here. That's what they want and that's what they're not going to get, by jeez." He thumped three times on the wall, and a *Vermont Life* calendar jumped. "Well, come on, then." He motioned her onward with his thumb.

"He's crazy over this, you gotta realize," Mert whispered. "Is all we can do to keep him from going up to Balls', tearing the place apart. He called his buddies up to Swanton last night to storm the place. Told 'em to bring tomahawks! Gwen and me had to call 'em off. Olen says he'll have him in jail, he goes up there—he got no legal right."

She nodded. "I can sympathize." Though sometimes, she thought, you do have to take the law into your own hands.

Russell was already at the burial site when she arrived; he was on his knees, sifting through the dirt. "He done that a hundred times this morning," Mert whispered, "found zilch. But he keeps hoping. I dunno, for a toe bone, maybe."

Now Russell was jumping up and running into the woods beyond the site, as though he'd seen something. Ruth squinted but saw only sun and trees. There was a path there, Mert said, that led through woods and out into the Balls' cow pasture.

"Hey!" Russell held up something shiny-white. It glinted in the late sun. It was a shell bead, he shouted. When Ruth and Mert caught up, she saw it had a tiny hole in the center.

"You have sharp eyes, Russell," she said.

He grunted. "Ball would of dropped it. He had his hands full." Russell gave a triumphant laugh and lunged forward through the path.

"No!" Mert hollered. "You're not going up there, Russ. They told you not to. You'll get in trouble if you do."

"Just look around a little," Russell yelled back, and he was gone, running swiftly around a curve in the path.

Mert sighed heavily, shaking his head. His hands dropped slack to his sides. "I can't make him stop. I can't do nothing. He'll have to take what comes, that's all."

Ruth knew Harvey Ball from Agri-Mark meetings. He could be negative, abrasive. He'd defend his own without a qualm. And Russell, she'd seen in the fiery eyes, would defend *his* own. Though why Ball would want a skeleton was more than she could figure. Except as a form of blackmail, as Russell had said, so that Gwen would sell her land.

She followed Mert back to the house. Gwen had arrived in her pickup, with Donna in the passenger seat, Leroy in back. The rear end was painted a lighter blue than the front, she noticed, a makeshift job. Gwen got out, smiling. She halted when she saw the frown on Mert's face. "What is it?" she called out. "Where's Russ?"

When Mert told her, she cried, "No! He can't do that." She climbed back in the truck.

"Let it go, Mother!" Donna shouted.

Ruth ran to the truck, held onto the door handle. "Are you sure you want to go up there? I could phone Colm. He might be able to settle things before Ball calls the police."

"I'm going up," said Gwen, determined. "Get out now, Donna. You have homework to do."

But Donna was grabbing the keys from her mother, shouting at her to "leave things alone. I don't want both my parents in jail. Don't go, Mother!" She ran into the house with the keys.

"I have to go," Gwen yelled, and demanded an extra key from Leroy, who handed it over obediently.

"Maybe better to stay here like she says," he muttered, but Gwen paid no attention, and seconds later, backed out of the driveway.

When Ruth went back to return her coffee mug, she found Donna sobbing at the table, beating her fists against the wood. "I hate my mother!" the girl cried. "I hate my father. Why can't they be like other parents? Other parents don't grow poison plants in their yards or attack people and accuse them of digging up graves. Every time I think about it I get depressed. I just want to be like everybody else."

Ruth put her arms around the girl. "I know, I know," she soothed. "Emily tells me that, too. She wants to live in town like other girls she knows. Not on a farm full of smelly cows. But Donna, are those other families any better off? Even the rich ones?"

She told Donna about the Unsworth boy addicted to cocaine, and a wealthy lawyer named Southwick whose son had victimized her own son. And Harry Rowen, whose parents belonged to a fundamentalist religion and wouldn't let him bring a book into the house. "I think it's wonderful that your mother grows these plants. She's ahead of her time, that's all. One day they'll legalize marijuana—for medicinal purposes anyway. Look, it was just rotten, rotten luck that boy fell into the nightshade."

The thought of nightshade started Donna wailing again.

"I think somebody turned him over, stuck his face in that nightshade," Mert said, standing behind the pair. "It's just a hunch I got. I seen a muddy footprint over beyond where he was—after the police was first here, I mean. Before they brought in the extra police. I smoothed it over."

"Why would you do that?" Ruth cried. "It was evidence."

He fumbled with a button on his shirt; the tattooes shone dark blue on the backs of his hands. "I thought it was somebody in the family might of done it—put that boy's face in it, maybe hit him. Russell. Gwen. Leroy. Even you, Donna, I didn't know, I didn't want to take no chances—you had a right. Don't you tell your mother about that footprint, don't you get her all upset." He laid a hand on Donna's shivery shoulder. She gazed up at him, as though surprised by the depth of his feeling.

Mert glanced over at Ruth. "I guess I better tell the police, though. I'll tell Olen. He won't want to hurt your mother."

"He'll put you in jail!" Donna cried. "That's all he cares about, the law. It's right or it's wrong." She appealed to Ruth. "He put Daddy in jail once for fishing out of season. He didn't think about Mother's feelings then."

They were both looking at Ruth now, as though it were her decision, as though she were the moral judge. Her shoulders slumped with the weight of their expectation.

She looked out the kitchen window; the silence behind her was almost palpable. Beyond the glass Leroy was getting the lawn mower out of the barn. There wasn't a lot of grass to mow—no more than an acre or two. Most of the land was wooded. But Leroy was cranking up the machine with a determined face. He was going to keep that grass under control. Though he couldn't mow near the hives, could he? Lawn mowers, she'd discovered when Tim went to cut near the hives, upset the bees.

Ruth thought of her farm, where the grasses and buttercups grew wild. Tim only mowed around the Christmas trees. She liked the land wild. People had to allow a little wildness in themselves. They weren't meant to be kept under wraps, controlled.

"Keep it to yourself, Mert," she told him. "The footprint's long gone. This family's been through enough without you in trouble. But off the record, do you remember the size of it? I mean, give or take an inch?"

Mert ran a hand through his sparse gray hair. "I didn't look too hard. I guess I was afraid to. It was a shoe, though, not a boot."

Russell, Ruth recalled, had been wearing moccasinlike loafers when he ran just now into the wooded path. Leroy, she saw, was wearing high black sneakers. Now she was disturbed at Mert for not reporting this footprint at once. It could have put them on the right track, after the right person. She still felt that Shep Noble's death was not an accident. And the police were, cautiously, according to Colm, calling Shep's and Camille's deaths "possibly connected."

But there was no point pursuing the subject. Mert was sitting in the kitchen chair, braiding a length of sweetgrass. He and Donna had twin expressions: both of them looking glum, defeated.

Ruth rinsed out her coffee cup and took her leave. The late sun was flooding through the windows, painting the walls and door white, making her squint. She called out a good-bye, headed out to her pickup. She still hadn't looked at the swamp where the nightshade grew, but she didn't need to. Mert had gotten there first. Worried about family, he'd blotted out evidence. Ruth thought of the Jane Austen biography she'd picked up in the town library: how Jane's extended family had burned letters, not wanting posterity to know certain things—about Jane, about themselves, their secrets. But they had a right, hadn't they? Ruth had named one of her cows Jane Austen, but her Jane couldn't speak.

Secrets, she thought. Shep Noble, Camille Wimmet—all of them, all of us—harboring secrets.

She waved at Leroy, who had turned to look at her, his face expressionless, and driven off. She had put off talking to him, hoping Colm would do it. A police car carrying two men traveled past as she rounded a curve on the mountain road. She prayed that one of them wasn't Olen Ashley—and on his way to the Ball farm.

"You're not afraid of me, are you, Ralphie?" Russell asked, and the boy pointed at Russell's earrings and said, "Shiny man." Russell held out the shell bead. "For you," he said. Awed, Ralphie held it close to his face. The boy was the only one home, Russell told Gwen when she arrived, out of breath, pleading with him to leave. He'd only rummaged around in the outbuildings, he insisted, he hadn't searched the house—just knocked on the door and Ralphie let him in.

"You come and see us, now," she told Ralphie, hanging on to her husband's arm. "But we have to go. Don't tell your father we were here, okay? Keep it a secret between us?" Ralphie's slanty eyes looked dubious, but finally he nodded.

Suddenly he cried out; the eyes rolled up in his head, his lips went blue. Before Gwen could get to him, he crashed to the floor; his body fell into a series of violent, rhythmic jerkings. Gwen knelt beside him, held up his head to keep him from swallowing his tongue. When the seizure was over, when the boy lay back limp and exhausted, she sponged off the perspiring forehead with a damp handkerchief. Ralphie looked up into her face, panting like a small animal, the brown eyes soft and watery.

"Are you all right?" she asked, and he stared back at her. For a time it was as though he were still in another space, somewhere she couldn't go. He held up a limp hand and she saw that he'd dropped the shell bead.

"Pretty," he wailed. "Ralphie lose his pretty." He crawled across the dusty floor to find it. "Ha!" he cried a moment later, and held up the bead.

"Good. You stay quiet awhile now," she told him. A serene quarter of an hour later, she shut the door carefully behind her.

Russell was already outside, his rear end wriggling out from under the porch. "She's here somewhere. I know goddam well she's here. I need a day. A whole day without the Balls around—

I'd find her, all right. That pack of filthy thieves!"

"Not a pack," she said. "Not all of them involved, I'm sure—if any of them. We can't prove it, Russ."

"They've got it. They took it," he said stubbornly. "No question." A cardboard *TAKE BACK VERMONT* sign was taped above the front door and Russell grabbed at it, but Gwen pulled him back. "It's his opinion," she said. "It's his sign."

Muttering to himself, Russell let her lead him to the pickup. They drove in silence back to the house.

When Gwen saw the police car in her drive, she put the pickup in reverse, backed into a wooded opening. But already Olen had seen them. He jogged over to the truck. "You weren't up at Balls', I hope," he said to Russell.

"How am I supposed to find her if I can't go look, damn it?" Russell lunged out of the truck, faced the officer, hands on his blue-jeaned hips. "Tell me that, Ashley."

Olen, she saw, was trying to be calm, professional. He kept his voice low, though Gwen could hear the irritation beneath the words, like an engine full of super fuel, trying to go slow when it wanted to race full speed down a highway. "We're on our way to question the Balls," he said. "But we can't search the place. We don't have probable cause." Sergeant Hammer got out of the car, hand on her hip, as though ready for an outbreak of violence. The Woodleaf-LeBlanc family seemed to have that reputation these days.

"No 'probable cause'? Tell 'em, Gwen, what I found on the path." Russell took a step closer to Olen. The anger hung, like a live coal, between the two men.

Gwen held her husband's arm. "They just stopped to tell us about it, Russ. They're going up there now, right, Olen?"

Olen stepped back. His voice softened. "Right, Gwen. We just stopped to see if you had anything more to tell us, that's all."

Scowling, Russell grabbed her arm and pulled her toward the house. "Sure, that's all," he called back over his shoulder. "That's why you stopped. It had nothing to do with seeing my wife."

"Quit that, Russ," she cried, her turn to pull him along now.

"Okay, LeBlanc," Olen hissed, scowling at Russell's T-shirt. "You were just taking a drive around your own grounds, right? But next time you'll be in the lockup. I'm warning you, now." His voice cracked. Gwen nodded briefly over her shoulder and followed her husband into the house. Mert was there with a teapot in his hand, along with Brownie, big-eyed and wary, home from school, glancing from one parent to the other, as though unsure if he should speak. Russell poured himself a tankard of beer. Gwen listened to the police car pull out of the driveway and then let out a long shuddery breath.

Ruth had exhausted Joey's memory of his real parents. He hadn't remembered a male relative at all, poor fellow—not until Tim came along. Tim was father, uncle, grandfather, all in one. Joey worshiped him—and vice versa. Now Tim wanted to legally adopt him, even though the boy was almost of age. Joey had smarts, Tim insisted, he'd improved a hundredfold since he'd left the Petits. "Not that they weren't okay to him," Tim said, "it's just that now the kid's got a one-on-one."

"It's improved you, too," she teased. "You don't turn the air quite so blue with your goddamns." Tim laughed, of course, and told how Zelda, Number One Ornery Cow, as he called her, had just rammed through "the fuckin' east pasture fence."

So now Tim would have occasion for more four letter words. Ruth was going to leave him right after the morning milking to go to the Papineau farm in Bridport.

"What in hell you going there for?" Tim cried. "You're not planning on a bigger herd, are you?"

"Lord, no." The Papineaus had a thousand cows, a brand-new milking parlor, the latest in farm machinery. "I just want to look around. I might get some ideas." She didn't want to tell him she was looking for information about Joey's relatives. Not yet anyway.

"So don't get any ideas I have to put in practice. There's enough work to do around here as is. Especially with you gone half the time solving some neighbor's headaches."

"When I've got enough headaches of my own, yeah, yeah," she said, and tossed a hardened cow turd at him. It hit the knee of his muddy jeans and bounced off onto the barn floor.

"Hey, lady," he said. "I can sue for damages, you keep doing that."

She thumbed her nose at him.

The Papineau farm was as grand and spanking clean as it had been pictured in the local *Independent*. She hadn't been there in ten years and since then it had quadrupled in size. They would think her pretty small potatoes with only thirty-two milking cows—but then they didn't have a Pete Willmarth wanting her to buy out his portion of the farm for a hundred thousand. No, it was down to seventy thousand now, but they were mostly loans, so how was she gaining on it? She was spreading around the debts, that was all. Pretty pathetic, Ruth, she told herself. You may be out of a job, woman. Quick.

She found Adele Papineau in the kitchen—the men were out discing the soil, getting it ready for planting. Adele's main job, it seemed, was to feed the hired men. She belonged to the grange, helped with the 4-H Club, was a staunch member of the Catholic church; a crucifix hung over the wall oven. There were blue polka-dot curtains in the windows, but practical blue oilcloth on the long center table where the help would come to eat. Thinking of the number of men needed to care for a thousand cows, Ruth was thankful to have a small herd.

"I feed twenty at breakfast and lunch," Adele said, following Ruth's eyes, "plus the four kids. Though Jean, the oldest—he's fifteen—he helps with the dishes. He likes doing it better than farm work. I tell my husband not to let the farm get any bigger. These kids aren't going to take over when he gets long in the tooth."

"I can relate to that," Ruth said. "My three have no interest in farming. For now I've just got Tim and his foster boy, Joey, to help. Joey's why I came."

"Uh-huh?" Adele poured hot coffee into a blue mug; it had a cow and *Papineau Farms* glazed on it. She sold the mugs, along with a video about the farm, in one of the Branbury shops. "Gotta pay off the loans," she said, grinning. One of her upper teeth was dark, needed extracting—or whitening. Did it really pay to have a state-of-the-art farm? It fed the male ego, Ruth supposed. But it didn't pay for the wife's teeth.

"Joey doesn't know anything about his family. But we heard that his grandmother worked for you. Nicole was her name, Nicole Godineaux. It would have been back in the late seventies, early eighties."

"Lord, that was twenty years ago, I was just married. I remember her, sure, she did chores in the barn, helped me with housework now and then when I was carrying. But I don't know the background. Grandpapa?" she shouted into the next room. "Come on in here. A lady has some questions about Nicole Godineaux."

There were thumping footsteps, and finally an old man with a large brown hairy wart on his chin appeared in the doorway. Adele introduced him as Emile Papineau, her father-in-law. He'd been hurt in a tractor accident, she explained, he had only one leg. "Roll up your trousers," Adele ordered, and he did, grinning. The prosthetic leg had several dozen signatures on it.

"Oh," said Ruth.

"She wants to know about Nicole," Adele shouted in his ear. "Where she came from. Where she went to."

The old man leaned back against the wall and considered. "Sure. She were here ten years or so. She been in that place down to Rutland. I took a chance on her, seemed a good worker. I don't know nothing about her folks, least I can't recall now, memory not what it was, but she got cancer, sure—breast, lungs, Jesus, it were all through her. We kept her in the trailer till she couldn't work no more. Then we took her to the hospice up to Bristol. She could of died there, I dunno, it were eight, nine years ago now." He shook his head—he had a healthy crop of white hair—and glanced up at the crucifix as though it would bless the memory of Nicole.

"I remember that," Adele agreed. "I remember they took her

up to the hospice, poor thing. She looked terrible, flesh all shrunk—just skin and bones."

Emile started to hobble away and Ruth stood up. "Do you know anything else about her—husband, or man friend? We'd like to know who our Joey's father was."

Emile bared his gleaming dentures, ran a tongue around the inside of his wrinkled cheek. "There was a fella come 'round once or twice, I recall. He was called . . ." He scratched his head. "Some name begun with an N. Norman? Ned? Anyhow, he asked about a job here. We didn't have nothing for him, we wasn't that big back then. 'Sides, Nicole didn't seem to want him here."

"Were they married, those two?"

"Well, I can't tell you that. But she knew him, all right. If they was married, she was glad to get rid of him. Too bad. She was a good looker till she got that cancer."

Ruth thanked them both, gave them her phone number in case they thought of anything more about Nicole.

Adele shooed her father-in-law out of the kitchen, and Ruth heard the television blare out a baseball game. "We record the games for him," she explained. "He goes to bed early, but doesn't like to miss a night game."

As she left, Ruth heard the old man holler, "Bad call. Bad call. That were a strike, you damn fool!"

"Say," Adele called out to Ruth as she was getting into her truck. "Any more news about those college murders? You think it's the same guy? None of us can sleep till they get him."

"They're working on it," Ruth called back. "That's all I know. But I don't think the professor's was a random killing. I think she might have been targeted."

"Yeah? What makes you think so?"

Ruth waved her arms. She didn't know, really.

Thirteen

Donna was in Hopewell's Dress Shop looking for a new blouse to replace the one Shep Noble had torn—she'd tried sewing it, but it still looked tacky. Tonight she and Emily were going to a birthday dinner—she wanted to look nice. She picked out a mauve, a pink, and a lilac silk—she liked the luxurious feel of silk against her skin. With her black hair, the warm pinks, mauves, and lavenders looked good. She was entering a booth when she saw the saleslady staring at her. "Just trying them on," she said.

"How many?" the woman asked. Donna could see the gray roots in her dyed red hair.

"Three." She held them up. The woman snatched them from her, one by one, as though to count them, as though she thought Donna had deliberately undercounted and might stuff one into the Guatemalan bag she was carrying. Donna didn't like that. But Hopewell's was the only dress shop in town and she had to have a blouse for tonight.

She chose the mauve silk, it was a perfect fit; it clung softly to her breasts, showed them off but not too much. She left the rejected ones on hangers and went out to pay. The saleswoman ducked back into the booth and swept the others across her arm;

she looked surprised, as though she hadn't expected them to be there.

Donna paid for the blouse with two dozen one-dollar bills she'd saved up from her library job at the college and refused to say thank you to the saleswoman. The woman didn't say thank you, either. She just crumpled the blouse into a white bag and left it for Donna to pick up.

Donna was pausing by the earring counter on her way out when a young girl walked in. Donna had seen the girl before. She was a junior in high school—she had the reputation of sleeping around. The girl stopped near Donna to look at the earring rack, not acknowledging Donna's presence, although she probably knew who Donna was.

"Hi," Donna said, to annoy the girl as much as anything. The girl looked at Donna a moment and jerked her head back. It was then that Donna saw what the girl was wearing around her neck. It was a necklace of copper beads. The beads had that dullish patina that age brings. Donna could see where the thin leathery string that held the beads together had frayed and been retied. "Where did you get those beads?" she asked.

Now the girl looked wary; she shook her head and left the store. The saleswoman glared at Donna with pressed lips like she'd made the store lose a customer.

Donna chased the girl to the corner. "I said, where did you get those beads?"

The girl spun about, staring Donna down. "They're a present, if you got to know. It's nothing to you. Now leave me alone!" and she ran down the street.

Donna ran after, grabbed her sleeve. "Who gave them to you, I said? They were stolen, I'll tell you that. Or maybe you stole them. You'll be arrested if the cops find out."

She had only seen the copper beads once, when her father first discovered the grave, but she'd been struck by the beads. It was high noon and they gleamed bright against the chalk white of the neck bones. It was a moment she'd never forget. She'd felt the awe of time passing, nothing left then of a young girl but her beads.

The girl stared arrogantly back. "I told you, I was given them. Now leave me alone." She dashed across the street and into the Ben Franklin store. A MacIntyre fuel truck swung around the bend, preventing Donna from following. But she was certain those were the beads. And she didn't think the girl—her name was Jill, Donna remembered now—had stolen that skeleton. It would have been someone else. Someone who wanted to please Jill. Maybe to sleep with her.

Well, Donna was going to do whatever it took to find out who that person was.

Ruth couldn't bear to go back to her hardscrabble farm after seeing the Papineaus' place with its six-row free-stall barn and state-of-the-art milking equipment, and so she steered her course toward the Brookview Reformatory in Rutland. She took an alternate route, following the Otter Creek as it carved its way through the Champlain Valley, winking silvery-green at each twist. She thought of her ex-husband's forebears back in the 1700s, rafting along the Otter to make their pitch in Branbury—on the same land she farmed today. How could Pete have walked away from it like that?

A horn blasted. A face glared at her as she took the last turn, too wide, into the oncoming lane. Mea culpa, she thought. Too much daydreaming. Now she needed hard facts, something to bring down the greedy, the prejudiced, the avengers.

She took three deep breaths before entering the door to the director's office. After Colm's experience, she was ready for a rebuff. If Nicole had been sterilized like so many "defective" persons of her day, it could be an embarrassment—even though sterilization had been legal up to 1973. Imagine! That late date! Ruth was twenty-three back in 1973, and three years married. In love with her husband, on the edge of a new world, and dreaming already of having Pete's children. Her eyes were closed to outside affairs.

How the climate had changed. Now there was global warming. But her own world gone cold with Pete's defection.

To her surprise a female voice called out a greeting. A middle-aged woman sat behind the desk. Mr. Godwin was ill, she said; she was June Keefe, his assistant. "I'm fairly new here," the woman apologized, "but I'll help in any way I can." She was a tall woman, an inch or two over six feet when she stood up to shake hands. She might have weighed close to two hundred pounds, but she carried it well. She wore a hint of mauve lipstick to express her femininity. She waited, smiling, for Ruth to speak.

Ruth told her about Joey; she asked about the Godineaux women; she didn't mention the word "sterilization." Once again, she felt like a schoolgirl going to see the teacher after class, needing information, but not knowing how to phrase her question. "Anything you can tell me about Nicole or Pauline would help. Pauline was in for petty theft or something, according to the foster care agent. It was after 1973. After the other records burned."

Ms. Keefe raised a blond eyebrow. She didn't know about any burned records. "Like I said, I'm new here." She clanked open a metal drawer, pulled out a manila folder. "Pauline Godineaux," she summarized, "in for stealing panty hose and underwear at J. C. Penney's. A microwave and radio at Sears. Bad checks. Punching out a sales clerk. Striking a policeman with a Coke bottle. It's a long list. Do you want to hear all of it?"

"No, thanks. Just the family connections. Is there any mention of Pauline's father? Or a husband or lover who might be our Joey's dad?"

Ms. Keefe scanned the document. It appeared to be only two pages—mostly filled with Pauline's misdemeanors. It seemed she'd serve six months, have six months off on parole, and bounce right back in again for another misdemeanor. "Oh, and she was pregnant the third time she came in," the woman noted. "In 1982."

"That would have been with Joey. Is there mention of the father?"

"Something here, but entered with a leaky pen." She stood up by a window; it had bars on it like all the windows in the reformatory. "Under visitors: just two names. Nicole—that, I gather, was the mother—and a Marcel Shortsleeves. Do you think this Shortsleeves could be your Joey's father?"

Ruth didn't know, of course, but she wrote down the name. Shortsleeves had known Pauline, at least, there would have been some relationship. She would look him up. This was turning into a merry-go-round of visitations. "Any mention of his whereabouts?"

The blond woman shrugged. "No. But I know a Shortsleeves here in Rutland. On Maple Avenue. You can try him—I forget his first name. He is or was a construction worker. He probably has relatives he can tell you about." She looked apologetic again, sorry she'd been of so little help. "I like to see families reunited. I was adopted myself. It took twenty years to find my real mother. And when I finally got there—she'd passed on."

"I'm sorry. You had no other siblings?"

"None that I know of. My mother was a teenager when she had me. She was here in the reformatory for a time. For stealing a television." Her face colored to the roots of her yellow hair. "I determined then I'd help these women. So many of them driven to stealing. Not their faults, really, they have to survive. A television may be a luxury, but it keeps the mind occupied. It brings a little laughter into one's life. Romance, sometimes."

She held out a hand to Ruth. Ruth clasped it warmly. She tried to think of the right thing to say to this woman who'd shared something of herself with a stranger, but the words didn't come. So she said, "Thank you. I'll look up that Shortsleeves."

She hesitated at the door. "I suppose you had to do a lot of running around to find your mother?"

"Like I said, twenty years."

But Ruth didn't have twenty years to find Camille's murderer. *If* she was even on the right track.

Why on earth was she now in a gas station telephone booth, looking up a Shortsleeves? What did a man named Marcel Shortsleeves have to do with the murder of a college professor?

Apparently nothing, according to the telephone that rang

eight times with no answer, not even a machine. Well, she'd try again. Right now she just wanted to go home. She wanted to see that new heifer calf Madonna had birthed last night. An easy birth, a strong, well-coupled calf. And there were more freshenings to come this spring. For now she just wanted to think birth. Future. Growth. She didn't want to keep milking the past.

She raced on home, taking the curves of the creek in and out, like a skier on a mountain slope, and waiting at the bottom, hot chocolate—and, for Ruth, new life.

Gwen was proud of the ethnobotonist, Jack Sweeney. He'd done his homework; he spoke eloquently, factually—first at the hearing, and now in court. The case had been brought by the state's attorney to determine whether Gwen was liable or not for manslaughter because Shep Noble died in her cultivated patch of nightshade. "The so-called bruises stemmed from the nightshade," Jack explained. "From the photos I saw, there was no evidence of blows from an outside source. Belladonna is extremely toxic. Small doses of it can cause coma, even death. People have been poisoned just by eating rabbits that fed on the berries of deadly nightshade."

Gwen glanced back at Sharon Willmarth, who was sitting behind her in the courtroom. Sharon winked at Gwen and stuck up her thumbs. Gwen hoped it was victory, although she wasn't sure what victory was in this case. If the judge ruled the death an accident, Gwen might still be sued by the Noble family for growing belladonna. But what about Camille's message? Well, they'd never know what it was, so she had to stop thinking about it. Beside her, Donna sat with her hands folded in her lap, her head sunk on her chest as though she'd fallen asleep. But her rigid limbs, her rapid breathing, belied her posture.

"Almost every part of the plant is poisonous," Jack went on, his auburn head nodding for emphasis, "but especially the roots and leaves. The victim in this case would have come in contact with the roots. And since he had a small cut to begin with"—he nodded at Donna—"and because the victim had asthma, the roots and leaves would have been especially toxic."

There was a murmur of voices in the packed courtroom—the whole town, it seemed, was caught up in this rare case of possible homicide. It was now being proven, Gwen felt, and the townspeople with her, that the death itself was not homicide, but an accident.

Warming to his subject, Jack described the history of the plant, how it "poisoned the troops of Marcus Antonius during the Parthian wars." The soldiers of Macbeth, he said, poisoned a whole army of Danes by mixing belladonna in their drinks. "The Scots murdered 'em in their sleep," he went on, the freckles pinkening on his round cheeks.

But he had overresearched for this court. "Stick to the case in hand," the judge grunted.

The defense attorney came back to the purplish bruise on the forehead. "It would have been caused by the nightshade, you conclude?" he asked the ethnobotanist.

Jack nodded. He was a convincing witness, Gwen felt; there was something of the Boy Scout about him, a look of artlessness in the wide blue eyes. He went on to describe the dilated pupils, the hot dry skin, the rapid pulse, the convulsions.

"But the bruise. The swelling of skin," the lawyer prompted, wanting it nailed down in words.

"It happens," Jack said. "Especially when the victim spent hours facedown in the plant. It wasn't actually a bruise—it was an allergic reaction, a kind of edema. And in this case the discoloration went away more quickly than a bruise would. You have the photo the mortician, um, William Hanna, took."

"It could have been a blow to the head, a glancing blow from a rock, a shoe," the prosecuting lawyer shouted, and William Hanna, a hunched-over man with cheeks like polished apples, stood up and shook his fist. "No, damn it! It wasn't there by the third day. And it wasn't the makeup, either, by jeez, I can tell you that. My makeup girl can't do it that realistic!"

The spectators chuckled, while the judge shushed both men for "speaking out of turn." The old man was yanked down into his seat by his son Colm.

Jack was cool. He repeated his analysis. "I can cite case histories. In 1984, for instance, up in Cabot, a child stumbled into a patch of nightshade. She was horribly bruised. Two days later, the bruise was gone. There were no lesions, no indication of violence—other than the nightshade."

The prosecuting lawyer gave up finally, and Jack sat down beside his wife, whose loud congratulatory whispers could be heard all over the courtroom. Gwen wanted to hug him, but it wouldn't be appropriate. Instead, she hugged Donna, who responded only by blowing her nose. When the girl looked up finally, her eyes were shiny with tears. Gwen reached for her hand, but Donna pulled away. There was no comforting her. She had been in the witness stand, was almost paralyzed by the experience.

Olen Ashby got up to testify next, and then William Hanna limped up to give the spiel that he'd already shouted out of turn. The attorneys gave their concluding speeches, and the jury tramped out. In the recess that followed, Sharon came up to apologize for her mother's absence. "Another cow freshened," she explained. "It's a bull calf, it got stuck in the vagina and Mother had to call the vet. She really wanted to be here, though."

Gwen waved away the concern. "That cow needs her more than we do. It's all in the jury's hands now. Though, either way—that boy died." Sharon put a hand on Gwen's shoulder from behind. Her long brown braid swung loose to hit Donna's cheek and the girl burst into tears. Sharon looked distraught, and Gwen patted her arm. "It's not you," she said, and handed her daughter a Kleenex.

A short time later the jury ambled back in, and the courtroom quieted. It was as though people were holding in their breath to hear the verdict. It came loud and nasal from the jury spokeswoman, Hetty Burdoch, a local resident. "We find the defendant Gwen Woodleaf"—she paused for dramatic effect—"not guilty. We conclude that the death was . . . accidental."

There was a cacophony of voices in the courtroom; most of the spectators applauded, some booed the decision—Gwen heard the word "witch." They were hushed by the judge's gavel.

He admonished the defendants to pull up the belladonna. "A child might walk into your woods," he warned, his eyebrows in a morbid V, "and fall into it. You are *not* to grow it, and that's final."

Someone in back hollered, "I seen it growin' down to the Branbury swamp. The gover'ment owns that land. Who's goin' to pull 'at stuff up?"

The judge banged his gavel again to quell the laughter. His features settled into a defensive mask.

Olen was outside the courtroom when Gwen and Donna came out, almost the last to leave after Sharon and Jack, whose freckles were crimson as he strode off, arm in arm with his laughing wife. Olen was now in plain clothes; he had the rest of the day off. "Have a cup of coffee with me," he urged Gwen. "That bagel place across the street. I need to talk to you."

He settled her at a corner table, leaned across his coffee mug to gaze in her face. "I want to apologize," he said, sounding breathless, as though it were a life-or-death matter with him if she didn't accept what he had to say. When she waved his urgency away, he leaned even closer. "It was accidental, that death," he said. "That was the jury's conclusion and I accept it. So I'm sorry about accusing your hired boy, or your, um, husband. Though he's in enough trouble without that, I'd say."

His voice had risen, and he took a deep breath, restrained himself. "I want you to forgive me, Gwen. I came on too strong. I wasn't thinking of *your* feelings. I wasn't thinking of *you*."

Gwen had to smile, he looked so terribly earnest, his face a blotchy red as if he were the one immersed in the deadly plant. "There's no need for apologies, Olen. You were only doing your job. You had to look at everyone. Me, even. I might have done it."

He looked shocked. "Not you, Gwen. Never you. I never once suspected you. You've got to know that."

He reached for her hand and she pulled it back. A woman across the room was looking at them. "Not here," she said. And then was sorry she'd said it. Not anywhere, not even at her home, was the true answer. "About Russell," she said. "He found a shell bead, you see, from the grave. It was on the path leading to Balls' farm. That was why he went up there. We went," she amended.

Olen settled back in his chair, cupped his mug—he hadn't drunk the coffee yet, while her mug was almost empty. "Even so," he said, the man of law again, "he should have called me. Or one of us. It wasn't his job to trespass—I heard about it from Ball. He can't do that, Gwen. You have to make him realize. I overlooked it this time—but next time, well . . . you know, I'd have to bring him in."

Gwen sighed, sipped the last drop of her coffee. Russell was so vulnerable, he wore his grievances on his sleeve. The thin veneer of Abenaki pride he wore masked generations of put-downs and prejudice. Maybe this was why he loved his work, underpaid as it was. The reenactments allowed him to run through the woods and defend his own; to *be* his ancestors.

"Leave him alone, Olen. I'll be responsible for him. I'll make him behave. Just stay away from him. Please."

They sat in silence while he finished his coffee. The cup trembled in his hand. He looked feverish; she told him he should "take a little time off, get some R and R."

He said, "You know why I'm in civvies?"

She looked up, questioning.

"I'm the top speeding ticket writer, and yet Fallon's grounding me for twenty-four hours. He says I ran some woman off the road. Not true!" His hands coiled into fists on the table's edge. "I mean, I've brought in twice the revenue for the station." He glanced at his watch. "Look, it's only eleven-thirty. I have the rest of the day to fill up. How? I have to keep busy, Gwen—my head, my hands."

She stared at him. "Good Lord, Olen, I'd love to have time off. But the bees won't let me. Today I go to Wolcott to split the hives there. I'd rather be home, the place needs cleaning. Mert can't do it. And Russell—well, Russell tries, but he's all thumbs."

She supposed she should ask Olen to come along with her to

Wolcott. But Leroy was coming, the pair wouldn't match. Leroy in his brand-new jeans—he'd even bought a secondhand car. Where did he get the money for that? Olen might wonder. Gwen thought, too, about something Leroy had told her about his Aunt Camille. She'd been married once, to a childhood friend. The marriage had lasted six months. Then she'd moved in with another friend, a woman. Leroy's smile told her that Camille might have been lesbian. That would have made her, too, an outsider. Gwen was beginning to understand why the professor had been so impassioned in her research on the so-called "degenerate" women. Poor Camille. Gwen wished she had gotten to know her better.

For some reason Gwen didn't want Olen to know this about Camille. Ruth, though, would understand.

"I have to go now, Olen, I really do. Why don't you go to Burlington? To a bookstore. A movie. There's a new cop film there, I saw it in the papers."

"I don't watch cop films. They're phony."

"Maybe you should see a doctor. Take something to calm your nerves."

She was sorry she'd suggested it when he jumped up, hovered above her stiffly, awkwardly, like a helicopter taking off, said he was sorry to take up her time. When she stood up, too, trying to smile, afraid she'd hurt his feelings, he said, "I think I'll take another look at Ball's place. That bead you said Russell found might give us just cause for an outdoor search, anyway. Like you say, it's possible the fellow did take that skeleton. That'll make it easier for you, right, Gwen? You won't have to worry about Russell's going up there if we find it?"

"Sure," she said. "But what about your day off? Aren't you supposed to keep on the civilian clothes? Lie low, like the chief said?"

"I still have my badge." He patted his blue shirt pocket. "I'm still a police lieutenant. I'm still on the force."

Pride shone in his face. He wore the badge like a knight wore his armor. Who would dare try to remove it?

Fourteen

There was more than one reason to celebrate on Tuesday afternoon. Jane Eyre had produced, without intervention, a beautiful black and white heifer calf. As always, Ruth was thrilled. Jane was a good mother, she practically purred while the calf nursed. The euphoria increased when Sharon burst into the barn, hollering, "Jack did it! You should have heard him. He was a hero!" She shouted a word-by-word account of the proceedings as they all went back to the kitchen for a coffee celebration.

"Hey, all I did was look up stuff in a couple of books," Jack said, the freckles blossoming on his cheeks. "Belladonna's an amazing plant. You gotta respect it."

Gwen did respect it, Ruth told him. "But I'm going over tomorrow to help her pull it up. I'm curious to see what it looks like—in case it's growing here. Vic's asthma, you know."

"I'd never do anything dumb like lying in a mess of nightshade," said Vic, who was home from school with a spring cold. He blew his nose for emphasis.

"Maybe not, but you never know. We'll have a little ceremony, Gwen says. Oh, dear. I suppose I should have apologized to these daisies before I cut them. Plants do feel, they say. Do you think so, Jack?"

"Of course," Sharon said before Jack could open his mouth. "You have to thank the flowers. *I* always do. Plants not only feel, they communicate. Isn't that right, Jack?"

Jack told them how he'd cut down an aging maple tree on his property, and the one still standing nearby began to shed its leaves. "It wasn't till I planted a new one that the second tree revived. I mean, trees do communicate chemically. They're connected through fungal strands to other trees."

"See?" said Sharon, to whomever might disbelieve.

"Jeezum," said Vic, "now who's being ridiculous?"

Vic, Ruth observed, was going through a negative phase. He thought his sister Sharon "kooky." He argued against his mother growing hemp, even Christmas trees. He helped with the calves, but otherwise wanted nothing to do with the farm. Obviously turned off by the whole conversation, he grabbed a plate of cheese and crackers and took it upstairs with him, where he could eat, read the O'Brian sea novels his father had sent him, and blow his nose in peace.

"What's with him?" Sharon asked, and Ruth just raised an eyebrow. What he really needed, she knew, was a father. But she couldn't do anything about that at the moment.

As if she'd read her mother's mind, Sharon asked, "What do you hear from Dad? What's going on with this farm deal? I thought he'd relent by now, come down on his price. I called him up, you know. I told him he was hurting all of us."

"Oh? How so?" Ruth asked.

"Well, you're our mother!" Sharon cried, her braid shaking loose with her indignation. "What happens to you affects us. If you go to the poorhouse we'll have to bail you out."

"For chrissake, Sharon," said Jack, who always took his mother-in-law's side, "your mother's not going to any poorhouse. Anyway, they don't have them anymore, do they?"

"They call them shelters now," said Sharon. "For the homeless."

"So that's it," said Ruth. "You're worried about my landing on your doorstep. Well, my dear, you don't have to worry about that. I can always sell the house and live in the barn. Snuggle up between a couple of cows, and who needs a woodstove?"

"Not a bad idea," Jack commented. "That's what they did in the old days."

Ruth shot her son-in-law a grateful look. "But seriously, Pete's not relenting. He wants his money. He's giving me more time, I can say that for him. I may get a bigger loan from my bank. They're considering. If I can get it, I'll have your father off my back."

"They're not getting along," Sharon said with a little smile. "Dad and that phony actress. They're still not married, you know. He pushed you into a divorce so he could marry and now he's holding off. I wouldn't get in a jam with too much bank interest."

"Ho ho," said Jack, nursing an O'Doul's. "Listen to who's talking. What's our credit card bill now—up to twenty thousand? At lemme see, ninety percent monthly interest?"

"Well, it's not all me!" cried Sharon, banging the table with her fists. "Two kids, and you work seasonally, and I work in the counseling service for peanuts."

"If you're going to argue," said Ruth, "do it at home. Where are the kids, anyway?"

"At Martha's Day Care. We've got to go get them. And Mother. It's not true about the credit card. We only owe twelve thousand. The mortgage on the house you know, and the car payments. But we're paying back. I mean, slowly."

"Who's going to bail *whom* out of debtor's prison now?" Ruth asked, smiling, and waved the couple off.

Afterward, though, alone in the kitchen, she sank her chin in her hands. At this rate, they could all land in the shelter: mother, daughters, son, and grandkids. Pete sent a minimal check each month to help out with Emily's college, but it didn't stretch far beyond. She still had Vic to feed, and a hired man who was willing to work for minimal pay and free milk and beef, but might not forever. At least Joey came free, God bless him. She was fond of that boy—though investigating the Godineaux, made her, for some reason, worry about him.

"I'm thinking of changing the name of Willmarth Farm," she

told Colm when she'd rung him up at his real estate office. "I'm thinking of calling it Stone Broke Farm. It fits—both words. What do you think?"

Colm laughed. "Is it really that bad, Ruthie? Look, I can give you another loan. I just sold a house on your road. The guy has two kids in Branbury College and wants to have a place for them to come to."

"College kids will be living in it? Whooping it up all night?"

"Come, now, Ruthie, you were in college once."

"On scholarship," she reminded him. "Anyway, I wanted to tell you. Tomorrow at ten we've got an appointment with a man called Shortsleeves. I don't know what he can tell us about Pauline Godineaux, but we'll try. He knew her back when."

"We, Ruthie? You and I?"

"What other 'we' would I have in mind?"

He chuckled. "Let me look at my calendar. If he's anything like that Godineaux up on the mountain, you'll need me. Four rifles in the rack and one pointed at me."

"Exactly my reasoning. I can't leave Vic without a mother."

"There's always Jane Eyre. Anyway, I've a real estate appointment, but I can change it. I'll pick you up at nine. We can take my car."

"Did you have the muffler fixed?"

"Not yet, but I've got an appointment for next week."

"We'll go in my truck."

"The John Deere might be safer than that."

She told him to shut up, and then laughed, in spite of herself.

Marcel Shortsleeves wasn't a gun-running man at all; on the contrary, he was as short as his name implied, a mild-mannered septuagenarian with a high-pitched tenor voice. He sang, he told her, in a men's quartet. They sang French-Canadian songs while another fellow played the fiddle. "We're trying to get better known," he said, handing her a brochure. "We do dances and weddings." He winked at Colm.

"I'll let the Board of Realtors know," Colm told him. "We have monthly meetings, they might like a little entertainment."

They never had entertainment, Ruth knew, but Colm liked to please people. That was one of his good points, and at the same time a fault. He'd lead people on, get them to hoping he'd buy this, order that. "Maybe your father would like a little entertainment at his wakes," she said, and smiled sweetly at him.

"Oh, yes, yes, indeed," said Shortsleeves. "We sing at funerals. Oh, absolutely." He handed Colm a pack of brochures.

Ruth explained why they'd come. "We heard you knew Joey's mother, Pauline."

Shortsleeves's demeanor altered with the name Pauline. He shrank back as though Ruth held a gun to his chest. His nose was a red pepper. He cleared his throat, fiddled with his top button, hummed tunelessly. Finally he said, "Pauline Godineaux. Well, that name does ring a bell."

"Your name was on her records," Ruth reminded him. "You came to see her. Several times. Nothing incriminating," she added as his face came to a boil.

"Oh, no, nothing incriminating, no," he cried, wringing his hands. "I only—well, we dated a little, you see. I didn't know she was shoplifting. I was horrified when I heard. I thought she'd been booked on false charges. She seemed a nice girl. Chain smoker, yes, but I wanted to help her."

"Were you lovers?" Colm asked, blunt as usual.

The face boiled over. Ruth sat upright, ready to give CPR. "It's all right," she soothed. "It's okay if you were, or weren't, lovers. We just want to know whose child Joey is, that's all. We'll keep it confidential."

Shortsleeves took several quick breaths. His skin cooled. He tried to smile, but it came out a smirk. Finally he said, "She already had a kid by another fellow. Whoever he was, he just up and left; poor girl, she had no support. I took her in, she lived in my house awhile. It was after my own wife died. Pauline was in her mid-forties then. She sang a nice contralto." He smiled, remembering. "I mean, I offered to marry her when she got pregnant, but she said she'd had enough of live-in men."

"By you?" Colm asked. "She was pregnant by you?"

The face heated up again. "Well, I never could be sure. I

mean, she was seeing another fellow, you know, when she lived with me. I didn't find out till later. I made her leave my house when I found she was seeing someone else. She went off with the other man, I guess, I don't know." He seemed upset, remembering; a little saliva dropped onto his shirt collar.

"So you might or might not be Joey's father."

"We-ll, at first she said yes, but then she told about this other one. It could have been his. I tried to find out where she went, I did! I tried to find out about the child. I'm Catholic, I didn't want her to get an abortion."

Ruth asked about the grandmother. Marcel said he'd met Nicole a few times. "She was a nice person. She'd been through the mill, you know, that kind. She'd bring things when she came to visit—fruit, a bottle of sherry. We got along. We got along better than we did with Pauline. Pauline wasn't always easy to live with. She had a quick temper.

"Personally," he repeated, "I think that other guy was the father, not me. I mean, my wife and I never had kids, you know. I had mumps as a boy. I never . . . well, can we leave it at that?"

Shortsleeves seemed relieved to hear that Joey had a good foster parent, but he showed no inclination to meet him. He reminded Ruth that he was "living hand to mouth on Social Security. I was in construction, you don't save up much."

Nor could he tell them anything about Pauline's father. "She never said much. He was a no-good, that's all I can tell you. He left Pauline and her brother when they were small. But he kept coming back for money, sex, you know. A real bastard."

"Have you any idea where we'd find Pauline?" Ruth asked.

Shortsleeves thought a minute. He sank his head in his coarse, scarred hands. "I had a postcard from her. Maybe three years ago. If I can think of where it came from . . ."

"Vermont?"

"No, not Vermont. Uh, New Hampshire, I think it was. That's right, New Hampshire. Some town begun with an A. That's all I can remember now. It begun with an A."

"The old runaround," said Ruth when they were back in her pickup.

Colm pulled out a wrinkled map of New England, spread it open to disclose the narrow state of New Hampshire. "Hell," he said. "Can't be more than thirty towns that begin with an A. You'll find her."

"*I* will? With no help from you?"

"I'm up to my ass in work, Ruthie. Real estate getting busier; the old man needs me in the death house, his arthritis worse; now the prostate acting up. And I do have a few hours to put in at the station."

"You're not coming to New Hampshire with me, then."

"Did I say I wasn't?"

"Don't play games with me, Colm."

"I mean, I'll have to see how things go. Though I'm thinking now it might give us some time together. Alone, you know what I mean?"

She did know what he meant. That sly look. The hand on her knee. What could she do but slap it—and then grin?

Gwen was waiting for Ruth at the bee farm in boots and slicker—it was raining lightly. She had a basket of tobacco leaves on her arm. Mert had made the basket out of sweetgrass. "Smell?" Gwen promised to give her a braid of it to hang for good luck in her kitchen. Oh, but Ruth could use a bit of good luck!

Gwen plodded ahead in her rubber boots, while Ruth walked carefully behind, examining the ground as she went—for a footprint, maybe, although Mert had smoothed over the one he found. And the police had tramped the area over and over, so what clues to the boy's death could possibly remain? Still, Ruth couldn't help but think that the death wasn't accidental at all. And here she'd told Mert not to report his footprint, putting the responsibility squarely on her own shoulders.

The woods were lush with thistle, wild columbine, and pink trumpet honeysuckle. The bees were happily sucking up the nectar. Water was seeping into her socks, but it was worth it just to smell the woods, that thick leafy fragrance. This landscape was different from her open pasture; it was like something primordial, the fragrance that dinosaurs had smelled, the Abenaki who'd hunted here, the Willmarth forebears, settling into a unspoiled land.

"Voilà," Gwen said, pointing, and Ruth saw a group of long-stemmed, vinelike plants with simple pointed leaves on top and, at the base, larger leaves with small lobes. The flowers were only in bud, but one could already see they'd come out purple. Later, there would be plump black berries, as poisonous to the tongue, according to her son-in-law, as the purplish red flowers.

"That poinsettia plant I still have from Christmas is poisonous," she told Gwen. "So really, why are we pulling this up?"

Gwen nodded. "The irony is, this plant does so much good." She explained about the atropine, its medicinal use. "It's a part of my income, too. But what's money?"

"Screw money. Get rid of it!" Ruth picked up a pile of pebbles and tossed them in the air. They both laughed.

It was time now for the ceremony. Gwen got down on her knees, spread the tobacco leaves at the base of the plants. She said something in Abenaki language; Ruth supposed the words meant "thank you," or expressed contrition of some kind.

"*Kway* is Abenaki for 'hello,' or 'greetings,' " Gwen said. "And *gici oliwni* means 'many thank you's.' It's an expressive language, isn't it? I wish I could speak it. But I've learned only these few words from Russell's cousin Mali, who is studying the language, hoping to teach it to Abenaki children. You know, of course, that Indian children were forbidden by the nuns in school to speak their own language? So it got lost. And part of their identity with it."

"A tragedy," Ruth agreed, imagining how it would have been not to be allowed to speak English in school, to have to speak a foreign language after a takeover of some kind. It could have happened after World War II. It was unthinkable.

The roots squealed as they pulled up the nightshade. "I'm sorry, sorry," Gwen kept saying, and still the roots complained. Who could blame them?

"We're all like the nightshade," Ruth said. "We do harm to others, and then we do good. We're so ambivalent."

"You've got it," said Gwen, scooping up the roots and leaves and stuffing them into a plastic bag. She would use the roots one last time for the atropine.

Afterward the two women walked through the woods looking for healing plants. Ruth had brought along a camera; she photographed a dozen she wanted to learn to recognize on her own land. Gwen showed her lady's slipper, with its variegated leaves and crimson "lip"—picked so often, she said, that it was virtually extinct. She pointed out feverfew—or corn marigold—it had daisylike flower heads with yellow centers. They were helpful, she explained, in curing headaches. "And over there, that woolly plant with the fernlike leaves: it's yarrow. I use it to help stop bleeding."

Ruth was starting late with this knowledge, but she'd learn a little and pass it on to her children. Although Sharon was already something of a healer. She was always bringing castor oil or peanut oil to Ruth to "make the warts disappear" or "cure the muscles" where Ruth had injured herself sprawling headlong on the ice outside the barn this past winter. After that tumble, Ruth ruined an upholstered chair with the castor oil Sharon had lathered on her aching knee.

Gwen sent Ruth off with a half dozen plastic baggies of dried herbs and a cutting of aloe plant—"for healing cuts." She offered a marijuana cutting from her jar, but Ruth reminded her that she had her hemp.

"Enough is enough," she said, and impulsively hugged Gwen as she left. She looked back at the woods one more time as she left. It looked so serene, so bucolic. Who would think a young man had died there?

Donna had left a message on Emily Willmarth's voice mail to meet her at the high school at three o'clock. She had a mission, she said. She might need help. "Try to borrow your mother's pickup. It's a matter of life and death," she'd added. And it literally was: her family's life and then the girl skeleton.

"I don't know where she lives," Donna said, explaining the mission when Emily arrived. "I don't even know her last name. That's why we're here, you see, so we can find out where she got those beads."

Emily was psyched. "I didn't have anything better to do—except work in the barn. I'm meeting a guy tonight for a movie. I don't want to smell like a cow."

"Did your mother give you a hassle about the truck?"

"Nah. I made a bargain with her. She's getting a whole morning out of me tomorrow. Though if it's a late night, it won't be any fun getting up."

Donna knew about making bargains with parents. She'd had her fill of bees in high school. In college, though, she'd wanted to make her own kind of honey. But since Shep Noble's death the guy situation hadn't worked out. Even with the death declared an accident, she felt herself under suspicion. Though everyone suspected everyone else, it seemed. Classes were quiet, no one wanted to speak up except for the usual swaggering males. With two college-related deaths, students and faculty alike were anxious, on edge; the campus was a ghost town after dark.

Donna just wanted to lead a normal life. For one thing, she wanted to get the "princess" back for her father. Get him back to work, out of the house. Out of her hair! Every minute he wanted to know where she was going, who she was seeing. He was obsessed with that skeleton. He was drinking too much, swearing, and then laughing like a crazy man, like he was some kind of manic-depressive.

"This guy I'm seeing tonight will probably turn out to be one more jerk," Emily said. "I can't seem to win this year. I've had it with Boze. All he wants now is to get inside my pants. I'm not ready for that. Not with Boze."

Donna put a warning hand on Emily's sleeve. The students were swarming out of the school now, climbing into buses and cars, milling about with friends. "Look for frizzy green hair—orange lipstick. You can't miss her. You look to the right, I'll take the left."

The strategy was to follow the girl, or the bus she rode on, or the car she drove home in. It wouldn't be easy, Donna knew, but she had to nail her down.

"Over there, a girl with greenish hair," Emily cried, pointing. But it was the wrong shade of green, Donna informed her, and the girl was skinny and flat-breasted.

"Jill has big boobs. Falsies, maybe." Donna had small breasts, but she rather liked them that way. They didn't attract the wrong guys.

One by one the buses pulled out until there was only one left. Donna slumped back in her seat. Jill had probably stayed home that day. Tomorrow Donna had an afternoon class; she couldn't afford to wait outside the high school. She groaned softly and Emily put a hand on her arm. "I know it's been hard for you. But there's some good news. We've got a new professor for soc class. She's coming down from the university to teach it. She's reading our papers."

"But she doesn't know us! She doesn't know the story behind our papers. She won't be able to judge."

"She'll judge just as well. She'll judge the paper on its own merits and not on us as students. Besides, she's nice. I saw her office door open and went in. She was interested in farming, she said, her grandfather farmed. She said she was looking forward to our papers. To getting to know us, even though it's practically the end of the year."

Was she interested in Native Americans? Donna wondered. Was the woman's grandmother an Abenaki? Most likely not. Indians made up only one percent of the country's population. And Abenaki, less than one percent in Vermont. What would this teacher care about some long-ago English girl who'd opted to stay with the natives? She balled her fists, squeezed her eyes shut.

She opened them wide again when Emily cried, "Is that her?"

Donna saw a green-haired girl burst through the door with two other girls, one of them in a blue and white cheerleading outfit. They were running to catch the last bus, which was already starting to pull out. "Hey, wait!" the girls cried, and, giggling, caught up with it. The driver swung open the door and they climbed in.

"Follow the bus," Donna cried, and Emily moved out behind it. "But not too close," she warned. "It'll make a lot of stops. I don't want Jill to see us. Maybe I won't even talk to her this trip—I mean, if there's a lot of people around her house."

The bus made eleven stops before it turned onto a side road and flashed its red lights in front of a gray trailer set back in a small woods. There was a pot of geraniums on a wooden step and a huge TV aerial poking out through the roof. There was no car in front, no sign of life inside. The girls watched from a turnout a few yards down the road as Jill climbed off the bus, a maroon book pack on her back. She was wearing the beads; they looked incongruous with her green T-shirt and white shorts. Shorts, and it couldn't be more than fifty-five degrees outside.

"Wait here," Donna said.

"Don't you want me to come with you?"

"I want you at the wheel so we can make a quick getaway if we have to. But if I need you, I'll whistle. I don't think anyone's home, but you never know."

"Could be an old grandmother."

Emily was right. Donna marched boldly up to the door and, before Jill, with a shocked face, could shut it on her, pushed her way in. An elderly woman was asleep and snoring in a tattered armchair, a *Good Housekeeping* magazine upside down in her spread lap. A TV actress cried, "I can't go on like this any longer!"

"What are you doing here? You've got nerve! Now go away." Jill pushed Donna to the door and Donna shoved back. Jill staggered a little, and then regained her ground. "Don't you push me," she cried. "Nobody does that. Nobody pushes me around." She grabbed a metal ashtray from a table and flourished it.

"I'll go if you tell me who gave you those beads. You stole them off a dead girl. She was buried up in our land."

Jill was obdurate. "I never stole nothing. Somebody gave them to me, I told you. We made a bargain." She still had the ashtray in her right hand. The TV actress was screaming at a hairy man in a red T-shirt. Donna felt a little dizzy. But she wasn't going to leave without the beads, without knowing who gave them to Jill. She lunged at the girl, knocked the ashtray out of her hand, shoved her back against a chair. She felt the sharp nails on her neck. "Now you tell me who gave you those beads or I'll call the police. You're wearing stolen goods. The cops could put you in jail for that."

"Don't you call no cops! Don't you tell about these beads. Here. Take 'em. I don't like 'em nohow. They're old. They don't do nothing for me." She yanked them off her neck and the thin strap broke, the beads clattering on the floor. "So pick 'em up. Go on. Pick 'em up you want 'em so bad." She dove head first into the chair and curled up in a ball. Donna crawled about the room to collect them.

"They's one under that table," the grandmother said, awake now. "I don't want 'em stuck in the vacuum. I told her them beads was secondhand. Cheap. I didn't like the looks of that boy nohow. He wanted too much for 'em."

"Like what?" asked Donna, reaching an arm under the TV stand, retrieving a small copper bead.

"Like her. He wanted her. She'd sell herself for a cheap set of beads! She's a bad 'un, that 'un. Her mother was alive, she'd keep an eye on her. I can't do nothing with her. Too old. Too sick. It ain't right, I brought up five of my own, don't need a sleep-around grandgirl."

"Oh, shut up, Gran," Jill said, unfolding herself from the chair. "I know about all your boyfriends till you got too old. You're just jealous. No one wants you no more."

"Don't you say that! I took you in. You could of gone to a foster home. I give you a roof over your head. You're ungrateful. Ungrateful little biddy."

Jill appealed to Donna. "She goes on like that all day. You see why I dye my hair? Gotta have somethin' in my life. Somethin' to make me forget . . . her." She pointed at the old woman.

Emily appeared in the doorway, her face anxious. "It's all right," Donna told her, "I was about to leave. I've got the beads. I just have to know one thing more." She turned back to Jill.

"Who gave them to you? What boy? He's the one stole our princess. He's got her. You tell me or I'm definitely going to the police."

"Princess!" Jill gave a sneering laugh. "It was just some old Indian skeleton, he told me. Who cares about a pile of old bones? The police won't."

Emily went to the phone, and Jill grabbed her wrist. "You put that down, damn it. You're not calling no police."

"They might want to know 'bout that hair dryer you stole at Ames," the grandmother said, grinning.

"Shut up. Just shut up!" Jill cried, wheeling about to accost her grandmother. Hearing Emily start to dial, the girl spun back. "All right. All right, I'll tell you. But you tell him you made me. You threatened me. He's got something on me."

Emily waited, the phone buzzing in her hand. Donna stared into Jill's eyes. "Tell the truth and we'll help you. We'll tell the police you had nothing to do with the theft."

"I didn't. I didn't have nothing to do with it! It was Tilden done it, he seen me stealing that hair dryer, said he wanted to sleep with me, he'd give me the beads. Jeez, he was a nerd. But he said he'd tell the cops about the hair dryer if I told him about him stealing those bones. Why'd he do it anyway? I asked. He had his reasons, he said."

Jill sank back into the armchair, her feet splayed wide on the linoleum floor.

"Tilden Ball?" said Donna. "You must mean the father—Harvey Ball?"

"Tilden," the girl said, crossing her arms hard over her chest. "Why would I go to bed with some old man? It was Tilden. He been after me a long time. Just looking at me, not saying nothing. Till that time he showed me the beads, said they was worth something. Like I could sell 'em somewhere if I wanted, and keep the money. So—I said I'd sleep with him." There were bitter tears in the girl's eyes. She pressed her lips together, hard, until they looked bleached, like lumpy flour.

When Donna and Emily turned to leave, she jumped up. "You keep your promise, now. Don't you say nothing to the police about me taking that dryer! It's a lousy one anyway—they can have it back. Don't you tell Tilden Ball neither I told on him. Tell him you grabbed the beads off my neck, that's all. Tell him I fought back. I did, too."

"Sure," Donna said, feeling the scratches flame up on her neck, "you did." She banged the trailer door shut behind herself and Emily.

Fifteen

Ruth was at the kitchen table bent over a spread map of New Hampshire; a bottle of iodine stood on one corner to keep the ends from curling up. She'd used the iodine on Donna; the girl had gotten scratched by a high school girl—Ruth was glad Emily hadn't gotten wholly involved in the fracas over the stolen beads. But Ruth had made Donna promise not to go after Tilden herself. "It's a matter for the police, not you," she'd warned, seeing the wild look in the girl's eye. "Your parents will see to it—your mother's policeman friend."

Finally Donna had agreed. She would spend the night in Emily's dorm, the roommate being away.

Ruth had been phoning the town clerks and chambers of commerce in all the New Hampshire towns that began with A, looking for a Pauline Godineaux. It could take weeks. Did she really want to do this? But Camille Wimmet had asked for her help. And Ruth was going to give it, no matter how long it took.

Andover, Antrim, Albany, Amherst—she wasn't through the list and already she'd counted eight A names. It was ridiculous. The New Hampshire border itself was an hour's drive from Branbury. How was she going to find time to do this?

She left the map on the table and got up to call Colm, with

no luck. She left messages with his office secretary and his father, and then went out to prep the cows.

But she could hardly concentrate on the task, thinking of tomorrow morning's trip. Would she go it alone? Colm had been so ambiguous, she couldn't count on him. "Tim," she called. The hired man was herding in the cows, his cowboy hat tipped back on his head. She tilted her head and smiled at him.

"Go ahead," he hollered. "You've got that look. You've got some damn fool thing to do, I can smell it. Tonight, tomorrow, I don't care."

"Tomorrow morning," she said. "Right after milking. I'll be back for evening chores."

"No sweat. But look, Ruth—Joey here doesn't have to know where his relatives are. He's got me, right, Joey? You got this old beat-up guy for a dad now?"

"Thath's right, I got you for a dad," Joey lisped, and gave Tim a punch in the arm.

"Watch it there, man," said Tim. "You got a mean left hook. I'm gettin' old. Christ, I'm one of these baby boomers, we're all in our fifties now."

"Do you have to remind me?" Ruth called back.

"Send Vic down here, we can use him to feed the calves, okay? Keep the kid out of trouble."

"Vic?" she called, running back to the house. "Get your arse down to the barn. Tim needs your help. And Vic, I'm leaving in the morning for New Hampshire. I'll be back for evening milking. I'll ask Sharon to be here in case I'm late. Okay?"

"Not again?" Vic hollered down the stairs. "You're always taking off. You're always going somewhere. Why do you keep this farm anyway?"

The question hung with her as she rolled up her map. Her youngest was growing up. Her pillowcase was soaked at night from the hot flashes. She could take estrogen, but how costly was that? How safe? She had these children to herd through their lives.

She'd have to think that question through. But who could

think around here? Not when the phone was ringing off the hook.

"Hey, Ruthie," Colm said in his real estate office, "I got your message. I been out walking land—nice day for it, huh? You really heading out tomorrow? You need a driver?"

"No, but I'll take on a passenger if you want to come. I found a Pauline Godineaux—or Godineau—or Gaudineau—in five of the towns. We leave first thing in the morning, after milking."

"Jeez," Colm said. "Milking's at, what—four-thirty?"

"It'll be over by six."

"Six-thirty?" he begged.

"All right, pick me up at six-thirty. I want to see Vic ready for school anyway. We'll go in your car. Emily has the pickup."

She put down the phone and picked it up again on the first ring. This time it was Gwen, looking for Donna, needing her help with supper—she was going out to Glenna Flint's again. "There's another swarm there—this time by her clothesline. The bees won't let her unpin her underwear."

Ruth laughed and explained that Donna was spending the night at Emily's. "She said she'd call you. She has some news you'll be interested to hear, but I'll let her tell you."

"She probably passed that chemistry test she was worried about. Mert will have to make his own supper, then—another peanut butter and honey sandwich, I'm afraid." Gwen was on her way then, apologizing for the hurry, and both hung up.

Donna rode back from the Willmarths' in a state of high adrenaline. She was excited and angry all at once. She rode right past her own place, where Brownie was out pitching a tennis ball at the side of the house, and on up to the Balls'. She was going to see Tilden. She was going to bring back the girl skeleton. She imagined the joy her father would get from having his princess back. She'd thought about telling him first, of course, but then she'd decided against it; he would only rush up there and threaten Tilden, the father would call the police, and they'd all be in trouble again.

Whereas she would approach Tilden slowly, tell him what she

knew, what Jill had told her—explain that she'd forced it out of Jill. He wasn't to touch that girl, no, not one more time. Then she'd ask for the bones. If he balked, why, then *she* would call Uncle Olen.

Tilden was there in shorts, working on his car. His long skinny legs were sticking out from under the chassis. Painted in red on the back end of the car was a huge angry-looking bee. Hearing her approach, he wriggled out from under, saw her looking at the bee, grinned up at her. "Killer bee," he said.

She leaned her bike against a tree, held out the beads—her hands glowed coppery red with them. She assumed a stance, legs apart, her demeanor cool, her heart beating like ten drums. She looked him in the eye for a long moment. Then she said, "Beads. Beads you stole. Where is she?"

He stopped grinning then, his eyes narrowed. "Where's who?" But his eyes were fixed on the copper beads. She took a step closer, one hand on her hip, the other holding out the unstrung beads. "I said, where is she, Tilden? I know you took the skeleton girl. I have proof. I have a witness. You can't hide it."

He stood there, like a tiger ready to spring. She saw the yellowish irises of his dilated eyes. He seemed to be baring his teeth. He was on something, she could tell that. She was suddenly afraid of him. But she couldn't back off, not now. Her feet wouldn't budge from the patch of grass they were sinking into.

"If you won't tell me, I'll call the police." Her voice was thin, like a plucked harp string. She managed to turn about, toward her bike.

And felt his hands on her. He wrenched her toward him. "Come on, then," he said, his voice sounding strangled. "She's in the forest. I'll show you."

"Let me go!"

"All right, then. But get in the car. I'll take you there. You'll get the bones back. Come on, then."

She didn't like the sound of his voice—there was something cold in its timbre. She hesitated. The sun glinted off the car and shocked her eye. There was a green smear on the passenger door. She squinted. It was the lime-green paint of her bicycle. Her heart froze in her chest.

"It was you. You were the one who tried to run me down. You could have killed me! You'll go to jail for that, oh, yes, you will." She sprang at him, pummeled his chest. He fought back, got her in a headlock, pulled her toward the car, shoved her in, into the backseat, which had no doors; and the car roared forward, sounding furious, like a killer bee, up the road and on into the wilderness of the Green Mountain Forest.

The Pauline Godineaux of Alexandria, New Hampshire, turned out to be a nine-year-old girl running a lemonade stand. Her birth name, she told them, was Mathilde, after her father's mother; she'd changed it to Pauline and her mother went along. "Anyway, my dad's gone now. He had an attack." She clapped a hand to her heart, and Ruth said, "Oh."

They bought two paper cups of lemonade from her, watched eagerly by the brown-braided child, for whom they were the first customers. "It's really yellow Kool-Aid," the girl allowed after they'd swallowed it down, and giggled at her ruse. Ruth slipped her an extra quarter anyway; the Kool-Aid had quelled her thirst.

The Pauline Godineau of Acworth, twenty miles south, was a waitress at a local diner—her overweight, octogenarian mother directed them there: "But they's awful busy this time of day. They don't like it you try to talk personal."

"We'll be discreet," Colm assured her, but she shouted after them, "Pauline can't afford to lose her job. You mind what I said, now."

"We'll order something and sneak in a question or two," Ruth told Colm. She could use a bit of nourishment; she'd only downed a glass of orange juice before Colm arrived at six-twenty-nine. "But you don't have to go overboard," she warned when Colm ordered bacon well done, three eggs sunnyside up, and then a serving of Belgian waffles.

"She's too young," Colm observed when the waitress dashed

off with their order. This Pauline's hair was dyed an orangy red, lips to match.

"Look deep. Under the makeup. She could be in her sixties," Ruth whispered. But the woman wasn't about to divulge her age, and no, she'd never, ever been in Vermont, she said in her crisp waitress voice that betrayed a slight Southern accent. "You on the wrong track here, folks. You want decaf or regular?"

"Regular," they echoed, and Ruth thought of Tim and Joey struggling with the postmilking chores while she sat watching Colm drown his waffles in maple syrup and then gulp down every saturated hunk, without once looking up.

She tried to make conversation, brought up Tilden Ball. "He's the one who dug up that grave, and stole the copper beads—or at least the girls are pretty sure he did." She told him about the visit to Jill's trailer. "Did you ever speak with Tilden? He was on Camille's class list."

He mumbled something through his waffle.

"Speak up, please."

"Leshbian," he said, swallowing. "He called the professor a lesbian, he'd seen her going into some bar in Burlington, he said—early last fall. She had her arm around another woman."

Ruth had heard about Camille's sexual orientation from Gwen. "How awful, to be spied on. I suppose he spread it around—that he'd seen her."

"I suppose."

"That adds another dimension to the case, doesn't it? It could be a hate crime, this murder. Hate crimes have increased in the state, I read, since the civil union legislation. All those *TAKE BACK VERMONT* signs?"

"They're not just about the civil union thing, you said that yourself."

"No, but for some people they are." She kept her eyes on him while he finished his waffles. "So what do you make out of all this? Camille's lesbianism—and then the theft of the skeleton. Where does it all fit in?"

Colm looked thoughtful. "Could be a motive—I don't know. We'll have to look into it. The bones thing, though—probably just a prank. So we'll bring him into the station, give him a good scare. Look, Ruthie, we're here. This was your idea, not mine. So let's get on with it."

"Then let's go," she said, and tapped her fingers on the table while he slurped the last of the heavily creamed coffee. She'd go crazy living with this fellow, who even chewed his ice cream twenty times—a legacy from his mother.

Colm was unruffled by her impatience. He'd live to be one hundred, she told him, and he laughed and said he hoped not—"unless you'll be around, too." He picked up the check.

"We'll split it," she said quickly. It was a small way to retain her independence.

"Why can't you let me do something for you?" His hand was still covering the check. "I'm not trying to own you, for chrissake."

But she was already in his debt. He'd lent her money toward the farm payment. That was enough, without owing him breakfast. She slapped down a five-dollar bill and stood up. "I'll pee, then meet you in the car."

Even then she had to wait five minutes for him.

By early afternoon they'd gone through two more dead ends in Ashuelot, Alton, and Alton Bay. None of the Paulines were the right age, none had relatives named Pauline or knew of any in the area. They were driving in circles, it seemed, skirting lakes and mountains where snow still filled the deep crevices of earth and swamped the crocuses and narcissi poking up through. "Granite outcroppings," she described the landscape, recalling the novel *Ethan Frome*—it had been her English teacher's favorite novel, back in high school. It was deeply depressing, she recalled: that miserable Zeena crowing over the crippled lovers in the end. She'd never name a cow Zeena. She wouldn't let the animal carry that crabbed image.

Of course, Colm wanted a hot turkey sandwich and french fries at one o'clock in Concord, just off the Thruway 89, and then a hot chocolate break at three. They had visited Amherst and Atkinson in the southwestern part of the state, both no-shows, and now veered north to Auburn, where the Pauline Godineau, again without the "x," turned out to be a voluptuous thirty-something brunette, tending bar in a lounge on the outskirts of town. It was already five o'clock and the place had just opened. Colm had to have a drink, and this time Ruth lost her cool.

"Why're we staying?" she cried. "This isn't the woman we're looking for—she's too young. You don't need a drink. You can have one when we get back to Branbury." And then, "No, I won't sit down, damn it" when Colm patted the stool next to him. "Get up off that stool, Colm Hanna, and take me home. We should have driven my pickup." She was close to tears now, it had been such a frustrating day. All those Paulines who had nothing to do with what she was looking for—whatever that was—and Colm acting like a—a lush, she thought, as the Pauline behind the bar slung a beer in his direction.

"Then I'll drive," she said, crossing her arms tightly over her chest. "And I'll take us straight home. I give up on Pauline and Nicole and all those other blooming Godineauxs. I give up on the whole damn case. I can't keep wasting my time."

"Nicole?" said the bartender, hanging over the counter, her long dark hair spilling onto the polished wood. One could see she was a leaner, the way her shoulders slanted forward even when she stood up to mix a drink. "I got a relative named Nicole. Lived in Vermont, don't you know. Some kind of great-aunt—she'd be in her eighties now."

Ruth felt a shiver of recognition run down her spine. "Alive? You knew Nicole? But I was told—"

"Dead, yeah," said Pauline the bartender. "I mean, she'd be in her eighties if she'd lived. Golly, it's hard to keep track of all the relatives. But Annette's still perking. Imagine! At a hundred years old. Sure, my mom goes to see her. My mom's from her son André's side. His was the good side. Stayed out of jail, you know. Old Annette, she had a tough life."

"Still alive, really?" Ruth mused, and ordered a beer—why not? They didn't have Otter Creek Ale, but anything would do, just to keep this woman talking. Something good had to come from this trip away from home.

"Like I said when you walked in looking for that other Pauline," said the bartender, "I don't know nothing about her. She's another side of the family—the bad side. My mom won't have nothing to do with that side—I'm named after my mom's sister Pauline. We're the respectable ones, Mom says. Mom's a beautician. She likes my great-grandmother, though, she's named after her. Annette Godineaux—with an 'x.' Fuchs was Mom's name. She dropped the Fuchs after she divorced my father—and took back the Godineaux, but dropped off the 'x.' Foolish, I'd say, but what the hell."

Colm was nudging her; Ruth almost choked on her beer. *See?* the nudge said. *You got mad and now you're sorry.* She elbowed him back. "Where is she now? This centenarian Annette?"

"Andover," said the woman. "Northwest of here somewhere. I never been there, but like I said, Mom goes up maybe once a year. You want I should call Mom for you? I mean, what do you want to see her for? You relatives, too?"

Ruth explained their mission, saying nothing about the murdered Camille but mentioning Joey. Pauline softened. "Oh, yeah, oh, golly, it's nice you doing that. It's nice knowing about the family. I gotta go meet that Annette 'fore she kicks off. I mean, she's a hundred and one, actually. She had another birthday, Mom took her an African violet."

"The question is," Colm whispered after the bartender had gone off to phone her mother, "has this old woman any memory left? What about Parkinson's, Alzheimer's, plain old dementia?"

"Not everyone gets those things. I want to see her anyway. She might have old letters, who knows? Family records. Anything to give us names: Nicole's father, Pauline's. Joey's father."

"Mom's at the beauty shop," Pauline announced when she came back. "She wants to see you in person before she gives out any address. And Annette's phone's unlisted, you see. Mom's afraid someone will spread the bad news around. About the wrong side of the family, I mean. Mom's got her reputation to keep."

She gave the address of the beauty shop. "But you better hurry," she added as Ruth reached for her wallet to pay for the drinks. She wasn't going to wait for Colm this time. "Mom goes bowling after work. She never talks to *anyone* when she's bowling."

Gwen had held back from calling Donna at the college—she'd promised herself not to interfere, the girl was eighteen now. Still, she reasoned, she and Russell were paying for all this. Even with the Native American scholarship there were books, meals, clothes, a dozen other expenses. Donna owed it to them to let her know when she couldn't perform her home duties. And today she'd shirked them. Thursday was Donna's afternoon to do the grocery shopping: She didn't have a late class and Gwen was in over her head with work. Gwen had convinced Russell to go back to Saratoga for his reenactment. He hadn't wanted to leave, with the grave site still empty, but what could he do, she'd said, hanging around? So reluctantly, with plenty of bluster, he went. Olen and his colleagues were questioning college staff, neighbors, the local hoods—taking fingerprints. She and Russell would have to have faith in the law. Or so Olen would say.

But now she was desperate. She had to go to Enosburg Falls to see to the hives there, it was a good hour and a half north. There was no milk in the house, nothing for supper. Mert couldn't walk the four miles back from town with heavy grocery bags in his arms. He'd already had one heart attack.

So she called Emily's dorm. It did seem odd, she thought now, that if Donna had had something exciting to tell her, she hadn't called. Ruth had said she would. Of course, she reasoned, more exciting things were probably going on at the college—a concert, a play, a dorm party—who knew? Gwen was more lenient than Russell; she didn't begrudge her daughter's having fun—especially now, with the stress of the two deaths, and then the grave robbery.

But Emily wasn't in her room. And the girls weren't at the Willmarths' when she called there. Ruth, according to the hired man who answered the barn phone, was in New Hampshire with

Colm Hanna and wouldn't be back until milking time—"if then," Tim grunted. So she had to trust that Donna was still on campus with Emily, and Gwen didn't have time to track her down. Anyhow, she'd surely be home for supper. *Mystery!* would be on, her favorite TV program, she wouldn't want to miss that.

"I have to leave," she told Mert. He was labeling baskets, getting them ready for her to take Monday to Dakin's Farm Center, where he would sell them wholesale. "I can't wait any longer. I'll bring home some Chinese. Tell Donna when she comes to make a salad. At least there's lettuce in the fridge, if nothing else."

"Will I pass inspection?" Colm joked, smoothing his hair as they walked into the Permanent Solution—a place that might harbor a host of centenarians, he joked.

"Or a crematory," Ruth added, thinking of World War II, although it didn't seem likely, what with the pink exterior of the building, and inside, a large woman with a puffy blond hairdo, paying her bill.

"I'd leave you a tip, but you *are* the owner, right?" the customer reminded the proprietress, a busty, big-hipped, sixtyish woman in a pink plastic apron with a head of dyed jet-black hair permed and teased into an elaborate bee's nest.

The proprietress gave a forced smile and accepted the woman's check. "Thank you," she said, glancing at Ruth and then Colm. Ruth felt herself redden as though she bore a degree of guilt for insinuating herself into someone else's life. Colm coughed discreetly beside her.

The woman lit a cigarette, inhaled, blew out the smoke. "She'll never see *you*," she told Colm. "She won't let a man come near her. She's been done in by too many."

"In what way?" Ruth ventured, but the hairdresser only turned her head away.

"You'll have to ask *her*. If you're lucky, she'll tell you a story or two. *You*," she told Ruth. "Not you," nodding at Colm.

"Jeez," said Colm, and Ruth had to smile.

"So what's this all about? Why do you want to see old Annette?" The younger Annette stuck her hands on her wide hips, the cigarette hanging out the corner of her mouth, and peered suspiciously at Ruth, who gave the usual spiel about Joey and his relatives. Ruth kept her eyes focused on the woman, her demeanor cool. She didn't want the woman to see how important it suddenly was to her. It was as though that centenarian held the key to a young college teacher's death.

Finally the woman sighed, stubbed out the cigarette. "All right, then. If it's only for that. But just you, not him, I told you. She's my relative, my father's mother. I don't want nothing upsetting her. Don't ask too many questions, okay? She gets tired easy."

Ruth promised. "I only want to know who Joey's father is, his grandfather—you know, the male line in the family? Names. I'm not going to dig up Annette's past. I just want to, well, help Joey." She flushed with the lie. But it wasn't exactly a lie, was it? She wanted to help Joey as well, and Tim, who was himself interested in Joey's background.

"Can you tell us who Nicole's husband was? None of the Godineaux women took on their husband's name, it seems."

The beautician gave a high-pitched giggle. "How could they? They wasn't married, except for Nicole—and she kept her own name. I was. Twenty-two years to a man named Fuchs. Well, I bit the bullet and took his name. Then he ups and takes off with another woman and I get back my maiden name. Who wants to keep the name Fuchs when you don't have the man to go with it?"

"I can understand," said Ruth, not wanting to go into her own life, although the invitation was out. Probably all of Auburn knew the story of this Annette Godineau's marriage to a man named Fuchs.

The woman lit a second cigarette, inhaled, then blew out a lungful. Colm coughed loudly. "Okay, then. She lives up on a mountain road in Andover. It's Annette's trailer, she owns the land. When she dies—well, we'll see who gets the place."

The hairdresser patted her beehive—did she think she was the rightful heir? She dabbed on red lipstick and said she had to "get on the road. I gotta bowling league, I'm already late. Now, you be careful with Annette, she's no spring chicken." She squinted meaningfully at Ruth, stubbed out the second cigarette in a porcelain sink.

Ruth was just climbing into the Horizon, choking back a laugh, when the woman came running out. "Say, you're not thinking of going there tonight?"

"Well," said Ruth, "as long as we're in New Hampshire. I've work tomorrow morning. I'm a farmer."

The woman's face was huge and pink in the passenger window. "You'll have to drive back tomorrow, then. It's after six now. Annette's in bed by six-thirty." She heaved her bulk into a canary-yellow VW.

"A nice motel?" offered Colm, turning the ignition key. "You can see her first thing in the morning while I have coffee in the local diner—if there is a local diner. What about it, Ruthie?" There was a coy smile on his lips.

She hesitated; she'd had two drinks at the Auburn lounge. She thought of Vic, home from school already, needing her help with homework; the morning chores he might skimp on without her.

"We can take two rooms, if that's what you want." His voice was soft and pleading. She turned to look at him; the eyes behind the dark prescription glasses were half shut.

"How can I, Colm? Sharon's coming over at five, but I can't ask her to spend the night—not with two children—can I?"

"You can," he reassured her. "She'll understand. Look, Branbury's two and a half hours from here. She'll have to put the kids down anyway. Unless Jack—"

"Jack's away at Cornell today with his mentor. He's starting a doctorate—as if they're not in enough debt already."

"Huh. Well, then, it's decided."

"But the milking, all the prep, and Elizabeth down with milk fever."

"We'll make two calls. One to Sharon, one to Tim. You can pay him overtime. I'll take care of the motel. You do the overtime. We'll be back by noon, sure thing."

"If the old lady complies. It may turn out to be another dead end."

"At a hundred and one? You may be right."

"Enough. Look—there's an outdoor phone at that gas station. Pull over."

"Of course, we'll be taking two rooms," she told Sharon, reddening as she spoke, as if she were the teenager, faced with her mother's frown.

"You're such a prude, Mother. Sleep with him, for God's sake. You know you want to. Take a night off motherhood. You've earned it."

"Honestly, Sharon." Her face was on fire now. She could only babble something about Vic's bedtime, clean sheets in the upstairs closet, towels on the outdoor line.

"Live it up, Mother," Sharon crooned into the mouthpiece. "I'll speak to Tim for you. I'll help him with the morning chores. So will Robbie—he loves to bottle-feed those little calves. He may be the one to take over the farm."

"I should live long enough to train my grandson," she said, laughing.

Still her face was scarlet when she stumbled back to the car; she was feeling the drinks. Colm was grinning at her. "Sharon approves, right?" he said, and in an unaccustomed burst of chivalry he ran around to open the car door for her. He looked almost handsome in the last sheen of sun, his hair curled a little at the nape of his neck, his eyes glinting Irish blue. "Madame?" he said, and tucked in a fold of her denim skirt. Why was she suddenly conscious of her scuffed boots?

She smiled and impulsively grabbed his hand. For a mad moment she was her young self, on a date with a dark-haired boy—on a night when anything might happen.

Sixteen

When Gwen got home from Enosburg Falls and Donna still wasn't home and had left no message, Gwen was fully alarmed. She called the dairy farm, but Sharon Willmarth answered to say that her mother would be away overnight. Did Gwen hear a smile in her voice? So she called Emily again and this time the girl came to the phone.

"But she decided to go home—after we found out about Tilden Ball," Emily told her, and went on with a wild story about a girl named Jill who had the copper beads that Tilden had given her.

"Tilden? But she didn't come home," Gwen cried, panicked now. "We haven't seen her since yesterday morning!"

"Oh, yeah," Brownie said—he was at the supper table, spooning up a dish of chocolate ice cream, "I heard her bike go past yesterday afternoon. I knew it was her—it's got that funny clanking sound since she fell off that time."

"Go where? What time?" Gwen demanded, the phone dangling in her hand, Emily's voice faintly calling, "Ms. Woodleaf? Are you there, Ms. Woodleaf?"

"I dunno, I was throwing a ball, I wasn't looking. But it sounded like she was riding up the road, you know, up toward the forest."

"Up toward the Balls' you mean," Gwen shouted at Brownie.

"She was mad as hops," Emily said on her dormitory phone. "She wanted to get that skeleton girl back. But she promised my mother she'd let you and the police take care of it."

"Your mother knew—and she didn't tell me?"

"Well, she wanted to let Donna tell you."

Gwen remembered now. This was the "exciting" news that Donna had to tell. But she hadn't told. She hadn't told because she wanted to find the princess for herself; she would have gone straight up to find Tilden Ball. And when she did, when she accused him of digging up the grave, stealing the bones, why, then . . . She clutched the phone in two shaky hands. Even then she could hardly hang on to it.

Tilden would be backed into a corner. He wouldn't want to be found out. He was a big, rawboned fellow. Not a boy—a man. No, a boy in a man's body. He wouldn't hurt Donna, would he? Would he?

She thanked Emily and hung up. She couldn't panic, she had to keep her wits about her. "Brownie, call Olen Ashley and tell him to come straight up to the Balls', would you? Tell him Donna's missing. Then clean up here. I'm going up myself."

"Mom, I have homework."

"Just do as I say!" she hollered, and abashed, unused to this strident voice, he obeyed.

"Dad's coming home," he said in a small voice as she started out the door. "He called this afternoon. He'll be here anytime now."

"Then send him up!" she yelled back. She needed her husband. It was his child, his daughter. Russell should be here.

Harvey Ball was incensed. There was no skeleton girl on his place, "goddam it all. Why'd I want some Indian bones for? They been up here lookin' around, I don't like it. I'll sue, that's what I'll do. A man can't work his farm without people coming around, accusing him of stealing a pile of bones."

"It was Tilden who took them. Donna has proof. She came up here to make him give back the skeleton. But she didn't come home. She didn't come home, Harvey!" The tears welled up in her eyes.

"She's at the college," he said, looking uncomfortable with all this emotion. "Go look. You'll find her."

"No, she's not at the college. She came to see Tilden, I told you. I didn't see his car when I drove in. When did you last see him?" She heard her voice go shrill with her impatience.

He licked his lips. She saw how purplish his tongue looked, how red and blotched his face was from the sun. Finally he said, "Yesterday afternoon. He didn't help with chores. He's probably at the library. Tell you what. You go there, see for yourself. They're both there, exams coming up. He knows he's got to pass."

Maybe. Maybe, she thought, though she couldn't believe it. Donna studying quietly in the library, skipping her chores, not letting her mother know where she was?

"He's gone off somewhere, Harvey, she's with him. He doesn't want her to tell. But we already know, you see. Emily Willmarth was with her when she found the copper beads. He'll have to come back and face the truth."

She heard the siren, Olen was coming on in style. Harvey's face went pinker still. When Olen burst in with a colleague and a warrant to search the house, Harvey had to let him do it. He stood aside, arms dropped at his sides, Ralphie beside him, grasping his hand, humming to himself. Russell burst in with Brownie, flushed, wanting to know, "What in hell's going on here?" Harvey looked like a man swept away by a nor'easter.

After a half hour's search they found the skeleton under Tilden's bed, wrapped in a blanket—Gwen was surprised to see again how tiny a bundle it was: a small round skull, neck and breastbone well preserved where the beads had lain—the copper salts had acted as a preservative. She'd been somewhere between three and seven years old, a tiny princess indeed. Russell scooped her up; he was weeping. He rocked the bundle tenderly in his arms, as if it were a living child.

Gwen remembered how he'd been at Donna's birth, how loving, how thrilled. Brownie had been a different story, he was a boy child. Russell hardly touched him until he was on his feet and running. Gwen saw Brownie watching his father cry; he was openmouthed, it was as though he were seeing him for the first time. He wouldn't remember how his father was when he was a child.

This was the time to go, Gwen thought. While they had the bones, before Russell demanded restitution. Although that would come: Russell wouldn't let the Balls get away with such a sacrilege. But they couldn't leave. Not without Donna.

They were downstairs, Harvey following, muttering to anyone who'd listen about how he hadn't known, had nothing to do with the theft. It was that son of his—"a disgrace," he owned, "a goddam disgrace. I'll see he gets his when he comes back. I'll deal with him," he assured Olen Ashley, who was standing in the outer doorway with his hand on his holster. Sergeant Hammer stood behind him, in the same posture.

"It's not for you to do that," Olen said. "This is a matter for the police. You have to go through proper channels. You can't take matters in your own hands, Ball."

"Damn right, he can't," Russell growled, the bundle still gripped against his chest. He didn't seem bothered that Olen was seeing him this way, the tears glazing his black eyes. He had his princess, he wanted to go home, return her to her proper grave, restore order. He didn't yet know about Donna, Gwen realized, he didn't know she was missing.

When she told him, he howled like a banshee and Olen had to restrain him. "Find her, Ashley, goddam it," Russell moaned. "Get out the sirens. Just find her." For the first time since he'd known Olen, his hands gripped the older man's arms. His eyes begged.

A cry came from the direction of the woods, and Sidney Ball appeared in the doorway, pulling along a distraught Tilden. "He was hiding in the tree hut," he told his father. "You gotta face up," he warned his brother, "You gotta tell them what you told me." Sidney's face took on a stiff-lipped aura of self-righteousness.

Tilden's face went dead white at the sight of the two policemen; he broke from his brother's grasp and ran to his father, embracing him. "For you, Dad, that's why I did it. For you! I thought you'd want it, I thought you'd be glad." When his father didn't return the embrace, he dropped, sobbing, at his feet.

"For chrissake, be a man," Harvey bellowed, yanking his son up by the armpits. "What made you think I'd of wanted you to do that? Dig up a goddam grave? You thought that'd help? Now you only made things worse. I was getting what I wanted, in my own way." He shoved the boy toward Olen. "Here's your thief." But the boy only sank down again at his father's feet.

And was jerked up by an irate Russell. "Where's Donna? Where's my girl? What've you done with her?"

"How'd I know where she is?" Tilden blinked up into Russell's eyes, his face a mask. He's like a marionette, Gwen thought, pulled by his father's strings—but he'd suddenly snapped out of control.

"Let me," she told Russell, pulling the boy around to face her, stronger than she knew herself to be. "Brownie saw Donna biking up this way. She was coming to find you, to bring back our skeleton girl. You intercepted her, didn't you? Well, didn't you?"

She saw Olen beyond the boy's shoulder, his mouth open, almost panting, like he wanted to get at the boy and she was interfering. *Wait*, her narrowed eyes told him.

She was screaming inside now. "If you hurt her, Tilden—if you did anything to harm her in any way—I'll kill you myself, I swear I will. Now tell me. Where's Donna?"

"Up there," he said, waving an arm toward the north. "In the camp—Dad's hunting cabin. I drove her up, she was going crazy, accusing me of . . . all kinds of things. I couldn't have her doing that. I just wanted to reason with her. I wanted to make her understand." The sweat was streaming off his brow, soaking his T-shirt. He wiped his forehead with a hand, smearing the dirt and ash.

"Where's this cabin? You lock her in?" It was Russell's turn to yank him back. Tilden was taller than Russell by two or three inches but seemed smaller in his guilt.

"I was coming down to get food for us, that's why. Then I was planning to let her go. Sure, I was, I—" He was trying to swallow, as though he had a huge lump in his throat that wouldn't go down.

"Where's that camp?" Olen demanded of Harvey.

It was Sidney who answered, sounding anxious, paranoid, as though he were guilty himself because his brother was guilty. "I can show you. I'll take you up. I got the truck outside." He ran out the door, Russell after him.

"Wait, Russ, I'm coming," Gwen cried, but the two were already out, the truck revving up.

"Hammer! Go with them," Olen shouted at his fellow officer, and the latter jumped into the back of the moving truck.

"I was trying to make her understand, why I did it, why I ran her down that time—I didn't mean to hurt her."

"It was you!" Gwen cried. "She called it an accident. All the time it was you. What else—what else did you do, Tilden? What other things that have happened around here? Omigod! I don't want to think . . ."

Olen yelped, his face suffused with red, a match for Tilden's. "You tried to run down that girl? What in hell you think you were doing, you little son of a bitch!" It was like a light breaking in front of Olen's eyes. "The fire in Gwen's truck. The hate calls—was that you, Ball? Was that you? And what about that teacher? You were in her class. You were failing the course, right? What'd you do then, did you—"

"No, no!" Tilden cried. "I never. Not that. I never!"

Olen slapped a pair of handcuffs on the boy, turned to Gwen. "We'll find out what he's done. He'll tell us, all right. You'll tell us everything, won't you, Ball? What else, who else you hurt?"

Harvey Ball was pressed against the wall, his mouth slightly open; he was rocking on his feet, as though trying to get words out. Finally he pitched forward, gripped his son's shoulder. "You tell him, boy. You tell him what you did. Wasn't that bad, was it? Stealing some old bones? You didn't try to hurt the girl, did you? Tell me you didn't do that. No son of mine would hurt a girl."

Tilden shrank away, refusing to make eye contact. He stared down at the handcuffs, like an animal caught in a trap, not comprehending where the trap had come from.

"Olen," Gwen said, "I want to find Donna. Make him take us up there."

"I have to take him to headquarters, Gwen. Then I'll be back. You go home now. Sergeant Hammer has gone after the girl, and your husband's with her." He started out the door, shoving the boy ahead of him, slamming the car door on him. She heard the cruiser pull away.

Harvey stood looking after it, hands dropped at his sides like a man who had lost a race. Ralphie was whimpering. He hugged his father around the knees, and Harvey gathered him up in his bulky arms. There was love enough for that one, anyhow.

"Take me to the cabin," she told Harvey; and sighing, pushing Ralphie off with a pat on the buttocks, Harvey started out the door.

But when they got there a quarter of an hour later, the cabin was empty. There were only a pair of dirty mattresses on the floor, a broken rocking chair, a board on two sawhorses to serve as table. She gasped. On the table was a package of Africanized bees. Killer bees! What was Tilden planning to do with those? All it took, she knew, was a lawn mower, operating within one hundred feet of a hive, to set killer bees off.

Behind the package she saw a familiar jacket. She held it up, hugged it. It was Donna's denim jacket. "Where are you, sweetheart?" she cried, squeezing the fabric. "Oh, Donna, love . . ."

She ran outdoors with the jacket. Donna was out there somewhere. She'd escaped, she'd gotten disoriented; she was lost. She was hurt—there were bears, snakes, fisher cats lurking about. Gwen's mind spun out disasters. "Donna!" she shrieked. "Russell! Oh, please, please, answer me!"

Ruth woke up, disoriented. This wasn't her room, the windows were in the wrong place; there was a large homely TV across from the bed—a king-sized bed. Someone was in it with her. He lay there on his back, in deep sleep, his salt-and-pepper hair like a bird's nest—why, there was even a tiny piece of leaf stuck in it! His skin was slack from sleep—she saw the coarse hairs on his chin and cheeks where he hadn't shaved, his arms bent back at the elbows the way a child sleeps, the breath wheezing like a bicycle unwinding from a long ride. She had never seen him like this, it was quite wonderful. He'd kicked off the sheet, yet his body was warm to the touch. It appeared lean and hard, any excess flesh fallen to the sides.

She stroked his belly. How long it had been. For months, even before Pete left, while he was fooling around with that "actress," there had been little sex. She lay back down, already delighting in the feel of a body next to hers, touching, both of them at peace. There was the familiar fullness in her groin, from urine, from lovemaking. She and Colm were like the two half-empty wine bottles that stood on top of the TV. She changed the wording: no, they were half full.

Then she remembered the cows and sat up. "Colm!"

"Wha'?" His eyes squeezed open a crack.

"Who's doing the prepping? Who'll help with the milking?"

He groaned, rubbed his eyes. "The what? Oh, you 'member. You called home. Sharon'll help. Ruthie, stay in bed a little longer, huh?" He touched her breast and she sighed. It was all right, then, she could have this time out. It had been months since she'd had a day away from the cows. She nestled into her lover's armpits, closed her eyes. . . .

When she opened them again she saw it was nine o'clock. "That woman, Annette. The reason we're here. I've got to see her." She struggled out of bed, stood on the bland gray carpet. Gasped. There she was in the dresser mirror, stark naked—she hadn't brought a nightgown. Her hair was wild, "like a middle-aged nymph," he told her, and she flung a pillow at him. She sucked in her belly. Was he still looking at her? She flushed like a sixteen-year-old. His watery blue eyes smiled back at her in the mirror.

"Annette's not going anywhere. You know what that hair woman said. She never goes out. Come back to bed." He held out his arms.

"I should phone her, at least. Would she be in the book?" She pulled on day-old panties, her bra; looked under the Gideon Bible for the phone book.

"Jeez, Ruthie, the phone's unlisted. Remember? You'll just have to go there, that's all. But first eggs and bacon, okay? Couple of Belgian waffles?"

Ruth was all business now. The honeymoon was over. "Go have your Belgian waffles—they'll keep your stomach occupied while I talk to the old lady. Or try to talk to her. I'll grab some coffee out in the lobby. You can save me a doughnut."

"Waffles?" he said, looking dreamy-eyed. But before she could pull on her shirt, a little sweaty from yesterday's running around, Colm was beside her, holding her, stroking. "You gotta live a little. You can't work all the time. Lie down couple more minutes. Just a couple, okay? Time out, Ruthie. We don't get many chances like this. Sharon's there, so's Tim. Please, Ruthie?"

His hands were on her back. She let him unhook her bra, pull her back down to the bed. Time out, time out, she told herself, and took it. Even enjoyed it.

Gwen was pacing the kitchen floor when the phone rang. A search party was out looking for Donna: police, neighbors, scouts—Russell, Mert, and Brownie, too. Her job now was to stay by the phone in case Donna had blundered into a house, called home. Breathless, she grabbed up the receiver. "Yes?"

"Ms. Woodleaf? It's Sergeant Hammer. You remember me, I was—"

"What is it? You've found Donna?"

"I'm afraid not, I mean, I don't know. They've got me down here at the station. I'm calling because Chief Fallon thought you should know we found out about the fingerprints."

Gwen waited. What fingerprints? She had no idea what the sergeant was talking about.

"In two places. On that pack of Juicy Fruit gum we found on the floor at the teacher's place. And then on the living room window." The voice was high-pitched, gaining in confidence. Gwen waited for the officer to make her point.

"And?" There was no time to waste. One of the searchers might be calling at this very moment, to say they'd found Donna.

"Well, they're Tilden Ball's."

The voice went on for a few more sentences, but she couldn't seem to concentrate. Tilden Ball, a killer?

Alarm bells rang in her head. Tilden had tried to run Donna down, hadn't he? He'd admitted that. And now Donna was missing. Had he hurt her? Had he—no, no, she couldn't think the word, or say it.

She hung up, held on to a kitchen chair. She knew now what it was to be helpless. She might as well be handcuffed, bound to the chair, for all the good she could do. She could only wait—and worry.

Seventeen

It was ten o'clock when Ruth arrived at the yellow trailer halfway up Bradley Hill and parked in the dirt driveway behind a dented black Honda. She'd gotten lost, had to ask directions in the country store, even though the town of Andover was small, strictly rural, except for the private academy at its center, bustling with boys and girls, who seemed to live in a kind of treasure island of their own.

The trailer was set back from the road, with no houses in sight on either side. It was in desperate need of a coat of paint. A porch had been built onto the front, too large for the trailer, like a sketch of what might have been. A pair of peeling green rocking chairs stood at one side of the front door, a rusted yellow swing on the other. A clump of daffodils nodded in a front garden; honeybees hummed in the unmown grass. Behind the house the woods were dark with evergreens and ancient-looking oaks. Through them she saw the glimmer of a pond. It's the right place, Ruth thought, for a woman who doesn't want neighbors nosing into her past.

She knocked, and after a few minutes the door opened; a tall, angular woman in her sixties, perhaps, stood there in denim shirt and blue polyester slacks, as though she'd been waiting for the knock, for *something* to happen, had watched from a window as the car pulled up. And yet she took a negative stance.

"If you're asking for money, the answer is no," she said in a monotone. She held on to the sides of the doorway to underscore her dissent.

Ruth explained her visit stammeringly, cowed by this woman, still disoriented from her night of loving. She gave the hairdresser's name: "Annette Godineau, a namesake. It's for my Joey, Joey Godineaux. Looking for roots, you see. I'm only wanting to help him."

Hunting the queen, Ruth thought, remembering the swarm of Gwen's bees in her trees, how Gwen had searched out the queen among the guarding workers—and suddenly there she was, long and bright-eyed and golden yellow. Would Annette look like that?

The woman examined Ruth with narrowed eyes; she might have been a bodyguard for the old woman and Ruth a suspicious person. Ruth wondered if the woman could hear her banging heart.

"Wait here," said the bodyguard, and shut the door in Ruth's face.

A book lay facedown on a ripped cushion of the swing. Ruth picked it up. The off-white paper cover read, *Poems by Annette Godineaux.* Ruth let out a whistly breath. She wrote poems, this old lady? It hardly fit the Godineaux image Ruth held in her mind. On the inside cover she read, "Ragged Mountain Press." Self-published, she supposed. But did it matter? Annette wrote poems! Ruth was blown away.

"They're not for you to read," the bodyguard said, reappearing in the doorway, holding out a hand for the book. Something fierce in her dark eyes made Ruth give it over. "That's where Annette sits, in that swing. You can sit here," she said, pointing to a nearby rocking chair.

"Come on out," she called, and a frail shrunken woman less than five feet tall, a long skinny braid of white hair down her back, plodded slowly along on a cane. She had on a red wool shawl over a purple print housedress, pinned with a copper brooch. The companion followed close behind, but didn't touch her, as though she were indeed a queen.

Annette lowered herself so carefully on the swing, she didn't set it rocking. She didn't look at Ruth, as though at her time of life she needed no contact with others, no new friends or companions. She seemed to be content with the one she had, still nameless, sitting beside her on the swing. Ruth could literally hear the silence: a protesting bird, a harrumphing frog in the lake, a buzzing insect. They could sit this way all day, Ruth thought, and she'd gain nothing. She had to speak up.

"Your descendant, Joey Godineaux," she began—unsure of what descent Joey actually was, though great-grandson came to mind, "works with me on my farm. I'm—that is, he—is anxious to know something about his family. He's a foster child, you see." She described her interview with Mabel Petit and then Evangeline Balinsky, while Annette stared ahead into space.

"This cushion is splitting at the seams," Annette told her companion, seeming to ignore Ruth's story. "I can feel it popping under me."

"I'll take it to that seamstress in town," the other woman said, lighting up a cigarette.

"No," said Annette, in a throaty voice stronger than Ruth would have guessed from a centenarian. "I'll do it myself if you'll buy some green thread."

"I'll do it, then."

"No, *I* will," said Annette, and that ended the subject.

"What Joey and I would like to know," said Ruth, blundering on, wanting to get to the heart of the matter, thinking of her cows, and Vic, who probably needed a bath, clean clothes, lunch money—"is who Joey's forebears are on the male side. I mean, his father, or grandfather. Or great-grandfather?"

"Nobody," Annette said, her eyes trained on a high point beyond Ruth's head, and for the first time Ruth realized that she was blind. "Nobody at all. Never stayed long enough to leave a name." She dropped her shriveled chin, appeared to look inward. "Not one goddam man among 'em worth leaving his name.

They were all liars. Who knows what names they had? Two or three, to escape the law."

"Oh," said Ruth, afraid she wasn't getting anywhere, but plowing on. "I met a Marcel Shortsleeves. He seemed a pleasant, honest fellow. He came to visit Pauline when she was in the reformatory."

There was a sound from the companion, and Annette smirked.

"Oh, you know about that, do you?" Annette gripped her hands together, rocked the swing with her body, though her feet didn't touch the porch floor. "You been snooping into our family secrets, have you?"

"Only to find out . . . for Joey," Ruth stammered. "The early records burned, they said."

"Sure, *they* burned 'em," said Annette. "They didn't want the world to know what they did to us." Her eyes were luminous with sun as she spoke. She rocked faster. The swing made a jarring sound, metal grating on metal. The companion stubbed out her cigarette on the porch floor and pulled another out of her pack of Kools.

"I know about the sterilization," Ruth said, taking the plunge. She couldn't hide the truth under the Joey umbrella much longer. "I need to tell you. A woman named Camille Wimmet, a professor at our local college, was doing research into the thirties eugenics project." She told the woman what little she knew about Camille's work. "But," she said, afraid to look at Annette, hearing her voice hoarse, "Camille was killed for it. Someone strangled her. We think it may have been because of the research she'd done. Someone who didn't want his or her reputation, well . . . blemished."

Ruth looked up. Was Annette ill? A funny, raspy sound was coming out of her throat. Why, the woman was laughing! It was a bitter laugh that rose up out of the saggy pot of her belly. She glanced at the companion, but the latter just sat there, still as a possum. Ruth wanted to pick the old lady up—she couldn't weigh more than eighty pounds—and shake her.

But she couldn't, wouldn't do that. She could only wait until the laugh died away and the woman was quiet again, except for the methodical creaking of the swing.

"So it's come to that, has it?" Annette said finally, and something like a groan came up out of her lungs. Ruth saw her glance at her companion, but the latter was staring straight ahead, the cigarette pressed tightly between her thin lips.

"This is why I've really come," said Ruth, leaning forward in the rocker, needing to be frank. "For Joey, yes, that's part of it. But for Camille as well. To find out who killed her, and why. That's why I want to know about the male side of the family—it was a man killed her, they think, the way the fingers had dug into the neck. Knowing all the names might lead us to someone."

Annette turned her head toward Ruth as though she could actually see her. The eyes, when the sun went under a cloud, were dark holes. The white braid that lay on her chest was a stunning contrast to the red wool shawl. She smelled musty, like old books and papers. Ruth waited for her to speak.

"I had four children: Nicole, Jeannine, Cosette, and André," she said finally, "by three different men—I only knew their first names. Jeannine died from scarlet fever, there was nobody to help. That Annette who does hair, she was André's daughter, she comes sometimes to see me, but she talks too much—I have to cut it short. Nicole married at sixteen, but the bastard abused her. Finally . . . well, he left. Nicole came back to live with me, we didn't have much. I stole some groceries, you know, we had to eat—other stuff we needed. Nicole got the habit, too, that eugenics woman 'round to talk to us, she thought she knew every goddam thing there was to know. She was the one got people sterilized. Her and the men with her."

Annette's voice was growing thin. The companion ran for water, but the old lady waved it away.

"They put Nicole's kids in the training school," she went on, "though they wasn't backward. Way I got us out was I made a bargain. Sew up my cunt in exchange for a pardon. I took it. I didn't know they did it to the kids, too—well, one of 'em anyhow, the boy."

The old lady leaned back on the swing, gasping, exhausted from the long speech.

"She's tired, can't you see that?" her companion said, looking annoyed; she stubbed out the second cigarette, tossed it over the railing. "She's not used to talking to people like this. Here," she told the woman, "drink this. Don't talk. You need your strength." She sat back down beside the old lady, put an arm around her shoulders, and Annette leaned into it. It was as though they were lovers—or had been, once, and now were simply close companions.

Ruth stood up. She'd obviously been dismissed, but there were still questions. "Do you know where Nicole's son is now? Where he came from? He might hold a key. You see, Camille Wimmet was trying to right a wrong, bring all this prejudice—this program—out in the open."

She felt light-headed, standing there on the slanting porch, looking down on this odd couple; she glanced again at the book of poems. It was all so incongruous. The reformatory, the sterilization, the poverty: How could you get a poem out of a life like that? Was there poetry in poverty?

But the companion was hustling the old woman up out of the swing, back toward the front door.

As she went down the rickety porch steps, feeling off balance, Ruth heard Annette whine, "Fix me a cup of hot chocolate, will you, Pauline?"

Ruth wheeled about. Pauline? Why, this woman was Annette's granddaughter. She was Joey's mother. "Pauline?" she hollered. "You know those names I'm after. It was your own father and brother. And Joey's father, who was he?" She stumbled back up the steps. "Pauline—don't you want to know about Joey? Your son, Pauline!"

A door slammed. Ruth stood on the top step, feeling shut out, like the day Pete left and she'd watched him drive off in the taxi to meet that woman in town.

She was still standing there, her feet as though nailed to the wooden step, when the door opened again.

"How is he?" Pauline said. Her eyes were half shut; she was staring at Ruth's car, or at a point beyond it.

"He's fine, fine and healthy. My hired man has been a caring foster father, he wants to legally adopt him. But we'd like your permission. And the father's. What's his name, Pauline? You know, I know you do."

Pauline stood frowning into space another moment, as though she might tell. Then she crossed her arms, thrust out her lower lip, and swiveled about.

"Tell me the names, Pauline. Call me! I'll leave my number on the swing." She drew pen and paper out of her pocketbook. "Call me or I'll come back. With a policeman this time."

Pauline pushed through the door. It banged behind her, and latched.

Donna had been sleeping in the leaves. She'd wandered off the path and now she couldn't find her way back. Once she thought she heard voices on the wind and she hallooed, but no one answered. She'd heard a helicopter overhead and waved, but the 'copter flew on. The trees were thick here, tall pointed pines so close together they made a canopy against the sun. The path she'd been on for what seemed hours would only lead back to the cabin. She didn't want that, oh, no!

They'd be looking for her, though, she was sure of that. Someone would find her. A friendly human, she hoped, and not a fisher cat. Not Tilden, no, not Tilden. . . .

"I could kill you," he'd said, "with this," and he'd held up his little finger. Looking up at him where she was bound to the only chair, she'd felt it was true. He'd tried to kill her once, hadn't he? He'd left the cabin, locking it behind, taking the key, announcing that he was going for food and she'd better make up her mind to listen to him, to "understand" why he'd done all those things: stolen the skeleton girl, run her off the road, gotten those killer bees. Oh, the bees were just a backup, he said—"in case." It was for his father's sake, he'd said, pleading with her—didn't she know what it was to want to please a father? It was the bones, he claimed, that were keeping her parents from selling their land. He'd removed that obstacle, that's all. She had to try and understand.

Why couldn't *he* understand why the bones couldn't be moved, why the land was sacred? she asked. But she was told to shut up. He was on something, it was obvious. She'd been afraid to cross him.

It took the better part of an hour to rub and rub the rope that held her hands against the splintered wood of the table, but the rope was old; eventually it gave; the lock that held the door was weak, and she pushed through. She stumbled up the path behind the cabin, in the opposite direction from her house to avoid Tilden, veered onto a less traveled path, thinking she could circle back toward her home. But the path disintegrated into brush; the day was overcast, there was no sun to orient her. She could only sit still—and wait.

When she heard the dogs barking, she thought it was wolves, and she hitched up onto the lower branch of a white pine and crouched there. But the barking was followed by voices, the high-pitched babble of children. The blood leaped in her veins. She jumped to the ground again and hollered, "Halloo, halloo, there! Here, I'm over here!"

And then she was surrounded by a dozen Girl Scouts in green uniforms, their sneakers caked with mud and mottled with grass stains. "Donna?" one of the girls said, and when she nodded, unable to speak, the girl burst into tears, and Donna with her. Now everyone was hugging everyone else. A stout woman panted up behind, grinning broadly. She blew a whistle that split Donna's ears and shouted directions into a walkie-talkie. Then Emily Willmarth raced up to fling herself into Donna's arms.

"You're cold," Emily cried, and yanked off her jacket. It turned upside down in the melee and the contents tumbled out: pens, paper clips, shredded Kleenex, earrings, sticks of gum, and something that seemed to surprise her—Emily dug down deep into the hemline, below where the pocket had ripped, and held up a disk. "Oh!"

She jammed everything back in the unripped pocket and wrapped Donna in the jacket, which was too big for the girl and smelled of barn. But it was all right, all right. A group of men and boys ran up, breaking a path with their boots and machetes, and suddenly Donna was in her father's arms—the two of them laughing and crying all at once.

Gwen was having coffee with Olen Ashley; he was explaining that it was a felony under state law to knowingly disinter human remains. He was determined to "nail the bastard. I mean, look what he did to Donna! Thank God she's all right, Gwen," and Gwen added a silent amen. It had been a poignant homecoming. She'd hurried Donna into a hot bath and afterward followed her around the house, unable to let the girl out of her sight until Donna cried, "Enough, Mom. At least let me pee in peace."

Olen leaned closer, planting his elbows on the kitchen table. "It could be more than a felony, Gwen, it could be murder. You heard about those fingerprints we found."

"But why would he do that?" she asked, thinking of Camille Wimmet, and maybe Shep Noble, too, although she'd no idea what connection Tilden Ball would have with that fraternity boy. Tilden had tried to get into a frat, been blackballed. After that he'd loudly proclaimed his disgust for fraternities.

She didn't get her answer because just then the telephone rang. It was Ruth Willmarth, on her barn phone, she'd been shoveling manure. "I'm glad you can't smell me. Robbie let in Vic's chickens by mistake, and Sharon didn't have time to clean up 'cause the baby needed her. So now there's cow *and* chicken shit on the floor."

Ruth was calling about Donna: "We're all so thankful she's safe." She told Gwen about her visit to Annette Godineaux. "But I didn't learn much beyond what we already knew—about the sterilization, I mean."

"The stolen honey," said Gwen, thinking of the sterilized women, and then the robber bees she'd found recently on the Earthrowl orchard. "Or maybe I should say, bitter honey."

"That's an oxymoron."

"Isn't everything these days? Love and war? Lies and truth? That's the reality of our lives. We're made of opposites."

"But I still don't know the male lines," said Ruth, going on with her train of thought, "although they might be on the disk Emily found. Imagine, the idiot. Camille's disk in her pocket the whole time. And Colm and I went on this wild goose chase."

"At least you had an outing together."

There was a pause. "Yes, yes, we did."

Gwen smiled to herself. They'd been there overnight. Well, good for Ruth, she thought, and changed the subject. "That Pauline sounds like a sly one. And I'd like to have met old Annette. Over a hundred years old! A real matriarch. A poet, you say?"

Now Ruth was making a loud noise with mop and bucket. There was a small crash, like she'd dropped the phone, and then silence. Gwen glanced over at Olen, who was looking at her, questioning. "Ruth Willmarth," she mouthed.

"What's this," he asked, "about a hundred-year-old Annette?"

"Oh, some woman from New Hampshire—Andover, I believe." She didn't want to have to explain. Camille Wimmet's death was a case for the police, Olen would insist, not for a civilian like Ruth Willmarth. "Ruth was just visiting," Gwen fibbed, and Olen nodded and swallowed his coffee.

Ruth's voice came back on the line. "Sorry. Zelda sabotaged me with her tail. Now there's a heck of a mess. And I spilled my coffee into the other stuff."

Gwen smiled. "You'd better go back to work. By the way, has Emily told you about Tilden Ball?"

"Yes, yes! She gave me the news. That's another reason I called. To tell you how glad I am you've resolved all that malice—the fire, the hate notes. What a relief it must be for you! And what a miserable character that boy is. I hope he's in custody."

"Oh, yes. Olen took him in. He's trying to hold him on a charge of felony. And, worse, they found his fingerprints in Camille's apartment."

"How does he explain that?"

"I don't know. Olen hasn't said." She glanced at Olen, but he was getting up from his chair, going over to look at the wall calendar. "I should be sorry for Tilden, he's a mixed-up kid, really, sick. But my God, he kidnapped Donna! She could have died in that forest."

"It must have been terrifying for her, Gwen—and for you."

"Olen's getting us through this, thank heavens. He's a brick. He's here." Gwen smiled at Olen, where he was pouring a second cup of coffee now, looking abstracted. "He's been a madman as usual, taking Tilden in, then coming back to help us bury the bones. We had a ceremony an hour ago, just before Russell left. I've rewarded Olen with coffee cake."

"Lucky man. Oh, and Gwen, you have the disk? Emily said it was still in the coat she'd made Donna wear."

"Donna has the disk, yes. I can run it over later this afternoon. I'm going in the opposite direction this morning. I told a farmer in Cabot I'd come—he has a swarm inside the walls of his house. I don't know if I can help with that, but I'm going. Oh, the man told me something interesting. Did you know that Alexander the Great was carried to his burial place in Egypt in a casket filled with honey? It preserved him, too."

"No kidding? Well, you'd better go. Anyway, I don't have a computer here to download—is that the word? But Emily can bring me a printout from her computer. I want to see if those male names are on it. I mean, I know it sounds like Tilden's our man, but until we know, I'll keep looking."

"Good. A week ago I wouldn't have believed that Tilden could kill. But now . . . I don't know." She glanced at Olen, who was staring into his coffee, looking cross. "Oh, and Ruth? You can always come over and use our computer."

There was another crash, and Ruth was laughing again. "It's Dolly, she just kicked the bucket."

"Literally, I hope. A tin bucket?"

"Oh, yes, you can hear her complaining. Listen." Gwen could hear the bellowing. It sounded like a mournful foghorn.

"What's this about a disk?" Olen asked when Gwen hung up, laughing.

"Oh, dear, I should have told you." She'd put her foot in it now. Of course the police should have the disk. But Ruth wanted it, too; she'd done just as much as the police had, hadn't she, trying to find the killer? The police, according to Olen, were still cross-examining college people, electricians, other workmen who'd gone into Camille's office or apartment for one reason or another. And they were building a case against Tilden Ball.

Olen was waiting for an explanation. He slapped down his coffee cup. He seemed upset with her—for holding back information, she supposed.

She explained about the disk, what it probably contained. Olen stood, arms akimbo, looked down at her sternly. "We'll have to have it, Gwen. I'll have to take it to the station. It's evidence. You can't give it to whatsername—Willmarth. I mean, she's just a civilian." The red was slowly creeping up his neck, coloring his ears.

"But I told Ruth. She's been working on this, too, helping Colm Hanna—he's one of your men."

"But *she's* not, I said. It's not her business. Now let me have that disk, Gwen. I promise I'll make a copy. I'll give it to Hanna, if that'll make you feel better."

Donna had put the disk into a box with her school files. Gwen had hardly thought about it after that, with all the confusion of the burial celebration, Russell's departure, Olen's visit. Olen had been so jovial then, was even cordial to Russell afterward. And Russell had removed his *ABENAKI NATION* license plate—his way of saying thank you to Olen for helping to locate Donna.

Now Olen had returned to his gruff cop's persona. The law was the law.

Reluctantly she handed it over, and Olen seemed suddenly jubilant, clapped it to his chest. He laughed aloud. "Good girl," he said. "You're a good girl, Gwen. This could make all the difference."

To find the killer, he meant, of course. She'd have to explain to Ruth. It was an error of circumstance. "But you will give Colm Hanna a copy?"

"Did I say I would, Gwen?"

"You did."

"And I will." Impulsively, he embraced her. His unshaven

whiskers—unusual for him—grated her cheek. "All the difference," he said again, and plunged out the door.

Gwen returned the file box to the computer table, idly looked through. These were mostly Donna's files, along with a few of her own for her beekeeping books. The disk for Donna's paper was in here, filled with quotes from Elizabeth's journal. "The Captive Who Wouldn't Come Home," she'd entitled the paper; the disk simply read, *CAPTIVE.* Another professor was reading it now, Donna had said. Though it wouldn't be the same, the girl felt. It was Camille who'd helped her with it; encouraged. Gwen felt all over again the poignancy, the horror of the killing. Someone taking the life of a bright young woman with a whole career in front of her. "Bastard!" she cried aloud. "Animal!"

When she replaced the disk, she saw that behind the *CAPTIVE* disk was another labeled *ANNETTE—COPY.* The title was stuck on with a yellow Post-It. For a moment she wondered if she'd given Olen the right one. He'd be furious with her if she hadn't. But no, this was Donna's handwriting, not Camille's. Donna had had the disk copied.

"Oh, Donna!" she cried aloud, grateful to her daughter for her foresight. Though she should have realized: Donna was always reminding her mother to copy her documents twice; Donna kept a second *CAPTIVE* copy in her room.

"Donna home?" It was Mert, emerging from the basket room. He was wearing an orange *DAWNLAND* T-shirt that Russell had given him. The name Abenaki meant "People of the Dawnland" or, simply, "Easterners," referring to their proximity to the rising sun. Each new day, Mert would say, the sun cast its first rays on the land of the Abenaki before continuing its journey west. It was Mert's habit to take a dawn walk just to see the sun rise.

"I got some nice new sweetgrass. Found it down the mountain a ways when I was walking this morning. I thought I'd show Donna. She might try a basket now, you see. Since she found them copper beads. Wrote that paper."

"She might," Gwen agreed, smiling at Mert's old theme song. "But no, that was just me saying her name aloud. It was something Donna did that was helpful. But you can ask her when she gets home."

"I'll get it started, then. That's the hard part, getting started. Then she can take over. Sweetgrass is nice for a young woman." Mert shakingly poured himself a glass of grape juice, nodded at Gwen, and padded back into his room.

Now it was Leroy at the door, ready to go to Cabot. He was wearing a new blue shirt and boots—Camille's "estate" wasn't settled yet, but he was borrowing against it on his charge card. He wanted to stop by at a friend's house in Cabot. But first she wanted to get the disk copy to Ruth. She wanted it out of the house.

"We'll check the Laframboise hives first, then stop at the Willmarths'," she told Leroy.

"Out of the way, i'n' it?" said Leroy, slouching in the doorway, hands on his lean hips. He wore his jeans low: A north wind could blow them down. The thought amused her. "*If* you're going to Cabot?" he added. Leroy had been haunting the kitchen since Donna's return. And still the girl wouldn't glance in his direction.

"A little. But there's a shortcut to 116 from the Willmarths'. I've something I have to leave there. Anyway, it won't hurt to take another look at those hives, see how the new queens are doing."

Leroy looked nettled; he pursed his lips. "Can we get going, then?"

She didn't care for the cross way he'd spoken. "We can," she told him, "when I'm good and ready."

Eighteen

Ruth had read halfway through the file Emily had printed out for her and still hadn't found any real clues to a killer. She wanted to finish reading the printout before milking. There was some vague sense of time being important, as though something might explode if she didn't get those names, and soon. "Superstitious ass," she chided herself, and reached for a doughnut.

It was a fascinating paper, really, a significant one—such a tragedy that Camille hadn't lived to complete it. Those poems of Annette's! Camille had only printed four as far as she'd read, but they were powerful, passionate.

There are bars everywhere
on windows walls doors
they hold in my bones
they crush my heart.

The lines made her feel as though someone had punched her in the stomach. She wished now she'd begged a copy of Annette's poems from Pauline. If she had to go back there, she'd do just that—despite Pauline's warning that the poems were not for strangers' eyes.

The phone rang in the middle of her reading about Annette's

bartering her reproductive eggs for freedom. She reached for the receiver, still reading. "What did I have to lose," Annette had written at the age of, what—forty-three? "I'd had enough of men and their hungry penises. But I didn't like what they did to Nicole. That wasn't right. She was a good girl. She was 26, that bastard husband hardly there but she had the boy. And they did it to him. A four year old kid. A smart kid—beat me at dominoes when he was 3. How'd they justify that?"

Camille had added in parentheses: "*(The boy taken from Nicole & put in foster home—must find out where, what's happened to him since. I'll look up Lafrenière. According to Annette, the boy's abusive father "too proud" to be associated with a Godineaux. Too irresponsible, she means. She obviously loathes the fellow.)*"

"Ruthie," Colm was shouting into the receiver. "Will you talk to me? I know you're there, I can hear you breathing."

"Lafrenière," she said, feeling the excitement down to her toes. "Do you know any Lafrenières in Vermont? Though he might have left the state, we have to realize that."

"Ruthie, I don't know what in hell you're talking about. Will you come back to earth? Anyway, you're talking with your mouth full. Better watch those doughnuts, you'll get fat. Well, look, I'm calling because I've read the document. I mean, Olen made a printout—seems he'd promised Gwen. But Ruthie, Tilden Ball's our man—I really think so now. He's got motive, he's got means. We've got proof he was in her apartment. Not on the key—we still have to determine whose prints those are—but on the gum wrapper and on the window, where he must have raised it, climbed in. Not too bright, huh?"

"The document is what I'm talking about. Emily printed it out for me—Donna made a copy, but please, don't tell Olen that. And right near the end—I just came to it—is the name Lafrenière. Someone Camille was looking for. Someone who might have a motive to kill."

"Near the end where?" His voice sounded ingratiating, the tone you'd take with a stubborn child. She was piqued.

"It's the next-to-last page, Colm. And on the last page Camille made a list of people she wants to look up. Annette's on it.

And André—he's Annette's son. Oh—here it is again. Noel Lafrenière, Nicole's husband. The name we've been looking for!"

"That name's not on my printout. Mine ends with Annette's getting her tubes tied, or however they did it."

"What? There's nothing about the sterilization of the little boy—? A four-year-old, Colm, and they neutered him! How could a four-year-old give permission for that?"

"Maybe something wrong with the printer here," Colm excused. "It's always fouling up. Anyway, I never got that last page you got."

"Or"—she felt chilled—"Olen didn't want you to see it."

"Why wouldn't he want me to see it?"

"I don't know," she said. "Maybe—maybe because he wanted to be the one to track down this Lafrenière—if he's the killer. Olen could be running for some police office, who knows? Then he'd be the big cheese. Get all the credit."

Now Colm was laughing. She wanted to hit him. "If you won't be serious, I'm going to hang up," she said.

"Okay. Well, you may be right on that," he allowed. "Olen's been acting nuts lately. Brought in four more speeding tickets last night. The guys think he wants the top job here. Roy's talking retirement, you know."

"Roy Fallon's always talking retirement."

"This time I think he means it. He's been taking more time off. Giving Ashley jurisdiction over us. Olen's a good cop, but he's too gung ho for me. I don't want to kill myself chasing some speeder just so I can bring back a couple more bucks for the till."

"Okay, then," she said.

"Okay, what?"

"Okay, then, you'd better hustle. Get to this Lafrenière—the son, I mean, not the old father—before Olen gets there. So *you* can get the credit, my dear."

"Do you really mean that?" he said. His voice sounded tender.

"Mean what?"

"Calling me 'dear'?"

"Did I? A Freudian slip, then." She laughed.

"Anyway," he said, laughing himself, "you should be on the force, not me. And Ruthie . . ." He cleared his throat, ready to make a pronouncement. "Like I told you, I'm convinced Tilden Ball's our man. Those prints put him in the right place at the right time."

"What does that prove?" She was feeling perverse. "He might have just dropped that gum when he went in for a conference. Opened the window for her."

"That's what he claims, sure; says he picked up the gum wrapper, then dropped it again. Likely story! But the woman who lives in the other part of the house says she saw him going in there when Camille was out. Through a window, she says—she's sure he's the one she saw. It's all adding up, Ruthie. He was failing the course, for chrissake. Not exactly motivation for most students, but for a sick kid like Ball? 'I did it all for Dad,' he keeps saying. 'Dad wanted 'em off their land.' Jeez!"

"Sad," she said.

" 'Sad' isn't the word for it. Look, Ruthie, you can go after this Lafrenière, but don't count on me. I don't have time for it."

"All right, then, if you're so sure you have the right killer, I'll find Lafrenière myself."

"Ruthie, honey, can we slow down a minute? This is your lover you're talking to. Things aren't the same between us now, they never will be again."

"They won't?"

"Sweetheart," he said, and breathed heavily into the phone. She had to smile at his sentimentality. *She* had to be practical, didn't she? She had thirty-plus cows to milk. Young calves to feed. Tim was waiting for her. She'd put an awful load on him lately.

"Love you," Colm said finally, and gave a despairing sigh. "I'll be over at seven, okay? We can have some supper together? I'll bring something from the deli."

"Make it eight. I have to get to the library. They keep all the phone books there."

"Phone books?"

"To look up Lafrenières. That's a good place to start, don't you think?"

He groaned. "You are determined, aren't you? Suppose he doesn't have a phone."

"Quit throwing obstacles in the way. I'll see you at eight."

"I can spend the night?"

"Vic's here, Colm, you know that. He's still a kid."

"He'll have to know, then. This is the twenty-first century. He'll have to accept that Mom has a lover."

"He's not ready yet, Colm. He's still close to his father. He's still in school. We'll talk about it when you come."

"Tell him you're going to Montreal this weekend," he said. "If there's a Lafrenière anywhere, you'll find him in Montreal." He chuckled and hung up.

He might be right, she thought—that she should look in Canada. But if so, she'd go alone. She certainly wasn't going to beg Colm's help.

There was more bad news in the barn when she walked in. Hester Prynn, Zelda's offspring, who'd produced her first calf, was down with ketosis. Ruth knew the symptoms, it had been coming on slowly; she'd been too busy with everything else to prevent it. A drop in milk, body weight loss, poor appetite—signs of nervousness. A nervous cow! She could relate to that.

"Should we call the vet?" she asked Tim, who was finishing up the milking. Then he'd get ready, he said, to plow the south meadow. The earth wasn't quite dry enough yet for planting—the second week of May was the usual time.

"Naw, we can deal with it. She only calved two weeks ago, right? And she's a fat one. Eats like a hog. You ever watched her?" He attached the tubes onto an udder after Ruth disinfected the teats.

"Not really. I've had my eye on Elizabeth. Ever since she got stabbed that time, she's been skittery, off her feed."

Tim pushed his feed cap onto the back of his head. It said *STONE BROKE FARM*—he'd had it made up for a joke, after she facetiously mentioned the name. "Yep. We'll have to watch her. Anyway, see that Hester gets more niacin." He paused while the last four cows were milking. When he lowered his head, she saw how gray he was getting. You didn't notice people getting old when you saw them every day. A small gesture like a hat tipped back on the head could suddenly add years to a person's age.

"Dug up any more lately about Joey's relatives?" he asked casually. She knew he wanted the adoption to go through without some long-lost relative coming back to protest. The boy was almost of age, but Tim had his heart set on this adoption.

She told him about Pauline and Annette. "Joey's mother and great-grandmother," she said. "But you needn't worry. Annette's a centenarian, Pauline isn't interested in motherhood. Though you'll want to meet her, maybe. You and I might take a drive back there—between milkings, of course. But look, Tim, do you know any Lafrenières? One Noel Lafrenière—an abusive fellow, I'm afraid—is apparently Joey's grandfather." When Tim whistled: "Now, you needn't worry about *him*—he disappeared long ago. But we'd like to find him. Or one of his heirs anyway, his son. Someone who might, just might be involved with Camille Wimmet's death. I mean, we've only a hint as to why he would, but you know me, I work on instincts."

"Jesus. You think so? Poor Joey. The kid had ten strikes on him when he was born. His aunt a thief, his great-grandmother—"

"A poet. An amazing woman. Joey should be proud. His grandmother was a good woman, too. She worked her butt off at Papideau's farm. And who knows? Young Lafrenière might be a minister—or a politician." For some reason she thought of the famous scarlet A. Emily had read Hawthorne's novel last year in a high school English class—she'd named Zelda's calf Hester. It was a Puritan minister who'd gotten Hester Prynn pregnant and wouldn't—couldn't—tell. Emily was angry with him at the time; she always took the side of the female protagonist: Hester, Jane Eyre, Ophelia—who was "psychologically abused," she claimed, by Hamlet.

"Hey, Joey, you ever know a guy named Lafrenière? Back in your murky past?"

Joey was stomping into the barn with a chicken in his arms. "It almost got run over, Tim, see? Got a hurt foot."

"Just leave him. It'll get better on its own, I expect."

Ruth wanted no more chickens in the barn, but she couldn't run off a fowl with a hurt foot. Joey stroked the fluttering chicken. If there was any violence in the family, it hadn't come through to Joey. Ruth patted his arm. "You're a good guy," she said, and Joey giggled.

"So's him," he said, pointing at Tim.

"You're givin' me a swelled head," said Tim. "Don't know any Lafrenières, but I know a family named Bruneau. Tom Bruneau. He bowls with me. And he's complainin' 'cause his son just changed his name to Brown. It's 'cause he's marryin' this Protestant girl and he's Catholic and her family's not crazy 'bout that. And so the kid wants to change his name. His family's all choked up about it."

"Ridiculous, the bigots. Well, look, Tim. You can finish up here as soon as I'm done graining the heifers, can't you?" She fired the rations from a five-pound scoop. "I want to check the phone books, see how many Lafrenières I can find. Do you think I'm nuts doing all this?"

"Do you really want me to answer that?" he said, jumping back where the last cow, Oprah, was galloping out the door into a field muddy from last night's rain. "Shit," he said, looking at his pants, and Joey laughed.

"Shit, shit, shit! Good stuff," Joey crooned, and ran out after the cows to see that they went where he wanted them to go.

"An A, Mother, she gave me an A!" Donna was dancing in and out of the kitchen, hugging her sociology paper to her chest. She was feeling good today for the first time since the trauma in the forest. Tilden Ball was in jail—though there was talk of bail. But he wouldn't try anything now, she was sure of that. Why, he was under suspicion of strangling Ms. Wimmet! Had he really done that? Nights, in bed, she was certain of it—she remembered that little finger he could "kill" with. In the daytime, she wondered about Tilden's father, who was known to be angry at any teacher who'd fail his son. Not because of the boy, of course, but because it reflected poorly on Harvey himself.

Her mother was smiling now, too. "Remember, it was your Abenaki forebears who helped with that A. Speaking of which, there may still be relatives alive from that union. I'm thinking we should look them up."

"Sure," said Donna, who'd agree to anything today. "That'll be another paper. And I'm definitely planning to major in sociology, no shit."

"No what?" said her grandfather, coming into the room. He didn't approve of girls swearing, although Donna had heard a few hot words coming from him when his basketry wasn't going right.

Now he was pulling her by the elbow into his workshop. "I got some nice sweetgrass here. Smell," he urged, thrusting the grass under her nose, and it did smell nice, he was right. She smiled at him. But today she was too excited to sit down and weave a basket. Things were going right for a change. There'd been no more hate notes or graffiti on her bike, kids were gearing up for exams; the fraternity hoopla had calmed, although the campus was still in a defense mode, with a murder unsolved.

"Later," she told her grandfather. "Later, I'll try it, Grandpop, I promise. Not now."

She ran out into the yard. It was a gorgeous afternoon, the daffodils her mother had planted were in full bloom in the garden, an early pink tulip was out. The perfume filled her nose. There were bees in the pussy willows. She wished she could see the mountains, but the trees obscured her view. Well, if she couldn't see the mountains, she'd ride up into them. She felt fully aware of her surroundings today, like she was entering a new world.

Hopping on her bike, she pedaled up the road, toward the forest. This time she knew where she was going. If you'd almost drowned, get back in the pond and swim, her pragmatic father would advise.

En route she passed the Ball farm, saw no one there. She pedaled rapidly past and up to the edge of the forest. Leaning her bike against a white pine, she walked up the trail. The evergreens gave off a pungency that filled her with purpose. Squirrels and rabbits dashed past, birds rustled through the branches. Once she saw a raccoon; its beady eyes took her measure, and it dashed off. A gray fox raced across a scant yard in front of her, and she laughed out loud.

It was in a place like this, she thought, that her ancestor Isobel had played as a child, a place where no one told her what to do or when. No teachers, no fraternity boys, no officious neighbors. Only freedom, absolute freedom. An intimacy with the beasts of the forest. Isobel had had her choice, and the wilderness was where she'd elected to stay.

Donna thought of Shep Noble again, who had no choices at all anymore. She couldn't get him out of her mind. Shep's friends and coaches had liked him, their testimonials at the memorial service proved that. Had she gotten to know him, she might have made him realize that Indian girls were every bit as smart and feeling as white girls or boys, that they should be treated with dignity, as equals to boys and girls of any race. That females of any race or culture should be treated with respect.

One day she'd be a sociologist and devote her life to educating Indian girls, giving them the opportunities she'd had—for she was lucky, she'd never before realized how lucky. She wanted to learn more about her French ancestry, too. Camille Wimmet was a Franco-American—she'd been a role model.

Donna suddenly wanted to ride home and run in the house and hug her mother, tell her how much she appreciated and loved her. Her eyes watered to think of it; she raced back down the trail and climbed on her bike.

Someone was in her path as she pedaled around a curve in the road. She swerved and ran her bike off into a forsythia bush. "I'm sorry," she told the bush, and tried to straighten the limbs.

"Soh-wy?" said Ralphie, standing there, looking down on her. He seemed concerned, and she smiled. "I'm okay," she said. "I didn't want to hit you, that's all." Ralphie was the best of the three boys, in her opinion. If you asked him an honest question, you got an honest answer. If he could answer the question at all, that is. He put a hand on her arm as she got up, handed her a broken stem of yellow blossoms.

"Ralphie sorry," he said, speaking of himself, as always, in the third person.

One of her pedals had fallen off; it lay there in the grass. She would have to walk the bike back to her house. It hadn't been right since Tilden ran her off the road. She shivered, remembering the night.

"Shiny," said Ralphie, pointing at her silver earrings. They were a present from her father, made by an Abenaki woman up in Swanton. "Pup-pies," said Ralphie, touching one of them.

"They're bears, Ralphie. That's my father's clan." She didn't say *her* clan, too, although she supposed it was. She'd have to give more thought to that.

"Nice," Ralphie said, "shi-ny."

"Nice and shiny," she agreed.

Ralphie soon tired of her earrings and went over to sit on a rock. He was taking things from his pocket, spreading them out on the grass.

"Shiny," he said, "come see." He held out a handful of objects. She saw a lucent stone, a dead orange caterpillar, a tarnished silver earring. "For you," he said, dangling the earring between his thumb and forefinger. "Pretty. Take it."

She shook her head. She didn't need a tarnished earring. But he insisted; he got up and pushed it into her pocket. "Ralphie find it. For you."

"Thank you. That's very sweet of you." She walked her bike back down to her house. The phone was ringing when she entered the kitchen; she dashed in to pick it up.

It was Uncle Olen with a message for her mother. "Tell her I've made a printout of that file for Colm Hanna. Your mother asked me to."

"Oh, you needn't have bothered," Donna told him. "I made a copy myself. She could have had that."

Olen was quiet. He was always quiet when he was annoyed for some reason. But how had she known he'd have to go to extra trouble for her mother? "You have it there, then," he said finally, "at the house?"

"It's in my file box."

"Good," he said. "Keep it there until I can get over. It's evidence, Donna. If the wrong person should get his hands on it—well, you know."

"Don't worry, Uncle Olen," she said, wanting to end the conversation. She had homework to do. "No one will touch it except myself."

But when she looked in the file box after she'd hung up, the copy wasn't there. Her mother, she supposed, had given it to Ruth Willmarth. Now Uncle Olen would be pissed.

This was exactly what had happened, she discovered fifteen minutes later when she was fixing herself a hot chocolate with whipped cream, ready to go over some history notes. Ruth Willmarth called to say she had the disk, Emily had printed it out. She had another question for Gwen—could Gwen call her back?

"I'll tell her. Say hi to Emily, okay? I suppose she got her grade back on the soc paper?"

"Oh, yes, she got a B-minus. Now she's blaming me because I gave her the material. I'm afraid I didn't spend enough time with her." Ms. Willmarth didn't ask what Donna's grade was. And of course Donna didn't tell her, although she was bursting with the good news.

But, "An A, I got an A!" she sang to herself as she reached into her pocket and pulled out the silver earring where it had stuck into her hip. She examined it. It was a fairly anonymous shape, like a crescent moon, or sun, or even a plump animal, like a woodchuck.

"Shiny, shiny," she said, smiling, and, feeling silly, she dropped it into the file box.

Ruth was at her wit's end, she told Colm when he arrived at eight. There were no Lafrenières in the Addison or Rutland County directories, and only three in the Chittenden. When she phoned them, she drew a blank. One was a single girl, a UVM college student; another was a young couple come lately from

Iowa; the third was a disconnected number. "That's probably the one," she told Colm. "And the fellow's taken off for Cambodia."

"There are lots more counties. And there's Montreal," he reminded her softly. They were sitting in the living room. Vic was upstairs doing homework. "We could go to my house?" he suggested.

"With your father roaming about? Lifting a knowing eyebrow, trying very obviously to stay out of the way but never does because he wants grandchildren? You've told me that, Colm. He doesn't care who you sleep with, he just wants a grandkid. Well, I've got news for him. At my age, I don't think I could get pregnant if I tried every night. And even if I could," she added, thinking of her cows and their artificial insemination, "I wouldn't want to. It's too late. Too late."

"It's okay, honey," he said. "We've got your three. They'll do. Dad could be a surrogate granddad. Pete's away," he reminded her—not that he had to. She hadn't seen Pete for months now. He'd come up a couple of times to see the children, but he and Violet had stayed at the Branbury Inn. He'd talked off and on about wanting weekend visitations with the boy, but it was obvious that the girlfriend wouldn't like that. Now Violet had a bit part in an off-Broadway play; it kept the couple in New York. And thank God for that. She'd had enough of Violet last winter, stuck with Pete in Branbury during a four-day ice storm.

She wished Pete would marry, as though his commitment would somehow free her to be on her own, make her own life choices. Was she still hoping that Pete would come back? She didn't think so. But then, who knew her own heart?

Needing to get back to business, sitting up straight on the shabby sofa, she said, "What does the name Lafrenière mean anyway? I took a year of French in high school, can't remember a word now, except *oui*, *non*, and *Où est la bibliotêcque, s'il vous plaît*? We had to learn those foolish phrases. Much good they do me now! I never did learn the French word for barn."

Colm had taken Spanish and flunked it twice; he had a lousy

memory, he said. He sipped his Guckenheimer—he kept a bottle in her pantry; he was moving in, inch by inch. He even kept clean socks on the pantry shelf—she'd threatened to make a stew out of them. He recalled that *la* meant "the." "Big help, huh?" He took back the inch she'd withdrawn on the sofa.

"Emily has a dictionary. She took French in high school. I'll look it up."

"You're wasting time, Ruthie."

"Wasting time because you've got the finger on Tilden Ball?"

"Maybe, but it's not that. You know what I'm talking about." He put a hand on her knee. She smilingly removed it and ran upstairs after the dictionary.

"I'm doing it," Vic called out, on the defensive. "I'm almost finished with the math. Then can I watch TV?"

"For half an hour," she said. "Then bed. You know the rules."

She heard him mutter, "This kid" could stay up till ten, schoolnights, "that one" till eleven. It was the old story. But those kids didn't have early morning barn chores.

"Nine-thirty, and that's *it*," she hollered, and ran back downstairs.

"The root *frêne* means a kind of tree. An ash tree," she quoted. "Lafrenières must've grown ash trees somewhere back in time."

"Ash trees?"

"Ash. That's a familiar root." She told Colm what Tim had said about his friend's son changing his name. "So he wouldn't be embarrassed by it when he wanted to marry a WASPy kind of girl. So the in-laws could keep up their WASPy reputation."

Colm was silent a moment. He rattled the ice in his glass. She disliked the sound of rattling ice. Her own father had been something of an alcoholic. Her mother had lived with rattling ice most of her too-short life.

"I know an Ashe in town," Colm said. "He's a jewelry craftsman—great guy, wouldn't swat a mosquito. There's an Ashworth just moved here from Massachusetts, a hockey coach—I'll check him out for you. I ran into an Ashby in real estate—from Winooski, wants a piece of land in this area. He's a musician."

He frowned, rolled his tongue around in his cheek. "Then there's Ashley. Olen Ashley. My colleague, a highly respected cop. A Freemason—pretty high up in the ranks. As a cop he's ready to kill anyone who breaks the law."

"Ready to kill."

"You know what I mean. He's a fanatic. I've told you that."

"Highly respected, you said."

"That's what I said."

"But he might have deleted the last page of Camille's print-out?"

"Might've been a printer error. I told you, Ruthie, we've had trouble with that printer."

"Might not have been the printer. He might have deliberately deleted it. So we wouldn't see it."

She jumped up off the couch, a fine layer of dust springing up in her wake—when did she have time to clean the house? He grabbed for her leg and missed.

She waved him away. She needed to make a phone call.

Nineteen

"Olen?" Gwen was surprised to find him in the kitchen, seated at her computer. She hadn't heard him knock.

He glanced up, his face the color of eggplant. "I came for that copy of the disk. You didn't tell me there was another copy, Gwen. We can't have it lying about where just anyone can see it." He held up the plastic file box. "Find it for me, will you, please?"

She couldn't understand why it was so terribly important when he already had a copy. "You gave one to Colm Hanna," she reminded him, "knowing he'd show it to Ruth."

"Please, Gwen." He was still holding out the file box. His face was resolute.

"I didn't know Donna had made another copy." She was angry now at Olen: for barging into her house so familiarly, for being upset with her for something she had nothing to do with. She glanced through the files. *SOC PAPER, ENGLISH LIT PAPER, HISTORY NOTES, CAPTIVE.* There were eight disks, but none of them Camille's.

"Only this," she said, trying to smile through her pique. "Now, what on earth is this doing in here?" It was a silvery earring, tarnished, slightly bent out of shape as though someone had stepped on it.

Olen ignored the earring; he was on a single track. He grabbed back the file box, fumbled through with shaky fingers. "She said it was here."

"Oh, *that* copy," said Gwen, realizing; she was feeling out of sorts from Olen's persistence. "I gave that to Ruth. I forgot, that's all, so much going on. I suppose I shouldn't have, but you were planning to make a copy anyway, Olen, right? You knew Colm would show it to Ruth. So what have I done that's so bad?" She stuck her hands on her hips, stared him in the eye. She wasn't going to let him browbeat her.

His eyes were a cloudy gray, his face like nightshade; he looked as though any second he'd reach out poisonous roots. He was in his blue dress uniform, coming from or going somewhere "important." His gray hair was slicked back on his head, belying his inner distress.

"Olen, did you lose an earring?" she teased.

But already he was out the door without a response or a good-bye. She heard a car door slam, an engine grind. Tires peeled off down the drive and out onto the road.

She looked at the earring, tried to flatten it out in her hand. It looked familiar, shaped like an animal—a bear, maybe. One of her men, or a friend of Russell's or Donna's, might have lost it. She must remember to ask. The back side was greenish, as though it had lain a long time in the grass. Perhaps Leroy had found it, mowing. Or Donna. She put it on top of the computer.

The phone rang and it was Ruth, asking about a Lafrenière, a Lafrenière who might have changed his name to Ashley. What did she know about Olen Ashley's background?

"*Olen's* background?" Gwen said, pouring a cup of coffee with her free hand. Why was Ruth asking this? Why would she want to know about Olen?

"Just an oddball question," Ruth soothed. "I'm trying, well, to think of everyone who might have been connected with Camille. We know that Olen was assigned to investigate the break-ins at her office."

It took Gwen a moment to recover. Her Olen, under suspicion? Unthinkable! It couldn't be Olen involved. "No, no, that's impossible," she said, thinking of Olen's almost maniacal regard for the law. Lafrenière—the name was familiar, but not in connection with Olen, she told Ruth. She'd seen the name somewhere, but couldn't think where. As for Olen's personal life, well, her memory brought up a few pieces of his past that he, or her dad, had told her about.

"For one thing, he was always looking for a maternal grandfather, someone named Goodpasture. He was descended from some Englishman who fought in the Revolution. Olen wants to join a group called Sons of the American Revolution. He's an intensely patriotic man, Ruth. He's a Master Mason, and that's a very big deal. I don't hold with all that secret stuff: the handshake, the symbols and signs. But they do admit men of all faiths. And they hang together, take oaths to protect each other."

"Do they admit women?" Ruth asked.

"Oh, no, it's strictly a fraternity. Donna doesn't care for that—she'd tease my dad—he was a Mason, too. But they do good things for people. The Shriners, who are some kind of offshoot, give millions to cure sick children."

"Oh, yes—they're the ones who scoot around in those funny little cars. They were in the Memorial Day parade, throwing candy. Vic loved them."

"Right. Brownie, too. Well, I suppose that's why Olen's a Mason and a cop, he has this thing about making the world safe for us to live in. It goes along with his trust in the great American system of justice. Dad used to rib him about that. My father didn't have quite such a blind faith in the system."

"Did Olen say anything about his mother? Who she was? Where she came from?"

"He never mentioned her to me. I don't suppose he knew. He has only what his adoptive mother told him to go on."

"He was adopted? Was Ashley her name?"

"It was his, I understand. I only know that he was adopted as a child by a couple who'd known the parents."

"Are the adoptive parents still alive? Would they have told him the truth about that revolutionary ancestor?"

"They died years ago. I never met them. But I don't know

why they'd lie about that ancestor. Unless to make him feel good about himself. There was always this need to be *somebody*. That's why he latched on to the Freemasons, I suppose; it gave him self-esteem. Pride. I never cared for that quality in him. That terrible pride."

She sipped her coffee; it was getting tepid. "Olen was good to my father—he saved his life once, did I tell you that? Dad was chopping down an old oak; it toppled toward him, took him by surprise. He gave the sign—the Grand Hailing Sign of Distress, I think they call it. Olen grabbed him in time—he risked his own life! I'll always be grateful to Olen for that. I think he'd give his life for Donna and Brownie, too, I really do."

"And for you?"

Gwen gave a soft laugh. "Possibly. Yes. He's stubborn that way. Loyal, you know."

"Is it possible that Ashley's not his real name?" Ruth persisted. "That his father could have been French-Canadian? Lafrenière? That's the name on the disk, Gwen. Not on the disk Olen copied for Colm—a page was deleted on that one. It was on the copy you gave me, the copy Donna made from the original."

Gwen was quiet a moment. She dropped into a chair as if someone had suddenly pushed her. She held the receiver close to her ear, in two hands. She felt she was betraying Olen, talking about him like this. But then, she rationalized, Olen himself would put justice over loyalty, wouldn't he?

She took a deep breath, told Ruth about Olen's frenetic visit, how upset he was at not finding the copy. How he'd rushed out, as though obsessed. "He didn't take the earring." She cleared her throat, coughed up phlegm.

"Earring?"

"Oh, a tarnished one Donna or Leroy found in the grass somewhere. I'm sure it has nothing to do with either death." Her throat felt like gravel now. The grounds had seeped into her coffee.

"Do you know where Olen was going?" Ruth asked. "When he raced out like that?"

"I've no idea where he's gone. Maybe to England. After that

famous ancestor." She tried to laugh, but it came out a gravelly cough.

After she'd hung up, Gwen downed a full glass of water, then slumped back in a chair, feeling exhausted. Yet it hadn't been a hard day at all. She'd visited four farms and every hive had been intact. There'd been no more damage—beyond the usual swarmings, trachial mites, robber bees—not since Tilden had confessed to the malice. Yet no one in her household had died because of it. There had been cruelties, yes, to the bees and her family, but they'd all survived. She'd destroyed the package of killer bees Tilden had left in the Balls' hunting cabin.

Tilden could have killed Camille Wimmet, yes, she felt that now. After all, he'd been failing Camille's class. And he did drugs, Donna had told her that. The drugs, whatever they were, could change a Dr. Jekyll into a Mr. Hyde.

She was glad when Russell called—briefly, because he was having dinner with two Mohawk men he'd met during the latest reenactment and was already late to meet them. She asked him about the name Lafrenière and he said he knew a fellow of that name up in Quebec. "A mellow guy—eighty-four years old. Wanna drive up some weekend and meet him?"

She didn't, but she'd tell Ruth about the man. She didn't tell Russell about a possible link with the name Ashley, though. The less Russell heard Olen's name, the better—although he'd approved of the way Olen "took care" of Tilden Ball. The two men seemed to have arrived at a kind of truce.

Finally, "Love ya!" Russell bellowed, and the phone went dead.

Next Donna arrived, and there were questions and explanations all over again about the extra copy. "I didn't know you'd taken it to the Willmarths'," the girl said. "Not till after I hung up and found it was gone. You should have told me." Donna was "done in"; she flung her jacket and book bag down on a chair. She had a "mountain" of work to do. "I'll need the computer. You're not planning on using it?"

"Not tonight." Gwen held up the earring. "This was in the

file box. What was it doing in there anyway? Where'd it come from?"

Donna laughed, tossed back her hair. It was looking especially lustrous; she'd just washed it in lemon and beer, she said. "Ralphie gave it to me. It was part of his shiny collection. I don't know where he found it. Why do you ask?"

"Oh, just curious, that's all." Gwen dropped the earring into a pocket. The nightshade death had been called an accident. She didn't want to pursue it. She didn't like Ralphie's talk about shiny men.

Donna shrugged and adjusted a gold bead earring where it had gotten twisted on its stem. She was at the refrigerator now. "I didn't have any supper. I was in the library. Exams are coming up and I still have two more papers. Well, short ones, but even so . . ."

"Can you give me a half hour in the barn? The place is a mess, and Leroy's got a cold again. I swear he's become more and more of a hypochondriac."

"Oh, Mother. Can't you? I'm starving. I've got this Frost paper due tomorrow. We have to analyze 'The Death of the Hired Man.' I haven't even read it yet."

Gwen gave up. If things were to be done around here, she'd have to do them. What was the point of having children anyway? Brownie was no better. He'd gobbled down his dinner and then she'd had to drive him to a friend's birthday party. In a couple of hours she'd have to go pick him up again. She supposed she should talk to Ralphie Ball, find out where he'd found the earring. After all, it could be evidence of some kind. But then she might run into old Harvey, and she didn't want to face that. Though he'd been lying low lately; there'd been no more calls about her selling land—not with Tilden a murder suspect. Did she hope they'd find the boy guilty? Or did she just want to keep Olen's name untarnished? In a way, she loved him, didn't she? Olen was family.

Gwen stopped by her hives on the way to the barn. All was contentment here, the bees busy at their tasks of gathering early nectar. By June the clover would be in full bloom, and the alfalfa;

the bees would be working like madwomen, they would keep the coffers full.

"Good work," she told a pair of honeybees murmuring in her newly opened tulips. She felt they could hear her, that they liked her approval. Bees were like people in so many ways: their complex social structure, their language. Through their special sense of smell they could recognize each other and their queen, tell one another where the food was, alert one another to danger. If they left a stinger in a person, Gwen felt, it was to mark the enemy, because the alarm odor would continue to be released, no matter where the enemy fled.

"Help us to find the truth," she pleaded, "whether we like the answers or not. Shep Noble's enemy, and Camille's."

The bees went humming along at their task.

When Ruth called the police department, a woman's voice informed her that Olen Ashley was off duty—she might try his apartment on Cross Street. But Ruth was not about to go there alone. "I don't know the man," she told Colm, who was sitting in her kitchen devouring her doughnuts. "You know him, you can tell him we just want to ask questions about a Lafrenière?"

"Uh-huh," said Colm, "I'm your fall guy. Look, Ruthie, I don't want to go to Olen Ashley's apartment. I don't want to ask questions about a Lafrenière. He's my colleague, for Pete's sake."

Now Colm's arms were folded, he was staring at the floor—it was a crunch of crumbs from Vic's evening snack. The boy ate like the birds at her feeder, kernels dropping as they swallowed the sunflower seeds.

"I called Emily to babysit," she told him, ignoring his attitude. Colm would come around, just so he didn't lose face. It was a game; she'd have to butter him up, offer a prize.

"Just this once, Colm, I can't do it without you. If nothing pans out, I'll give up on the Lafrenière quest, help you with Tilden Ball. Maybe there's French blood there, too. Maybe there's a Lafrenière in their past."

"Now you're talking sense," he said, unfolding his arms, sighing, then going to the phone. "Dad?" he said to his father. "I can't come home now. I'll help with that cremation later to-night. . . . Look, Dad, the guy's dead, he's in no hurry. I've got something else to do—it's for Ruth. . . . No, Dad, I'm not mak-ing love to her—not at the moment. . . . Why not? Well, I don't know why not. Ask her. I'll call when I can, Dad." He hung up, grimaced at Ruth.

"He didn't really ask you that. If you were making love."

"He did. It's his dearest wish, I've told you. He says Mother wanted me married. So *he* wants me married. In his lifetime, he says. I've got a responsibility to him, Ruthie."

"Let's go," she said, ignoring the responsibility part. "We'll take my truck. Your car sounded like a freight car when you pulled in. If Olen's guilty of anything, he'd be out the back door in seconds."

"Sure, Ruthie," he said, placating her. "Why not? I'm prac-tically out of gas anyway."

Vic was surprised to see a policeman when he opened the door. "Uh-oh," he said, thinking of his mother's hemp and the trash barrel down back—Vic didn't like her burning trash, it wasn't good for the environment. They'd been talking a lot about the environment lately in school. It would serve his mother right if she got caught.

The man was smiling, a nervous kind of smile; he kept shift-ing his weight. "It's all right, son," he said. "I just dropped in to see your mother. Nothing to worry about." Vic saw him glancing about the kitchen, his eyes coming to rest on Emily's PC. "She home, son?"

"Gone off," Vic told him. "With Colm Hanna. You know him? He's a cop, too."

"Yes, yes, I do. I was looking for him as well. Do you know where they went?"

Vic shrugged. He wanted to get back to his program. He was watching *Jeopardy*. A man with a bronze-colored mustache was really raking in the money. Vic would like to go on *Jeopardy* himself one day. He could buy a humongous telescope with the money he'd make just answering questions. He'd help his mother pay off what she owed the bank. All you had to do was answer the questions right. Sometimes Vic knew the answers when the contestants didn't—like, 'What novel did the character Eustacia Vye appear in?' Heck, Eustacia was one of his mother's cows. She came right out of Thomas Hardy's *Return of the Native*. Vic hadn't read it, but he knew the title.

The man repeated his question, and Vic said, "Looking for something, I don't know. Police business, I guess."

A vein bulged in the man's neck, his cheeks pinkened, and Vic wondered if he should offer a glass of water. Back in the living room he heard the audience cheer and he decided not to offer the water after all; he wanted to get back to the program. "I'll tell Mom you were looking for her. Unless you want to wait here?"

"Oh, no," the man said, gripping his hands together. "I'll get ahold of her later. I'm on my way out of state."

He was turning to go when the door opened; Vic saw him jump. Jeezum. It was Joey, thumping noisily in, staring openly at the cop. He would have seen the police car outside. He probably came in for a close look at the uniform. Joey was crazy about uniforms. Colm Hanna never wore one, but he'd look better if he did—this was Vic's personal opinion.

"I never rode in a police car," Joey said, fingering the man's buttons, gazing up into his face.

The man started to pull away, then took a breath and smiled. "Maybe one day," he said. "But I have to go now, on business."

"Out of state," Vic informed Joey, who looked disappointed.

The door opened again and it was Tim. Vic would never get back to his program now. He could hear the audience yelling and he'd bet the guy won a million dollars. Lucky guy. He was a minister, too, he'd said. What did a minister need a million dollars for?

The policeman stepped back. With Tim, it was like a whole barnful of cows just walked in. That was one way to get the man out of here. You could see from the way his nose twitched that he was smelling it, too.

"I can't leave yet, we got a sick calf," Tim told Joey.

"But Tim, I got my job," Joey whined, sticking his hands on his hips. "I gotta get there, Tim. Maybe he could take me?" He pointed at the cop.

The man was halfway out the kitchen door when Tim asked, "Officer? You heading downtown? Joey here needs a ride, it's his night at Greg's Market. I can't take him, I got a sick calf."

Vic saw the policeman put a hand to his nose, like the smell was too much for him. Or maybe it was Tim's question. Himself, Vic wouldn't have asked. Cops were busy. They had speeders to chase, con men to capture—that killer that was on the loose around here. That worried Vic, too. The kids in his class talked about it all the time. Yes, it might be interesting to be a cop; Vic would think about that. Would he turn his own mother in? Well, probably not. But he'd give her a good talking to about that hemp.

"Greg's Market," Joey was saying, "I gotta go there. I pick up carts and stuff. I missed last time. They say, 'Joey, you get here on time or you lose the job.' "

Joey squeezed out the door ahead of the man. Vic knew he'd jump right into the police car, that was Joey. Joey was missing something upstairs, he didn't read all the signals people gave out. Vic liked him, though, the guy helped around the place.

"Well, just to Greg's Market," the policeman said to Tim. "It's out of the way; I'm on my way east of here. But okay."

"He'll be thrilled," Tim said, following the others out. "Thrilled to ride in a police car. Just drop him at the main entrance, Officer. He won't give you any trouble."

The door shut behind Tim, and a moment later Vic heard the police car peel off. He went back to his program. But when he plopped back down on the couch, the commercial came on. Loud. The program was over. "Jeezum," he said, disgusted, and headed back into the kitchen to make himself a sundae: vanilla ice cream with chocolate sauce and a maraschino cherry on top. His mouth watered.

Only there weren't any cherries in the refrigerator. Some days a kid couldn't win.

* * *

The place was ablaze with lights, but there was no answer when Ruth banged on the door. Olen wasn't home. "What now?" Ruth asked.

"We go home," he said, turning back.

"Hold on a minute. Check the windows. There might be one open." He still didn't move and she ran around back.

"You can't do that," he said, following her, "you can't just break in. We don't have a warrant."

She'd discovered a bedroom window that was open an inch, enough to squeeze her fingers under. It was a warm night. A light rain was misting her hair. "See? We don't have to break in after all." She shoved it wide.

Colm said, "Jeez, that's funny. He's a stickler down at the station for turning out lights, shutting windows when it rains."

"He would've left in a hurry, that Noel Lafrenière."

"What! You don't know that. About Lafrenière."

"Ten bucks on it, Colm. Think about the name 'Olen'." She climbed through the window, scraping her elbow on the splintery sill. She was glad to be inside where it was dry. Colm followed, with a "Jesus! I shouldn't be doing this, Ruthie."

It was a spare bedroom in the literal sense of the word: a double bed with a plain pine headboard, a pine bureau, nondescript wooden chair, a closet. Clothes were spread out helter-skelter on the bed as though he'd been in a hurry to leave. He had to be wearing his dress uniform, Colm observed, because it wasn't in the closet. A day uniform was hanging there, though. And in a corner, apart from his shirts and pants: a dark jacket and a white apron, fringed and trimmed with badges and symbols, a pair of pristine white gloves pinned to it. She recalled Gwen saying he was a Freemason. She'd seen pictures of Masons in the local paper, wearing those fancy aprons.

The living room was equally spare. An uncomfortable-looking black vinyl couch, a hard-backed rocking chair, a couple of massive mission chairs, a large oak desk littered with papers, a small oval blue rug on the hardwood floor. Yes, it was a man's apartment. If Olen had had any women on and off, there were no signs. He'd been married once, Gwen had told her, but the female touch was gone now.

Colm shuffled through a pile of papers on the desk, held one up. "Sons of the American Revolution," he read. "Here's an application from the New Hampshire chapter. Why New Hampshire?"

"I don't know. Maybe there isn't one in Vermont."

"Dated, um—1994? Jeez, what's it still doing on his desk?"

"A reminder of who he might be? Hoped to be?"

"Ruthie, there's nothing here about a Lafrenière. Let's go, before he comes back. He could shoot first, then ask questions! I have to work with the guy. He could be our next chief."

"Just a minute." Ruth held up a genealogical book entitled *The Goodpastures of America*. There was no Lafrenière in the index. She wandered into the entryway, plucked a wrinkled map off the floor. "Map of New Hampshire," she called back to Colm. She unfolded it; a town in the central area was circled in red. She gave a shout. "Andover, Colm. Look! That's where he's gone. To Andover. Looking for Annette."

"Whoa, there, woman. Aren't you jumping to conclusions? How would he know she's in Andover? And why?"

"She could be a relative. He could be the son of a Noel Lafrenière who got a Godineaux pregnant. He's, let's see, in his late fifties now? Sixty? So Annette could be his grandmother." She refolded the map. "But what do you suppose he'd want from her?"

"To do her in?" He was smiling, playing along with her, she knew the look. "He's been hanging around the Woodleaf place, you said. He could have heard about our going there."

"I suppose Gwen could have said something. He was there when I called her about going to Andover." Now she was really worried. If she'd put that old lady's life in danger . . .

"Ruthie, cool it. I'm leaving. You can stay here and get caught if you want to. Ashley'll have you arraigned for breaking and entering."

"You'll have to walk, then," she reminded him. "I've got the car keys. The only way to find out," she said, as much to herself as to Colm, "is to go there."

"Tonight? But I'm supposed to help Dad cremate a guy. And Emily won't like it, either."

She considered. "No, she won't. But she'll do her homework and go to bed. I'm her source of milk and meat, she'll do what I say. Your dad has a fellow he can call on to help, hasn't he? Come on, Colm. You might be right. He really could kill her."

"Hey, I was kidding. Why would he want to do that? You haven't got any proof."

It was true. They'd broken into a policeman's apartment—a policeman with a sterling reputation, as far as she knew. What reason did they have? What evidence? Just a name, a hunch. A deleted page from Camille's disk.

"To keep her from talking, maybe?" Colm was interested now, he had her hands in his, was squeezing them, smiling at her. Placating her, yes, but respecting her concerns. "Her and Pauline—though he may not know about Pauline yet. He may not have known where they were till now."

"To keep them from telling the world he's a Lafrenière, not an Ashley, right? To keep them from telling *us*. He doesn't know that we know."

"*Olen* . . ." Colm mused. "Switch the letters around—if the son had the father's first name—you've got *Noel*. Hey!"

"See?" she said. She'd already figured it out.

Colm was hooked now, she could see that. He said, "We'd better damn well find out before somebody else gets killed."

She followed him out through the bedroom window, dropped to the ground with a thud. It was still misting; she couldn't see the house next door for the fog—a fog that matched her brain. "We'll have to stop at the farm first, Colm. You can call your dad. I have to see to Vic. Ask Tim to stay till Emily gets there."

"No so loud. You want the landlady to overhear us? Call the cops?"

"But you are a cop."

"Never mind. Just get in the car. I'm driving."

"Not my pickup, you're not. Get in the passenger seat, mister. I'm driving."

Twenty

The brakes screeched as Olen paused at a stop sign in New London. He'd gotten off the thruway too soon. It would cost him an extra twenty minutes to get to Andover. No one was coming in either direction, but out of habit he waited, to be sure. The boy was in the back, asleep. Greg's Market had been out of the way, it would have cost him a good fifteen minutes to backtrack; he was on police business, he told the boy. And when the boy clapped his hands and pleaded, "Can I come, Officer? Please? Can Joey Godineaux help?" Olen had kept going. He didn't know why—it was the shock of the name, maybe—Godineaux. Afterward, driving up over Bread Loaf Mountain, he was sorry he'd said yes. The boy was talking nonstop, nonsense. At the foot of the mountain, though, at the turn onto Route 100, the kid fell, thankfully, asleep.

Olen was on his way to find his grandmother, Annette Godineaux. He'd long ago heard from his foster mother that she was living in New Hampshire—no one knew where. He'd assumed that by this time she'd be dead, like his mother—he'd read about Nicole Godineaux's death in the local paper, felt only surprise, maybe relief. He'd traced her to that Bridport farm but never went to see her. She'd never bothered to look him up, had she? She'd given him away. He recalled little about his father except the name Noel Lafrenière, passed on to him, along with his father's allergies. Well, there had been men in the house, he remembered that. Some of them mean to him: he recalled a cigarette burn, bruises he woke up with on his face, chest, and arms. Not his father, no.

When he turned eighteen he'd switched around the letters in his first name, changed the surname to Ashley, and moved to Burlington. He worked his way through a year at the university, got a job as a rookie cop. Married and divorced—she wanted kids, he couldn't give her any, he couldn't tell her why. He'd transferred to Branbury. A new man, a clean record. He met Donald Woodleaf—he'd saved Woodleaf's life that time. It had felt good to do that. Gwen was just a kid then, nine or ten. But she knew, she saw. He had a family now.

Hearing Annette's name in Gwen's kitchen had sent a series of shock waves through him. Annette, his grandmother—still alive . . . his sister Pauline, living with the old woman? He'd kept track of Pauline awhile through police records—she was a suspect in their father's death. He'd howled when he read that! She'd disappeared, probably into drugs, he figured, dead from an overdose. By then he had a reputation, he was a police lieutenant—he didn't need any relationship with a murder suspect. He was a Master Mason, men looked up to him. Women, too: Gwen. What would she think if she knew he came from a family of degenerates?

"Where we now?" the kid said in the backseat, waking up.

"Almost there," he said. "Keep quiet, now. I got to concentrate on my driving. I don't want to miss the next turn."

Every ticket he gave, every break-in he went after, every drug case he busted—it was all to purge those lawless Godineauxs out of his life. To prove he was smart, clean—no stains on Olen Ashley. He was a success, a success!

Then one night he picked up that college kid for speeding. Found his name on the ID: Shepard Perkey Noble. Perkey—an all-too-familiar name. He was stunned. It was Eleanor Perkey had come busting into his mother's trailer that day back in the thirties, nosing around, asking questions, getting them on the list of degenerates. Degenerates! And him, a kid. Christ Almighty.

The boy, Noble—bombed, stoned—told him, yeah, his grandmother'd been a social worker in these parts. She'd gone to Branbury College, yeah. The kid had family records, he thought he might use them for his sociology paper. Get him an A, absolutely. He could use an A. His grades weren't so hot. "I'm an athlete," he'd said, preening, flapping his wings, a young rooster. "That's why I'm here. I play baseball. Had a .300 batting average in prep school."

Olen released him—with a stiff fine. It wasn't the first time, he found out, that the boy had been caught drinking, taking drugs, making a racket in the fraternity. Olen despised those college boys. They were privileged, they thought they owned the town. He'd doubled the fine.

Then that night coming back from the Masons, hearing the motorcycle, seeing Donna on the back, he'd followed them up the mountain, worried about the girl. He'd parked on the road, walked up, heard Donna cry out. But then he saw the Boulanger kid intercede, saw Donna run to her house. He left, came back hours later; found Noble on his back in the nightshade, drunk. Who dragged him there? Leroy? Probably. On an impulse he'd turned him over, rubbed his face in the stuff. Served him right, he'd thought, the bastard. Let him sweat it out.

But Jesus, he didn't think it would kill him! He didn't know the kid was an asthmatic.

He was sweating himself now, he turned up the air-conditioning. Someone was behind him, honking.

"Where we at *now*?" Joey said. "This Greg's Market?"

"No, it's not Greg's Market," he snapped. "The sign says Andover, two miles." He supposed the boy couldn't read, he had some missing links. Olen didn't like that. It reminded him of the bad seeds in the family, the degenerates. Siblings sleeping together, the poverty, the overcrowding. Breeding degenerates. He felt the bile come up in his throat. He'd slept in a bed with his mother up to the time she was caught shoplifting, thrown in Brookview that last time, and him with her. That's when they did it to him, just a kid.

And she knew, that college professor. He'd gone into her office that afternoon, after she'd called the station saying it had been vandalized. She told him what had been on her screen, her paper. Her paper about the eugenics project—someone might have copied the work, she said. The words hit him like a rock. For a time he couldn't speak. When he pulled himself together, he told her he'd find out who did it, who stole the work. One thing led to the next, like a waterfall, the water cascading down, rolling him over and over, among the rocks.

His one thought then, his single purpose in life, was to destroy that work. No matter what it took.

And now he had the disk. He knew the worst. And so did that farm woman, Willmarth. Bad luck that Donna had made a copy! And Colm Hanna—a fellow cop.

The kid began talking again, gibberish, something about Tim, cows, his job at Greg's Market. Would Olen take him back now. Christ! He should have made the kid get out in Branbury, he could only be in the way here.

"Not now. I have business, I told you. Stay in the car and keep quiet."

"But I hafta go peepee."

"Jesus," Olen said.

"I swear he said east, he was headin' east. New Hampshire? Boston?" Tim said when Ruth ran into the barn, begging him to stay just another half hour till Emily got home. "I asked him to drop Joey off at the store. But then the store called, said he hadn't checked in. And when I called the police station, they said Ashley had called in sick. He didn't look sick when I saw him."

"How long ago did they leave?"

"Forty minutes, maybe. Not that long. But long enough to get Joey to Greg's Market." Tim didn't like it. He took off his cap, mopped his brow with his bandanna.

"He's probably taken Joey with him. I think he has relatives in New Hampshire."

She wasn't exactly telling a lie. Olen did have relatives there:

Annette and Pauline. But she didn't want to worry Tim unduly. If Joey was in a police car, he'd be easy to spot. Should they call now? she asked Colm when Tim had gone back to work. "Or wait till he gets to Andover? I suppose there's nothing at this point we can prove. We have to catch him in the act."

"What act?" Colm asked, looking grim, and Ruth felt suddenly ill. "Let's just go, then," he said. "He's not that far ahead of us, he doesn't know where the place is. We do. Too bad we can't get a phone number. We could warn them."

"We could call the New Hampshire police, ask them to go up there."

"He'll just tell them he's visiting relatives. Bringing another Godineaux with him."

Ruth's head was aching. Joey was a Godineaux, yes. And Pauline wanted no part of him. It might be interesting, though, to see the woman's reaction to the boy. That is, if Olen gave her a chance. Would he hurt her? His own sister? But why?

Pauline had been to Camille's apartment, the visit was on the disk. Who knew what they'd talked about? Pauline might suspect it was Olen who'd killed Camille, threaten to turn him in. Who knew the scenario in Olen's crazed mind?

"Get back in the car," she said. "And we're on our way."

Olen stopped at the Andover convenience store to inquire about Annette. He had her great-grandson with him, he told the storekeeper. The woman's eyes popped to see his uniform. He tried to smile, but couldn't force it. His heart rate was climbing. *Hurry up, hurry up*, it was telling him. They'd know he had Joey, they'd be on their way.

"She know you're coming?" the woman asked.

He dropped the car keys—they made a clatter that rang in his ears; he felt her eyes on him as he bent to pick them up. She gave him the directions anyway, the uniform worked. "She expects us—her directions were fuzzy." He tried to act casual, taking deep breaths in and out, the way he did on a late-night call. He bought a candy bar for the kid, and that did it. She pointed up the road. "Two miles or so. Yellow trailer on the left. Go too far, you're at Bradley Pond."

He remembered to thank her, his police training. Outside, a strong wind had come up. He was suddenly chilled. He tossed the candy bar at Joey. The boy caught it; he was looking, impressed, at the gun in Olen's holster. "That gun loaded?" he asked.

"Yeah, it's loaded," Olen said, his heart louder than the car engine, churning up Bradley Hill Road. "Now eat the candy and keep quiet. I told you I'm here on business."

There was the trailer at the top of the hill, patchy yellow in the headlights, a run-down front porch, sticking out like Joey's buck teeth. A black car that belonged in the junkyard. Degenerates, he thought, they were all degenerates.

He had to know things, though—before he did what he'd come to do. There were good seeds in the family. In the Lafrenière line—his father's father. Those Goodpastures his foster mother told him about—somewhere back in the family history. Annette would know. If he was lucky, he'd find them.

"You can't come in," he told the boy when they pulled into the yard. "I won't be long. You wait here." He climbed the porch steps. Christ! His foot caught in a crack. The place was a dump. He banged on the door. And banged again. She had to be here. Where would a hundred-year-old woman go at this time of night?

"Fire!" he shouted. "Open up!" And when no one answered: "Woods on fire up the road, burning in this direction—a south wind. You're in danger!"

It worked. A light switched on inside the trailer. Eyes peered at him through the glass. He waited. A key turned in the lock. A moment later the door opened. A tall gaunt woman filled the doorway. Pauline. Looking scared, blank, she didn't recognize him. How could she? It had been years. But he knew her, he'd seen her photo in the police files. He'd read of his father's death from a hundred bee stings. It was odd, suspicious: after all, his father, he recalled, was careful, always carrying around his plastic case with the Adrenalin. Lucky for himself he hadn't inherited the allergy, in view of Gwen's bees. On the last page of Camille Wimmet's disk, the page he'd deleted, was a note that Pauline lived in Andover, New Hampshire, where his father, according to the file, had died. But no one back then knew where Pauline was.

He shouldered his way inside. "Just a min—" she cried, taking in the uniform, the badge. "What fire? No. Stay out!" The wind followed him through the door, the door banged, he glanced at the key, still in the lock, then back at his sister. She was almost as tall as he, her eyes black scars, the irises an ugly yellow. Everything about her ugly: the dress that dipped down at the sides, the hair gone an ashy gray when he remembered it brown, the pocked face indicating to him she'd picked up some disease—sexual, he didn't doubt it.

"What is it? Who?" Here was the old lady now, his grandmother. He had a bone to pick with her.

"Hello, Annette," he said. "Do you know me? Noel Lafrenière?"

She looked at him—no, through him. Christ! Was she blind? "Noel," she said, her eyes like empty plates, her skin papery white, like she was a ghost. "Noel? No!" She was thinking of his dead father, of course, she hadn't seen Olen since he was a child. He wondered if he looked like his father. He had no pictures. No one had ever taken a picture of *him*. Not until Gwen, anyway.

Pauline had gone from the room. It was all right, he'd deal with her later, he had questions to ask his grandmother. She was in her nightgown, a pale blue shift that barely covered her bony knees, her wrinkly feet shod in cheap pink slippers, the furry kind you buy at the discount stores. She smelled of urine—or was it the dusty plants filling the narrow room that gave off that fetid odor? A dead African violet sat on a windowsill.

"I'm his son," he said, "young Noel. Remember me? That reformatory in Rutland? You let them do it to me, didn't you, sterilize me? You wanted to get out of there, you'd made a bargain."

It was in the teacher's notes. He'd seen it the second time he went to her office, found her papers. He'd left in a hurry then, someone coming. He'd been in plain clothes; that was lucky, they'd only seen his backside.

"What do you want here? How dare you barge in!" He could tell she was hovering between wanting to see him and wanting to preserve her pride, her sanctity. He could knock her down with a stroke of his hand, the thought occurred to him. He had that power over her. Still she stood there, defiant, in her flimsy nightgown; you could see through to the frail frame of bones—no breasts at all. The waxen face was full of gullies and hollows, the forehead dented in like someone had taken a hammer to it. The white hair shagged down over her shoulders, a mockery of what she'd been. The Godineaux women had been handsome, he recalled that. His mother Nicole had strong curving cheekbones, they were there in the photograph above her obituary.

He didn't sit down, she didn't ask him to. He saw the packing boxes in the hall, beyond the narrow room they were in. They were going somewhere? There wasn't a chair in the place that would hold his weight. It was a room for females: narrow raggedy chairs, the kind you found at the Salvation Army, a cot covered with a red throw, grayish lace curtains at the trailer windows. An unpleasant room at best, but he had his questions to ask.

"My ancestor, Robert Goodpasture," he said. "I need documentation. It was the Agneaus told me about him, my foster parents. They said it came from you."

There had been nothing on the disk—no mention of family before Annette. The Goodpasture connection would have come through his father. He'd tried for years to get back to that father, then found he was dead. By his sister's hand, he was sure of it. She'd taken that away from him. Patricide! It couldn't go unpunished.

Annette crumpled into a chair like a pile of old bones. She was wheezing. Or was she laughing? He wanted to yank her up, shake her, tell her to shut up and talk to him. She had to know how important this was to him, that he sprang from a deeper, purer source than these poverty-driven roots. This crowd of thieves and murderers!

"You knew my father," he said. "He lived with you and Pauline till you got in Brookside for the last time. I lost track then. But Pauline—oh, Pauline knew where he was. When he came here to look for her, she killed him." The words incensed him, raised the pitch of his voice, heightened the buzzing in his brain. "My father's ancestor fought in the American Revolution. Goodpasture. The name's on a monument down in Boston, I saw it myself—that's when my foster mother told me, she took me there. She said, sure, it's your ancestor, Noel."

"He was a *good* one, all right, our father." It was Pauline, back in the doorway, a cigarette burning in her left hand. "Good in bed, good at keeping the locks broke on my bedroom door. Good at beating up Mother. You don't remember those bruises on her head and chest? Ones she said come from tripping over the cat, banging into doors? Well, it was him. Your father. Noel Lafrenière. A good one, oh, yeah, a regular good ole beat-'em-up boy!" The laugh rose, then fell, strangled in her throat. She stuck the cigarette between her lips, inhaled. Blew out the smoke. He took it as an insult.

"You can't kill for that!" He lurched across the narrow space to confront her. He had business with Pauline anyway, it was mainly why he'd come. "You have to turn yourself in, Pauline. You can't get away with killing. It's the law. It's in the Bible. 'Thou shalt not kill.' " *He* hadn't, had he? Killed that Perkey boy? It was an accident, the judge declared it that. It was the asthma, a cut on the kid's face—*he* hadn't dragged him there! One day, though, he'd tell someone what he'd done. He'd have to. For his soul's peace. . . .

"Pauline," he said, "I have to take you in."

He stopped, shocked. He was looking into the mouth of a .45 handgun. Behind it, she was laughing, the cigarette between her teeth like a stuck-out tongue; she pulled it out with her free hand. He felt the wind blowing through a crack in the window; he was shivering.

"You're taking me nowhere, man. And you're not telling nobody what we did and where we live. 'Cause we won't be here after tonight." She nodded at the packing boxes. "And if you're smart, you'll go back to your snug little nest in Branbury, Vermont—oh, sure, I know where you live—and keep your mouth shut. You always were a snotty-nosed loudmouth little bastard. Just like the old man."

"Tell her to put down that gun," Olen told Annette.

"Gun? No! Put down the gun, Pauline." The old lady struggled up out of her chair, stumbled toward her granddaughter. "Tell him what happened, Pauline. Tell him who killed your father. Let him take me, I don't care, I'm an old woman. Tell him, Pauline. Put down the gun now!" She clawed at Pauline's sleeve. Pauline lowered the pistol. The cigarette smoldered in her left hand.

"It wasn't her. I'm the one killed him," Annette said, defiant now, her voice sounding disembodied, like a robot's voice. "I invited him up here—he'd found where I lived. This was years ago! I didn't want him bothering Nicole no more. Sure, I emptied out the bees into his glove compartment—with a little smoke, you know. Later he'd open it and out they'd come, wide awake and mad as hell. It was cold out, he'd have the windows shut. I took away his adrenaline syringe, you see, that case he always carried. Well, I took a chance and it worked. They found him next morning—the car run into a telephone pole. Noel full of bee stings and the heart stopped."

She turned her face toward Olen; she looked to his blurred eyes like an antique doll, missing some parts. "They didn't know who he was, where he been. Pauline wasn't living here then, she wouldn't tell anyway. I'll tell the fuzz, why not? What've I got to lose?"

"Me!" Pauline shrieked at her grandmother, the pistol loose in her hand, her breath coming hard and angry. She dropped the cigarette stub on the floor, stamped it out. "I'm what you got to lose. They find out who I am. They find out about—" She stopped short. Annette was pointing a trembling finger.

Pauline's eyes darted from her grandmother to her brother.

The blood leaped in her neck and cheeks. The black eyes were sly on Olen. She backed up a step.

Olen's legs were trembling, his hands. "They were *yours*, the fingerprints on that key," he said, his voice hoarse, the breath trapped like a small animal in his chest. He looked back at the front door, at the key with the purple blotch of paint. He'd only half recognized it when he came in. It wasn't Tilden Ball, it was Pauline who'd strangled that professor. He was reeling with the knowledge, his body off balance—he grabbed the back of a chair to steady himself.

Though he might have done it if he'd had to, if he'd been pushed to that extreme; the guilt of what might have been tortured him. The relief he'd known to hear she was dead, that someone *else* had killed her! He'd hardly been able to contain his jubilance that night, when the call came through. His hands had been violent with it. And the others thought him upset over her death. . . .

"How did you know," he asked, his hands still clutching the chair back, "about *her*?"

Pauline leered at him, her stance more casual now, her weight on the left foot, the gun in her dropped hand like a tool she might use to pick a lock. She was enjoying his surprise, his shock. "Eugene Godineaux," she said. "The teacher went to visit old Gene with her busybody questions, she left her card there." Pauline snorted at the thought of a business card. "Gene called me. What business she had, he told her, poking into his life like that? He was right. I thought, they find Granny and me here—then what? I went to see the woman for myself. I told her to stop. You can't say I didn't warn her."

Aware again of his uniform, she said, "I didn't go there to kill her. I just went to wreck the computer, take her goddam notes. I saw her go out. But she came in on me unexpected. I . . . reacted."

He fought to regain his breath; his chest was hard, like marble. The grandmother a killer, too. His own blood! He felt sick; he clapped a hand to his mouth.

Pauline laughed. "Don't tell me you're not glad. You wanted

that thing printed? What'd they find out about *you*? Who *you* come from!"

"The Goodpastures," he murmured.

He heard Annette snort. "She made it up, your foster mother. Noel Lafrenière's father was a no-good, he got shot breaking out of prison up to Quebec. His mother was a Passamaquoddy. They were poor, dirt poor. Like the Godineauxs."

Pauline was laughing again. They were both laughing at him, all teeth, gums, mouths, splitting their faces. He was hot, his brains burning up. He rushed at Pauline. The gun swung up in her hand, fired—punctured his shoulder. His gun out in an instant, a reflex. He shot her—twice, three times, four—he was on fire, couldn't stop! Emptied his gun. He'd never felt such fury, such hate for all that poverty, that depravity. The old lady was screaming, stumbling to find Pauline.

He ran out of the trailer, banged into someone on the windy porch. "Hey!" A male voice, yelling at him. He jumped in his car, his shoulder a torture. Raced down the mountain, left hand on the wheel. The kid awake when he took the curve. "Hey, mister, we going home now? I'm cold, mister."

Joey worried about his job at Greg's Market. Tim wouldn't like it if he got fired. But the man wouldn't talk to him—he was going too fast, Joey didn't like *that*. "Slow up, mister!" But the car speeding along, crazy, lurching in the strong wind, zigzaggy, like the cow Zelda when she took off down the road once. The man breathing hard, coughing, blood on the wheel.

"Hey, mister policeman, you cut your arm?"

No answer, only the man hunched over the wheel like he got to win a race. Joey heard a siren behind, a police car, a truck, it was like a chase. Joey'd seen them on TV, cops in their cars, going fast, too fast, crashing—wham, bang! Now Joey in a chase. He liked it better on TV.

"Stop! They after us, the cops!"

But this man a cop, too. He couldn't figure it out. The cops after a cop. Then, bang! A shot. And the car swerving, skidding, crashing in a pile of shrubs. The man putting bullets in his gun, then staggering out.

"Stay put," he yelled at Joey, and Joey stayed put. The engine still running. In the headlights he saw the man run, run toward the woods. His hat blowing off. Another shot. Bang!

The man's arms high in the air, like signaling somebody. Dropping his gun. Whirling back, smack in the arms of another cop—like they loved each other. "I killed her," Joey's cop howled. "I killed my sister."

Another bang then and Joey's cop falling. His chest bright with blood. The second cop stooping down, his face broken up, like he'd lost something big. Joey's cop saying something Joey couldn't hear, and his head dropping down.

Then the van, taking away Joey's cop.

Ruth! Lifting Joey out of the stalled car, crying, hugging him. "You all right, Joey? Answer me, Joey!" Blood on the front seat, the wheel. But not on Joey. Joey's clean. Ruth crying now, all over her pretty blue shirt.

"Take me home, Ruth?" he begged.

"Yes, yes, I will," she cried. And kept on crying. That's a woman for you, right? That's what Tim would say. That's a woman for you.

Joey didn't mind. He didn't mind being cried over. He didn't want Ruth to let go.

Ruth arrived at the trailer with Joey just as the medics, summoned by Colm, were loading the gurney into an ambulance. "It's Pauline—she's pretty well gone," Colm shouted, and the doors clanged shut; the vehicle raced off, taking the first curve on two squealing wheels—or so it sounded in the dark.

"I can't believe you drove off without me," Colm accused, giving Joey a bear hug, embracing Ruth as though she'd come back from the dead. "Didn't you see me running after you? I tripped in a goddam pothole, skinned my knee. The wind almost blew me away. And off you drove."

"They needed you here. It was Olen who killed Pauline—all those shots we heard? He confessed to it. He told a local cop she'd killed Camille. The cop told me himself, after they took Olen away. But why didn't Olen just bring her in?"

"She'd turned a gun on him—I don't know why. It was on the floor, she'd fired one shot."

"It was self-defense, then. But he must have provoked her, don't you think? It's weird, but the other cop was a Mason, he said he saw Olen do some kind of distress signal. Then Olen shot himself. Why, why did he do it? Why, if he didn't kill Camille?"

"Jeez. Is he dead?"

"I don't know. He looked bad."

"I mean, he's got things to tell us. Though I found this in the door, and he held up a door key with a purple blotch. "It matches the one Pauline would've dropped in Camille's apartment."

Colm ushered her and Joey into the trailer, where Annette Godineaux was in her chair, the stick legs splayed out, chin sunk, ducklike, into her chest, the hair like raggedy feathers on her shoulders.

"Annette?" Ruth said. "It's Ruth Willmarth. I'm so sorry about Pauline." Not knowing what else to say, she said, "This is your great-grandson, Joey."

Annette raised her head an inch, her face expressionless. Joey clung to Ruth. Who was this ancient creature? his look said. It was no one he knew. No one he wanted to know.

Ruth made the old woman a cup of tea that Annette waved away. Colm brought her a snifter of brandy he'd found in a kitchen cupboard; she drank it down. Glancing slyly at Ruth, Colm threw one down himself. Then, seeing Annette shivering, he wadded up his handkerchief to fill the crack in the window.

"We can stay the night with you, so you won't be alone," Ruth offered. Though where she and Colm would sleep, she didn't know. There was a single boxlike bedroom beyond the sitting room, a cot that Pauline perhaps had slept on. Would she and Colm have to share it? He could sleep in the truck, she decided. After all, Annette frowned on men in her house.

“No,” Annette said, acknowledging Ruth’s presence for the first time. “I don’t need you here.”

“Then come home with us. I see you’re packed.” She nodded at the boxes.

“Those are Pauline’s. I never said *I’d* go. They’ll have to come and get me.” The head fell forward again on the sunken chest.

Twenty-one

What will they do to Uncle Olen?" Donna asked in a small voice. The Woodleaf-LeBlanc family was sitting around the supper table, except for Russell, who was in Buffalo and didn't yet know what had transpired. The call had come in that morning from the New Hampshire hospital: Olen was on the critical list—the bullet had punctured his lungs, not the heart; he would survive. He'd kept trying to talk, he had things to tell the world, he insisted; but for now, the doctor said, they would keep him sedated.

The family was exhausted but wired; they'd sat up half the night before while Ruth and Colm wound out the horrific story.

"I don't know." Gwen shook her head. She was going to see Olen tomorrow, beg the nurses to let her in. "It had to be self-defense. Pauline, Colm said, shot Olen in the shoulder. It was after he'd made her confess, I suppose, that she'd killed Camille. He told the local police about that. But there were six bullets in her," she said softly.

"Overkill," said Brownie, who watched taped videos of *Law and Order* with his grandfather. "They'll make him pay for that."

Gwen nodded. She was still in shock, to tell the truth, that Olen would react so irrationally to Camille's research. So he was a Godineaux, as Ruth had discovered. What was wrong with that? There were black sheep in every family, and Olen was a cop, people respected him. Well, that was the problem, she supposed. He'd created a new identity, worn it like an expensive new coat—he didn't want people to see what was underneath.

If only he'd talked to *her* about it! She would have made him see that Camille was trying to *defend* the family, show the world how those Godineauxs were unfairly judged and persecuted. Camille's paper, in the end, she was certain, would have enhanced the family's reputation, not destroyed it.

"Poor Camille," she said aloud, "she had every good intention. And now the poor woman is dead, for all her resolves." She thought, too, of Shep Noble. And Pauline, whom she'd never met. Though Pauline was obviously a more violent sort, in her own way, than Shep. But Pauline would have had her reasons. They would probably never know the roots of that terrible anger.

"People don't like that," Mert said, chewing on his salmon steak. "They don't want to be out there for folks to judge. Now, when I saw that Perkey name on the motorcycle—"

"What?" They all turned their heads toward the old man. He swallowed his fish, dabbed at his lips with a paper napkin.

"You did what, Mert?" Gwen asked. "When you saw the Perkey name on the motorcycle—what?"

"I knew the name," he said, gazing into his water glass. "It was the Perkey woman snooped in *my* family business—I told the teacher that. It wasn't just the Godineauxs Perkey was after. Took my aunt to that place, you know, they done it to her. Wanted to *help her*, they said. They had no goddam business."

"So what did you do when you saw the name on the motorcycle, Grandpop?" Donna was leaning toward him, her fork halfway to her mouth, motionless. This was something, Gwen saw, the girl had to know.

"I moved the damn thing off our land," he said. "Then I—well, I found the boy. It was that moon. I was taking a walk. He was asleep, dead drunk. I don't know what come over me. I took him by the feet and I drug him. Drug him over by the nightshade—wasn't far. Serve him right, I thought, bringing my grandgirl home, and him drunk like that. And him a Perkey."

Gwen reached in her pants pocket; it was still there, the tarnished earring. "Is this yours, Pop?"

He held out his hand for it; nodded, dropped it into a shirt pocket.

Donna wasn't looking at the earring. There was something else she needed to know. "You put his face in it, Grandpop? In the nightshade?"

Gwen saw Donna's mouth drop open. She was holding her breath. Her own heart was hammering; she could barely hear Mert's answer.

"Naw, naw I didn't do that, just left him on his back, that's all. I hear him wheezing some. I know what it is to be out of breath. I was sorry then I'd drug him, but I couldn't drag anymore, I didn't think it would hurt him on his back. I thought he'd come to in the morning, go home."

"He must of turned himself over," Brownie said, and Donna nodded. She sounded relieved, got up to clear the table.

Gwen served the dessert: honey cakes topped with vanilla ice cream. Her head was churning, there'd been too much talk to absorb. She felt bloated with these new discoveries; she didn't want any dessert.

She excused herself and went outside. The bees were humming in the clover, which was just starting to bloom. It was early this year, from all the warm rain and sunshine. It was white clover that brought the honey, white clover that the bees would see as blue. When she looked closely at it, yes, it did have a bluish hue. Or was she beginning to think like a bee?

"It smells so good out here," Donna said, coming to stand beside her mother. She waved at Leroy as he drove off in the secondhand Suburu he'd bought through a loan—an advance against his small inheritance from Camille. Leroy looked surprised, then grinned and waved back.

"Sometimes I envy the bees," Donna said, "getting to drink up those juices."

"It's delicious, I can imagine."

The two were quiet, listening to the bee song. Gwen smiled

at the *KEEP VERMONT CIVIL* sign Donna had stuck in the grass by the hives in memory of Camille. The Balls would have to see it when they drove by, she'd said, looking sly. It's more than a political slogan, Gwen thought, it's a metaphor for all our lives. She wondered what Olen would think of it. Olen's mind wasn't always as open as it should be.

"Lafrenière," she said. "The name haunts me. Where have I seen it before?"

Donna turned toward her, surprised. "*You* know, Mom. It's in Elizabeth's journal. There's a Lafrenière married one of Isobel's grandchildren. Sometime in the late 1800s. Why, he could be related to us! Uncle Olen, I mean, for real."

Gwen drew a quick breath. "He could be, at that." A Lafrenière had married Isobel's granddaughter. Mali, yes—she should have remembered. She and Olen might really be family. He has a revolutionary ancestor after all, she thought. What an irony.

For some reason, out here in the spring evening, among the clover and the bees, the old superstition came to mind again: how you should tell the bees about a death in the family—how she hadn't done it after her father's death. If not, her father had told her, there might be another death.

"It was a terrible thing Olen did," she said. "Shooting that woman over and over. But I can understand it, that anger. Why, when Tilden Ball kidnapped you, Donna, then confessed to running you down, I could have killed *him.* Right then. Without a thought. Over and over, I was that angry.

"But you're alive, thank God," she said, watching the girl kneel in a patch of clover, breathe in the fragrance.

Impulsively, she knelt beside her daughter: the two of them, like honeybees, embracing the clover, sucking up the nectar.

"What do you suppose Annette meant when she said, 'They'll have to come and get me?' Who are 'they'?" Ruth asked.

She and Colm were sitting in her kitchen, splitting a bottle of Otter Creek. Colm was staying the night—Vic was at a friend's sleepover party, there was no school tomorrow. Ruth hadn't been able to get that old woman out of her head. A social worker had brought the news of Pauline's death just before they left Andover; the woman was settling in for the night, in spite of Annette's protests.

"She probably meant the social workers—trying to put her in a home. Who else would want to come and get her? Not the police?"

"No, I wouldn't think so. But I can't imagine her in one of those nursing places, can you? She just wouldn't fit in. She's the kind who has to be independent to the end. Live free or die—the state slogan, you know."

Ruth took a deep swallow of the ale.

It seemed to have a life of its own, the way it traveled down into her chest and spread there in a warm pool.

"Free or die," she cried, shaking a fist. "The way I want to live my life!"

Colm said, "Don't I know it, Ruthie."